Black Rainbow

ALBERT WENDT

Black Rainbow

University of Hawai'i Press
Honolulu

First published by Penguin Books 1992
Published in North America by University of Hawai'i Press 1995
Printed in the United States of America

95 96 97 98 99 00   5 4 3 2 1

Library of Congress Cataloging-in-Publication Data
Wendt, Albert, 1939–
Black Rainbow / Albert Wendt.
p.   cm.
ISBN 0–8248–1586–6 (alk. paper)
I. Title.
PR9665.9.W46B58   1995
823—dc20   95–30291
CIP

University of Hawai'i Press books are printed on acid-free
paper and meet the guidelines for permanence and durability
of the Council on Library Resources

Acknowledgement is made to Hone Tuwhare and Richards
Literary Agency for permission to reprint "We, Who Live in
Darkness" on page 196 of this book.

For
Ralph Hotere

Contents

one

On Maungakiekie

I slipped into the sitting room and the rich scent of ripe fruit. She didn't turn round as she stood at the windows and gazed down the street. The light was fading.

'Summer's ending,' she said.

'Yes,' I said.

'How was it today?'

'It was all right.' The evening glow lay easy upon her. I thought of children's hands, my daughters', finger-painting with yellow acrylics.

'Let's go home before winter comes.' In her faded denim shorts and floppy T-shirt she looked like a teenager.

'Got another eight months,' I reminded her. I went to the fruit bowl on the coffee table, picked up an apple, wiped it clean on my sleeve, changed my mind and put the apple back between a banana and a pear. She always had a lot of fruit in the house.

'Got a call from our second daughter this morning,' she said, as she continued surveying the street.

'How is she?' I picked up the banana and started peeling it.

'Okay. Got an A for her first Sociology assignment.'

'That's good.' Half the banana was mushy, overripe. I broke off that half, put it in the ashtray, and ate the rest. Too sweet. Texture of wet dough. 'What else did she say?'

'Nothing much.' She scratched her right shoulder. A familiar nervous gesture.

'Is there any cold beer?'

'In the fridge. Put it in over an hour ago.' Folded her arms and remained at the windows.

As I went into the kitchen I thought about One Tree Hill

and how it overshadowed our neighbourhood — I preferred its original Maori name, Maungakiekie — and its phallic obelisk memorial to the Maori tribe who'd once occupied the hill as a fortified pa.

Opened the fridge. Unpleasant smell of leftovers. Got out a stubby, opened it and returned with it to the sitting room.

She was now sitting on the arm of the settee, facing me. The light from the windows lay on her back. She glowed as she looked at the Hotere lithograph on the wall above my head. *Black Rainbow/Moruroa*. She'd bought it the month we'd shifted to Auckland. I didn't understand it but I liked it. Can you really have a black rainbow? I wanted to ask her but asked instead, 'Did you do your weekly shopping today?' She nodded. The icy coldness of the stubby was burning my fingers. I swigged it. The bristling cold stung my throat. 'Great!' I sighed. My eyes were watering. Swigged again. 'Bloody good!'

'Yes?'

'Yeah!' I said. 'You want one?' She shook her head. (I always forgot to offer her a beer.) The last light was colouring her hair a luminous gold.

'Went to Foodtown this morning. Everything's gone up . . .'

'What else did my daughter say?'

'She doesn't like the hostel. Wants to go flatting next year.'

'Not if I'm paying for her education.' She looked at me. 'You tell her that.' I sucked back until the stubby was empty.

That night after Chinese takeaways, we watched TV. She went to bed at ten. I fell asleep watching an old Clint Eastwood western. Woke at 1 a.m. to a crackling screen. Switched it off.

I paused in front of the Black Rainbow. I looked at it closely. Recognised the thick black arch to be the rainbow. But the numbers, 1 to 14, on either side of the upsurging cloud? The countdown to what?

I tried not to wake her as I slid under the blankets. She snuggled into my side. I turned off the bedside lamp.

I remained still, listening to her deep breathing. And counted.

'Time!' She shook me awake. I rolled away from her. 'Time!'
She was already in her sports gear. My shorts landed on my face.
She was doing stretching exercises. 'Get up!'

'Okay,' I muttered.

Fifteen minutes later we were striding up our driveway to
the street. The gravel crunched like dry fish bones under our
running shoes.

As usual, she set the pace. My knees hurt, so did my lower
back, but I kept up with her. Left-right, left-right, left-right!
(We tried to walk for an hour every second morning.)

Ahead, above the trees and houses, rose Cornwall Park
sloping up to One Tree Hill and the memorial. Already it was
drenched with sun.

We turned onto Pah Road. A truck thundered by and
dragged the silence of the street behind it like a protesting
animal. Otherwise the street was empty. The houses watched
us. So did the gardens and letterboxes.

'There's a countdown, isn't there?' I asked. She glanced at
me. 'In the Hotere lithograph.'

'You're a bit slow,' she smiled.

We turned into Beckenham Avenue. I exhaled loudly
through my mouth, then sucked in air.

'Awful, isn't it?' she said.

'What?'

'That!' She pointed at the Memorial.

'Bit slow, aren't you?' I quipped. She punched my shoulder
and quickened the pace. I kept up but wished she wasn't so fit.
(I couldn't lose weight because I drank too much beer and ate
mountains of snacks between meals. That's what she kept telling
me.)

Past the dairy, across the street into the park and up the road
lined by hefty oak trees lush with leaves that were as green as
ocean depths.

The paddocks were parched from the summer heat. Groups
of sheep. A few cows. Stench of sheep shit and piss. Steeper now.
My legs were heavy, the muscles taut with the strain. She drew
ahead.

'Slow down!' I said. She shortened her steps. She refused to look at me. Our shadows touched as I drew alongside her. Round the bend rushed two runners. Middle-aged, balding, not an ounce of fat.

At last the Sorrento Restaurant at the top of the rise. We turned right at the fork and took the level road round the eastern side of the hill. To our right, the hill fell away to Royal Oak and Onehunga, and sprawled further out to Mangere now alive with morning sun.

We walked to the summit only once a week. The rest, we covered the road that circled the base of the Hill. One hour ten minutes it took us.

My sweatshirt was soggy with sweat. With my thumbs I wiped the sweat off my forehead. A young woman, with thick pink thighs and a long lope to her stride, avoided eye contact with us as she ran past.

Even when we didn't go up to the Memorial I sensed it behind me, just over my shoulder, watching my every move.

Twin Oak Drive is a stand of huge oak trees that casts a sea of dark shadow. Cool respite from the sun. As we entered that sea, she asked, 'They're still here, aren't they? The Pakeha have changed even the vegetation but *they're* still here.'

'Who?' I pretended I didn't know who she was referring to.

'The original people.'

'Their presence, you mean.'

'Even without that monstrous memorial, they'll always be here.'

I was putting the fruit salad, coffee and toast on to the table when she emerged from the bathroom, drying her hair with a towel. 'Have you noticed?' she asked.

'What?'

Her face and ears were flushed apple-red from the exercise and the heat of the shower. 'Our neighbourhood's full of old people's homes and hospitals.' She sipped her orange juice. 'And flats and apartments for them.' I poured my coffee and sat down.

'No, I haven't noticed,' I lied.

'A lot of houses up for sale too. A whole generation who can no longer care for themselves selling up and going into the homes.'

'Guess so,' I said. 'I feel great. It was a good walk.'

She nodded. 'But soon the cold'll make it tougher, less enjoyable.' I caught her looking at my paunch.

We finished our breakfast in silence.

That day she was going to go to the laundry, finish knitting a jumper and catch more sun, she said, as she stacked the dirty dishes in the sink. Enough to fill her day. No need for me to worry about her.

After a hot shower I turned the cold tap on full blast. Slapped my body as the icy cold attacked it. Dripped and shivered as I stepped on to the bath mat. Remembered what she'd said about the gerontocracy in our area, as I dried myself. In our street, in their gardens in front of each home, stood an old couple, trowels like weapons in their hands. Porcelain white with age. Staring at us as we headed for the park. Above them loomed Maungakiekie, wings outstretched to gather them into its heart, its beak — the Memorial — thrusting skywards like an admonishing finger. That vision left me gradually as I dressed in my uniform. I looked in the mirror. Not a spot on my blue shirt, black tie, black trousers. All ironed perfectly. Black shoes. On went my black coat. Perfect. A-tten-shun! I snapped to attention in the mirror. Sucked in my belly.

'You look great,' she said from the doorway. I reached out. She moved into my arms.

'What do they want from us?' she said.

'Eight more months,' I whispered.

'But they may change their minds again.'

'Not this time. I promise.'

'I want to go back to my house, our son, our community.' She buried her face in my shoulder.

The car, as usual, was on time. It stopped right at our front door. John got out, held open the back door and waited for me.

'See you tonight,' I said to her. She handed me my black brief-case. I glanced at her face. John waved to her. I brushed past her. She smelled of shampoo. I would hold that inside me all day, as a healing balm.

As the car pulled away, I looked back. She raised her hand.

'Mornin',' the driver said. A new man, but in his navy blue uniform and cap, he looked like the other drivers I'd had.

'Morning,' I mumbled.

John handed me that morning's *Herald*. I waved it away. He read it. We performed the same ritual every morning, had done so since he'd started collecting me. He never asked why I didn't want to read the paper. Not that we talked much. I knew his first name, what he looked like (more or less), was familiar with his meateater odour, but knew little else about him.

The driver switched on the radio. FM86. Rock music. 'Turn it off!' John ordered him. The driver muttered sorry, and did as he was told. John never asked why I refused to listen to the radio as we drove.

Heavy traffic on Manukau Road already. 'Motorway,' John instructed our driver.

Down Green Lane West, on to Gillies Avenue. Each name and street clicked into my memory. It was the same every morning.

'Are you married?' I asked John, and didn't know why I was asking that.

'Naw,' he said. Turned the page. I realised he was about the same age as my older daughter. Baby-faced, with spiky blond hair, long slender fingers, and sea-blue eyes that hid much.

'Are you gay?' I pursued, expecting him to be offended, but he just mumbled, 'Naw.' 'Not gay?' I wasn't giving up.

'Naw. Not that I know of. I play rugby though!'

'You do?' I couldn't connect my last question to his playing rugby.

'Yeah, in the Ponsonby Senior A team.' He folded the paper.

'You must be pretty good.'

'Not bad. Our coach reckons I should make the rep team this season.' From under his peaked cap he peered at me and asked,

'You play rugby where you're from?'

'Used to. But our community banned it.'

'Yeah? But why?'

'Caused too much violence among supporters.'

'Yeah? What kind of violence?'

'A few people were killed with stones and sticks.'

'Did you play?'

I nodded. 'But I was hopeless at it.' I put an end to our connecting. He reopened the newspaper.

I noticed we were now on the motorway, a swiftly flowing river of traffic vying for advantage. One careless move by our driver and we'd drown. I envied her at home, in the quiet, safe.

We stopped, as usual, at the security booth at the front gate. John held his pass up to the security guard. 'Right on, mate!' the guard said. The steel bar swung up. We drove in.

'See ya later!' John called to the guard.

Ahead was the Tribunal Building. Today we were meeting in Room 1303 on the thirteenth floor. I recalled her morning scent of shampoo and hugged it with all my resolve.

'All my family are vegetarians,' I told them. 'My father was one because he was allergic to meat. One taste and he swelled up as if he'd been stung by a swarm of bees. My mother became one — a vegetarian, I mean — so there would be no meat in the house.'

'Are you claiming meateating is an addiction?' they asked.

'I wouldn't know because I've never tasted meat. My parents raised me as a vegetarian. I didn't rebel against that because the smell and sight of meat has always upset me.'

'And your wife?'

'She came from a family of extravagant meateaters who even ate dog but, within a year of our marrying, she was a confirmed vegetarian.'

'You must've conditioned her,' the Chairman said.

I shook my head. 'She chose to become one.'

'And your children?'

'They have never questioned their vegetarian upbringing.

They are staunch supporters of Animal Rights.'

'Are you and your wife supporters too?'

They never relented. 'We don't believe in being part of a group fighting for a cause. We are our own persons,' I said.

'How would you describe our society?' the Chairman asked. A diversion.

I pondered and then said, 'It is meat. Your country is all grass which you turn into meat. You even turned Maungakiekie into pasture and therefore into meat.'

'But they were meateaters too!' he insisted.

'Who?' I asked.

'The savages who once lived there,' he replied. 'And they were eaten by other meateaters.' The other members of the Tribunal laughed. They stopped laughing when they saw I wasn't amused.

'My wife is the best cook I know,' I declared. 'An artist. A priest.'

The days grew colder but we didn't deviate from our simple daily routine. We walked the park. John came for me every morning (and dropped me off at night). She shopped, wrote letters, paid our bills, gardened, read, slept, read some more. At night we ate her delicious dinners. (She experimented with every available vegetable.) We then watched TV, went to bed, and promptly forgot the programmes we'd seen. The neighbours left us alone.

'On this side,' she said one night as we lay in the dark, ' are the Hurleys. He's a retired businessman who made a comfortable living out of selling toilet bowls. Was good at tennis and squash, but is now paralysed in the left leg. Their daughter ran away with the Moonies.'

'And to our left?'

'The Cousins. He came here from Bristol fifty years ago. Set up a lucrative fashion shop, married a nurse who died of a stroke three years ago. Now he's going to be put into a nursing home by his only child, a son who's a Remuera lawyer.'

'And behind us?'

'A retired teacher, Ms Thurstin, and her young companion, Ms Rost. Ms Thurstin's bedridden. Been like that for five years. Ms Rost goes out a lot with other Mss.'

How come she knew a lot about our neighbours, I asked. 'Mental telepathy,' she laughed. But just when I thought I was safe, she said, 'You've been lying, haven't you?'

'About what?'

'About our returning home. By not telling me, you've been lying!'

I grasped her hand under the blankets. She jerked it away. 'I'm sorry,' I admitted finally. 'I didn't have the courage to tell you.'

'Tell me what?' she demanded. When I didn't reply, she sat up and repeated, 'Tell me what?'

'That they want me to stay longer.'

'How much longer?'

'They couldn't say.'

'Tell me what happens when you go to see them, then.'

'You know I can't. Please don't ask me.'

'You don't want to leave, do you?' she shouted. She jumped out of bed and dragging a blanket behind her, stamped away into the dark of the sitting room. 'You like it here. You enjoy what they're doing to you!'

'But I'm free!' I protested. 'We can leave any time.'

'Let's leave tomorrow then!' she taunted me. I couldn't answer that. 'See, you're not free. You don't want to leave!'

She suffered but never cried. Not tears.

She woke up at 5.30 a.m. for our walk. No trace of pain in her. 'Hurry,' she said.

As she walked to the front door, I noticed she was carrying a small haversack on her back. I didn't ask her about it.

We tried to weave into the cold southerly. Leant forward, pushed. It was still dark but the sky was opening with light above Maungakiekie. 'Slow down!' I asked her but she ignored me. I puffed as I tried to keep up to her. The cartilages in my knees creaked and cracked and the pain was sharp and unending.

17

Maungakiekie, I forgot to say, is an extinct volcano. The road up to the summit follows the ridge that is the eastern edge of the cone. The grass was still sparkling with dew. Our breath smoked. For once the smell of sheep shit was absent. As we climbed, the swirling clouds in the heavens dropped lower and seemed to anchor themselves to the tip of the Memorial. I gazed down at the bottom of the cone. A few sheep were grazing among the boulders. She continued to pull away from me, striding bravely.

When I got to the carpark around the Memorial and the lone pine tree that grew a few metres away, she was already on the concrete platform that was the base of the Memorial. I hurried up the steps.

We stood and looked at the city that spread out in all directions, at the other dead volcanoes, the harbours, bays, horizons and islands of the Gulf. The mattress of dark cloud cast its shifting silence over everything. The southerly stirred.

'It's getting cold,' I said.

She unzipped her haversack. Out of it she took the Hotere lithograph. For a while she examined it. Her sweat dripped on to the glass. She wiped it dry with her sweatband.

'Once all this and that city was forest,' she said. She gripped the lithograph with both hands.

As she circled the Memorial, she held the lithograph out in front of her, like an icon. In it the sky and the full swing of the city were caught. Every shade, shape, light, twist, change and impermanency of them. Reflected there for a time and then lost as she circled.

Was she reinvesting everything with mana? Warding off evil spirits? Or what?

The cloud cover in the east began to thin out. The morning sun became visible, a faint ball of orange. She stopped and, facing it, held the lithograph above her head, with the Black Rainbow pointed at the sun. As the sun rose the lithograph's clock of doom recorded its rising.

Then in an ancient language I'd not heard before, she sang to those who'd been there before us.

Later, on our way down, she started jogging. I hurried to catch up with her. Our shadows ran on ahead, separately. It started drizzling. The tiny raindrops were icy needles that pricked at our faces and arms.

'Was Hotere a descendant of the original tribe?' she asked, more to herself than to me.

'Don't know.' I looked up. There was no rainbow in the swirling heavens.

John was on time as usual. I was eager to go with him. It was now raining steadily.

As I walked towards the car I looked back and saw her putting the Black Rainbow back on the wall.

I counted.

two

No History/Herstory

I woke. My wife was gone. I couldn't find any trace of her (or anything that was hers) in the house, garden or grounds. I imagined the house clean even of her fingerprints. (The Hotere lithograph was gone too.) I experienced no guilt: I hadn't wished her away.

'Don't worry about her,' John said that morning when I got into the car. Whatever John and the Tribunal told me I believed because they'd never betrayed, harmed or threatened me. They always kept their word, and their word was always for our good.

No reference to her was made during that day's session, as if she'd not been part of my life.

When I got home that evening I didn't expect her to be there. I felt no loss. But when I noticed the space where the Hotere had been I regretted its absence. She'd taken it. I didn't resent her for that, though. The Tribunal would protect the Hotere.

No leftovers in the fridge. They'd reprovisioned my fridge completely. Whoever had done it knew my tastes, allergies, calory intake, etc. I stir-fried some mushrooms, green peppers, tomatoes and celery in the wok. Remembered how delicious her cooking had been but didn't miss it as I ate mine in front of the TV.

I was washing the dishes when the announcer said her name. I turned to see her smiling face filling the screen. John had taken that photo at the airport when we'd arrived in Auckland. Her shoulder-length hair wove like smoke around her head in the wind that had gusted across the tarmac. An accident.

Silver Enlai Lancer buckled up against the bridge railing . . .
'She died instantly,' the announcer was saying. 'The driver of the
other car is in a critical condition . . .' The phone rang. Jangled
in the centre of my head. I hurried over and picked it up. Tried
to steady my trembling hand.

'Don't worry,' John said. 'We've faked her death so ya
enemies'll stop lookin' for her.'

'Thanks,' I whispered.

'Next week, ya daughters'll disappear too.'

'Thanks,' I whispered.

'Soon ya'll be one happy family again.'

I ate two heaped dishfuls of hokey-pokey ice cream, my
favourite, as I watched the Bill Cosby Show.

Later I couldn't sleep. I emptied my head of memories
except the Black Rainbow, the Hotere lithograph, on which I
counted away the minutes, the hours, and relaxed.

I didn't walk the next morning. She'd taken our routine with
her, and she wasn't there to nag me about my weight.

I have no history. She has no herstory. Our children's history
began with us but that's all — there is no time before that. History is a curse, the Tribunal has ruled. We must be free of it to
be.

I believe them.

'Would ya like a companion?' John asked as we drove to work.
I didn't understand. 'Another womin?' he added. I shook my
head. 'Jus' ta clean up and cook and look afta ya house . . .'

'No!' I was surprised at my heated refusal. 'I can look after
myself,' I apologised.

He shrugged his shoulders. 'Suit ya self, mate. But if ya ever
need one, jus' ask.'

'Okay,' I said. In the grey autumn sky above Auckland
Hospital hovered a helicopter. Blade spinning, spinning, but the
machine remained motionless, poised as if to drop. I held it up
with my breath.

We drove off the motorway. I couldn't see the helicopter any more.

'Ah hear ya're a vegetarian,' John interrupted. I nodded. 'Ah need lotsa red meat, as a rugby player. Lots of it. Don' ya get sicka vegies?' I shook my head. The helicopter blade spun in my head.

As usual I entered and sat down in my chair, facing the Tribunal's desk and the throne-like chair of the Chairman.

It didn't matter what room we had the session in. They were all the same size, shape, appearance, and with the same furnishings. The light never altered: it was white neon, skull white, emanating from the walls and ceiling. Always the same temperature, tropical, about 75 degrees. And soundproof and smelling pleasantly of roses. Without windows. An egg in which I felt secure, unafraid.

At the centre of the back wall above the Chairman's chair was the massive portrait — an oil painting — of the President with an out-of-focus face and mouth like a wound slit open by a scalpel and just starting to bleed. The Tribunal's chairs had high backs that peaked at the corners and gave them the appearance of having wings.

The thick black Book of Rules lay on the desk, in front of each chair.

My hands sweated as usual. I wiped them on my thighs. The back door slid open noiselessly. Into the room shuffled the Blind Recorder.

'Good morning!' he called.

I greeted him.

'Beaut day, isn't it?' He placed his computerised recorder on his table which stood to the right of the Tribunal's desk. Once again, I wondered if he was really blind: he never faltered, stumbled, or walked as if he couldn't see, behind the thick sunglasses he wore. He didn't seem to age, either. He'd been at all my sessions since I'd come to Auckland. I'd aged visibly, going grey, but he was as on that first session. Perfectly groomed, not a hair out of place, long unwrinkled face, long hands with the gold ring on the middle finger of his left hand. And smiling, always smiling.

He pressed the red button. Out of the centre of the Tribunal's desk emerged an intricate computer panel.

He sat down behind his recorder.

The back door slid open again. The Tribunal filed in.

Strange, but I didn't worry about the rooms not having a view.

A red Huntsman Colt was parked in my garage when we got home. John opened my car door. I hesitated and looked at the Huntsman. 'Id's okay, mate. Id's for ya use.' I glanced at him. 'No restrictions — you can go anywhere.' I got out. I looked at him again. 'Don' worry. The Tribunal says id's alright. Ya won't run away, will ya?' I shook my head. He chuckled as he drove off.

The cold was like injections. I hurried into the house. Stopped just over the threshold. The whole house smelled of garlic and cooking oil. Sizzling vegies being fried.

I opened the sitting room door. Blazing wood fire in the fireplace. Its warmth enveloped me immediately. I took off my overcoat and hung it in the corridor.

She stood in front of the stove, with her back to me. Same figure, same fall of hair, same firm roundness of flanks and calves. I started to speak. She turned. I didn't speak.

'Hello,' she said. 'I didn't hear you come in.' Her seagreen eyes lingered on my face. 'I hope you don't mind. They asked me to come and take care of your house.' She looked away.

'It's okay,' I said. I went back to the sitting room.

'Dinner'll be ready soon!' she called. Similar voice.

I settled into the soft chair in front of the fire. It was good having someone else in the house. Uncanny, the physical resemblance. The Tribunal thought of everything. They knew I found it difficult adjusting to other people, so they'd provided a companion like my wife.

Why was I out-of-body watching my body — a transparent

plastic replica — swallowing water, filling myself from toes upwards? I watched as the luminous water rose. Up to my knees, then belly button, chest, as heavy as mercury . . .

'Are you all right?' the voice whispered. 'Are you okay?'

And I was back in my body, spluttering, drowning above my throat. 'Yes, yes, yes,' I gasped. Arms around me. Tears streaming down my face. I couldn't understand why.

'You okay?' she asked. I nodded. 'Was it a bad dream?'

'I don't dream.'

'Never?'

'Not since we came to Auckland.' Her arms were a warm shield.

She switched on my bedside lamp. Quickly I wiped away my tears with the corner of the sheet. I glanced at her arms. 'Sorry,' she murmured, and released me. She got off the bed.

'Thank you,' I said, not looking at her.

She went to her bedroom.

Why had I lied about my dreaming?

I tried to read a novel by Kundera. Couldn't. Her scent of Charlie perfume and musk kept entering the nostrils of my thoughts. Her smell was that of my wife. The Tribunal thought of everything.

'Is she useful?' the Chairman asked. I didn't comprehend. 'Your new companion?' I nodded; smiled.

'Good,' he said. The other two judges nodded also and opened their papers.

Our session began.

The Tribunal were my family — that's how I thought of them, even though the three changed every week. When replacements came they knew exactly where the sessions had ended and the questions to ask to continue my narration. Though they changed physically, they seemed the same people. I imagined the Tribunal an indefinite line of threes, much like a hive, functioning to the same purpose, pattern, design. Like me, they were ordinary people. Like me, they were with little history/herstory. That didn't mean they weren't different people. For instance, the latest three were, according to the notes provided by the Blind Recorder:

(a) Chairman

William B. Yeast, 45, schoolteacher of Omokoroa. Married with three children. Hobbies: beekeeping, stamp collecting and whistling. No police record. Utterly faithful.

(b) First Judge

Evelyn W. Evening, 52, housewife of Titirangi. Four children, one in the Air Force, one in a reordinarination centre, for burglary. Hobbies: The Society for Expurgating Swear Words.

One arrest for demonstrating against submarines. Has been unfaithful to husband six times.

(c) Second Judge

Tom Dudley Scott, 56, unemployed plumber. Divorced. No children. De facto wife: Jane Samuels. Hobbies: Beer drinking, palmistry, sleeping, and bird watching. No police record.

And like their predecessors, they were reluctant judges: they always emphasised that during the session. 'But, like our Illustrious President, we have to do our duty,' Mr Yeast declared. 'Some of us are chosen to be judges, others to be judged.'

He wore a splendid pair of goldrimmed spectacles. Every time he looked at me, my reflection was caught clearly in their dark-tinted lenses. To that reflection I addressed my answers. Every Chairman seemed a reflection of myself, and our sessions were like self-confessions, conversations with myself: whole narratives prompted from my depths by his and the other judges' questions and remarks.

'What do you think of children?' Mr Yeast asked.

'I enjoy their company.'

'Would you mind explaining further?' Mrs Evening helped me. She had a slight lisp.

'I'm from a family of thirteen children . . .'

'Unusually large for our economy . . .' Mr Scott interrupted.

'. . . six boys and seven girls,' I ignored him. 'We managed. There was much love between us. That made up for the lack of material possessions.'

'Is that why your family didn't eat meat?' Mr Yeast asked.

'You couldn't afford it,' Mr Scott helped me.

'No. We were vegetarians because we were, and still are, allergic to all meat.'

'Says so on his medical report,' Mrs Evening pointed out.

'Bad for our economy if everyone was like you!' Mr Yeast joked. We laughed.

'Your children. What are they like?' Mrs Evening asked.

'My son is a mechanic. He's eighteen. Our daughters are at university . . .'

'And very beautiful,' Mr Scott said, holding up a photo of them.

'Yeah!' applauded Mr Yeast.

'They do TV ads sometimes,' I said.

'Where are your brothers and sisters now?' Mr Yeast asked.

For the next hour or so I gave them a detailed account of where and what my brothers and sisters were doing. The Tribunal were interested in their wives and children too.

As I resurrected my relatives, I felt close to them again, even to the ones I'd never liked and had avoided since my childhood.

That night my new companion and I watched TV. I discovered she liked the same programmes as I did.

Before she went to bed she made me a cup of Milo, kissed me on the cheek unexpectedly, murmured goodnight and hurried off.

The warmth of her lips burned. I tried to concentrate on the TV. It burned bone-deep.

The next evening she suggested we visit Queen Street. Perhaps see a movie. I agreed to the visit but not to the movies. I hadn't been to the city for months. Auckland was too sprawled out, like a camping ground, radiating out from its dead volcanoes.

She drove. She was a confident driver and hummed 'Nothin' to Lose' by the Switchblades as she drove. I turned on the heater.

We parked in the underground carpark at Aotea Square. The enclosure was choking with exhaust fumes. We hurried up the stairs on to Queen Street.

My ears started stinging from the cold. I pulled up the collar of my overcoat. She reached over and straightened it. She wore woollen gloves, a red overcoat and knee-high boots.

We started down Queen Street through the silent stream of pedestrians. Ahead a neon sign said: BUY HARDLY TO PUT STEEL INTO YOUR CHEST.

'Everything's still the same,' I said. She glanced up at me.

'You didn't expect it all to have vanished?' she joked. I shook my head. The evening traffic was thick and loud.

As we strolled past the Mid-City cinemas, she said, 'They're still here.' She nodded towards the groups of young Polynesians sitting on the benches under the trees by the footpaths. 'An unkempt lot, if you ask me. With nowhere to go.'

'Street kids?' I asked. She nodded. One group had a huge cassette player around which they crouched as if for warmth.

'They cause a lot of trouble. And a burden to us hard-working taxpayers.'

I thought of my children. I slowed down in front of a group of four youths, all wearing navy blue duffel coats, patched jeans, and balaclavas — a uniform.

'Got a light, mate?' He was taller than me. Handsome, utterly in command. Blond-tipped hair that swept down to his shoulders.

'Sorry, I don't smoke,' I replied. He nodded, backed off, waved once. Black crosses were tattooed on the backs of his fingers. He could've been my son.

I sensed she was frightened. We hurried away.

'No one can reform them. They get rounded up periodically and put into reordinarination centres, but they come right back to the streets. Must be in their blood.'

'What is?'

'Their refusal to be like us, be law-abiding citizens.'

'A passive rebellion?' I tried joking.

'Yeah, with all their lice and dirt and stench!'

I didn't say anything. I was glad to be lost in the crowd. 'What's their story?' I asked her.

'Whose story?'

'Theirs, the Polynesian kids?'

She looked at me surprised. 'No one has a history: we have no histories,' she reminded me.

The city throbbed around us. We were in one of its veins. A beast of steel and concrete and people like us living wholly in the present, the eternal instant, as prescribed by the Tribunal. Young always. When the Hotere clock pushed into my thoughts, I pushed it out again.

I looked back. The Polynesian street kids were still in front of the cinema. I felt safe. They would always return to the heart of the city. I didn't understand why.

My son. My daughters.

'What's the matter?' she whispered.

'Let's go home.'

John explained, as we drove home in the winter dark, that my daughters were now safe; their existence, even at Victoria University, had been erased from all records; they had new identities and were with their mother, protected by the agents of the Tribunal.

'And the boy?' I asked.

'Ya son's a cracker mechanic, isn't he?' John tried me. I didn't reply. 'Well, he agreed to our plan. He'll disappear on a fishing trip . . . .'

'Good,' I interrupted.

'Ya're lucky,' he said. 'Soon ya'll be with ya family. Doesn't happen often.'

'What doesn't?'

'Most hearings before the Tribunal go on for hang of a long time, mate. Some never end.'

'How long?'

'No one can remember when some started, that's how long.'

The black sky reflected the lights of the city. No stars. The motorway was a roaring flood of traffic. I thought of her waiting with a blazing fire, chilled beer, and her green under-standing eyes.

'Are there people who never have to appear before the Tribunal?' I asked, remembering the street kids in Queen Street.

'Naw. We all have to sooner or later.'

'Even you?'

'Yeah. But, as ya know, there's nothing to be scared of. The Tribunal's our family, they're doing it for our good, eh.'

Our car crunched over the gravel of the driveway into my house.

I opened my door. The smell of compost rushed in. 'See you tomorrow morning,' I said to John. His blond hair was gold in the inside light of the car.

'See ya, mate!' He waved. 'Ya lucky bastid!' I shut the door.

three

Monopoly

I dressed quietly and left the house at 6 a.m., bundled up in a balaclava, scarf, track suit, jersey, football socks, leather gloves, and the army overcoat my daughters had bought me at the surplus store. Must've looked like a bear; I certainly felt like one.

I'd slept fitfully; the dream of drowning had recurred whenever I'd fallen asleep.

My breath steamed as I marched up Liverpool Street. Everything was wet, the colour of lead, even the light. My running shoes squeaked over the sleek black tongue of road. The light mist that covered Maungakiekie and the Memorial stretched over the city and was being sucked up by the grey sky. I avoided looking at the houses.

I sensed my wife beside me. I hadn't walked since she'd disappeared a few weeks before and was therefore very unfit. The Tribunal had her at a safe hideaway, that's what John had told me. Concentrate. Left-right. Left-right. I struggled against the pain of my joints and lungs that threatened to choke. Left-right-left. Soon only the tip of my nose felt cold, as if it didn't belong to me.

I stopped for breath at the bottom of the road that meandered up through the paddocks to the top of the hill and the Memorial. My heavy hide of clothes weighed a hot sticky ton. I undid the overcoat. Wet, bedraggled sheep watched me from beneath nearby gum trees. Go! My left shoe stepped forward. Dewdrops sparkled on the wire fences. Step by step up the steep incline. Looked only at my shoes. Tensing. Hillary. Everest. Oxygen.

Where the road forked near the top, I stopped again. Heart

thumping wildly in my throat. Spat. Wheezed. Must lose weight.

She was beside me. She moved ahead. I followed. The mist began to shred around us. Shred and lift.

I circled the Memorial. 360 degrees. To survey the whole city and horizons. Once. In the mist and grey, the Harbour Bridge, Rangitoto, the hills, the forests of buildings and the bays and harbours had the sheen of ancient bone. Twice. Recalling how my wife had circled the Memorial, with the Black Rainbow held out like an icon, to bless the earth and protect it from the clock of doom that ticks in our pulses.

Soon I'd be with her and our children. Again. My exhaustion vanished. I didn't care any more if winter ever lifted from the earth.

Below, the city sprawled out like an orderly graveyard. Ships hooted from the harbours. Owls were gods once, my wife had said.

The original inhabitants of Maungakiekie were still here. I felt them through my skin, in the stinging air.

As I descended the hill, I cried silently. In joy? Sadness? Regret that it was over?

'Where did you go?' she asked me as she put out our breakfast.

'A walk.' I refused to talk about it. She moved around me as if I might shatter.

We ate. She avoided my eyes.

'It's over, isn't it?' I had to ask. She continued eating. 'Isn't it?'

She nodded once without looking at me. 'You'll be able to go to your family.'

'And you?'

'Oh, I'm a full-time employee of the Tribunal. I'm a companion. No shortage of work for us.'

I wasn't hungry any more. 'How long have you been doing this?'

'After university and a year's practical training at the Institute of Services.'

31

'Do you like your work?'

She shrugged. 'Some of us have to do it. It's our duty. Last year I was awarded the President's Medal for Companionship.'

She helped me put on my uniform. As I looked at myself in the mirror, she brushed my clothes. 'The Tribunal's proud of you,' she said. 'They have your full history and you are now free of that burden.'

As John and I drove away from the house that morning, I realised I didn't know her name. I'll always remember her seagreen eyes, their everchanging depths.

Mr Bernard Smith (Chairman), Mrs June C. Woolf (First Judge), and Mr James K. Tracter (Second Judge), who made up the Tribunal, were already in their seats when I entered. Their smiles filled the room.

'Sorry,' I started apologising.

'Don't be, we were early,' said the Chairman.

'This is your special day,' smiled Mrs Woolf. I sat down and tried to steady my trembling.

'There's a surprise for you,' the Chairman nodded at the sheet of paper on my table.

'Yeah, ya should read it,' chuckled Mr Tracter. My vision was blurred by tears.

'He seems overwhelmed with joy,' the Chairman declared. I nodded.

'Perhaps, Mr Chairman, ya should read it out for 'im,' Mr Tracter prompted.

I wiped my eyes with my hands. Through the blur I saw the Chairman pick up his copy. He coughed; straightened his glasses. The Hotere clock stopped ticking in my ears and I listened.

In the dramatic baritone of the stage actor he'd once been before becoming a wealthy real estate agent, the Chairman read out my final reference:

TO WHOM IT MAY CONCERN

We, the Supreme Tribunal, Servants of our Almighty State,

declare that the bearer of this reference is now the ideal citizen of our State. He has undergone and survived with A's the prescribed process of Dehistorying. He submitted his soul, his history, to us, with total admission, honesty, and frankness.

We, the Supreme Tribunal, after consulting our Illustrious President, who lives forever, grant the bearer of this document complete freedom and the privileges of that status.

Our state is his. Nothing is to be denied to him.

We, the Supreme Tribunal, Guardians of All Truth, assume total responsibility for his history and the crimes and sins of that past.

We, the Supreme Tribunal, declare that he is, that he is now of Us, forever.

Signed — The Supreme Tribunal

They each hurried off the platform and shook my hand. There were tears in their eyes. Mrs Woolf kissed me on the cheek. 'Bless you,' she whispered.

I stood hugging the reference to my chest as they waved and left the room.

Slowly the Blind Recorder, who'd kept the records of my years of interrogation, collected his papers. I watched his every move. His departure would end my relationship with the Tribunal. He turned to go. Stopped. 'You're very lucky, mate,' he said. 'Congratulations. Not many people get the freedom of the State. You can do what you like now, with total immunity.' He started shuffling towards the door.

'But . . .' I called. He turned. His dark glasses glittered. 'But — what if I don't want it?'

He took off his glasses. The eye sockets were bare. 'How can you refuse freedom?' He put his glasses on again. 'It's what we all dream of, mate. To be free of our past, our guilt . . .'

'Why didn't you take it?' I interrupted. He continued to the door. 'Why?'

He looked back over his shoulder. 'I was never offered it!' he declared. The door slid open. 'Enjoy it. Go to your family.' He stepped over the threshold. 'By the way, don't ever lose that reference.'

'I'll throw it away!' I threatened.

He smiled. 'That's your choice, but you'll be killed if you do.'

'Don' lose this,' John whispered, handing me a plastic kit. 'In id's a map and directions about gettin' ta ya missus and kids.' He opened the car door. 'Ya're one lucky joker.' He got in beside me.

We drove out through the front gate. The guard nodded. I glanced back at the Tribunal Building. It seemed a monument carved out of the air and winter sky.

It wasn't even mid-morning. Unusual to be returning so early. I couldn't resist opening the kit. 'Not here, mate. We don' wan' others ta know, do we?' John cautioned. I zipped it up again. 'When ya get home, memorise id then burn id.'

We didn't know what to say to each other. We'd been together for so many years it didn't seem natural that we were parting.

As we left the motorway and started up Gillies Avenue, I had to ask, 'What do I do for money?'

'Easy, mate. Jus' use ya Reference. Id'll get ya anything, anywhere.'

'Sure?'

'Yeah, mate. Yar've got ta trust the State. The Tribunal's word's worth more than gold.'

For once, he walked me to the door of the house. The air was crisp, the sky clear. 'Watch the telly nex' Saturday,' he said. 'Ya'll see me playin' for Aucklin'.'

'Congratulations.'

'Aw'm goin' ta be the bes' number eight in the bloody country!'

'Yeah!' I said. 'I'm sure!'

He put his arm around my shoulders and patted my back. 'Aw'm goin' ta miss ya, mate. Id's been a long time, eh.'

'Yes, a long time.' We shook hands.

'Yeah, ya're one lucky bastid!' he said. I watched him walk back and get into the car. 'Look afta yaself!' he called.

'I will!'

He waved. 'See ya!' I waved once in reply.

The car disappeared up the driveway and was soon swallowed up by the noise of the street.

I entered the watchful silence of the house. No trace of my companion, nothing except my memories of her — and those were illegal.

After drawing the curtains of my study, I unzipped the kit and studied the road map of the North Island and the instructions about the possible routes to my destination. They were only for part of the journey. Once I got to the end of the first phase I would find further instructions for continuing my search. At the bottom of the page was the usual truth:

THE TRIBUNAL IS YOUR FAMILY. YOUR SEARCH IS FOR THE TRUTH OF THE TRIBUNAL. THE TRUE CITIZEN NEVER GIVES UP.

I memorised the instructions and the map, and then burned them in the fireplace.

The whole afternoon lay ahead of me. I changed into some working clothes and boots, got a spade, and started digging up the middle section of the garden. The spade's sharp head crunched cleanly into the black earth every time I pushed it down with my right foot: CRUNCH! Black water seeped out of each cut like blood. I remembered the Polynesian word for earth and blood was the same: *eleele.*

After showering I packed my suitcase and duffel bag. I folded the Final Reference and fitted it into my wallet.

That night I slept well. No nightmares of drowning.

I didn't look back at the house.

At the top of Pah Road I drove into the service station, and while the young attendant filled the tank, checked the oil and tyres and washed the windows, I got the morning bulletin out of the automatic news dispenser and flicked through it: a half-page photo of the President opening a new ordinarination centre at Palmerston North; two smiling patients being awarded certificates for surviving a new treatment for AIDS; a record year for dairy exports. It was all good news, as usual. Our earth was at peace.

I sweated as I drove on to the motorway south but relaxed when I encountered only light traffic. I even increased speed. It was warm in the car. I pushed in a cassette: my second daughter's favourite group. A short while later my hands were drumming on the steering wheel to their loud beat:

> *Eat the day away*
> *Eat the sadness in your heart*
> *'Cause yar got nothin'*
> *To gripe about in our happy state.*
>
> *Eat yar darlin's love*
> *Eat ta yar heart's content*
> *'Cause all's well under*
> *Our President's philosophee of Grace . . .*

I hadn't been out in the country for a long time. The limitless green was flowing into me again, kilometre after kilometre, through my pores. 'It's one paddock,' my six-year-old son remarked when we'd first flown over the North Island. He'd refused after that to look down at it.

The pale sun sang above the Bombay Hills as I drove up them, weaving round the bends, then down the other side into a stretch of mist in which all sounds were muffled. I switched on the car lights and slowed down. Everything was bandaged in white. A few trucks edged by like whales groping through limestone seas. I started sweating again. I switched off the cassette player and concentrated on steering my vessel through the eerie sea of white which had no tongue.

When I broke through the whiteness I was driving along the banks of the Waikato out of which the sunlight seemed to be bursting and spreading over the land. Again the Hotere clock ticked in my unwilling ears, bringing with it chapters of the history of the Waikato tribes. Like the people of Maungakiekie, the Waikato tribes had been turned into grass and meat. History is madness, the Tribunal has prescribed. So I silenced the Hotere clock, pushed down on the accelerator, and sped away from history.

I opened my window. The wind gusted against my face. I sucked it in. Held it down in my centre until I was with and of the moment again.

> *Eat eat and be free*
> *Eat of the Tribunal's everlasting Peace*
> *Don't listen to historee*
> *That's all guilt and insanitee . . .*

Mid-morning. Hamilton was to be my first compulsory stop. I entered it through the long street of motels displaying a gauntlet of garish signs advertising vacancies, cheap rates, free video, saunas and waterbeds. *Fourteenth motel on the left; ask for Unit 13*, I recalled my search kit.

After the tiny receptionist showed me into my unit, she dropped the key into my hand. 'Have a pleasant stay,' she said. She left behind the heady scent of Opium, and the purple glitter of her thin smile. I locked the door behind her. *Your first clue is under the pillows.*

I folded back the bed cover, turned over the pillows on the double bed and found an envelope:

Read the contents of this carefully then proceed to your next stop and collect $1,000 to pay for the next stage of your journey.

DO NOT DEVIATE FROM THE ENCLOSED INSTRUCTIONS OR YOU WILL FORFEIT WHAT YOU HAVE WON ALREADY.

My hands shook as I ripped it open.

Leave this city immediately. Agents are here already looking for you. (Besides, Hamilton has no worthwhile attractions for searchers.) Proceed to Rotorua and 247 Tangata Street. Ask for Mr Heremaia Clatter.

Flush this down the toilet.

As a youngster I'd enjoyed Monopoly. I was enjoying this

more because it was for real, full of risk. The Tribunal certainly knew how to give meaning to our lives.

Rotorua stinks. It stinks of sulphur (not my favourite smell). And bubbles with hot pools, dying geysers, and other thermal activity. It feeds off tourists, mainly Japanese and American.

On my way there through the rolling man-made pine forests, I'd kept looking into the rear-view mirror to see if I was being followed.

The city was crowded. It was about 2 p.m. I parked in the main street and looked for Tangata Street on my car map. A short while later I drove up the main street, stopping often because of pedestrians and the heavy traffic. *Up you too!* signalled one beanpole of a man when I horned him as he crossed in front of me. He scooted onto the footpath when I aimed the car at him.

There was little traffic in Tangata Street. I drove up and down it twice. Neatly cut lawns and hedges, houses that wanted to be inconspicuous, the odd housewife gardening. Once I was certain no agents were about, I parked round the corner and walked back to Tangata Street and Number 247.

Two sprawling gum trees hid most of the front of the house. Through the sulphur stench I breathed the aromatic scent of eucalyptus. No one about. A garden gnome stood in a patch of bamboo, fishing.

When I raised my hand to knock on the front door, I discovered I was dripping sweat, heavy drops of it, on to the doormat. I wiped my forehead with my handkerchief.

I knocked. No one. I backed off, hurried to my car, and waited.

I felt I was being watched but couldn't figure out who by and from where. An hour or so later cars and people returning from work went by and into some of the houses.

He was waiting for me, I think, because as soon as I knocked the door swung open and he pulled me into the house. He turned and hurried into the sitting room, mumbling, 'You're late, mate.'

I followed him. 'You almost lost your entry fee.' Suppressed chuckling. 'Come.'

From the back, he appeared squat, solid, as if carved out of lava. His long black hair was tied in a topknot.

One step into the sitting room, and I stopped dead-still. From wall to wall and across the floor was an army of wood carvings. 'My whanau,' he smiled. He was totally of it, among it. Chiselled classical Maori face, ebony colour of wood, heavily muscled arms and legs. 'Fearsome, eh!' he laughed. 'Io, te Atua.' I didn't understand what he was referring to. 'All my life I've explored the wood for Io's face.' Though the carvings varied from the size of a knuckle to ones that towered to the ceiling, they were all stylised faces. From those recognisably traditional to the highly abstract. And they were fierce.

I walked in and among them. A garden, a forest, his imagination, his search for Io's face.

'Here,' he handed me a thick envelope. 'A thousand dollars, mate. You've earned it. Your directions are inside too.'

'I'm sorry to be endangering your life and these,' I said.

'Don't worry, mate. I'm just one of the network. Doing my bit for the country.' A glow was emanating from the skin of his face. 'I'm just a humble carver.' I turned to leave. 'You want some kai?' I shook my head. 'Here.' He took the pendant from around his neck. I backed off but he insisted on tying it around my neck. 'For luck. Io's face. It's only beef bone anyway. Sell lots of them to the bloody tourists.'

'Thanks,' I said. I caressed the pendant. It was still warm from his body. 'They're very beautiful,' I pointed to the carvings.

'A lifetime's work. Don't want to sell any of them. Don't need the bread. The Tribunal pays me well.'

Parked under an isolated stand of willows on the shore of the lake, I opened the envelope.

> Proceed south to Wanganui. Stop there. Go to Wally's Book Centre and buy a copy of Janet Frame's *Faces in the Water*. Check into the White River Hotel. Read the novel. It will tell you where to go next.

P.S. Janet Frame once lived in Wanganui. Otherwise that town is a spiritual desert for searchers.

Destroy this immediately.

I pushed in the car lighter. When it was hot I used it to burn the message. I stamped the ashes into the sand of the lakeshore.

Night was walking across the water and stretching up into the heavens. In it I caught for a moment Heremaia Clatter's face, the eyes of Io.

I retreated into the car.

I checked into the most expensive hotel, soaked for a long time in the bath, then gorged myself on a dreamless sleep in which there was no sulphur stink.

Wanganui City is on the river that drains out the heart of the North Island. I'd never been in it before but it wasn't difficult finding Wally's Book Centre, buying the Frame novel, and checking into the White River Hotel. My room on the eighth floor had a clear view of the countryside as far as the eye could see. The river swept by below, snug in its bed.

Though I'd read a lot of New Zealand fiction I wasn't a Frame fan. Her first novel, *Owls Do Cry*, had frightened me with its bleak vision of Pakeha society and humanity. It was midday. I wasn't hungry. I lay on the bed and read and floated on the easy sound of the river.

When it was evening I switched on the bedside lamp and ordered vegetable quiche and hokey-pokey ice cream from room service. I didn't look at the face of the waiter who brought it.

I ate as I continued reading. And read until my eyes threatened to tear themselves out of their sockets.

As I dressed for bed I remembered James K. Baxter, the poet, was buried upriver in Hiruhirama, Jerusalem, a small Maori settlement where he'd found some peace in the river that was now singing past my window and taking Baxter's poems to the sea:

> . . . *going step by step in solitude*
> *To the middle of the Maori night*
> *where dreams gather* . . .

At breakfast I didn't look at the couple at the far end of the dining room. I got fruit, croissants, tea and toast from the self-service bar. I sensed them watching me but I chewed and swallowed my food as if I was enjoying it. Other guests came in. Surreptitiously I glanced at the couple. His back was towards me. Grey suit, thinning hair, large ears, slow gestures, long slender hands. She had a sharp profile: all nose and teeth. Alabaster skin.

When they got up to leave I let them get to the door then I swivelled round and caught her scrutinising me. Startled eyes. She looked away and they hurried out.

The Huntsman would be too slow. So after packing my gear, I drove round until I found a car dealer with an array of powerful cars. Princess Anne, that's who that woman reminded me of.

The spacious building was a glittering dome that magnified the sunlight on the cars, making them look as if they were on fire, powerful creatures waiting to claim their owners. I steered clear of them as I moved among them. Two men in the office kept glancing at me but didn't bother to come over. I had to beckon. The younger hurried to me as I laid my hands on the steel-blue Enarisan. Smooth and cold.

'Yeah, mate?' He reminded me of a Doberman, but without the breeding.

I breathed in deeply. 'How much?'

'How much what?'

'This.' I ran my fingers over the bonnet. He winced at my fingerprints.

'A lot of money, mate.' His face was a pan of pale makeup and purple lipstick.

'I can afford it, *mate!*' I leant with my elbow on the car roof and just stared at him.

He emphasised each number of the exorbitant price, smiling.

'Will a cheque do?' I tested him.

His purple mouth curved into a grin. 'Sorry, chief.'

'Why not?'

41

'We don't accept cheques.'

I wasn't going to argue any further. I unzipped my brief-
case, took out my wallet and said, 'Tell your boss I want to see
him.'

He didn't move; he kept grinning at me. 'Out here?'

I nodded. 'Out here and quick!' He chortled as he minced
off.

I watched them talking and then laughing and looking at
me.

I swallowed him with my eyes as he sauntered over, hands
in his pockets, belly overflowing his belt. The bottom half of his
face hung down to his collar bone. 'Yeah, mate, I hear ya wan'
ta see me.'

I pulled It out of my wallet, snapped it open with my left
hand and held it down to his face.

Each word of the Reference kicked his smile and arrogance
away, hunk by hunk.

'And I want *this* car, chief!' I said. 'See that car?' I pointed
to the Huntsman. 'You can have that.'

After ten minutes of their rushing about and gracious attention, I was in the Enarisan with the ownership papers signed,
the keys, my luggage, and their profuse goodbyes and promises
of fulfilling my every future wish concerning vehicles.

I couldn't believe it, the Reference worked. I could get anything with it!

You have finally passed GO. The chase is on. But don't worry,
if Janet Frame could survive Cliffhaven you can survive the
hunters.

I found the instructions in the glove compartment of the
Enarisan.

The couple, in the black Mao, were waiting for me in a side
street just over the Wanganui Bridge. They pulled out behind
me. The Enarisan purred around me. Into every nerve it poured
power, until I was part of it. You have passed GO, so go!

The Mao was centred in my rear-view mirror. Sleek and
inescapable as a conscience.

Monopoly

I will write about the season of peril. I was put in hospital because a great gap opened in the ice floe between myself and the other people whom I watched, with their world, drifting away through a violet-coloured sea where hammerhead sharks in tropical ease swam side by side with the seals and the polar bears. I was alone on the ice.

— Istina Mavet, in *Faces in the Water* by Janet Frame

There was purpose to my life again: the search for my family, while they, the hunters, stalked me.

four

Cocaine

Danger is a true searcher's cocaine. It keeps him high, unafraid, alert to his every nerve end. I can't remember where I read that.

The woman was driving, with black sunglasses that covered almost half her face. I pushed down on the accelerator and the Enarisan surged forward. So much power to control.

She drew up almost to my back bumper then dropped back to about twenty metres. More power and I pushed ahead, but she clung to the twenty-metre bond that tied us.

I settled into an easy 150 k's. The Enarisan had to be kept in harness, it was rearing to go but I didn't have the courage for it. Not yet. The road fingered dizzily ahead. The Enarisan swallowed it and the paddocks and hills, but I couldn't break from her. Parakina. Marton. Bulls. Over the Rangitikei River that was brown with swirling silt. Himatangi. Foxton. Coal Flat. I had to admit she was a gifted driver, putting just enough pressure on me to drive at the edge of my fear, forcing me to challenge my limits. 160 k's. She pushed me further. Every time I caught her face in the rear-view mirror I imagined her smiling to herself. Push him. Push. He's scared shitless.

Though it was winter the sky was an open dome of broken cloud and mellow light, stretching high, as I settled into the chase south. Tied to the speed, the frantic road, destiny, her purpose and mine.

Maintain a steady pace or you will forfeit 100 k's of your life. Don't dare the hunters yet. They too have a purpose: they will teach you, the hunted, survival techniques, evasion, the sweetness of danger.

They weren't trying to catch me, I decided. So I relaxed. Opened my jacket. Quickly the air-conditioning dried my sweat. I looked back. Her black glasses were unwavering. The country's imagery flicked over its surface like escaping fish.

I slowed to 120 ks. She did too. Levin. Ohau. Manakau. Otaki. I pushed in my son's favourite cassette — the Scalpers, reggae:

> *Fuck I say ta romance and chivalree*
> *The belly can't get no sustenance from that*
> *Fuck I say ta capitalists and Reds*
> *I ain't no ideologue bound for the guillotine . . .*

I wondered what she and her partner were listening to in their car. Steep rise then round a sharp bend and off the main road into a rest area that overlooked the land sloping down to the sea. Crunched to a halt. Out behind some bushes, pissing and pissing. *Nothin' like a good piss and shit ta relieve life's agonee*, the Scalpers would sing.

They shot past, saw me, but kept on. I jumped into my car and followed. I pushed to within twenty metres of them and held that. She tried to pull away, through lanes of tall pines and the smell of sheep shit. I kept up. More. I followed, held. Now she was teaching me to go beyond my competence and fear, into daring, the sweetness of risk.

Her wheels screeching, burning, as she hugged the curve. I didn't panic. (Steve McQueen in *Bullitt!*) I leant into it and held the edge as she'd done, then out of it. Down the hill. I imagined her laughing, head flung back, the man congratulating her on her teaching skills.

> *Don't try ta kiss ma arse man*
> *It ain't meant for sympathee . . .*

Their car hit a bump and lifted. Thumped down again. I followed up, landed smoothly, leaving my breath in the air for a moment. *Bullitt*, all right! Real car chases imitate art.

> *Our planet's made of milk and blood*
> *and razor-teethed creatures that eat glass . . .*

Following the coast. Waikanae. Rising on our left to hills and behind them the Tararuas. On to Paraparaumu. Paekakariki. The sea sweeping in from our right. From Kapiti, once the sanctuary of Te Rauparaha.

For almost 200 k's she'd taught me.

Now a colder southerly was gusting in from the Pole to engulf us, with the Scalpers mapping out my son's defiant creed:

> *If ya can't speak da simple truth*
> *Then up ya too with da President's Tool . . .*

Above Pukerua Bay, in a mist of salt spray, seagulls hovered. I couldn't hear their cries. Alistair Campbell, the poet, used to live on the top peak overlooking the bay. The peak looked unreal through the spray.

I clung to her as she sped up the hill. She overtook one, two, three cars. I copied her, risking the oncoming traffic. She overtook again. I ducked out, overtook, and pulled in behind her. Good, good, she seemed to be saying.

I pulled back as they headed across Paremata Bridge. Heavy traffic now. She overtook. I didn't follow suit. Once over the bridge she veered off onto the motorway into Wellington. I turned left, swiftly, and sped along the shore of Paremata inlet, into Sam Hunt's Bottle Creek, uphill and down into Oak Avenue and the crinkled expanse of the inlet. I took the winding road as fast as I could bear. A few punts on the water. On the other side, lead grey hills. Whitby above to the right, famous for suicides. I looked back repeatedly. No sign of the hunters.

The Enarisan hummed through the Sam Hunt farms and hills, past Moonshine Valley into the Hutt Valley. Past high noon now. The car dug into the buffeting southerly. Thick traffic but I danced through it. Suburbia, stretches of houses that looked like bone in the wintry light.

At Upper Hutt I knew I'd lost my pursuers. I turned down through the rugged hills and range and headed towards Reikorangi.

Soon I was following the river through the wide gap in the

hills. The pale sun, caught in a bed of cloud, hung over the western range. To it I gave the face of my wife.

As in others' lives your search will often demand your doubling back, your retracing of the path, to avoid danger, to learn from your footsteps. In Reikorangi lies the end of the first phase. Avoid sentimentality and win another $1,000.

I stopped on the wooden bridge. The river surged like smoke over the rocks and boulders, swung in an arc and sent spray up into the bush. In the spray was a barely visible rainbow.

The dirt road into the farm was not far away. Before I reached it, I pulled off the road, hid in a stand of trees above the river, and watched the main road. No sign of them. Vehicles passed. I waited and liked the waiting. The fuzzy sun dropped behind the range. The landscape turned a bluish grey. I waited, letting the eternal swishing of the river wash through my head.

Crickets were suddenly chirping in the core of my ears. I jerked awake. It was dark, and out of the dark rushed the lights of vehicles. Whisssh! and they were past me. Whisssh! Wiped my eyes with my hands. My back and legs were aching from the sitting. It was time.

The Enarisan's lights caught the front gate and mail box. The gate was open. I drove in and up the road that swung round behind a high wave of hills. The eyes of sheep and cattle flashed in my lights. The southerly was gone, blocked off by the hills.

Hedges and macrocarpas surrounded the house and outbuildings. I switched off my lights and edged towards the lights bursting from the house's front windows. I turned my window down a few centimetres. The sound of a radio. I stopped. Got out quietly, stretched the pain out of my joints. I recognised the record on the radio, the Moonshine Rockers. I crouched and shuffled forward. Stopped. Surveyed the house again. No sign of people. I circled until I was on the back porch among pot plants, sacks of potatoes and decaying fruit.

The launch the *Joyita* had been found adrift in mid-ocean, without crew or passengers, but everything else, including the meals, was ready. Goldilocks had found the Three Bears' home that way too. The bears had returned to wake her from her innocent sleep. That's how my family's sanctuary was when I arrived.

I inspected every room. Fingered, smelled, embraced, absorbed every evidence of them. I switched off the oven, took out the lamb roast and put it on the table set, by them, for five. Put out the vegetables, gravy, mint sauce, salt and pepper. Sat down in my chair at the table's head. Bowed my head and said grace.

And then ate. At first slowly, listening to and conversing with their empty presences. Until the pain of their departure shattered my fragile pretence, and I started cramming the food into my mouth, gullet, gagging and choking as I swallowed and swallowed.

> Dearest Darling
> Don't worry. Enjoy the meal. They have taken us to a safer place. They'll leave you instructions to follow. We had to leave in a hurry because our enemies' agents had discovered our whereabouts.
> Trust the Tribunal.
> We love you very much.

This note, in my wife's handwriting, was on the dressing table in our bedroom. I was able to sleep after that.

Next morning, and it was bitterly cold, I found an envelope crammed with $1,000 and a note congratulating me on surviving the first phase:

> Go into Wellington City. Check into the West Plaza Hotel. Ask the receptionist for messages. In this phase you will have to confront your hunters. Don't retreat. If you do you will forfeit a loved one.

I shouldered my heavy duffel bag and pushed through the revolving glass door into the lobby, out of the night's chilling wind.

As I unbuttoned my overcoat I looked around. The dining room to my left was noisy with diners. Scrumptious smells of food. The chairs in the lobby were occupied by a uniformed Japanese tour group, sipping tea and wrapping up the goods they'd bought.

I sensed it. Glanced across at the reception desk and caught the look on the receptionist's face. Knew what I was in for, my past was here again. I swallowed and headed into it.

She was serving two other customers. I stood at the counter. She refused to look at me. In the wall mirrors to my right I saw an unshaven, rumpled man. I tried not to inhale my unwashed smell. The other receptionist, a middle-aged man, locked his drawer, said goodbye to her, and left. I waited. A porter came and, carrying the other customers' bags, led them towards the lifts. She pretended she was busy reading the register. About twenty, hair dyed silky black, heavy yellow makeup, dangling black coral earrings. She turned to the files behind her. Other guests were queueing behind me.

'What do you want?' she asked me over her shoulder. I didn't reply. She turned her head, her earrings swung back and forth. 'There are other people.'

'I have a booking here,' I replied. She looked away again.

'Name?' she asked. I told her. 'No name like that here,' she said without looking at the records.

'Have a fucking look!' I said. Her head snapped round, her eyes stabbing at me. 'Yeah, have a fucking look at your records!'

Her hands shook as she fumbled through the cards, pulled out my card, thumped it on the counter and refused to look at me. 'Fill it here.'

'I know what to do!' I emphasised. She didn't move to give me a pen. I held out my hand. She thrust her pen into it and edged away to serve the next customer. 'Here!' I pushed the card at her. She continued serving the other man. 'Look here, I haven't finished!' The other man stepped back; he smelled of cigarettes. 'What's my room number?' She pulled the key out of the slot and dropped it in front of me. 'Get someone to carry my bags!' I refused to shift until the porter arrived and picked up my bags.

A few paces away from the counter I remembered and

returned to her. Ignoring the customer she was serving, I said, 'There are messages for me.'

'No there aren't,' she said, without looking at me.

'Check!' I said. She sighed and looked in my slot. When she found the envelope, she hesitated. 'Next time, open your fucking eyes!' I pulled the envelope out of her hand.

Once in my room, I sat on the bed. Good cleansing anger, a feeling I'd not allowed myself to enjoy since the Tribunal had summoned me to Auckland. And I wanted it to continue. Picked up the phone and dialled the Manager's number. No reply. I dialled his Assistant. I told him someone had collapsed outside my door.

Five minutes later he was ringing on my door. A squat security officer, who looked like a lock forward gone to fat, was with him.

As they followed me into the bedroom, I took It out of my wallet. Introduced myself. Before they could reply, I held up my Final Reference. I didn't say a thing as they read It.

'Thank you, sir,' the Assistant Manager said. 'Thank you for letting us know you are one of the Chosen Ones.' His spindly physique couldn't fill out his uniform. The black mole on his small chin was like a watchful eye. 'Where is the person you reported, sir?'

'Your receptionist,' I said. They looked puzzled. 'The one on duty right now.' They looked more puzzled. 'She discriminated against me, *sir*.'

His thin body contracted further. 'I'm sorry, sir, but our hotel is famous for its hospitality and policy of equal treatment.'

'She was bloody rude.'

'She's young, sir, just out of our four-year managerial training programme . . .'

'Are you saying I'm lying?'

He was now as thin as a question mark. 'Certainly not, sir.' He glanced at his partner.

'That's right, sir,' his partner echoed. 'We will interrogate her and get the truth from her.'

It was all back: my life, my family — our history of being

discriminated against, a history the self-sacrificing Tribunal had assumed the guilt and responsibility for but which the hunters, the receptionist, and now these men had brought back.

'What's your hotel got against my money, my appearance, my vegetarianism?' I demanded.

'Nothing, sir!' they chorused.

'Your money's as good as ours,' said the Assistant Manager.

'And your appearance is of our day and age . . .'

'And I'm a vegetarian too, sir. Our receptionist isn't feeling well — it's that time of the month. That's why she may've treated you . . .'

'Unwisely, unjustly,' offered his partner.

They jumped when my fist slammed down on the bed. 'I could've killed her!' I snapped. They straightened up.

'Is that what you want us to do, sir?' the balding security officer whispered.

'No!'

'But it's your privilege, sir. As a Free Citizen the Tribunal has ruled that your every wish should be obeyed,' the Assistant Manager said. He was inflated to his full size again.

I glanced at them: they were soldiers ready to obey my commands, and I was scared of the power the Tribunal had bestowed upon me. I thrust the Final Reference into my back pocket. 'No, it was my fault,' I denied that power. 'I've been travelling for three days. I misinterpreted her actions.'

'But she shouldn't have been rude to you, Free Citizen,' the Assistant Manager declared.

'No, sir. It's the wish of our Illustrious President and our all-seeing Tribunal that our Free Citizens, who've earned the Freedom of our State, be treated well. And obeyed utterly!'

'We have to sack her, sir,' the security officer added.

'Too right!' his mate pronounced sentence.

I tried but I couldn't dissuade them. Nor could I stop them from shifting me into their most lavish suite which even had a telephone and TV in the toilets. And for free, on the house.

Next morning as I walked to the lift I knew, from the feel of the hotel air and the smiles of the three Polynesian room attendants I met, that the hotel staff had been alerted to my status and instructed to satisfy my every wish.

I hurried back to my suite and buried the Final Reference at the bottom of my suitcase.

The southerly bit at my face, ears and hands. I hurried along Manners Street but I couldn't escape the unkempt man in the ridiculous army overcoat who raced me in the glass of the shop display windows. Finally, I turned into a hairdressing salon, the Floating World.

All mirrors, red carpet, plastic and glitter. I hesitated, wanting to leave again, but the attendant, a youth with a bristling mohawk and smelling of Poison perfume, held my arm and said, 'We've been expecting you, a good luck person, our first customer of the day.' Before I knew it I was lying back in a soft dentist-like chair, and he was washing my hair. He twittered in my ears about the weather.

'You certainly need a new personality,' another person whispered into my left ear after I sat down in the hairdressing chair. In the mirror, beside me, was a striking woman in flowing silk robes, dark hair that cascaded in ringlets down to her shoulders, and a face which was painted in the perfect Noh mask of a princess. 'I'm your hair artist and psychologist, Noriko James Oe,' she declared. 'Relax and enjoy.' She started massaging my neck and shoulders. Her relaxing scent of Sake slipped into my nostrils and into the centre of my resistance. I started relenting. And shut my eyes.

I floated in her curing touch, her flow and care, the snipping of the scissors, and the warmth of the room. Forever in the world of appearances, floating, in flux.

'Is that all right, sir?' Her whisper drew me out of my floating. I opened my eyes.

In the mirror, staring at me inquisitively, was the man I'd looked like over a decade before. 'Yes, yes,' I whispered.

She unwrapped the cape from around me. Brushed the snippets of hair off my neck. 'In a Noh play there is always the spiritual resolution,' she said. 'A spiritual balancing of good and evil in a world that is becoming.' I turned my profile this way and that, admiring my new appearance. 'A haircut and shave isn't everything,' she whispered. The smooth back of her hand felt like tingling electricity as she ran it down my cheek. I was alive, again, but I edged away from her. 'New clothes, ' she said, 'for new adventures and dangers.' She bowed and shuffled, like a Noh player, into the next room.

I paid the eager attendant four times what he normally charged, and asked for the best men's clothing shop in the city.

Two hours later, I'd shed my old skin and was marching down Lambton Quay in new underclothes, new three-piece suit — the latest cut for portly men – greenstriped shirt, pink silk tie, black shoes you could see your smile in, and a mohair overcoat, no longer feeling cold in the aggressive wind. A new wardrobe of suits, jackets, shoes, shirts, ties and socks was being delivered to my hotel. After all, I could afford anything in the Floating World.

And in the shedding of the rumpled man in the smelly army overcoat, I *felt* new, properly attired to suit my new status and the challenge of the hunters. Farewell, my lovely, to the poverty-stricken, unshaven Phillip Marlowe. Greetings to the neatly cultured Hercule Poirot and perhaps the suave James Bond. (I would have to lose weight, though.)

five

The Sisters

I opened the envelope when I got back to my hotel:

> Try and lose weight. The hunters are very fit. Let them find you. Be patient. They'll lead you to your family. Hunters have families too, and they are capable of falling in love.
>
> Remember, don't retreat.
>
> By the way, your Hotere is safe. It is counting.

To be safe one should cultivate invisibility. I should've learned that from Ralph Ellison's *Invisible Man* and the persecuted minorities of the world. Yet I'd allowed the hotel staff to discover who I was, and they were now competing lavishly to prove their servility to me. More so now that I was groomed and attired in the manner they believed befitted my status. Whenever I moved around the hotel, I was a target for their attention, which in turn drew the curiosity of the other guests. So I stayed in my suite and watched video or read and dieted. And waited. Three days of this and I was ill with boredom.

Hurry up, hunters. I need you to save me from this purposelessness.

Every night the Hotere clock ticked in my sleepless head.

The phone rang as I was finishing my breakfast of muesli and dried fruit. 'Yes?' I asked.

'They've arrived,' was all the woman said. Click. The silence buzzed in my hearing.

I trembled as I dressed in one of my new suits which now sat easily on me because I'd shed a few kilos.

It was Sunday, I remembered, as I left the lift and strode through the lobby towards reception. I avoided looking at the guests. Many of them became curious when the Manager, with his glinting teeth, appeared to greet me, accept my key, and ask if I needed anything. I told him. He led me to the most conspicuous table in the centre of the lobby, pulled back the soft chair. I sat down. He beckoned to a waiter and whispered to him. I thanked him. He backed off.

In a few minutes, I was pretending to read the morning paper, while I sipped a cup of Twining's tea with a slice of lemon. I observed the lobby periodically. Focused on the revolving front door, on everyone who entered.

Apart from staff I wasn't being watched, I decided an hour later, and strolled to the bar.

My life was imitating film thrillers. It might even attain the existential truths of *Breathless* by Louis Malle.

This wasn't a pub as described in most New Zealand fiction. This was a bar, a stage set of upmarket glitter, soft lights, padded chairs and glass tables, carpets as lush as a bowling green in spring before it was mowed, rows of any drink imaginable, and wall mirrors in which to boost your ego. And you didn't have to go to the bar to get a drink.

A waiter, in dinner suit, sat me down and asked what I wanted.

Four other customers: a slim woman on a barstool, with her back to me, nursing a long glass; three businessmen huddled over a calculator and yellow notepads.

I put some notes on his tray. The young waiter said, 'It's on the house, sir.' He returned my money. 'To save time,' I said, 'whenever you see my glass is empty, bring me another one. Okay, mate?'

'Yes, sir.' His name tag said Bernie.

'Thanks, Bernie. God'll reward ya!' I raised my glass. 'Do you like working in this joint?'

He laughed politely. 'Ah, yeah. It's good money. Lotsa tips.'

'And no Poms?'

'Yeah, no bloody Poms either!'

'Good place awright!' I downed my whisky-and-Coke-with-lotsa-ice. 'Bloody good, mate!' My teeth were stinging from the ice.

We talked in this relaxed, matey way for three more whiskies, two literary stereotypes conversing in the Kiwi tradition of social realist fiction, with a dash of Damon Runyon, Dashiel Hammett, Ross Macdonald, and other imports, in a bar not a pub, while I courted the attention of the hunters.

The woman at the bar staggered, steadied herself, turned to face the front entrance and, while everyone watched, steered herself out, head held high, trying not to appear drunk.

'Comes every Sundee, same time. Leaves the same time drunk to the gills but able to walk out under her own steam,' Bernie said.

'Why Sunday, why here?'

'Beats me, mate. Why do we do anything?'

I remembered she wore enormous glasses with red frames.

The bar filled. The cigarette smoke threatened me with cancer and stung my eyes. I drank steadily. Caught no sign of the hunters. Over the hi-fi system thumped the incessant beat of the Ballbreakers:

> *Luv ya man true*
> *Luv him blue*
> *Break his juice*
> *if he's untrue ta you . . .*

I got up to go for a piss, found my head and body were waterlogged, decided to go back to my rooms. 'Ya won't say no to a tip, Bernie?' I asked. He shook his head. 'Here!' I stuffed a handful of notes into his breast pocket. 'With the compliments of the Tribunal.'

As I swayed out of the bar, nausea started swirling in my head and nose. I staggered into the lift, tried not to breathe on the lift crowd, bid them goodnight and ran to my suite.

The bed held me down. I kept my head dead still, to quell the nausea.

Caring hands undressed me, wiped my face with a wet facecloth, drew back the duvet and sheets. I slid under. 'Thank you,' I kept murmuring as the hands kneaded the cold facecloth into my forehead.

Sometime, somewhere, in the dream, I saw those hands — long delicate fingers with lead grey fingernails — slide a hypodermic needle into the vein on the inside of my arm, pump a transparent liquid in, and then expertly pluck out the needle and rub cooling alcohol over the puncture. A woman's hands. Like my wife's. Sometime, somewhere, in that dream I saw myself waking, my vision as sharp as diamonds. I didn't know where I was and started panicking.

'Relax,' said the voice. 'Sorry to wake you.' Somewhere in the crystal clarity of my vision I saw the red frames, the glistening spectacles, then the stubby nose that carried them and the intensely amused eyes that the lens magnified.

I tried but I couldn't sit up; tried but couldn't lift my arms and legs. 'Don't struggle. We have many things to discuss.' I struggled again, saw I was fastened, at my wrists and ankles, to the corners of the bed. 'You're a very attractive man.' I looked at my chest, belly, and down. I was naked.

'Yeah, very attractive!' another female voice crooned. Over my genitals I saw them sitting side by side, in chairs, at the foot of my bed: the woman from the bar and the woman in the Mao. 'Soon you'll be erectly awake,' she added and puzzled me.

'He doesn't know yet,' Red Frames whispered.

'He will soon. Then his most secret fantasies will come true.'

They watched me. I glanced at my arms, hands, body. No transformation. Looked at my captors. 'No, you're not turning into a werewolf . . .'

'Or Mr Hyde . . .'

'Or *Metamorphosis* by Kafka . . .'

'Soon your most cherished fantasy . . .'

'Yes, most cherished . . .'

'Will materialise, thanks to biotechnology, and we will help you fulfil it, Mr Free Citizen . . .'

'We have studied, in minute detail, your full history in the

57

bottomless memory banks of the Tribunal's Puzzle Palace . . .'

'Every word, figure, fabrication, truth, fact, lie, fantasy . . .'

'Which our thorough Tribunal collected and extracted from you, voluntarily, all these years. We know every shred, every atom, every DNA of you . . .'

'From the second you were conceived to now.'

'By the way,' Red Frames said, with a slight bow, 'I'm Sister Honey . . .'

'And I'm Sister Ratched — Big Nurse.'

'You'll recall I was in Janet Frame's overpraised autobiography-cum-novel, *Faces in the Water* — melodramatic tripe.'

'And I was libelled and slandered in *One Flew Over the Cuckoo's Nest*. Kesey became impotent, his mind cells burnt out by LSD. Just punishment . . .'

'And Istina Mavet, through Frame, portrayed me cruelly as a sadistic nurse . . .' As they chorused their criticism, obviously a well-practised one, I wanted to believe I was in a nightmare I was going to wake out of soon.

'I suppose it can be said I was fortunate to feature in a bestselling book and film. But the actress who portrayed me was God-awful.'

'She won an Oscar for it.'

'Some consolation!'

'And I should be flattered Frame's Gothic autobiographical novel is studied by Stage One students. At least they'll know who I am, even if they end up despising me. Don't give a stuff, anyway. That book cost me my job at Cliffhaven; I had to find another one. Lucky me, I found my true vocation. This . . .'

'Detective work!'

'Yeah, hunting wayward souls . . .'

'Saving them from themselves and the Tribunal.' They leaned forward and peered into my eyes.

'He's bloody resistant,' said Sister Honey.

'Yeah, strong all right. It's taking the Erectol a long time . . .'

'Maybe we should've doubled the dose.'

'Shit no. He'd be a raving, rampaging maniac!' Big Nurse said. They chortled and clapped their hands.

At the back of my brain a warm, pulsating caress was spreading, getting hotter, waking other cells and nerves; connecting, firing my whole head then shimmering down through my spinal cord and radiating out, plunging down through my belly and thrusting my penis up, up until it was ready to burst. And they clapped.

'Amazing. Never fails,' echoed Big Nurse. The cry burst through my clenched teeth. 'Just hold your randy horse!' she said. 'All in good time.'

'Erectol III is the latest in aphrodisiac drugs,' Sister Honey explained. 'The Tribunal won't let it on the market. Just imagine a world of raving sex fiends; no one would have time or the energy to work. We'd intercourse ourselves to death!' Her companion giggled and ran her fingernails over my belly. My body twisted, burned, bucked.

'Not bad!' laughed Sister Honey.

'Yeah, not bad!'

I raged against my bonds. 'This is what you've always yearned for secretly, isn't it?' Big Nurse taunted me. 'But you kept it from your wife . . .'

'And the ten others,' Sister Honey laughed. 'You were unfaithful to your wife, weren't you?' The bed was soaked with my sweat. I could've eaten my bonds.

'Now your wish for the everlasting fuck — pardon my crudity, for the permanent erection, is about to come true,' whispered Big Nurse.

'And in return for it you must tell us where your family is.'

'A fair exchange, eh!'

'Shall I go first?' Sister Honey offered.

'Why not. He won't see your wrinkles, the ravages of age, not now, not in the state he's in.'

Sister Honey jumped up and, gazing at me like Salome in *Samson and Delilah*, started dancing.

'Ping!' Big Nurse laughed, as she flicked my raging erection.

I was a helpless bell of lust that rang and rang.

I don't want to contribute unnecessarily to the torrid ocean of pornography that exists by describing, in detail, the torture the Sisters subjected me to. (A thriller shouldn't go off on tangents that slow down its pace.) So I'll be impressionistic.

I was raised to fight evil even if it cost me my life, but the Sisters' technology, their Erectol and other serums, their relentless familiarity with my weaknesses, proved too strong. The Sisters and their helpers — two pin-ups out of *Hothouse* and one male out of *He-Man* — were artists at their torture. Imagine a happening choreographed by Marquis de Sade and filmed by Brian de Palma, based on *The Story of O*. The Sisters instructed their helpers and observed and talked to me.

My erection refused to blow, as it were. Every time I mounted to that crest, so to speak like Barbara Cartland, they stopped their delicious torture. The price for their continuing the exquisite pain was for me to talk, to sing, to betray. I was no macho Mike Hammer or Joan of Arc.

They wanted to know if my family were still alive. I resisted for fifteen minutes — a record, Sister Honey congratulated me. 'What about the accidents?' she asked. The massive gay out of *He-Man* stopped pumping.

'Accidents?' I slobbered.

'Yes?'

'Faked by the Tribunal!' I told them the truth. I arched up. 'Please!' My rider continued.

They wanted to know about John. I resisted for five minutes — Big Nurse timed it. Then I slobbered out everything I knew about John. The location of the Tribunal? I begged them not to let me betray that. Two minutes. And I was Judas again.

'Describe the sessions you had with them.' God, I really sang about that.

'Hurry!' Big Nurse urged her sister torturer. 'We've got to break our previous record of three hours, fifteen minutes and a death.'

By then I was screaming with pain and pleasure but desperate for more of both. They wanted to know the people and the safe houses I'd followed on my way south. I resisted for a minute, and told them. In my guilt I wept but begged for my torture to continue.

'We're working overtime now,' one of the pin-ups protested.

'Triple-time rates!' Sister Honey promised them, if they broke their previous record. They really attacked my honour, my truth, my upbringing and belief in protecting all human beings against injustice. For the price of an orgasm that never blew, I sold all that and the people I loved.

'You see, Mr Citizen, you're caught in our most basic contradiction as human beings: we want to love others, defend them, protect them, but, for the right price, we'll sell them!' said Big Nurse.

'And for most of us, pain is our pleasure, our aphrodisiac,' crooned Sister Honey.

'We're gods with arseholes: we excrete death, our deaths . . .'

'No, we're arseholes who want to be gods!' exclaimed Sister Honey. Their helpers laughed.

'Now what do you think of *that* arsehole?' Big Nurse whispered in my ear, while the gay thumped at me.

'What's going to happen to them?' I cried.

'The ones you've betrayed?' Sister Honey paused and said, 'Reordinarinising. We don't kill people any more, you know that. The Tribunal has outlawed that primitive art and punishment. Our merciful President has abolished capital punishment and unchosen death . . .'

'Old age won't even kill us now unless we choose to die that way. Look at us. We've aged since Frame and Kesey libelled us and misrepresented our truths, but we can't die.'

'Time's running out,' Sister Honey urged her. 'Thirty minutes left!'

'Mr Citizen, tell us where your lovely wife and beautiful children are?' Big Nurse murmured like Peter Lorre in *The Maltese Falcon.*

My weeping broke into sobbing. 'I don't know. That's the truth. I'm in search of them too!' The gay rider stopped. Sister Honey pumped more Erectol into my veins and I was a quivering mess begging for the orgasm's release. 'Please, please, I don't know where they are!'

Sister Honey stopped her stopwatch. 'Record. He's telling the truth!' The others clapped. My rider jumped off.

'Please,' I pleaded. 'Don't leave me like this!'

'To escape this, you'd even accept death?' Sister Honey asked.

'Yes!' I cried.

'Then die!' Big Nurse laughed as she injected another drug into my arm.

Soon sleep was pouring into my eyes from inside my head. I started relaxing.

'Mr Citizen, intellectuals never last the course because they're all in the head!' Sister Honey caressed my forehead. 'Bye!'

'Yeah, bye, Big Boy,' Big Nurse murmured and winked.

In the blur of what I welcomed as my death, I saw them dress, collect their instruments of interrogation, and leave.

six

Erasures

I wasn't dead when I woke. I switched on the bedside lights. The
suite looked in perfect order. No evidence of the Sisters and their
torture. My watch said 6.30 a.m., my usual waking time. No
puncture marks on my arms. Must've been a nightmare. Lifted
the sheets and duvet gingerly. Peered down. Still there. A bit
shrivelled, that was all. Pushed back the covers. Touched it. No
pain. Normal.

I hummed as I shaved and showered.

I hummed as I shovelled down a breakfast of bacon, eggs,
sausages, kidneys, tomatoes, toast and coffee. I sang as I dressed
in one of my new suits:

> *Hey Mr Square wake up and take a dare*
> *Before the planet's destroyed by your snores*
> *Hey Mr Square your eyeballs need shining*
> *With spittle from the President's despair . . .*

After ringing the desk and being told there were no messages
for me, I switched on the TV news channel. As usual the news
was all good. Switched it off again. Stopped. Switched it on. At
the top corner of the screen, the date. Glanced at the date on my
watch. I was a day behind.

'Are you sure?' I asked the hotel exchange about the date.

'Yes, sir, dead sure.' I must've set my watch incorrectly
before leaving Auckland.

In the lobby, a short while later, the manager who greeted
me was a new one. 'Mr Jimson has been promoted to our hotel
in Bangkok,' he informed me when I asked after his predecessor.
'He left yesterday. He wanted to say goodbye to you, sir, but you

didn't want to be disturbed.'

At the bar I was told Bernie was on a week's leave and had left no address.

Fifteen minutes later, after a quick walk up Manners Street, I was in front of what I expected to be the Floating World salon. I inspected the shops on either side.

I entered. Long shelves and racks of health foods. On the far wall: *Eat well, eat here.* A few customers. A skeletal shop assistant in a white smock hurried to me.

'Can I help you?' she asked. I stepped back from her garlic breath.

'How long has your shop been here?' I asked.

She pondered. 'Six years. Why?'

'I thought there was a hairdresser's here, called the Floating World.'

'I'll ask my husband,' she said. 'Jim, do you know a place called the Floating World in our street?' A pause.

'Naw. Sounds like a Chinese restaurant to me!'

I remembered the men's store where I'd bought my clothes. It wasn't there either.

As I headed back to the hotel through the rising southerly and crowd, I tried not to run.

No messages written or phoned. The receptionist double-checked at my request. 'I'll be in my room. Ring me as soon as any message comes in. By the way, tell your Chief Security Officer to come up and see me.'

He wasn't the lock forward gone to lazy flab. He told me my man was now head of a security firm in Greymouth.

'May I speak to Mr Bonner?' I asked the firm's secretary over the phone.

'Mr Bonner isn't in at the moment, sir.'

'Where is he? This is an urgent call.'

'I'll check. Hold on.' I waited. 'Mr Bonner is at a funeral . . .'

'Are you sure it's a Mr Christopher Bonner?'

'Of course. Shall I get him to ring you?'

'Is your Mr Bonner about fifty, about eighteen stone?'

'No, sir, he's barely forty and is a compulsive jogger . . .'

I thumped the phone down as if to block off a threatening creature that was snaking up through the line. Sweat was soaking right through my shirt and waistcoat into my suit coat. In the mirror, I saw that my hair was plastered with sweat to my scalp and neck. My face was blistered with large beads of sweat.

I stripped and dried myself with a bath towel.

I'd missed a whole day. The hunters had that start on me.

Histories can be erased, I remembered the Tribunal telling me. Erased and replaced with histories that please us.

I couldn't wait for instructions from the Tribunal.

I packed a few casual clothes in my duffel bag, and made sure the suite looked as if I was still occupying it.

Took the lift down to the First Floor, sneaked out the back entrance, hurried to a rental car firm and hired an inconspicuous but powerful Range Cheever, under the name Elmore Leonard.

My attention was again focused on the chase and its dangers. No time to be afraid as I sped towards Waikanae and Reikorangi.

As I raced the river through the gap, I thought the hills were straight out of an early Colin McCahon painting. Strange how we see reality through art and the other cultural baggage we carry. The Sisters were certainly imposing theirs on the trail I'd created.

I hid the Cheever in the bush by the river and crossed the hills on foot until I was hiding behind some bushes, observing the farm buildings below. Someone was moving about the house. There was a red pickup near the front verandah. The grey sky breathed a little drizzle. I zipped up my oilskin and slid down towards the house. My arse got soaked on the wet grass. Must be an easier way of defeating evil, stopping the rewriting of history.

Footsteps thudding through the house. I slid under the back verandah and landed on a greasy, stinking carpet of sheep droppings and chicken shit. But held my breath. Not a move.

Waited. No footsteps. I started crawling towards the slats of light under the front verandah.

I heard the rifle's click and froze. 'You twitch another muscle, mate, and I'll have ya balls for garters!' I started backing out. 'Quicker!' he called. 'Ya mus' love sheepshit!' He laughed.

I stood up and began brushing the sheep droppings off my front. 'Bin watching ya since you slid like a greasy duck down that hill. Yeah. You mus' be some kind of nut, mate!' Three of his front teeth were missing from his false plate. His laugh was more a frog's wheezing through pink gums. 'Whad the bloody hell are you doin' sneakin' up on me farm?' His lean face was a continent of freckles.

'I'm sorry,' I said. 'I thought people I've been following were hiding here.'

'Shit, mate. What people?'

'Have you been here all week?'

'Yeah. Whad's that got to do with you?' He lowered his rifle. I told him I was a private investigator looking for two women and perhaps a man who'd stolen important papers from a client's firm. 'You're not bullshittin' me?' he asked.

'Name's Elmore, Elmore Leonard,' I introduced myself.

He shook my hand. Vice-like. 'Jake, Jake Crump, mate. Come in and wash that muck off. You look cold too.'

He tossed me a not-too-clean towel and pointed to the bathroom.

When I emerged free of sheepshit, he handed me a steaming mug of tea. 'Sorry but I can't help ya. No one's bin here all week. Wouldn't've minded those sheilas you mentioned visitin', though. Haven't dipped me wick in ages!' He wheezed some more. He was the stereotyped cow-cocky-cum-good-keen-man out of much New Zealand realist fiction. An actor set in place by the Sisters? I looked at his hands. Large, calloused, deeply ridged palms, dirt ingrained under the nails. Farmer's mitts all right. But the Sisters could've faked that too.

Wally's Book Centre had been erased. In its place was a thriving mini-supermarket. I asked the short checkout girl if they sold Janet Frame's novels.

'Who's she? We sell lotsa Mills and Boon, but neva hearda her.'

'She writes science fiction,' I said. 'And she used to live here.'

'Here, in Wangarnoowee? Mus' be kiddin'. No writer'd wanta live in this one-horse town!'

I was holding up the queue, so I left. She was a stereotype too. The Sisters weren't very original or imaginative. Their characters were coming straight out of bad Frank Sargeson, Ian Cross, Maurice Gee, Maurice Shadbolt, Fiona Kidman, and the grey fifties.

When I got back to my car I wondered what the Sisters had done to the people they'd erased.

At the end of their trail of erasures were my family.

No use going to Rotorua and Hamilton. Too late to help Heremaia Clatter and the motel in Hamilton.

I hired a helicopter and pilot at Wanganui Airport. In my pocket, I held the bone pendant Heremaia had given me. It was warm like a live animal.

I didn't experience any fear of flying. The pilot tried to make conversation. I told him my wife was ill in Auckland Hospital. He sympathised and let me be. There was a brown birthmark on his neck. That was all I'd remember about him.

As I watched our helicopter's shadow fluttering over the countryside, I had to agree with my son that Aotearoa was one endless paddock. In every gully and ravine and stretch of bush I saw my wife and children. The chug-chug-chugging of the propeller echoed my heart's beating.

At mid-morning, we landed on the helipad on the roof of Godrake Enterprises, the biggest owner of reordinarination centres in the country. Soon after, I was in a rental car heading for the Tribunal's headquarters, hoping I was ahead of the hunters.

As I drove I searched the glove compartment for instructions from the Tribunal. Nothing. But I refused to give in to the

feeling I'd been cut off from the source of salvation, abandoned
to search alone.

The building was only one of twenty-seven identical skyscrapers
that were the Tribunal's headquarters. The complex had been
designed, at the President's wish, after the Altar of Heaven in
Beijing: three circular tiers, with streets radiating from the
sacred circle at the centre. I recalled the President reciting on
TV a poem about the Altar of Heaven:

> *As a boy I'd wanted to be*
> *a tree   skeleton branching*
> *into green sky legends*
> *and down into earth's fertile*
> *tales of genesis*
>
> *When I met the Cypress of Nine Dragons*
> *in the Temple of Heaven   I recognised*
> *the tree I'd searched*
> *to live as   But I was now*
> *another creature unable*
> *to believe in dragons*
>
> *Fast in the cool*
> *of the Cypress of Dragons   and*
> *in your opium dreaming   invent*
> *the sacrificial Altar of Heaven:*
> *three tiers of green and white marble circled*
> *by balustrades   surfaced*
> *with stone slabs in multiples*
> *of Heaven's number*
>
> *Pause   Suck on*
> *the pipe that knows*
> *the secrets of illusion*
>   *Out of your owl eyes   fish*
> *the circular stone*
> *to heart the top platform*
> *Place it at the centre   (Feel*
> *its breathing body under*
> *your fingers?)*

Pause   Then in
the mathematics of shamans construct
concentric circles of 9/18/27 until
the ninth of 81 slabs   and
the tapu is contained
utterly

Don't be afraid   Carry
your offering of live bone
to the stone heart of the Altar
*   Stop   Raise it to*
the Fire that created
the cosmos   Speak softly
Your prayer will echo
from the balustrades
(No one else will hear it)
*   You are atua*
*   You are the offering*

Like the Altar, the façades of the buildings were green and white marble. Ninety-nine storeys high, with dark-tinted hexagonal windows which had black steel frames.

The streets were crowded. I drove carefully; I didn't want to attract attention. The crowds were mostly civil servants who dressed anonymously according to the wishes of the President. 'We are all extensions of one another,' was one of his famous truths. Another: 'The group is us; we are the group.'

The treeless streets were canyons through which the wind funnelled. In summer the canyons were oppressively hot because the buildings emptied the motors of their airconditioning into them. It was said the streets, shops, malls and apartments were modelled on some of the President's favourite films: *Blade Runner, Star Trek* and *Who Framed Roger Rabbit?*, some of my favourite films too.

No live vegetation was allowed in the complex. All of it was art, 'a hive of art', so the President called it. Each piece, including the inhabitants, was a cell of the hive that was the city that was part of the nation and so on until 'we are one with the dynamic organism that encompasses the universe in one mass

mind, heart, soul, body, that is without history, and is forever.'
He'd said this in one of his nationally televised appearances.

I gazed up at the towering buildings and wondered where
the President lived and delivered his messages from. No one
seemed to know, and no one felt the need to find out because,
as he said, he was 'an ordinary bloke like us,' and he was everywhere, therefore, and in us.

It was uncanny, but one trip out of Auckland and I was now
feeling an intruder in the complex. But I hoped the Tribunal
would keep its promise and help me save my family. I also
wanted to warn it of the hunters' treasonous activities.

The same security guard was at the gate. I stopped beside
his box. 'Yes?' he asked. No smile, no sign of recognition.

'I used to come here every day,' I said.

'Your pass, sir.'

'I used to come with John, one of your senior officials.'

'John who, sir?' He was polite. I tried to describe John. 'We
have many employees of that description, sir,' he said.

I remembered. 'Will this do?' I held up my Final Reference.

Immediately he was smiling. 'Sorry, sir.' He bowed and
raised the bar. 'Very sorry. Go right in. I'm sure they can help
you at Reception, sir.'

The receptionist was formal but polite. I gave him the information about John and he punched it in. 'Anything else, sir?' I
shook my head. His eyes were grey marbles in which I was
reflected. 'John will be playing for Auckland at Eden Park at
3.30 this afternoon,' he recited.

'Thank you,' I said. 'Please don't tell anyone I was here.'

He smiled. 'As far as I'm concerned, sir, you don't exist.' His
eyes held me.

I turned to leave. 'Have other people been asking after
John?' I enquired. He shook his head.

I'd seen him before, I concluded as I left the building. But
where?

On my way to Eden Park, through bright sunshine that was

cold, I stopped and bought a pair of binoculars.

Thick traffic as I neared the stadium. Spectators choked the footpaths. At the gate behind the southern grandstand, the security guards stopped me. I showed them my Reference and they waved me through. I parked in the VIPs' area. As I went to the turnstiles I turned up the collar of my overcoat to cover the lower half of my face. I surveyed the people around me. No sign of the hunters. I joined the queue and bought a seat near the entrance into the dressing rooms under the grandstand.

Both grandstands were filling quickly, but there was only a sprinkling of spectators on the terraces. I took my seat and tried to look casual as I checked the opposite grandstand through my binoculars, then the terraces and the rows behind me.

Fifteen minutes to go.

My wife was a rugby fanatic before we married. She couldn't explain why. (Who can explain an addiction?) Her family didn't like rugby; the schools she attended didn't make a big thing of it. But *instinctively* she had a passion for it, she said. As a child she'd insisted one of the family TV sets be reserved for her rugby viewing. It was the President's game too, so her parents had pandered to her addiction. Sports were good for the national soul and spirit, the President emphasised. Rugby developed fit and loyal citizens.

Rugby was our country's biggest spectator sport, and the professional players made huge salaries and large sums from endorsements. She knew the life and game histories of each star, especially the Polynesian ones. She bored her family and friends with that knowledge. But there was a strange twist to her addiction: she refused to watch live games. She was afraid to, she admitted when we met. It was 'more real' on TV — you got the replays, the slow motion action, the games explained, she said. And you didn't have to be part of the crowd which could get out of control like a beast . . .

'You look like him,' she said one night not long after we started living together.

'Who?'

She showed me the photo in the rugby book she was

reading. 'Him. Bryan Williams, the greatest winger ever.' She pointed at the All Black who was poised to fend off a tackle. 'A Samoan superstar of the sixties and seventies.' Flattered, I got her to tell me about Williams. She did.

'Are you fast?' she joked at the end of it.

'Yeah, real fast!' I laughed.

Another time while we watched a Shield game between Auckland, her favourite team, and Wellington, she said, 'A rugby game is about other rugby games. So are the players, don't you think?'

Puzzled, I said, 'Yeah, like a story is about other stories.' And it suddenly made sense to me.

She made me read the biographies and autobiographies of the players, and the histories, novels, and plays about the game. I told her I liked Maurice Gee's *The Big Season*, and Rangi Aotea's *Season of the Panther*, but still preferred American fiction about sports.

'Such as?' she asked.

'*The Natural*, by Malamud.'

'A cop-out,' she said. 'It imitates the Greek epic fall of a natural hero. Too big. Rugby's real. It's a game. Malamud mythologises the sporting hero . . .'

'But so does TV!'

'That's how you view it.'

'And you?'

'As a game played by real flesh-and-blood people. I ignore the frame, the ideology, put on it by TV.'

'You're getting heavy,' I joked.

Uncanny (and unnerving) too that she never cheered, applauded or heckled while we watched a game. The only signs of excitement were the brightness in her eyes, the quickening pace at which she munched her chips and downed her beer. Otherwise it was a silent absorption, an osmosis, an expert reading. And she *was* an expert reader. Ten minutes into a game and she could predict which forward pack was going to dominate and how they were going to do it. Also where the weaknesses were in the other team. Where the attack was going to concentrate, why, and how it was going to be done. When she wasn't sure, she gave alternative readings and, as the game unfolded, reduced the alternatives.

After our first child was born I never again saw her watch rugby. I didn't ask why. But sometimes, when reading the sports pages, she gave an expert critique of the players. 'He's a fucking waste of time — he's got no liver, he won't last,' she said of a first-five who was being hailed as Frano Botica's heir. (She was right: the heir was dropped from the Auckland team soon after.)

When our son was born, she stopped critiquing too. Our children never knew she'd been addicted. I didn't tell them. Our son took to soccer and fishing, our daughters to the martial arts.

Sharp sound of sprigs running over concrete. I looked down into the channel out of the dressing rooms. Both teams were surging up and out onto the field. The crowd erupted: shouting, clapping, horns, rattles. John, with his number eight jersey, was fourth in the Auckland line. Chunky, heavily muscled thighs, legs and shoulders. A coil of energy bouncing over the artificial turf.

The teams lined at the centre line. A deep hush fell. We were on our feet, facing the huge electronic scoreboard above the western terraces. Standing at attention with his right hand clutched over his heart, the President appeared on the screen. Behind him the World Flag rippled. Our anthem started reverberating around the stadium. We sang along with the President's strong baritone:

> *We are one with the Earth*
> *at peace forever*
> *We have outlawed war   strife*
> *hunger   poverty   and disease*
> *We are equal in the World State*
> *free of individual selfishness*
> *crime   deviance   and intolerance . . .*

Silence again at the end of the anthem. The camera zoomed in on the President's face. There were tears in his eyes. 'Fellow Kiwis,' he began, 'every time I hear you sing our beloved

anthem my heart melts with happiness. Every time I see you
moved by it, I know our planet is now a paradise of peace. You
and your missus and kids and I with my missus can live forever,
free of the ills that once threatened to destroy our beloved earth
. . .' He spoke before every major public event. He said what we
felt and believed. He was one of us yet the One who had brought
us the peace we now enjoyed. 'Today I wish both teams well.
Play the game, play it to the best of your ability. Winning isn't
important. Taking part is what counts. And don't forget I'm
with you and will be with you, always . . .' (Presidents were
about other Presidents, I thought). He faded from the screen.
The teams started warming up on the field. Waves of clapping
and cheering surged across the stands and terraces. I found
myself shouting too, for Auckland, for John who was conspicuous with his spiked blond hair.

I'm not a good reader of sports, but knew enough about
rugby to conclude that John was a talented and courageous
player. He hurled himself into the mauls and rucks without hesitation. On attack he was always there to back up the ball car-
rier. He anticipated well, covered and defended bravely. I marvelled at his boundless energy: a coiled spring that went down
and sprang up again and was into the thick of play. I now
understood why the fans had nicknamed him 'Boing-Boing'.

Thirty minutes into the game and Auckland was ahead 12
to 3. John had gone over with one of the props to score the first
try.

Just before half-time a set scrum collapsed. The whistle
went.

The players untangled themselves. John lay writhing on the
ground. The referee signalled the St John's first aid people. A
man and woman ran on and examined John. A stretcher was
brought on. They rolled John on to it.

I edged towards the entrance into the dressing rooms. The
crowd clapped as John was carried towards me.

They went past. I followed them into the dark that stank of
sweat and liniment. They took him into the first aid room. I
waited a few paces away.

Not long after, they brought him out on the stretcher. He was asleep, sedated. Three ambulance people and an official. I turned away. They hurried by. I followed as they carried him towards the ambulance behind the grandstand.

I rushed to my car. As the ambulance left the grounds I followed it.

It cleared Eden Park and picked up speed. I hung onto it.

It didn't head towards the hospital.

One of the St John's attendants people who'd gone on to the field to examine John had been a woman. Slim and blonde, with sunglasses. I closed in on the ambulance. Slowed and hung back.

Ponsonby had once been the home of working-class Polynesians. Now it was a forest of high-rise apartment buildings, clones of concrete and steel designed after what the President believed had been the Tower of Babel. Business executives and civil servants lived in the apartments. I followed the ambulance along Ponsonby Road. Little other traffic and few people.

At the corner of Jervois Road, the ambulance drove into the parking area under one of the towers. I parked on the street and hurried into the lobby.

Two security guards were at the desk monitoring the wall of TV screens which covered the entrances and corridors. I pretended to be looking for an address on the list of apartments.

Soon I found the TV panel I wanted.

Sister Honey and her male companion were back in their civvies. A dazed John, now in sports jacket and trousers, walked between them, his arms around their shoulders to hold himself up. The TV monitor followed them up the lobby and to the lift. Sister Honey waved to the guards. 'Had too much to drink!' she called. The guards laughed at John.

As the lift zoomed up, I followed the floor numbers. Thirteenth floor. But which apartment? I showed the guards my Reference, and asked for John's apartment number.

'You mean, Ms Combs's, sir?' they asked. I nodded. '1327,' one of them said.

I found a house phone by the lift and dialled Sister Honey's apartment.

'Yes?' she asked.

'This is security, Ms Combs. There's an urgent message here for you.'

'Read it out.'

'It's sealed. Confidential, Ms.'

'Okay, bring it up.'

It was so easy, the lying.

I sweated like a sponge being squeezed in the lift, lost for my next move. Remembered Dashiel Hammett's advice: If you're stuck with your novel, have a guy break into the room with a gun. I took off my overcoat.

It was as if I'd become someone else. I didn't hesitate. Raised my right foot, tensed, and drove it at the door lock. The door burst back and I rolled in after it and across the carpet. Was on my feet as Sister Honey's companion sprang at me. I side-stepped, and drove my knee upwards. Crunncchh! He cried in pain and clutched at his balls. His mistake. I chopped my karate hands down across his neck. The bone snapped. He slumped onto the floor.

I ran into the bedroom.

The hypodermic gleamed in Sister Honey's hands as she reached down to inject John. I slapped it out of her grip. She screeched and drove her nails up at my face. My hands reacted automatically. Down across her collar bones. She screamed.

I pushed her away from the bed. She rolled across the floor, whimpering, unable to use her arms. 'Ya bastid. This isn't a novel — it's real. Ya dumb fuck!'

I tore off a strip of bedsheet and tied it around her mouth.

I filled the bath with cold water and lowered John into it. He started shivering. I held his head above the water. A few minutes later I took him out, dried him, wrapped him up in a blanket and stretched him out on the sofa.

I dumped Sister Honey and her companion in the bedroom and locked it.

As evening fell over the city, I sat beside John watching him break free from the drugs. When the fear threatened to turn me into liquid panic, I got a beer out of the fridge and emptied it in two long swallows. Another man, a coldly efficient weapon, had broken into the apartment, and I'd watched him demolish two people. It hadn't been me. What was happening? I emptied another beer bottle and switched on the sitting room lights. One man was dead.

I jumped out of my chair when John sat up unexpectedly. 'Whad's the bloody score?' he asked. I held his shoulders. 'Where the shit am I? How did I ged 'ere?' I told him what had happened.

He hurried to the bedroom. 'Shit, mate, they're both dead!' he called after a while. I rushed in.

Sister Honey was curled like a foetus on the floor; her head was slumped across her left shoulder.

'She was bloody alive!' I said.

'Ya don' know ya own strength, mate. Anyway, she bloody well asked for id!'

'But I didn't kill her!'

John looked at me. 'Id doesn't matter, mate. My people'll take care of id. No one'll know.'

'I'm not capable of killing anyone.'

'Yeah, ah believe ya.' He scrutinised me again. 'Do ya feel okay? Ya look differen'.'

I sat down on the bed and told him I'd panicked at the way I'd become someone else, a savage, in order to save him.

'Who, mate?'

'I don't know. Someone who felt nothing at hurting people.'

'Are ya sure?' He looked into my face. 'Like Jekyll and Hyde?' He chuckled.

'Don't joke,' I said. 'It was like that!'

'Mate, that shit's true only in novels. And this ain't a novel.' He was echoing Sister Honey. 'As the President says, we are each many selves.'

'But I've never killed anyone before!'

'Doesn't matter. It was in self-defence. And remember, mate, no one ever dies permanently. There's reincarnation. The

77

President, the Tribunal and the State can rule to reincarnate anyone . . .' As he explained, I felt consoled.

'Pity we can't question that sheila,' he said.

'Sister Honey?'

'Jeez, was that her name?' I nodded but didn't tell him she'd come out of Frame's novel; he'd think I'd gone crackers. 'Strange name.'

I told him about how she and her companion had hunted me, and erased my trail back to him and my family. 'Boy, ah'm lucky, eh. Thanks ta ya, mate!' He slapped my shoulder, and told me he'd nearly pissed himself worrying about me after he'd lost my trail in Wellington.

'Where's my family?' I asked.

'Safe, mate. Safe as Batman in his Bat Cave. We had ta shift them back ta Aucklin'. Id's safer in the labyrinth of this city . . .'

'Where?' I was surprised at the menace in my question.

'Ah can't tell ya. The senior people in charge of your case know. They'll tell us in good time. We have ta get ta my apartment. Ah'm sure there'll be further instructions for us there.' I remained silent. 'Have faith in the Tribunal, mate.'

'What about the other two?'

'The stiffs? Ah'll send people to erase them for good. Ah'm a master eraser, eh!' He laughed.

He dressed. 'Ya look great, mate. The search for ya missus and kids is putting steel into ya liver again.'

'But I'm risking the lives of the people I love.'

'That's whad makes id the most invigorating danger, mate. When we risk everything. Danger is an aphrodisiac.'

Fifteen minutes later as we left the apartment, he stopped and, searching my face again, asked, 'Are ya sure ya don' feel like someone else?'

'Like who?'

'Like that bloke who croaked the two stiffs in there, mate?'

I shook my head. 'That shit's only true in novels!' I reminded him. He laughed and patted me on the back.

'How did ah play today?'

'Great!'

'Fuckin' pity ah can't remember anything of the game.'

'My wife would've been able to tell you every detail if she'd seen it.'

'Yeah? Is she a rugby freak?'

'Used to be.'

The cold crisp air licked at my face as we hurried to my car. I wondered why John was now afraid of me.

Around us the forest of cloned apartments held up the dark with its millions of eyes.

seven

The Labyrinth Club

As soon as we got into his apartment, John switched on the wall computer and punched in our request for information. I went looking for a cold beer. John was a *neat* rugby player and dresser but his apartment was a mess. Unswept, dirty clothes everywhere, magazines and books left wherever he'd been reading them. The kitchen was worse. It stank of rotting food. I retreated from it.

My instructions were on the computer panel:

Tonight at 8 p.m. go to the Labyrinth Club, Karangahape Rd. Your contact will approach you. He will talk about Jorge Luis Borges, the famous unweaver of labyrinths. Being an expert on Borges, you will be able to untangle your contact's Borgesian talk, and follow that untangling towards your lovely family. Don't — we repeat, don't — be distracted by whatever else happens at the Club. Your hunters, as you know already, are expert distractors.

As Borges might have said: Life is a labyrinth that unweaves eternally.

Good luck. And enjoy.

'They're really poetic, eh!' John remarked. 'Who was that Borges bloke?'

'A blind cook.'

He didn't get it. 'Yeah? He mus've bin a bloody good cook ta find his way out of la-by- . . . How da ya say id?'

'La-by-rinths?'

'Yeah, that.'

'I guess he was that.'

'Don' know aboud yar, but ah'm hungry.' He disappeared

into the kitchen. I refused to follow him.

He put some cold chicken and wilted lettuce salad on the dining table. 'Here, good stuff!'

I sat down reluctantly. Tried to switch off my taste buds, and ate only the salad. Just shoved the food down. It didn't help my appetite to see the piles of unwashed dishes and leftovers through the kitchen door.

'Got any beer?' I asked.

I took two quick beers to wash down the mess.

'Good chow, eh, mate,' he said. I nodded. His taste buds, eyesight, and nose must be blind (like Borges).

Among the mess in the bathroom I found a new toothbrush and cleaned my teeth. I tried not to look at the technicolour posters of naked men who were imitations of Arthur Schwegger, the latest Mr Universe. Embarrassing that their genitals were almost lost among their bulging treetrunk thighs. There were a few pictures of naked Ms Universes. All breastless and heaped muscles like the men. And oiled.

I had to confront the Labyrinth and didn't want to be aroused sexually. So I hurried out of the bathroom.

After removing the jetsam on the sofa, I stretched out on it. 'Wake me at 7 p.m.,' I said to John.

'Ah'll have all the info ya need by then,' he said.

I expected the fear to swamp me again. It didn't. I dreamt of whales, and watched them surge and dive and surge again through lime-green tropical waters. I dreamt in their haunting singing.

Information about the Labyrinth Club was on the computer when I woke. I memorised it quickly. (And was surprised I was able to.) John called up maps of the Club and surrounding streets and buildings. I asked after specific details. He zoomed in on those, on the maps and diagrams.

'Ya gettin' fuckin' good,' he said.

'At what?'

'Detection work. And surveillance, mate.'

'And surviving,' I mumbled.

'Yeah, that too.'

'I've got my family to save.'

I tried not to breathe the stench of the bathroom. The cold of the shower slapped awake all my nerves and cleared my head.

As I was dressing in the bedroom — another mess — John came in. 'Ya've lost aloda weight, eh,' he said.

'Yeah, from being shitscared. I've got permanent worry diarrhoea.'

He chortled. 'Ya're starting ta look and move like someone ah used to read aboud.' I looked at him. 'A famous bloke, bud ah can' remember who. Mus've been a detective from a thriller series. Ah used ta be crazy aboud thrillers . . .'

'This ain't fiction!' I said. He laughed about that.

'Ah'll keep ya covered all the way in and oud, mate.'

'Better,' I said. 'There're monsters in the maze. And I've not been in a nightclub for years.'

John dropped me off a block away from the Labyrinth. 7.45 p.m. Shoved my hands into my overcoat pockets and started walking. Steady streams of people because it was Saturday night. Many families shopping for their pleasures. No signs of dirt or poverty.

Karangahape Road was one of Auckland's three Thera-peutic Zones, advertised as 'The Street of Preferences'. These Zones had been established throughout the world by the Tri-bunals and the Council of Capitalist Presidents, based on the principle that our urges were natural preferences determined by our individual genetic codes and upbringing. To deny those preferences resulted in deviance, neuroses, 'sin', psychoses, ill-ness, violence and crime. ('Look at the twentieth century,' the President pointed out. 'That was the last century of puritanical denial, and vicious maladies resulted from that.') For the human personality to flower our preferences had to be given free expres-sion (but guided scientifically). So the Zones offered every pleasure imaginable, and what our genes demanded. There were even parlours for children who craved simulated suicide. Theatres for literary freaks who needed their weekly fix of *Ulysses* or *Finnegan's Wake* or *Invisible Man*, or the latest best-seller. If you were into religion, the choice was endless. Glue sniffers had the pick of the world's choicest glues (but without the brain damage). Drinkers could choose from any booze or the purest water from the Himalayas. Any kind of sex and fetish, including vampirism with your own favourite Dracula. Smell addicts had the Smello-World in which they could swoon in the smell(s) of their addiction. You name it, the Zone had it or could improvise it on the spot. Whenever any *real* violence occurred, the client was referred to a reordinarination centre where his preferences were altered and he could return to enjoy the Zones without harming himself or others.

All the nightclubs, parlours, restaurants, theatres, gyms and stadiums were really clinics run by qualified psychiatrists and therapists who acted as hosts, victims and whippers, preachers and confessors, surrogate partners — whatever role you wanted them to play. So the Zones were totally hygienic and safe, though they maintained the atmosphere of dangerous and illicit 'sinning', free-for-all swinging and lawlessness, as described graphically by some of the President's favourite twentieth-century novelists: Burroughs, Genet, Céline, Ross Macdonald, Elmore Leonard, Dashiel Hammett, Damon Runyon, Hemingway, Calvino and Barbara Cartland. In fact, the whole physical façade of Karangahape Road was kept as it had been in the 1980s, the President's PhD research topic. Behind the façade though, the Road was the latest in psychology, therapy, electronics, architecture, simulation and healing illusion. And it was heavily subsidised by the State so that every citizen could afford it. 'Crime, violence, drug addiction and mental illness cost the suffering taxpayer billions in previous centuries,' the President was fond of saying. 'Compared to that, our Zones cost us peanuts.'

I'd not enjoyed the therapies of the Zones ever, but, as I walked through K Rd, I didn't feel alone or exposed. The alert bird, that was my heart, was perched in its cage of ribs, watching.

The Club was in a sidestreet, in what had once been the Mercury Theatre. The theatre façade and lobby remained.

I walked up the front steps to the ticket office.

The ticket seller wore a silver wig, silver lipstick and nail polish, and a silver body-tight uniform.

'What's on, baby?' I asked, following my memorised script.

'Your choice, luv, of any flick of the eighties,' she replied. She fluttered her silver eyelashes.

'Okay. How about *Mad Max 2*?'

'Gosh, you've got good taste, luv. Bet you've got good taste in love too.'

'Yeah, but some other time, doll.' Ridiculous lines out of a B-movie. The Tribunal needed better scriptwriters.

She giggled. 'That'll be $4.50, luv.' I paid her. 'Have a good time, luv. You can always come back to me if you don't.'

'See ya, baby,' I said. What an awful line! Bogart would've spewed; Edward G. Robinson would've had it rewritten.

I was surprised at the amount of history my mind was allowing to brim out of its depths. I wasn't afraid it was happening, either.

More people were lining up at the ticket booth as I mounted the carpeted stairs.

The people who occupied the padded furniture in the top lobby were sipping softdrinks or drinking coffee or munching popcorn. I bought a bowl of popcorn and a large Coke, as instructed. I hated Coke so I pretended I was sipping it.

At 7.59 p.m. the swing doors into the theatre opened inwards, with an almost inaudible swish.

The blackness inside was like a solid sea. We hesitated.

'What the shit!' exclaimed a wizened old woman as she stepped forward. 'C'mon, son, let's go see what this bullshit's all about!' She dragged a short bald-headed man after her. The black sea swallowed them up.

I sensed others looking at me. I was the biggest there. I pushed myself into the darkness.

A soft hand held my arm. 'Welcome to the Labyrinth, sir,' the husky voice crooned into my left ear. My flesh broke into goose pimples larger than measle spots. Perfume fingered its sweet way into my nostrils and perched in my head, as the black sea, like a live creature, caressed me through my clothes. 'Come, start your greatest adventure in courage,' she whispered. Marilyn Monroe's voice. She led me forward. I couldn't see a thing.

A perfect circle of dazzling white light opened in front of me. I turned to my guide. She was still in the darkness. 'Sir, go into the light out of which we all came.' I hesitated. She edged me forward. 'Go into the original labyrinth, the genesis, sir.'

I stepped into the light and, for a breathless exhilarating time-lessness, went through the final sequence of brilliant hallucin-ations in Stanley Kubrick's *2001: A Space Odyssey*. Words merely represent experience. The experience is not the descrip-tion of it. So if you really want to understand what I experienced in the light, see Kubrick's classic film and live out the psychedelic experience.

Through it, I found myself in a pub — of all places.

It was as if I'd been reborn. Without fear. Without guilt. With the unquenchable thirst to know, experience, explore. Yet when I walked into the pub and looked into the wall mirror, I saw a middle-aged man with streaks of grey hair.

Sawdust floor, stools, wooden bar with red chromium-trimmed top, a rotund barman filling jugs, large photos of rugby stars on the walls, smell of piss wafting in from the toilets. Replica of a fifties pub. But the few customers were of our time.

'A jug, mate,' I followed my instructions.

'Nice day, eh, mate?' The barman started filling my jug. 'Bloody slow today.' His hair was done in a bun at the back. Yellow jowls with a day's growth.

I paid him and took the table against the far wall. Filled my glass, drew back on it, long and slow. My throat, chest, and belly unclenched as the cold beer slid down. I waited.

The old man at the other end looked like a plucked rooster — his head and neck, that is. He nodded rhythmically as he sipped his beer and gazed into himself. The couple by the door into the toilets were necking. Slow drunken motions. They wore identical shirts and jeans.

Thirty minutes later he entered and shuffled up to the bar. *Nervous, dark, with perhaps a touch of Indian blood, and wears a skimpy, petulant moustache*, was how my instructions had described him.

He got a jug and came towards me. His movements were slow, deliberate.

'My name is Maneco Uriate,' he introduced himself, placing his jug beside mine. A Spaniard, what was he doing here? We shook hands. 'I've been looking for you for a long time. They told me you would be here.' I poured him a beer. The jugs dripped condensation.

'Yes, my friend,' I followed my script. He drank. His face had once been beautiful. You could still tell that through the thick ebony skin which had been ridged and wrinkled by sun and age.

'Ahh, such a smooth and healing taste!' he sighed. His eyes, when he gazed at me, were full of forgiveness. 'It's been a very long time, compadre.'

'Yes, my friend, such a long time.'

'You know me then?'

I nodded. 'I know one of the stories of your life.'

'As reported by Borges, my compatriot?'

'Yes, as written down by the unraveller of dreams.'

He poured me a beer. When he raised his glass to drink, I was astonished at the lean fitness of his body. 'I have kept my body fit for this meeting,' he said as if he knew what I'd been thinking. 'But we grow old, compadre.'

'And fat and slow,' I patted my belly.

'It does not matter,' he whispered. His eyes burned brightly. 'It is the weapons that remain fit. They outlast us. They propel us to our destinies, compadre.'

'Yes, my friend. It is the weapons.'

He patted my shoulder and smiled. 'Strange that we should meet here in a bar in a city in a country so foreign and so far away from our last meeting.'

'Yes, my friend. Strange but inevitable.'

He emptied his glass. 'Stories don't end, do they?'

I shook my head. 'It is as Borges wrote.'

'Yes,' he whispered. He sat back on his stool and, with his black eyes on me, asked, 'Tell me the story of our last meeting, compadre, as the master wrote it down.'

I did. I recited what Borges had written.

There were tears in his eyes when I finished.

'I have never heard it told so beautifully before,' he whispered. 'Thank you.' He wiped his sleeve across his eyes. 'What title did he give our story?'

'"The Meeting".'

'Yes, "The Meeting". Such an apt title. I am not an educated man but I know a beautiful title when I hear it.' He shut his eyes. I imagined his smell to be that of the pampas.

'And it is *our* story,' I admitted finally.

'And who is to write down the story of this meeting?'

'Someone in the bar observing us . . .'

'Or someone who will hear it from someone else . . .'

'Who heard it from someone else . . .'

'Who heard it from someone here.' We laughed and drank.

You must improvise from here on, improvise according to what Maneco Uriate does, I recalled my instructions.

'Tell me about the weapons again. I have lived with their terrible beauty all my life and in my search for you.'

My description came straight out of Borges' story.

He closed his eyes and tasted every detail. '*I still remember how Uriate's hand shook when he first gripped his knife, and the same with Duncan, as though the knives were coming awake after a long sleep side by side in the cabinet. Even after their gauchos were dust, the knives — the knives, not their tools, the men — knew how to fight. And that night they fought well,*' he repeated the ending of my description. He should've been a poet.

I bought two more jugs. We continued drinking. More people, blurred presences, came into the pub.

'I have never forgotten your last words, compadre. They

have haunted me since. Do you remember what they were?'

'No, my friend,' I lied.

'*How strange. All this is like a dream.* That's what you whispered. So true of our existence, don't you think?'

'Yes, my friend.'

'Let's drink to that, compadre!'

We clinked our glasses and then emptied them. He wiped his mouth with the back of his hand. A line of froth remained on his moustache. 'Have you ever forgiven me?' he whispered. I leaned towards him. 'Have you?'

I gazed into his face. 'Yes, Maneco. It was not us. It was the knives that controlled us. We did not fight. The knives used us as their weapons.'

'Yes, I forgot that. Yet why have I carried this guilt since?' I hesitated. 'Why, my brother?' he repeated.

'Because you started the fight. You allowed the knives to use us.'

The fire in his eyes died. 'Are you sure?' he asked. I nodded and refused to look away from the cold blackness of his eyes. 'But it was you who cheated at our game of poker.'

I was facing the choice of retreating or fulfilling what the story had reported.

'I did *not* cheat,' I emphasised.

'Once again you insult me, compadre. But I will not take offence, not this time.' He looked away but I could feel his anger.

Is it recklessness or true courage when you have nothing to lose or gain but you dare take that step into the possibilities of violence? I'll never know what made me do it. Uriate was offering me the chance to retreat with my honour intact and thus change the ending of Borges' story. My instruction was to improvise.

'But it was you who cheated,' I chose.

He looked at me, sadly. 'You have chosen the ending the Master gave to our story?' I nodded. 'So be it, compadre.'

'It is already written.'

He stood up and unbuttoned his suit coat. When he displayed both inside pockets, it was as if he was displaying his rib-cage and heart to me. I heard the silence in the pub. I sensed they were watching us.

Out of the left pocket he pulled a narrow object wrapped in cowhide. He placed it on the table in front of him. The other pocket produced a longer object wrapped in a red bandana. The two lay side by side on the table. Maneco looked into my eyes. Then down at the parcels.

'The Master's story does not say what happened to the weapons, does it?' he asked. 'No, but it says the knives outlive their weapons, we, who are used by them. How I recovered them is another continuation of their story. Enough to say, I traced them through the long line of their duels.'

He peeled back the cowhide. *I saw a glint of steel*, Borges wrote. Maneco then unwrapped the other, in caressing move-ments. It was a dagger, with a U-shaped crosspiece, longer and more showy than the knife. 'Beautiful, aren't they?' he whis-pered. The weapons were breathing. Their shining blades sucked in the Labyrinth's light.

'Yes,' I murmured.

'Last time, I chose first, compadre. The Master's story implied I did it because I was afraid and wanted the longer weapon. He is correct. But I have matured. I have fought other duels since and have earned my courage. So, you choose.'

As reported by Borges, I picked up the wooden-handled knife with the stamp of a tiny tree on the blade. It gripped my hand and forced my fingers to wrap themselves around its handle. Its power surged, like adrenalin, into my hand and up my arm. My hand shook.

When Maneco picked up the sword-like dagger the same thing happened to him.

We were young men again.

'I am a Spaniard,' he reminded me. 'Tradition demands we should not fight in the house in which we are guests.' I agreed.

I looked around. The pub was half-full. They were watching us, in hungry silence. 'Come, my friend,' I invited Maneco.

We pushed our way through the front door. The others followed.

We were on a lawn. The moonlight held us. The others spread out around the edge of the lawn.

'*This looks like the right place*,' I repeated Borges' dialogue.

We moved to the centre of the lawn, not quite knowing what to do. I certainly didn't, for I'd not fought with knives before.

A voice rang out: 'Let go of all that hardware and use your hands,' Borges wrote.

But we were already fighting.

I can't describe the fight as excitingly as Borges did. So read Borges' story.

Suddenly my blade seemed shorter, for it was piercing Maneco's chest. And I was pushing my knife (and Maneco) away. I was supposed to lose the duel.

He lay stretched out on the grass. The round moon floated in his eyes. '*How strange. All this is like a dream*,' he repeated what I'd said centuries before.

I bent over the body, sobbing openly and begging to be forgiven, as he'd done when he'd been the victor.

'Now we are equal,' he whispered into my ear. 'My search for your forgiveness is over, compadre.' He thrust a piece of paper into my coat pocket.

'Fuck the crows, he's killed the other joker!' someone was shouting.

'It's supposed to be therapy . . .'

'Yeah, make-believe!'

'He's a *real* deviant . . . !'

'He needs reordinarinising!'

I sensed them closing in. I wheeled. Their circle surged back, away from the knife in my extended hand. The lawn and moon were gone. Stage lights were on full blast. The dagger sticking out of Maneco's chest and his blood were real.

'Get the cops!'

'Yeah, get the bloody police!'

90

I wheeled full circle again, knife out. No obvious exits around the circular stage. Just a solid wall, a painted backdrop. All labyrinths were designed by people. There was a way out of each one. Think.

The old man with the plucked-rooster look stripped off his mask. He was young and tough and eager to be a hero. He danced towards me, arms outstretched like a knife fighter. 'Now, come on, mate, be reasonable. No need for that. You're just reverting.' My knife lunged. Nicked his right hand. 'Sheeettt!' he cried. He sucked at his wound. 'The bastard's a real deviant!'

The necking couple by the toilet door split and circled, one to my left, the other to my right. 'We're doctors, sir!' the taller of the two said.

'We can help ya, mate,' said his partner. 'Jus' relax, no one wants ta hurt ya.'

The knife jerked forward and up every time someone edged forward. I followed it. It lunged at the doctor to my left. He dived out of the way. It was clear to the wall. The knife grazed the belly of the doctor to my right. He screamed and clutched at his wound.

I ran at the wall. I expected a solid rebuttal, but it burst open with a ripping bang as I hit it.

And I was free and running through what looked like a cave.

'Stop the deviant!' I heard them shouting.

The cave floor was wet and muddy. A greenish glow emanated from the walls and lit my way.

My sweat-drenched clothes clung to me. Thrust a hand into my coat pocket for tissues. None. Only a piece of folded paper. Remembered Maneco had put it there. I stopped, panting, crouched against the cave wall and read this message:

Hail to the Victor; by now I would have found your forgiveness. But you must go on living and searching for your family. That is as good a purpose for living as any other. The Labyrinth Club is only the gateway into the more frightening

91

labyrinth that is this city. Your wife and children are being kept in the heart of the maze, at a place called the Puzzle Palace.

Don't trust their Guardians.

May the ancient gods protect you.

Do not lose your Knife.

Through the cave walls I heard them searching for me. I was surprised I wasn't afraid.

I ran the plan of the Club through my head. Found what I wanted and headed for it.

Icarus and his father escaped the Minotaur's maze by flying out of it. (Their story ended in the tragedy of self-love.) Joyce escaped his labyrinth, Dublin, by living in exile. Esther Zhao, the great explorer of Jupiter, obliterated the Creeper Maze with laser weapons she fashioned out of the wreck of her spaceship. My Hunters thought they had me trapped.

I found the crack in the wall. Plunged my knife into it, and twisted it round and round. Cool air gushed through the hole. Soon I had a circle of holes pierced in the wall. I rested for a few minutes.

Then watched my other self. He recoiled, clenched his strength into a tight ball, and karate-kicked the circle. POW! He didn't wait. He dived through the hole.

I crouched in the spacious wine cellar stacked with barrels and shelves of wine bottles. The bouquet of the wines started getting me high. I dragged a stack over and covered the hole with it.

Quietly, I moved from wine rack to rack. Found the shelf I wanted. 1989 Vaipe Red produced by Vaipe Winery. Wiped the dust off the two bottles and shoved them into my coat pockets (that wasn't in my instructions).

The steel-shiny corridor was empty as I moved down it. On both sides were laboratories and offices. Only a few technicians were at some of the equipment.

NO UNAUTHORISED PERSONNEL
BEYOND THIS POINT

The wall ahead was of white steel. Its door needed the appropriate identification cards to open it.

Gamble. Risk. I thrust my Final Reference into the slot. Click-click. A soft purring. I was ready to run. Click. And the gleaming door slid open. Short corridor of blazing light ahead. Then the control centre of the Labyrinth.

I was certain they were still monitoring my every move. (John was monitoring theirs, I hoped.)

Surveillance was the all-pervasive, all-healing art of our times, the President reiterated every Xmas. It preserved family, community, national and international peace. No more dark secrets, conspiracies, plots, hoarding, megalomania, individual dreams of being more powerful than your neighbour, which had been the curse of previous centuries. Privacy had been a hindrance to our loving one another, to our sharing everything, including our thoughts. Surveillance meant genuine equality. Ours was a truly *open* society; we knew what one another was doing, thinking, dreaming.

The centre of the Club was a glass cocoon that was suspended on a cushion of air and an alarm system. I stood at the walkway, and checked the centre. It pulsed and glowed as if it was ready to give birth to a miraculous monarch butterfly. Through the glow I glimpsed its innards of computers and other electronic equipment.

From the plans I'd memorised, I knew the secret path across the chasm of dark air, and through the alarm system.

I knelt down on one knee, and bent forward so they couldn't see what I was doing. Tapped off the cork and the top of one of the reds with the knife. Poured the wine into my shirt, lap, and down my trousers. Expensive blood.

I dripped as I staggered across the path, leaving the stains on the air cushion.

At the cocoon's invisible entrance I dripped a line of stains across the threshold. The door slid open. I slipped into the cocoon, groaning and clutching at my belly as if I'd been stabbed.

'Welcome, sir, we've been expecting you!' I looked in the direction of the voice. 'Welcome, I see you're badly wounded and bleeding to death!' I couldn't believe it: a younger version of the famous Yul Brynner as the Keeper of Hades in Cocteau's film, *Orpheus Descending*, in all his baldness and black dinner suit. I shut my eyes. My wine blood continued staining their carpet.

He helped me to my feet. Strong grip and arms. 'Heroes of epics don't bleed to death, sir. Here, sit here.' He pushed me into a soft chair. 'We considered you too important a person to leave to our underlings to welcome!'

'You've got to help me!' I pleaded.

'But heroes don't feel pain, sir,' he replied. I was in the middle of a melodramatic and badly told epic. Through half-closed eyelids, I surveyed the centre quickly. 'I believe you've met Miss Ratched?'

The bulky figure in black emerged from her chair. 'Pleased to meet you.' The man beside her stood up. 'Meet Brother Peter. He's been helping me track you but you've not met.' He reminded me of an immaculate Bible.

I leaned forward, arms pressed into my belly. 'Please, I need medical help.'

'Heroes don't die, sir,' the Keeper reminded me.

'They either become legend or ride off into the sunset . . .'

'Or are crucified to rise again . . .'

'Or win the king's daughter's petite hand and live happily ever after . . .'

'Or commit suicide instead of allowing us, villains, the pleasure of killing them . . . '

'Or jet off into outer space in search of other worlds, other adventures, other villains to conquer, other virgins to save . . .'

Their well-rehearsed chorus ended in taunting laughter which reminded me of Darth Vader, the twentieth-century evil prototype. Together the feel of the unholy trio was that of the Inquisition, the Nazis, the keepers of the Gulag and of Auschwitz, etc. Villains were about other villains and about our darkest fears.

The Keeper and Brother Peter held my arms and hoisted me

to my feet. 'Come, hero, you must see the wonders that we offer here,' the Keeper whispered. His breath stank of garlic.

'Yes, before you bleed completely into our carpet.'

I didn't feel the injection. Just a short *slittt!* sound. 'That'll wake him up for a while,' she said. Within seconds my brain was clear, alert.

The Keeper swept his arms across the panelled walls. 'Choose, sir. Any panel will reveal to you the pleasures and cures our Pleasure Dome decrees for our lucky customers.'

The cocoon was of crystal, glittering, throbbing, inviting my fingers to press whatever key I craved. I hesitated. They led me to the greenish panel.

'Now here, for instance, is the way into the tropics. Into the paradise writers, filmmakers, dreamers and beachcombers created of the South Seas. We understand you are a South Seas fancier. That monograph you wrote about it, is brilliant, quite brilliant, sir.' He paused, held my right hand and placed it on the centre button of the panel. 'Just caress it, yes. Just a little caress!' he whispered. I held back. 'Yes, remember the title of your paper? *AIDS and Poverty in the South Seas: a Crime against Humanity.* Go on, just give it a flick, a push. Don't be shy. We won't tell anyone about your pleasures . . .'

'Yeah, we promise!' Big Nurse said.

Brother Peter pushed up against me. Wound his arms around my neck. His scent was that of fresh South Seas trade winds. 'C'mon, lover. Give it a push.' He ringed his hand around my forefinger and pushed the ring back and forth. 'Yeah, lover, just a slow gentle push.'

I pushed the button. 'Wow!' he sighed.

I didn't know how long they kept me in the South Seas, wallowing in the 'ecstasy' of islanders dying in droves from the AIDS epidemics. But when I broke out of it, I pretended *satisfaction.*

'How can a hero like you enjoy death, the death of others?' Big Nurse complained.

'We all have our preferences,' the Keeper reminded her. That shut her up. He then switched on the entire panel.

Around us every type of labyrinth came alive. 'Behold!' the

Keeper said. 'The World of Preferences as we offer them to our customers!' In each labyrinth was a customer or group of customers.

'Yeah, ours is the greatest Pleasure Dome invented,' sang Brother Peter.

'The most effective therapies and cures . . .'

'For every twist, quirk, pulse, yearning of the heart . . .'

'And mind . . .'

'And flesh . . .'

'And spirit . . .'

'Thanks to our illustrious President and Council of Presidents . . .'

'And Tribunal . . .'

They were riveted to the scenes in the panels. Humankind's dream for every imaginable escape, pleasure and preference had come true.

'It's disgusting!' I pretended to be angry. 'You're sick voyeurs enjoying other citizens' private . . .'

'But privacy is against the Law,' Big Nurse said. 'We all must share everything, even our deepest fears . . .'

'And secrets, sir,' the Keeper whispered.

'Yes, there are no secrets.' Brother Peter caressed my cheek. 'So, where is your family?'

I played true to the stereotpye of the hero. Gritted my teeth and shook my head furiously.

'Valiant but futile,' the Keeper played true to villain. 'Utterly futile . . .'

'As you know, there are no secrets in our world. The Tribunal has made that a reality,' Big Nurse said.

'You won't get me to squeal!' I recited out of a heroic thriller. 'Not on your bloody life!'

'Remember the last time you resisted,' Big Nurse reminded me. 'One injection and you were squealing even on the ones you say you love.'

God, they were corny villains. I groaned and collapsed to my knees. 'Please, I'm — I'm dying!' I murmured. They pulled me up to my feet again. 'Haven't you got any mercy?'

'Mercy's a virtue that became obsolete after our utopia was created,' the Keeper said.

'To replace the horror of other predicted futures . . .'

'Such as *1984, Animal Farm, The Island, Das Kapital, Mein Kampf, Atlas Shrugged, Star Wars, The Empire Strikes Back,* and *Return of the Jedi, Alien* and *Aliens, Blade Runner, Mad Max 2, Planet of the Apes* . . .'

'Such as *The Holy Barbarians of Planet Z, The Happy Replicants, The Amazons of FM, My Perfect Society,* etc., etc.'

'By the way, why do you have a thing for the twentieth century?' Big Nurse asked. 'Why that awful century that suffered three World Wars, nuclear pollution and AIDS epidemics? Is it because it was the President's research topic?'

'I don't know why,' I moaned. 'Do you know why you have a thing for soiled underwear?'

Her slap stung the side of my face. 'Jesus, you're an awful hero. You're supposed to fight fair!'

'Yeah!' her cohorts chorused.

'He's not a genuine hero,' she declared.

'But it's not over yet, madam,' the Keeper said. 'His epic adventure is just continuing. He may yet prove to be a true hero . . .'

'To prove that, he has to defeat us, right?' she asked. 'Well, I don't want him to prove his stuff over my dead body, my defeat. Let's croak him now!'

'Our mission is to find and erase his family,' Brother Peter said.

'That is correct, madam.'

'Stuff that!' she cried. 'Heroes always win!'

'Not in this epic!' laughed Brother Peter.

'No, Miss Ratched. In this story we are the heroes. He is the villain. He is a serious threat to the very basis of our utopia.'

'Who says?' she demanded.

'It is written,' Brother Peter replied.

'By whom?'

Brother Peter and the Keeper looked at each other, alarmed. 'It is not for you, madam, or us to ask that!' the Keeper said.

'It's sexist discrimination!' she spluttered.

'Sexism's been outlawed for centuries,' Brother Peter replied.

'Bullshit!' she cried. 'That may be true in the law books but in practice we women still get shafted. For instance, why haven't I been told who scripted the epic we're now in? Yeah, why?'

'We can't tell you, madam.'

'See, I told you!' She punched her thighs, stamped her feet, and spun around. 'Fucking discrimination. I'm sick of it. Hear me, sick of it. It's about time a woman was made President!'

The other two closed in to console her.

The knife moved swiftly. Four short slashes and the Keeper and Brother Peter were helpless on the floor, clutching at their severed Achilles tendons. (I was alarmed at my ruthless expertise.)

'That's unforgivable!' cried the Keeper.

'Savage, uncivilised!' screeched Brother Peter. Blood was seeping through their fingers.

I turned to Big Nurse. Her eyes were as large as footballs. 'No, no!' she whimpered, backing away. The knife jumped. Zip-zip! Zip-zip! The buttons of her jacket scattered across the floor. She clutched her lapels together to hold in the reason Ken Kesey had called her Big. 'You wouldn't!' Quickly, I peeled her jacket downwards to trap her arms. 'You're no gentleman!' she snapped. I kicked her feet from under her. She lifted up, landed with a winded *Uhhhh!* on her backside and rolled over. 'You're — you're still a savage!'

Within a few minutes I'd reprogrammed the control panel. I pressed the master switch. Instantly, in the panels all around, I glimpsed the pleasures turning into comedy, horror, boredom, disgust, pain.

'You fool, you blind fool!' the Keeper called as I hurdled over him for the door.

I found the line of stains on the threshold. Stopped. The alarm system was on, the whole cushion of air was live laser rays. I glanced along the threshold stains and found the path of stains across the cushion.

'The epic isn't going to end the way you think it is!' Brother Peter called.

I started following the stains across the deadly abyss. Below, there was screaming, escaping footsteps, the cacophony of panic.

eight

Tales in the Safehouse

I sheathed the knife in the inside pocket of my jacket and merged with the torrent of frightened clients gushing out of the Labyrinth. Cops everywhere. And more arriving in loudly sirening cars.

Once on K Road, I stepped out of the torrent and was soon at the entrance of the alleyway John had pinpointed as my third escape route. I waited in the shadows. Sirens, screeching of brakes, people shouting, from the direction of the Labyrinth. The knife was warm against my heart. I'd challenged the nerve centre of the Labyrinth and gotten away with it. Just as the trickster Maui had stolen the fire from the atua. (How had I acquired that memory?)

I scanned the alley. No one. The light from the windows above was slabs of white and yellow on the asphalt. Dust floated in the light. Stirred and rose.

Quietly, I headed for the end of the alley. Maui had been crushed to death between Hine-nui-te-Po's thighs when he'd challenged her. (The Tribunal's most strict taboo was against the remembering of such mythology — after all, we'd defeated death.) For a moment I couldn't push out the picture of her enormous thighs squeezing, grinding around his head, his eyes bulging as he choked and his head started cracking inwards.

As I reached the car John had waiting for me, Maui's ballooning eyes popped like bubblegum.

I examined the street. No one. I slipped into the car.

Further instructions were in the glove compartment. As I drove up the street, I read:

Go to 5 Sunnyside Road, Mt Eden. It's one of our safehouses.
Our housekeeper will protect you. She is a wizard storyteller.

Sunnyside Road was a narrow one-way street, with islands to
slow down the traffic. Still and in darkness except for the three
streetlights. Old villas. Maungawhau, the dead volcano, was a
black wave looming above the houses. I turned into the
driveway of Number Five.

A yellow front door bordered by stained glass windows.
Scent of ripening tamarillos. I walked across the wooden verandah under creepers that garlanded the eaves. I knocked. Footsteps from deep within the house.

As Dashiel Hammett would've described it: *She filled the
doorway.* No fat; just massive muscle, and she was larger than
Arthur Masashi Schwegger, Mr Universe. In a red and yellow
chequered bushshirt, tight jeans and black boots. I stepped back.
I caught her smile. 'Welcome, searcher.' She extended her hand.
Mine was lost in her grip. 'It's a privilege to have you in my
humble home.' She stepped aside. I entered the warm corridor
which smelled of seafood cooked in red wine. I noticed she wore
a sheathed dagger at her side.

Fifteen or so minutes later, after a quick whisky — she
drank orange juice — I was seated in a bentwood chair at the
head of her antique kauri table. 'I specialise in cooking seafood,'
she said. Before me was an artistic array of seafood: mussels in
the shell cooked in wine and cream; thinly sliced paua lightly
fried in butter and garnished with parsley; rock cod steamed
whole and served with black bean sauce; kina sushi — six in a
row within a border of rose petals . . . 'The iron taste of the sea
is good for the soul,' she was saying. Her mellow contralto voice
was like the hands of a skilled masseuse. 'I can dish up an
unlimited variety for any kind of soul. Unrepentant souls,
repentant souls, pure and impure souls, troubled souls, happy
souls, souls cracked like marbles, mouldy souls which have been
denied the healing rays of truth, piebald souls which don't know
their true single colour, souls like zebras that cross the black and
white territory between Good and Evil, souls without hearts,

souls without eyes, funky souls, rock souls, souls with flat feet which police the endless streets of our dreams . . .'

'I'm a vegetarian,' I interrupted. 'I'm sorry.'

'Souls with baby's hands that caress you to sleep at night, souls the colour of mist, souls as black as Dracula's cape,' she continued as she rearranged the dishes, putting all the vegetarian ones in front of me. 'Souls that sing to whales, souls which dart and spark, webbed souls which trap the insects of our fears . . .' Vegetable salad, tofu, cheese — twelve varieties and crackers — the sushi . . . 'Go ahead, don't mind my chatter.'

I started eating. 'Souls which dance the two-step and the tango, souls which hide in cupboards and eat flies, war souls armourplated with dollar signs, hopeful souls which sigh and sigh and write poems to dead elephants . . . '

'I'm a realist,' I interrupted through a mouthful of sushi.

'Yes, I also cater for the souls of realists who piss on the dreams of idealists, souls which suck the milk of elephants, crazy souls which feed on money and spit out the bones of the poor, saltless souls, instant souls that live in television sets, the souls of eagles and hawks . . . Eat, eat, searcher.' I did; I was ravenous, I'd killed Uriate, defied the Labyrinth, and I wasn't hungry for souls. 'Souls that protect the President, souls that haunt the nightmares of bats . . .' Her litany moved in and out of my attention. She certainly knew how to cook for souls. 'Yes, I know what you're going to remind me of: that the Tribunal has outlawed metaphysics, but what's a soulkeeper-housekeeper-storyteller like me got to talk about?' I shoved another sushi into my mouth. 'Do you believe in souls?' She caught me. I couldn't escape her gaze. Her eyes were the colour of turquoise glowing in rich tropical light.

'I don't know. I've never thought about it.'

'Dangerous answer,' she said. 'Souls don't exist, that's official. Remember?'

'I'm sorry.' I wished she'd stop scrutinising me.

'You're not very sure of yourself, are you?' I didn't reply. 'They tell me you're turning into a very skilled and fearless searcher, though. I envy your purpose. I apply every year to be a searcher. No luck. For twenty-five years now. By turning me down, the Tribunal makes me feel as worthless as shit. I mean, what's wrong with me that stops them making me a searcher?'

'The Tribunal knows best,' I reminded her.

'Of course they do. I didn't mean to imply that they don't.'

'I'm sure they'll appoint you soon.'

'And you're a Free Citizen, the ultimate preference. Look at me, I've been before the Tribunal nearly all my life and I'm still a nobody. Every time they turn me down, the compulsion to build up my body becomes overpowering. I'm three hundred pounds, no fat. I pump iron five days a week. I take mountains of vitamins and steroids, eat a prescribed health diet, don't smoke or drink or fuck around. I'm just a puny soul caught in a mountain of worthless muscle. I despise Arthur Schwegger, he's the lowest of the low, yet I build muscle to look like him.' Bowed her head.

'You're gentle and kind.'

'But ugly. The Tribunal must believe that, otherwise why haven't they made me a searcher?' I handed her a serviette. She blew her nose and wiped her eyes. When she looked at me again, I felt as if I could linger in her eyes forever.

'You are very beautiful,' I said. 'And they tell me you're a wizard storyteller.'

'Who told you?' I handed her my latest instructions. She read them. 'Yes, I suppose I am. Kind of the Tribunal to consider me a good storyteller.'

'Thank you for the delicious dinner. You *do* cook for souls!'

Mirth in her eyes. 'And you *can* eat!'

I noticed then that the vegetable dishes were empty. 'Sorry for being such a pig.'

'I love cooking for big eaters, for large souls.'

I helped her stack the dishes and cutlery in the dishwasher. I felt small beside her, yet safe. Any hunter would have to get past her to me. I also sensed a shield of mana around her. 'Are there any other guests?' I asked.

She shook her head. 'I'm entitled to only one VIP guest at a time.' I must've looked puzzled. 'Oh, yes, you *are* a VIP. Not just because of your mission, but your status as a Free Citizen.'

She served Chinese tea in the sitting room. We sipped and talked, comfortable in our plush soft chairs and warmth and dim light. 'My house has everything you may need. If it doesn't we can bring it in.' The room was walled with book-filled shelves, from floor to ceiling. 'This is my hourless, timeless room,' she said. No windows, I noticed then. 'In here, the temperature is always that of a mild summer day, the light doesn't change either, no clocks, nothing to indicate the passing of time. The whole house, in fact, can be made timeless.' I unzipped my jacket and took off my shoes. 'In this room, among the dreams of the world in my books, I don't age, not inside. And in those dreams, I dream my own stories, stories that shield me and whoever I am protecting at that time.' She poured me another cup. Hers was the sweet aromatic scent of feijoa, a compulsive favourite of mine.

My mission, the hunters and their threat seemed far away, unimportant.

It was then that I referred to the dagger at her side. 'It is very beautiful,' I said, She didn't understand. 'Your dagger.'

'Oh, yes, it's a family heirloom. It's passed down from the eldest child of each generation. I'm the fiftieth to receive it.'

'May I see it?' She hesitated. Looked at me. I didn't back off. So she undid her belt and pulled the belt through the sheath. She extended the sheath with the dagger in it, with both hands.

I was surprised by its weight. The sheath was of animal skin studded at the edges with diamonds. It was lined with metal. 'It's crocodile skin; the metal is platinum.' I pulled out the dagger. The handle was of woven gold, with a steel handshield edged with hexagonal designs. It seemed to grow to fit my grip. I held it up. The twenty-five-centimetre blade glistened like teeth. 'The steel is Japanese, fashioned in Kyoto, by the great sword maker Sadao Takayashi.' The blade glowed whitely. Through that glow I saw that her eyes were fixed upon it. 'I don't show it to many people,' she whispered.

'Does it have a name?'

'Strange, but no. After fifty generations, it has no name, yet it is itself and can be no one or no other dagger.'

It warmed in my hand. I resheathed it. 'It's beautiful.'

'Yes, It is the mauri of my line.'

I returned it. She laid it on the coffee table beside her. 'Does it fight well?' I asked.

She understood. 'When it has to, which is not often. And it is very gifted.' I reached over and touched the back of her hand. She looked at her feet.

'I have one too,' I said. She glanced up and took her hand away. I pulled the knife out of my jacket. 'It is very plain and ordinary. Like a kitchen knife.' I handed it to her, handle first.

'But it has perfect balance,' she said, placing it across her right hand. 'And history . . .'

'It is a scarred and mangy dog.'

'But fearless and unrelenting and very expert.'

'It has killed many times. Both its owners and its challengers.'

She ran her fingers over the long blade. 'Yes, it is expert at its art,' she said. It was then that she raised her eyes to mine.

For what seemed a time beyond time, we held each other's loneliness. 'I fill my life with stories,' she said. I leaned towards her, into her heady feijoa scent, and ran my hands up the backs of her arms that goosepimpled and shivered. She started pulling away.

'You are very beautiful.' I held her arms. She pushed me back effortlessly.

'Wait,' she said, 'I have a story to tell you.'

She held my knife between her hands as she spoke. Her eyes were hypnotic stars which drew in my breath and awe.

A tale is about other tales; it is also the teller and her telling, my wife would've said. A story written down loses because written language is an artificial technology. That story has to fictionalise a readership and its author. So in my writing down of the house-keeper's tale(s), I risk losing the teller and the full mana of her tale. But here it is anyway.

A searcher, through the act of searching, determines what

she will find, she sang. One certainty is the path she has covered when she looks back at where she started from. The other is the uncertainty that is in her footsteps into the darkness ahead. What happens when the history, the looking back, is outlawed, bred out of our breath? Our search is then utterly in the ever-moving present. It is its meaning without *was* or *will be*.

Once there was a woman — the story doesn't give her a history or details about her personality, appearance, or life — who was summoned, one winter morning, to the Tribunal building. She went though she didn't know who'd summoned her or why. She didn't even ask the shy messenger, a one-legged man who wore a purple crêpe-paper party hat and a false black beard.

When she arrived at the front entrance — no time or date is given — she was told (the story doesn't say by whom) to take the third lift up to the Interrogation Room. There's no description of the lobby or lift, no information about the location of the Interrogation Room and whether she was afraid or not.

At the Interrogation Room door, which was shut, she was told by the receptionist — there are no details about the receptionist — to wait.

The woman sat down in the black leather armchair, which smelled of crushed mint and reminded the woman of that summer day she'd made love in a field of clover. (No information is given of the lover or the field or how she'd felt.)

She waited for thirty minutes exactly. (Why thirty minutes? The story doesn't say.) The door slid open. She didn't hesitate. She stepped over the threshold into the circular room.

The windowless room was odourless and full of bone-white light. In the opposite wall was a replica of the door she'd just come through. She hurried across the parquet floor to it. She didn't notice that the floor was not catching her reflection. She was full of hope because, like all of us, she'd been raised to believe that doors were merely entrances and exits into rooms, out of rooms, into views, treasures, meanings, surprises, and so on.

She waited in front of that door for exactly thirty minutes. (We don't know if she had a watch and whether she waited in another black leather armchair). The door slid open, and again she stepped over the threshold into a repetition of the empty room she'd just passed through. Again she wasn't disappointed; after all the longer the surprise is withheld, the more excited we become.

She hurried over the polished floor to the third door. Again she waited for thirty minutes before the door opened. Again another repetition of the empty room. But she kept journeying, full of hope, through doors that all looked the same. She didn't bother to study the doors, to read their shapes, surfaces, messages. Doors were merely conveniences, openings into vistas. She never once thought doors could be entrances into prison cells or torture chambers or lairs of savage beasts. No. For her, doors opened to the future, to new knowledge, visions, truths, revelations, progress.

Years later — the story doesn't say how many years or how she came to know it was years, she decided to change strategies. She turned around and began walking through what she believed were the doors she'd come through, but discovered she was repeating what she'd done going 'forward'. Again she didn't think of studying and reading the 'reverse' sides of the doors. She came to believe soon after, that the purpose of her existence was to keep on going on through doors and empty rooms that might yield revelations. And sooner or later, she would be rewarded for her persistence, her dogged determination.

She knew she was getting old. (The doors and rooms remained ageless.) She knew she was getting old by just looking at her limbs. They were wrinkling and shrinking. Her joints became arthritic, but she defeated the pain by moving, exercising, walking on.

One day she stumbled and landed face down on the floor. As she pushed herself up, she noticed she had no reflection in the mirror-like floor. She walked, stopped, bent forward and looked into the floor. No reflection still. She repeated this many times, but all she saw was the reflection of the blue-domed ceiling which reminded her of the summer sky under which she'd made love in the field of clover.

She came to accept her reflectionlessness as part of the reality of her journey, too.

From door through room to door through room to door, she walked. Until one day, old and breathless, she sat down on the floor and leant with her back against the door she was going to go through. As usual, she waited for thirty minutes. When she went to rise to her feet, she couldn't. She kept falling down every time she tried. 'Get up, body; get up, soul!' she whispered to herself. 'One more door to pass through, one more room to cross . . .'

At her seventeenth attempt to regain her feet, she collapsed against the door and died.

She (and we) would never know what lay behind her final door. (We can also ask the story why she died on her seventeenth rising.)

If only she'd bothered to read the doors, she would've found the 'meanings' to her life, early. If she'd read the surface of the first door, there would've been no stoic journey, no door to room to door to room fate. For on both sides of each door was this message:

ALL DOORS ARE ABOUT OTHER DOORS
THEY ARE THEMSELVES

And she would have gone home to her husband and children and not wasted her life chasing hope, salvation, meaning, through doors and doors and more doors.

If only she hadn't obeyed the summons, this story, her story, would have been different.

When I tried to embrace her, she held my arms and stood up, raising me to my feet. 'No, I'm so unworthy,' she repeated. I tried to hold her closer. She half held me off. I didn't let go as she backed out of the room, cauled in her rich feijoa aura and gentleness. Down the corridor, like a dance. 'What about your wife,' she insisted as she backed into what turned out to be her bedroom and gym.

'What about her?'

'Trust, faith . . . ?'

'Remember, the Tribunal has rid us of all that. We must share our love and give uninhibited expression to our desires and needs . . . '

'It's time for my training.' She pushed me away. I waited. 'Do you?' she asked as she took off her boots. I shook my head. She mounted the exercise bike. 'I'm a compulsive!' She started pedalling. Her jeans bulged and rippled. 'I hate doing five hours of this daily but I can't stop.' The bicycle seat was a squeaking wedge against her crotch and between her thighs. I burned as I watched.

The summer-warm room was baby blue, even the carpet. To the right was a round waterbed covered with blue satin sheets. Above it was a large smiling portrait of the President; his eyes were riveted on her buttocks. Weight-training equipment occupied the rest of the space. Colour photographs of world body-building champions covered the far wall. Arthur Schwegger was in the centre. I sat down on the edge of the bed.

As she warmed up, she stared into her reflection in the wall of mirrors in front of us.

Dark streaks of sweat began to appear on her shirt. She unbuttoned it. A moment later she peeled it off and dropped it to the floor. My breath almost stopped. Her arms and back were a perfect symmetry, a luminosity of clearly defined muscles clustered in groups, dancing under the tanned skin glowing with sweat. Her eyes swam in her reflection. My breathing was a rip-and-tear.

I looked into the mirror, into the groomed and trained geography of her chest and belly, bulging and retracting in time to her peddling.

She dismounted and with her back still to me, unzipped her jeans and rolled them off. Her lower body was a dazzling harmony with the top, trim flanks and buttocks flowing down massive thighs and legs in quivering currents of muscles.

When she came towards me I stood up and she moved into my arms.

We lay on the bed. 'I'm sweaty,' she murmured as I licked the sweat off her lips and face. Her arms wrapped around me and held. I didn't want to be released, ever. I'd been so long without wife, family, love, sex. On the run, at the edge of danger and death. And when her legs opened and I slid into her depths, it was as if I was being absorbed into her.

'It's never been like this for me,' I whispered.

'Not for me, either.'

'You're more beautiful than Schwegger and all the other atua of our earth,' I said, holding her tighter.

It was then that she started her second tale. It punctuated, gave rhythm, memory to our love-making.

Once she was told by a famous Tribunal psychiatrist that she believed herself ugly because of the circumstances of her birth. 'You see, my parents were brother and sister,' she continued. 'I know incest is no longer taboo but I've had to live with an inexplicable sense of guilt. When I was old enough to understand the nature of my birth, I left home.' She paused. 'Should I be recalling my history?'

'Why not?' I said, rocking back and forth in her flow. 'No one else will hear.'

'Remember the Law of Surveillance . . .'

'Let's dare it.'

'That's good, really good,' she whispered. 'Is it good for you?'

'Beautiful, very beautiful.' Her thighs hugged me closer.

'It's hard and hot . . .'

'Not too fast. Let's make it last.'

She kissed my left ear and continued telling her story into it.

She escaped to her uncle's and aunt's, Ben and Lustrous, who'd always been kind to her. She didn't tell them why she'd left home. They didn't ask. Ben was an expert carpenter who specialised in building homes. Lustrous taught at high school. 'But within a few weeks, Uncle Ben was trying to get into my pants.'

'The bastard,' I admitted my jealousy.

'So you too are capable of emotions supposed to have been bred out of us,' she said.

'Sorry,' I replied. 'No, I'm not jealous and I don't believe in sin or psychosis. Go on with your story.' I caressed her buttocks. She did the same to me, and my nerve endings tingled to her playing.

'My shame was like death,' she said. 'But I had to hide it from my friends and teachers in case they found out I had quirks considered abnormal. And I couldn't tell my aunt because she would've laughed at my shame and encouraged Uncle Ben to re-educate that shame out of me. One night while she was out, Uncle Ben tried again. I pretended *normality* and he fucked me. After that, we got together whenever Lustrous was out or asleep. And I thought I'd rid myself of the shame and guilt.' She paused and slid her hand down between our sweat-slippery bodies. I stopped moving as she fondled my balls. I ran my fingers down her arse groove. 'Uncle Ben taught me a lot about sex, though I later learned that, apart from Aunt Lustrous, he'd fucked only two others, a cousin and his partner at work — both men . . .'

'Bloody deviant!' I couldn't stop myself.

'Hey, you're a real savage!' She held up my head and looked into my eyes. 'Homosexuality is normal, mate,' she reminded me. 'What century are you from?' I nuzzled my face into her neck, to hide. 'Never mind, your secrets are safe with me.' She ground her thighs playfully around my hips. 'Anyway, soon after Ben started making music with me, I found myself training to Schwegger's prescribed body-building plan. I also joined the weight-training class at school, and Aunt Lustrous bought me a home gym recommended by Schwegger Enterprises. Both Ben and Lustrous loved watching me train at home . . .'

'I loved watching you tonight,' I interrupted. 'It was a most beautiful dance.'

'You're a bloody good flatterer too!' she laughed. 'How can you love ugliness? A body that is larger than life, a caricature of what a normal body should be?'

'Don't ask me why, I just do!' I started moving faster. She responded with a long pulling, clutching rhythm. Our conjunction, so to speak like a fifties novel, squished, slurped, gurgled, farted and overflowed. 'God, it's great, isn't it?'

'Let's do it forever!'

'Yeah, yeah, yeah!'

'When I left high school, I trained as a body-building instructor and worked in an Arthur Schwegger Fitness Centre on K Road . . . Not too fast . . . That's it, just right . . . Anyway, I wanted to shift to my own flat but my aunt and uncle insisted that I stay. "I can't do without you!" Ben pleaded. "But love and selfish possession of the loved one are banned," I told him. "I don't give a stuff about the Tribunals laws," he declared recklessly. "I love you." So I stayed. But then as Aunt Lustrous watched me at home, training, the guilt and shame got to me again. Her eyes, their stripping feeling on me, made me feel disgusted with my body, my self. It was my fault they — Ben and Lustrous — had reverted to emotions that were dangerous to our society's survival and well-being.' (I too was reverting.) 'One evening I refused to strip and train. Aunt Lustrous wept and pleaded. Ben finally threatened to betray my shame and guilt to the police. "What about your lust and jealousy?" I countered him.

She stopped moving. I stopped too and caressed her cheek, looking at my reflection in her eyes. 'I did *love* them,' she whispered. 'So once again I relented and stayed and performed for them. My self-disgust led me to train harder, to turn my body into a monstrous caricature.'

I nipped her nipples with my teeth. She shivered. 'Wow!' I nipped them again. She hugged me closer and stilled my movement. I waited.

'I killed him.'

'Who?'

'Uncle Ben.' I remained silent. 'When I didn't want to fuck him, he slapped me, tore off my clothes!'

'Barbaric!' I cried. 'Rape's been outlawed for centuries.'

She pulled the blankets up to cover us, and then she told me the rest of the second tale.

While Uncle Ben was ravaging her and raving about how much he loved her, she just stared into the ceiling, remembering her parents and their denial of her, and Aunt Lustrous and the lies she hid from the Tribunal. Her self-disgust mounted into nausea. She wept and didn't realise what her monstrously strong body was doing.

When she broke out of her self-disgust, she found him crushed between her thighs.

She was put into a reordinarination clinic where they discovered she had a talent for storytelling. She was a model patient because she wanted to be cured. Two weeks later she was free from her shame and guilt. However, the doctors told her those feelings would recur whenever she was attracted to anyone sexually. 'For instance, witness my shame when I found myself hooked on you tonight!' she laughed.

She was transferred to the city's Storytelling Unit. She was one of Professor Thinkus Circle's nine pupils. (Nine was the Professor's lucky number.) Her apprenticeship there was a story she would tell me another time. Enough for this tale that she graduated A+ in the art of Talk-Story, and a specialist in Icelandic, Tangata Moni, Red Indian and Tamaki Makaurau oral traditions.

For five years she worked at Auckland University, in the Department of Talk-Story. The head of her department was Tohunga Paratene Paki Matchet, Keeper of the Gates and the last bone flute player in the country. That too was another story she could tell me if I wanted her to.

Unexpectedly, the Bureau of Safehouses recruited her. Her training, for three years, was yet another story.

'I've been a housekeeper now for eight years,' she continued. 'I love my job. I'm doing something important for the Tribunal and our society. I enjoy doing it because I'm allowed to be myself, and I'm providing a safehouse for searchers who're on their dangerous quests for understanding. One day, the Tribunal willing, I too will be a searcher in need of safehouses . . .'

I slipped off her. As I lay beside her, watching the white light of the bedside lamp playing gently on her face, I ran my right hand over the hard geography of her body. I felt ugly and unfit beside her magnificent beauty. 'We each specialise in our individual talents. So my house offers an endless repertoire of tales and stories. I hope it is proving satisfactory?'

'Yes, *very* satisfactory!' I was combing her pubis with my outstretched fingers. Her right arm, on which I'd been lying, lifted and curled me back onto her.

'Bloody flatterer!'

'And very unfit!'

'Would you like me to put you through a fitness programme?' She was serious. 'Once, you must have been very fit.'

'No, I've never liked sports or too much physical activity.'

'I could persuade you. How are you going to last in your search if you're not fit?'

'I'd love that, but I don't have time.'

'Yes, I forgot. My guests never stay long.' She turned her face away. 'Have you always been a searcher?'

I shook my head. 'Until recently, I spent years before the Tribunal.'

'Must've been very exciting.'

'Yes, I was lucky to be awarded the Final Reference.'

'Are you free then to tell about your appearances before the Tribunal?'

I hesitated. I suddenly didn't trust the room. 'I'd love to but I'd be jeopardising your life.'

'I forgot,' she whispered. 'Sorry.' I held her face between my hands and kissed her deeply.

Then for what seemed a whole summer stretch I told her about my years with the Tribunal, all of it: names, times, locations, questions, answers, confessions, guilt, shame, secrets.

'I'm forbidden from knowing the missions of my guests,' she reminded me when I started telling her about that. 'Thank you for allowing me into your past though. I'd love to confess to the Tribunal. Perhaps you could put in a good word for me?'

'Of course I will, honey.'

'Are you sure? I've waited so long.'

'Once my mission is over, I'll recommend you.'

She said, 'You're hard again.' She sheathed my cock in her hand, squeezed and pumped. 'I thought you said you were unfit!' I jerked it through her hand. 'It's spoilt, isn't it?' Opening her legs, she slid it in. 'There.'

'It's so smooth and velvety, wet — and hot.'
'Tell me about your wife and children,' she urged.
I became the storyteller; she, my listener.

I met Margaret, my wife, at the bank where I was chief clerk, in a small South Island town called Okarito, famous in the twentieth century for its whitebait, whale suicides, and a novelist who wrote about bone people. I was tranferred there from Stratford where I'd been a teller, and she'd come down from Auckland as a secretary-typist. We didn't know each other's pasts beyond that. But within a week of our hands touching accidentally at morning tea time — it was electricity — we were madly in love.

It *was* love, Margaret and I agreed. We couldn't bear to be apart. So we got a flat together. It was beautiful, all of it — the sex, the talking, the eating, the living and working together. It was perfect, the way the Tribunal wants relationships to be.

'It's like something out of my favourite storyteller Arabarb Landcart,' she interrupted. 'But go on, it's so inspirational!'

We both wanted three children, two girls and a boy. Why that number and combination? I was the third person Margaret had made love to and we'd made love three times during our first night together, and three was my lucky number. Margaret wanted two girls to remind her of her two sisters who'd disappeared during the night of the electric storms. I wanted a son to continue my genes, illegal though that was.

'I've wanted kids all my life, but haven't been permitted to,' she sighed into my shoulder. 'Rest for a while. Just hold me.'

Margaret and I were average, law-abiding, God-fearing Kiwis. We'd done averagely well at everything. We thought therefore that the Tribunal would not allow us the three children, two more than the legal limit. But it did for its own reasons which I've not tried to fathom. And with the three kids we became an exemplary, exceptional family. Our kids excelled in everything: in sports, at school, at church — everything. Each month we received a congratulatory message from the Tribunal about them and the way we were raising them. The Tribunal also sent pamphlets about the latest child-rearing methods and maximising the development of exceptional children.

For Anis and Elem, our daughters, the Tribunal recommended the martial arts as practised by the Samoan master Alapati Tuaopepe and his followers.

'I was into that for a while,' the housekeeper said. 'But I found the spiritual demands and its metaphysics too difficult. I coped with the physical side of it okay. I even got a blue belt — the lowest!'

It was as if the Tribunal knew exactly what the girls were talented at. Anis and Elem took to the martial arts Way of Tuaopepe like ducks to water, pardon the cliché, or, like cannibals to steak, ravenously, passionately, giftedly.

For Leahcim, our son, the Tribunal prescribed the career of a mechanic, what it called 'a mechanic of life'. He had to start with car engines, then what made trees live and grow, then sheep, the most numerous creatures in our town. When he was a teenager he was into the mechanics of fish and other waterlife. We noticed that as he progressed through that hierarchy, he could heal, with an inexplicable mana, ailments such as rheumatism, ringworm, acne, piles, athlete's foot, and, most strange, alcoholism. And just before he left us two years ago to join the Fisheries Department in Wellington, he could fish the anger, jealousy, envy and other soul maladies out of anyone.

'Is he as manaful as you?' she asked, jiggling her hips. We laughed.

Everyone loved him. The girls and many of the boys tried to seduce him but he stuck to the basic law of his apprenticeship: no sex because that drained the mechanic of the power of healing, of fishing.

The teachers in our small town couldn't cope with their precocious gifts. The Tribunal arranged for them to attend the Wellington School for the Gifted. Our bank transferred us to Wellington.

Three years later, we woke, on a bitter winter morning, to two messengers, at our front door. They were dressed in the black top hats and long frock coats that gamblers wore in the

cheap western movies of the twentieth century. They apologised
for waking us so early and for bringing a summons from the Tribunal. 'If it's any consolation,' the grey-bearded one said, 'we
would love to appear before the Tribunal. Look at us, we're old
from waiting and being constantly disappointed.'

Our dinner that night was a celebration.

'Do you believe in reincarnation?' the housekeeper asked.

I pondered. 'Of course I believe in it,' I replied. 'The Tribunal and our President have defeated death through the practice of reincarnating people as other lives.'

'So do you think you and Margaret and your kids have lived
as others before you were a bank clerk?' She caressed my back
and looked into my eyes.

'I don't think so. I've never *felt* I've been another person.'

'Never?' she pursued me. I shook my head but remembered
the savage knife dueller, killer and detective I'd been in the
previous few days. 'Are you sure?' she emphasised.

'Of course I'm sure. I was — and still am — a harmless bank
clerk.'

'But now that you're a searcher?'

'Well, I've had to survive, even fight for my life.'

'And you're becoming courageous and daring?'

'I suppose so. I mean, look at me: I've never let myself
indulge wildly, recklessly, and passionately in anything, and
here I am . . .'

'Fucking yourself silly with a state housekeeper who's supposed to be protecting you?'

'Yeah, yeah!' I laughed. She laughed too. 'And I *love* your
protecting!'

And so we continued, making love and telling stories, in the
house which had outlawed time.

We and the sheets and the room stank of sex and sweat when I
woke. The bedlamp was still on. She was asleep with her back
to me. I ran my fingers over her shoulder. She didn't stir. I
slipped out of bed. I didn't know what time it was, and didn't
care. My body ached, my back muscles hurt as I walked.

Once in the corridor I searched for the bathroom.

Small lithographs in silver frames lined the corridor. Black circles within black circles within black. Not Hotere. The bathroom was next to the kitchen. Mauve walls, blue plastic curtain around the shower, round mirror above the sink. Someone had put out shaving gear, a towel, a dressing gown, slippers and a change of underwear for me.

For a moment I stared into the mirror and listened to the hushed stillness. No windows. I shaved, the buzzing filled my ears like water.

The shower kicked up steam when I turned it on. When it was as hot as I could bear, I stepped under it. My aches and pains started thawing.

I'd not met anyone like her before. More myth than woman. More everything than anyone I'd known before.

She wasn't in the bedroom when I returned. The bed had been stripped and fresh sheets put on. My dirty clothes were gone. I sat on the bed. When I looked at my reflection, I felt it didn't belong to me. I smiled, turned my left profile, winked, bowed, and it copied me. I lay back on the bed. Wondered where the knife was.

Whitebait, millions of laser spots, flicked and shot through the bubbling black water in which I was immersed, with my feet buried in mud. My hands darted out but were too slow for the whitebait.

'You don't love me!' I cried. They flicked — ping, ping, ping-ping! My hands began turning to green bone. I woke. The room was exactly as I'd left it. The man was still in the mirror, watching me.

I pushed open the wardrobe door set into the wall behind the bed. All men's clothes. New. My size. The Tribunal thought of everything. I put on a pair of black trousers, a black polo-neck jersey, black socks and shoes, and a leather jacket. Remembered I was a vegetarian and dropped the jacket to the floor of the wardrobe.

I was ready to leave. I had a mission. But decided, after wandering from one piece of weightlifting equipment to another, watched by the man in the mirror, there was no need to hurry.

Smell of miso soup. I followed it to the kitchen. She wasn't there. On the table was a tray of Japanese pickles, steaming miso soup, noodles, a bowl of steamed rice decorated with bamboo leaves. I sat down and started eating. A single, long-stemmed red rose stood in a narrow vase at the table's centre. I watched myself watching that rose as I ate. My reflection in the vase watched me.

After putting the dirty dishes in the dishwasher I wandered back to the bedroom, sat down on the bed, watched the man in the mirror and waited for her.

Her reclining form stretched across the horizon, outlined against the sky in which the Holere clock was drawn in black. The invisible clock hands ticked and moved, pulse-beat by pulse-beat, towards noon. The fourteen numbers cast their reverse reflections on her skin. I watched myself swimming through green seas towards her. With each frantic stroke I remained where I was.

'Don't cry, you're safe,' she whispered into my head. I was in her abundant arms, in the bed, weeping. 'You're safe, there's no need to be afraid.' She nestled my face into her neck and wrapped her arms around me. Her warmth and smell was that of fecund earth. 'Hush, there . . .'

I never wanted to leave her.

We each are a Puzzle Palace for our own unravelling, she sang. But most of us are afraid to do it. Maui tried but couldn't unravel death. So the President and the Tribunal have built a Puzzle Palace on Earth, for the truly brave searchers who want to unravel to their most hidden depths. Built into the Palace are all the possibilities of death so that those searchers who succeed know the most exquisite tastes of life having overcome death and its frightening traps . . .

nine

Tangata Maori

I sheathed her ancient dagger in my belt and my knife in the inside pocket of my jacket. After drawing the sheet up to her chin, I kissed her lips gently and switched out the light.

It was night and cold and threatening to rain. I shut the front door behind me. I checked the shadows in the garden and around the car. For a moment I held in the strong scent of tamarillos.

It started raining, a fine spitting. Once inside the car, I punched the dashboard computer. Focused, my heart thumping. Seven days! Seven days lost! Ample time for the hunters to get to my family. Ulysses and the Sirens. But I dismissed that thought.

Swiftly, I backed out of the driveway. A black fox terrier barked at me, jumping up and down behind the gate opposite. A red-haired woman watched me from the verandah. I waved and pushed the car forward, weaving between the traffic islands. Behind me, Maungawhau was lost in the darkness hissing with rain. I switched on the windscreen wipers, the heater and demister. Seven days. Again I'd been distracted. Deliberately? I checked the glove compartment. No instructions.

Once on Wynyard Street, I turned right and was soon over the railway crossing and on to New North Road, heading for the heart of the city.

Light traffic. I checked each car, every side street. Rain washed in waves over the windscreen. The wipers fought them off. I'd lied to her about the Tribunal and my trial, about my wife and children — an invented history with enough 'truth' in it to persuade her (and whoever she was gathering information for). But I'd not lied about how I felt about her. I'd not invented that. How else could I explain the lost seven days.

I switched to the news channel on the car TV. A few minutes later, as I sped into the maze that was the city, I was on the news. A mug shot of me. Wanted for questioning in relation to the killing of a man in the Labyrinth. *Extremely dangerous. Approach with caution.* I turned up my collar to hide the bottom half of my face. I breathed calmly, surprised at my detachment; that, intuitively, I knew what I was doing and where I was going.

Cars lined up behind me when I stopped at a red light at the bottom of Wakefield Street. Pedestrians. Green light. I turned down Queen Street, moving slowly as I scanned the footpath, shop doorways, verandahs. The buildings were canyon walls of black glass that deflected the light. The rain washed off them like mercury.

I saw the young woman first. She was in a thick woollen overcoat far too big for her, red scarf around her neck. Beside her, leaning against the shop window, was a young man in a yellow plastic raincoat and dangling bone earrings. To his left, a few paces away, was another youth with a stained sheepskin waistcoat, torn jeans and sandals. They looked cold and hungry and unreal behind the sweeping screen of rain.

I stopped at the curb, lowered my window, and beckoned to the youth in the yellow raincoat. He pulled the hood up over his head and ran to me through the rain.

'Fifty bucks,' he said as the rain splattered over the hood. He peered into my face. 'Fifty for the usual, fifty more for every extra you may want. And no fucking violence, mate.'

'And your friends?' I'd not done any of this before, yet it seemed *natural.*

'Both of them? Shit, mate, you must be desperate or something, or not satisfied with what you can get at K Road!'

'All of you,' I said.

'One fifty for us for the usual . . .'

'Okay, get in then.' He waved his friends over.

He got in beside me. The others got into the back. The wet

steaming stench of their clothes fogged the car windows immediately. 'Neat machine!' their leader said.

'Yeah, bloody neat,' the young woman echoed.

I drove towards the bottom of Queen Street. Their studied
manner and silence were those of people much older; the tough-
ness of sadness and suffering.

'You must be rich,' she said. Words but no genuine
enthusiasm. In the rear-view mirror, her pale face bordered by
wet ringlets reminded me of someone. 'Are you rich?'

'No, the car belongs to my company.' That silence again.
They gazed straight ahead.

'Are you a hunter?' their leader asked. I shook my head. 'A
searcher then?'

'Yes,' I replied eagerly.

'Stop the car then, mate!' he ordered. His companions
leaned forward. I felt her breath on my left ear. 'We don't go
with searchers. It's against the law.'

'Who's law?'

'Shit, mate,' she said. 'Where have you been? The Tribunal's
law, your fucking law!'

'Searchers are supposed to go it alone,' their leader said. I
kept driving.

'What if I was just looking for company for the night?' I
manoeuvred.

The two in the back whispered between themselves. 'Speak
up!' their leader ordered them.

'One night can change a searcher's search,' she told him.

'Who's going to know?' I said.

'The Tribunal's everywhere, mate. You made it that!' he
said.

'Aren't you afraid of deviating from the law?' she asked.
'You can get your brains castrated!'

'I know, but I love the feel of deviating,' I lied.

'Enough to risk your life?' he asked.

I turned along the wharves. 'Yes. Look at you guys: you've
spent all your lives deviating.'

'Yeah, but look where we are: fucking poor, fucking cold,

fucking hungry . . . ,' she said.

'Shut up!' he whispered. I kept driving. Only the swish of the wipers cut the silence. 'Okay, mate,' he said. 'Three hundred bucks for all of us for the night.'

'In advance!' she said. I pulled out my Final Reference and gave it to him.

He glanced at it and started laughing. 'Shit, man, that's for your world.' He handed it to the others who studied it.

'Yeah, mate, in our world this piece of paper is worth shit!' she whispered. 'Just plain manure!' She shoved it back into my coat pocket.

'Then you'll have to wait for your money until we get to the hotel.'

It was then that they spoke to one another in a language I understood only in bits and pieces — the English bits and a few Polynesian pieces, the rest was street pidgin, their coinage.

'How do we know we can trust you?' their leader said. 'You could fucking well sell us to the pigs!'

The car was hot, I was slightly nauseous from their smell, so I lowered my jacket collar. 'Hell, the bastid's the same tan as us!' she exclaimed.

'Another Tangata Maori, eh?' he said. 'Where you from, mate?' I told them.

'Are you Tangata Maori?' she asked.

'I don't know,' I had to reply.

'Jesus, they've fucked you up good too, eh. Like they've done to most of our people!' she said. I didn't understand. 'They've left you brown on the outside and filled you full of white, other-worlder bullshit.'

The other youth, who remained silent, looked up into the rear-view mirror and said, 'We're the only true ones left, eh.'

'I've got only my wife and three children,' I said, not knowing why.

They spoke to one another in their language. 'So we trust you,' their leader said. 'But it's still three hundred bucks. Okay?' I nodded.

'And if you sell us out, we just tell the cops you tried to rape me!' she declared. 'That's real serious deviation that'll send you to the reordinarinising crazy house, man.'

I turned up Albert Street. A black van swished by in the wet.

'Where are we going?' their leader asked.

'I have a suite in the Regent,' I lied.

'Man, when they see us they won't let you back in,' he said.

'Mate, you must be the dumbest searcher around!' She leaned back into her seat, shaking her head. 'You've got a lot to learn.'

'Yeah, hell of a lot!' I tried joking. But they'd withdrawn into their huddled silence. I'd decided on the expensive Regent because it was a most public hotel. No one would think of looking there for a killer on the run.

As I drove into the Regent, they lowered themselves into their seats. 'You're not going ahead with it, are you?' the leader said.

'Too right, I am,' I said.

'What's going to happen if we get kicked out?' she said.

I stopped under the overhang over the entrance. The entrance attendant, a tall Polynesian with a crew cut and black suit, rushed down and opened my door. 'Good evening, sir!' he said.

'Good evening.' I started to get out. He saw my guests and looked at me. 'Please put my car away,' I instructed him. He hesitated. I held up the Final Reference. He bowed and stepped aside. I started up the front steps. The car doors opened and shut and I heard them hurrying to catch up to me.

We snaked in through the circling door. ' What do you think you're doing?' she whispered. 'You'll get us all in the shit!' I kept walking through the lounge. It was fairly crowded. Most of the people avoided looking at us.

The guests around the reception desk parted as we approached. The three male receptionists, formidably sleek in their black suits, pretended we hadn't arrived. My companions fidgeted. I snapped open the Final Reference and held it forward as if I was holding a cross to ward off Dracula. The effect on the receptionists was immediate: they paled, backed off and then leant forward with the kindest smiles I'd ever seen.

'Good evening, sir!' the most senior said.

'And guests!' his companions added.

'No, my children,' I corrected them. 'They've just been to a fancy dress party to raise funds for the Tribunal's favourite charity, World Orphanages Enterprises.' My guests were dripping all over the plush white carpet.

'We raised five million tonight,' she said. The receptionists bowed. I told them we needed their largest suite. 'And not on the fourth floor,' she added. 'Four is unlucky in Japan.' We settled for the thirteenth floor. When they asked me to sign the registration form, I told them I was travelling incognito, on a mission.

'No one is to know we're here,' I threatened them.

'No one will know, sir,' the senior receptionist promised.

'Not even the hotel staff,' I added.

'Very well, Free Citizen. Anything else?' he said.

My companions were huddled together beside me. 'Yes, tomorrow morning send up someone to take our orders for clothes. We didn't bring any luggage. We're also very hungry.'

'I'll send up our senior waiter, sir.'

As we followed the chief porter to the lifts, I noticed a group of French tourists talking and looking at us. 'Fucking wankers!' she hissed. The lift doors slid open. We got in. She turned and, as the doors shut, she jabbed her V-fingers into the air at the tourists.

Ten minutes later, after the porter had shown us through the palatial suite, they stood in the centre of the lounge and looked at me.

'You've got mana, man!' Manu said.

'Yeah, real mana!' she laughed. The other youth smiled but maintained his charismatic silence.

'I thought you didn't give a stuff about *our* world and its values,' I said.

'We don't,' she countered. 'We just use it to survive . . .'

'Yeah, to con a bit of bread to stay alive.'

'How would you like to make a lot of bread?' They looked at me. 'From me. Working for me?'

'What doing?' he asked, warily.

'No sex, nothing like that?' she added.

'I'm too old for that!' I tried joking again. No reaction. 'I want you to help me find my family.' Puzzled looks. 'Sit down.' They did, close together. 'Some people are trying to get at my family. My search is to find my family. And save them, if I can, if it's not too late.'

'Why don't you go to the pigs?' he asked.

'Or the Tribunal?' she added.

'The Tribunal has set my family's rescue to be my mission.'

'Shit, man, you live in a crazy system. The Tribunal can rescue your missus and kids, yet it has set everything up, like a fucking game, for you to play that role and risk your life?' he said.

'Remember, in their world there are searchers and hunters and judges and the judged. And there are other fucking categories . . . ,' she chanted.

'That's enough!' he silenced her. 'Do you know where they're being held?'

I nodded. 'In the Puzzle Palace.' They looked at one another and started giggling. 'What's the joke?'

'Everyone knows where that is, mate!' she exclaimed.

'I don't,' I said. They laughed some more. I sprang up. 'What's bloody funny?' They stopped. 'Okay, the joke's on me. So tell me what it is.'

'Don't get angry,' she said. 'It isn't a joke, mister. Everyone in *our* world knows where the Palace is.'

'We forgot some of you jokers don't,' he explained. Their silent companion started giggling again.

I went to the bar. Poured myself a whisky. They wanted beer. I opened the fridge, and tossed them some cans. 'Cheers!' I said. We drank. The whisky warmed my chest.

'Fucking good brew, *sir*!' she said.

'You could all die looking for the Puzzle Palace,' the silent one said.

'Why did you have to say that?' she demanded.

'Why not? It's the truth!' he insisted.

'I know that. All the possibilities of death are built into the Palace,' I said.

'You must love your family a lot, mister,' he said. He drained his can while we watched him. He had lurid burn scars over the backs of his arms and hands.

Right then the waiter knocked and entered. 'You can order any food you like,' I told them.

'Anything?' she asked. I nodded.

The red-haired waiter, face spotted with pimples, kept smiling as he wrote down their orders which they gave, altered, gave, altered. I savoured the memories of my children doing the same thing. Finally their leader decided for them: six servings of fish and chips; six king-size burgers — two cheese, two egg, two meat; six thickshakes; and three large Cokes with lots of ice. 'And three pork and puha!' she added. The waiter was lost. 'And make sure it's hapuka, mate.'

'Madam?' the waiter stuttered.

'Shit, I forgot you Pakeha don't know real kai and fish from pimples, eh!' she laughed. The waiter hurried out, his freckles a bright red.

Later, while they devoured the food at the dining room table, with their fingers, ignoring the expensive cutlery, I rang reception and told them to bring up $600 in cash.

I waited and watched my guests. They looked to be in their early twenties. Without their overcoats, which had given them bulk, they seemed fragile, vulnerable. They were in their self-contained silence again, feeding a hunger that seemed endless.

'The bastid's even brought us hapuka!' she exclaimed. 'Great place you got here!' she called to me. Her irrepressible, cocky daring reminded me of Elem, my second daughter. I got another whisky. Remembered I'd not touched hard alcohol for years. With each sip I relaxed.

The doorbell rang. I went and took the money from the senior receptionist. He wanted me to sign for it. No signatures,

I reminded him of my secret mission. He nodded con-
spiratorially.

I dropped the wad of notes beside the leader's plate. They
glanced at me, then back at the money, and continued eating.
'Your pay for today and tomorrow. Three hundred a day, okay?'
I said.

He shook his head slowly, chin shiny with grease. 'We still
haven't decided if we're going to work for you,' he said.

'That's why I'm paying you six hundred. You take tonight
and tomorrow to decide.'

'Time's running out quickly,' the silent one mumbled
through a full mouth.

'Fuckwit, why do you always have to be serious, eh! Why
do you have . . . ?' she said.

''Cause this poor joker here . . .' he glanced up at me '. . .
may lose his aiga!'

'Why should we give a stuff about that, eh. Why? He's one
of them. And they've fucked us up for centuries . . . Let him find
out what the fucking Tribunal and all its sick bullshit is like. Let
him get buggered by his almighty President . . .'

'That's enough,' their leader whispered to her.

'Young lady, while you're my guest don't blaspheme against
what I believe in!' I tried not to sound angry.

'Young lady, me left tit!' she snapped. He held her arm. She
stopped.

They continued eating as if I wasn't there. I said, 'I'm tired.
I'll see you in the morning.' He nodded. 'If you need anything
just ring reception or room service. Good night!' I glanced at
her. She refused to look at me. I turned to go.

'What is it you want us to do to help you?' he asked.

'I want you to get me into the Puzzle Palace,' I said.

'That's fucking easy,' he said. 'Everyone's allowed in any
time.'

'I want to get in there without anyone knowing.'

'Can you trust the Tribunal?' she asked.

'Can I trust you?' I replied. She looked away. 'Good night.'

I trembled as I went to my bedroom. I still trusted the

Tribunal. It was my life. They wouldn't betray me. And my family.

I fell asleep quickly, and the Hotere clock ticked in the centre of my dreaming.

They were digging into a hefty breakfast of bacon, eggs, tomatoes, sausages, toast and coffee when I went into the dining room. 'Good morning!' I said. They glanced up, she smiled, then went back to the feeding. They'd left me the place at the head of the table. I sat down. 'Did you sleep well?' I asked. She smiled again, the other two kept their heads down. She started passing me the food. I noticed they were back in their shabby street clothes.

I heaped some food on to my plate and started eating. I realised I was very hungry as I tasted my first mouthful of bacon and tomatoes. We ate in silence. I waited. Though they appeared to be preoccupied with the feeding, they were observing my every move. I poured myself some tea. When I finished my plate of bacon and tomatoes, I started drinking my tea and observed them.

'What's the matter?' I asked, trying to sound casual.

'Nothing,' she mumbled.

'Then why are you afraid of me?' I asked. They looked at one another.

Their leader wiped his mouth. The other two stopped eating. 'Why didn't you tell us?' he asked.

'Tell you what?'

'That the pigs are looking for you, man?' he emphasised.

'I didn't think it was necessary.'

'Shit, not necessary!' she said. 'We're with you, mate, and, if they're looking for you, they'll get us too.'

'Sorry about that,' I said. 'The hunters are after me too, as you know.'

'Jesus, you really are in shit street, eh,' she said. He glanced at her and she kept quiet.

'Well, tell us why the pigs want you?' he asked. I told them about the Labyrinth, the bar, Uriate, and the duel.

'What about the other two at that Ponsonby apartment?' he asked.

'What two?'

'A woman and a man, acquaintances of yours, the TV said.'

'I didn't kill them,' I started. He continued staring at me. 'Well, I didn't mean to. I had to save a friend they were going to kill.'

'How did you kill them?' she asked. I held up my hands. 'But they said you're just a bloody bank clerk.'

'Of course I'm a bank clerk . . .' I insisted.

'Bank clerks aren't experts with knives and their bare hands, mate,' he said. Their quiet companion spoke to them in their language. 'Yeah, and what about the woman in the Mount Eden house?'

'I don't understand?' I replied.

'The one in 5 Sunnyside Road?' She couldn't resist it.

It was as if a giant hand was throttling my breathing. I struggled to my feet, my hands clutching the table's edge. They watched as I tried not to drown. He poured me another cup of tea. I took a sip and gagged, clutching the serviette to my mouth. 'It was on the TV this morning,' he whispered. I sat down again. 'We found out about the others from the TV last night after you went to bed.'

'I didn't kill her,' I murmured. 'Even if I'd wanted to, I wouldn't have been able to . . .'

'Shit, man, you must be an expert at . . .' she interrupted.

'Shut up!' he ordered her.

'But he must be!' she insisted. 'They said she was a champion dagger dueller and member of the Army's crack anti-terrorist unit.'

'How was she . . . she killed?' I asked. He looked sceptically at me. 'I did not kill her,' I said. He looked away.

'You don't need to get angry with us,' she said. 'Your war's between you and the pigs and the hunters, eh. Got nothing to do with us.'

'Yeah, as far as we're concerned, the more you otherworlders exterminate one another, the better,' he said.

'How was she killed?' I repeated, emphasising each word. I watched them.

'With one expert thrust through the ribs into her heart,' he said, watching my reaction. I didn't react. 'Her house was a bloody wreck. A fucking big fight it must have been, between her and her killer. There were cuts and slashes on her arms and hands. She must have used her bare hands to fight him, eh.' I remembered I had her dagger, the keeper of fifty generations of her family.

'If you didn't stick her, who did?' he asked.

I said nothing. They got up and cleared the table.

Since my return from Wellington, the hunters' erasures had taken a different form so I'd be hunted by the police as a killer. Why? They were keeping me alive so I would lead them to my family. Why had Uriate warned me about the people protecting my family in the Puzzle Palace? They were of the Tribunal, my protectors. What about John? Why was he afraid of me? Was he still following my movements and protecting me? Trust no one, Uriate had written.

'You're in real shit street,' she fished me out of my thoughts. I glanced up at them. 'We're sorry about that woman . . .'

'You don't have to work for me,' I said. 'It's now too dangerous. Everyone I've come in contact with recently has been erased or harmed.'

'Are you sure you're just a bank clerk?' the quiet one asked. I nodded. He shrugged his shoulders.

'It's all part of the President's "Game of Life",' she ignored him. 'A searcher is given a mission, the hunters are appointed to hunt him down, make his mission worthwhile. Anyway, no one dies permanently if the Tribunal rules for their reincarnation . . .'

'The President did *not* prescribe my family's arrest. The Tribunal is protecting them from my enemies and the enemies of our society!' I insisted.

'Suit yourself, mate,' he said. 'But right now your arse is in extreme jeopardy!'

'Shit, where did you learn that fancy vocab?' she laughed.

Ignoring her, he said, 'And if we stay with you, we're in shit street too.'

'Why didn't you leave last night then, after you saw the news?' I asked.

'We had to earn our six hundred bucks, remember. We need the bread.'

'You could've taken the money and disappeared.'

'Shit, man,' she said, 'we're honest, in our own way. And we wanted to enjoy the comforts of your suite. We deserve it, eh!' She started laughing.

'I wanted to meet a real, fair dinkum knife-fighter,' the quiet one said. 'Yeah, a real fucking expert!'

'Are you expert at karate too?' she asked. I sipped my tea. 'They said on the telly, you broke those jokers' necks with single karate chops.'

I looked straight at her. 'I've almost had enough of your — your insensitive bullshit,' I whispered. She backed away from the table. 'One more smart alecky crack out of you and I'll . . . !' I stopped, and felt foolish.

'G'on, say it, you bullying motherfucker!' she came at me. 'Say you'll break my fucking neck . . . '

'Shut your bloody gob!' their leader ordered her. 'One more squeak out of you, and I'll . . . !'

She backed off into the lounge. Once at a safe distance, she cried, 'You fucking jokers are all the fucking same: fucking sadists and bullies and selfish wankers!'

'If you don't like us, just bloody well leave,' he called. 'Go on, and see where that gets you!'

She stamped her feet and then slumped down into a soft chair, grasping her face. 'That's not fair, you heartless creep!' she cried. 'You're my bloody family!' She jumped to her feet and, tears streaming down her face, yelled, 'And where the shit am I going to go, eh? Our whole fucking country's a prison, a loonybin!'

The quiet one went over and handed her his serviette. She wiped her face.

'By the way, my name's Manu,' their leader told me. I told

him mine. 'She's Piwakawaka, my sister. (Everyone calls her Fantail.) And his name's Aeto. We found him.' He paused. 'It's still three hundred bucks a day?' I nodded. 'And all expenses paid?' I nodded again. 'You must be fucking rich.' He went off to his sister and Aeto. They talked for a short while. I waited anxiously.

'Okay, sir, it's a deal,' he said, extending his hand, and smiling for the first time. We shook hands.

'And he's got to accept us the way we are, warts and all!' she called.

'Is that okay?' Manu asked.

I jabbed a mock punch at his belly. He jumped back, smiling. 'Now, we're all in the shit together,' I said.

Soon after, I got reception to send up hairdressers and clothes designers. Conservative greys and blacks, ties and white shirts, short back and sides. As expected, Fantail objected. Temporary camouflage; the streets and her former life were still awaiting her. 'Let's play the President's "Game of Life" properly,' Manu persuaded her. 'I'm doing it only because I'm now working for you,' she said. I ordered different clothes from what I wore normally, and had a haircut that helped change my appearance.

While 'my children' were being transformed, I rang John's number, but got no answer. Reception had no messages for me either. But I wasn't so afraid any more.

Just after midday, they filed out of their bedrooms. I stared. I had to stop myself from laughing. They were now of my world, and looked trapped in it. Fantail appeared incongruous in her flowing black dress, stockings, white shoes, hair cropped short and swept back sleekly, light makeup and eyeshadow, black and white earrings, and a pearl necklace. She stood glaring at me, daring me to laugh. Aeto looked like the son of an undertaker in a cheap fifties western: black frock coat and black tie, white shirt and black shoes, black hair plastered down over his scalp. He fled back into his room and slammed the door.

'Don't!' Manu cautioned when I looked at him.

'Who's the insensitive wanker now!' she cried.

'You're beautiful!' I said.

'You bloody pervert!' she said, smiling.

We enticed Aeto out of his room with promises of a heavy lunch.

As we ate I had to suppress my laughter, and pretend not to notice how they were trying to ignore their awkwardness, their being snared in appearances they'd always despised.

'So what do we do now?' she asked.

'We've got to work out a plan,' Manu said. 'The hunters'll have our guts for garters, for sure, if we don't.'

I called the City Council offices and got maps of the city delivered immediately. We spread them out on the dining table. 'He can't read,' Fantail said of Aeto, who rolled his eyes at her. 'He can't read language and maps but he sure can read food and suckers you can milk, eh!'

'I'm not dumb, you dumb broad!' he said.

'Ya sure ain't!' she mimicked him.

Using the maps, they took me block by block, street by street, through the inner city. Names of businesses, buildings, places, gossip about those, recent happenings, some history, stories of crimes and daring deeds they'd committed against those people and places. They even filled in what wasn't in the maps, especially when we descended into the labyrinth below the inner city, into a world I knew nothing about. Sewage systems, tunnels, communication and power links and lines, forgotten byways and drains, nooks and crannies they used as home, as safehouses. A city underneath a city, holding it up. 'A city is layers of maps and geographies, layers of them, centuries of it. We were the first, our ancestors, no matter what lies the Tribunal says. So our maps are at the bottom of the bloody heap. They're still there though the bloody otherworlders have tried to fucking well erase them. As long as we survive . . .' Manu said.

'Yeah, as long as we stay alive, the bastids can't wipe out our maps!' she declared.

'Time for tea, I'm hungry,' Aeto reminded us. We looked up from the maps. It was evening.

We went to the lounge windows and watched the darkness creeping in over the city like a black-furred sea. The street lights blinked on, millions of them.

'Awful, eh?' I remarked about the city.

Yeah, but it's all that we have,' Manu said. 'It's our home.'

'Even though it's been turned into a madhouse,' she murmured.

They got me to order otherworlder food for dinner. 'But not too bloody fancy,' she quipped.

I marvelled at their appetites and their relentless style of eating.

'Good kai,' Manu said after they'd finished.

'Yeah, not bad. Especially when I can't pronounce the names of most of the dishes, eh. What was that one with the pigeons and peaches?'

'Man, that was great. The worst one was that liquid stuff with the meatballs,' Aeto said.

'Even the mussels were fancied up. What did that fruity waiter call it, eh? Yeah, the paua dish?'

'Abalone with black bean sauce,' I replied.

'No wonder you stick to your vegies,' she laughed.

'How come you're a vegetarian?' Manu asked.

I told them.

'Shit, the Tribunal was right, if all of us ate vegies, our economy'd collapse like fatless fat!' she continued the joke.

'If God hadn't meant us to eat meat, He wouldn't have made us of meat!' Aeto said. When we didn't laugh, he started giggling. 'That's a joke,' he prompted us. 'I heard it somewhere.'

'That's not a joke, man,' she said. 'It's the bloody truth.'

Later we agreed the hunters and the police had us under constant surveillance. We had to give them the impression we didn't know, so we would shift hotels every day.

We gave ourselves a week to prepare for the Puzzle Palace.

'I want to see the Palace tomorrow,' I told them. They looked at one another.

'Okay,' Manu said.

That night in my dreams, Big Nurse Ratched, Brother Peter

and the Keeper sat on my chest. It was difficult to breathe. 'Drown. drown, drown,' Brother Peter kept murmuring.

As we drove out of the hotel the next morning, I didn't bother to check if we were being followed. 'Where to?' I asked Manu. He nodded up the street. 'Is it far?' Fantail and Aeto chortled. We rounded the corner.

'Stop,' Manu said. I pulled over to the curb. He pointed ahead and up.

'But that's the Government Insurance Corporation!' I said. They started laughing.

'Its popular name is the Puzzle Palace,' Manu explained. 'Don't ask me why it's called that.'

'It's just another fucking ugly office building, eh,' Fantail added.

I sat gazing up at it in disbelief. Twenty storeys high, stained by rain, sightless rows of windows. 'Are you sure?' I had to ask.

'Shit sure,' she replied. This wasn't playing true to my archetypal version of evil and its lair. Uriate's note and the Eden housekeeper's references and stories about the Palace had given it legendary, mythical proportions in my imagination.

'Just hundreds of offices inhabited by nine-to-five people, desks, filing cabinets, paper, memories, paperclips, rubber bands, Twink, word processors and computers . . .' Manu recited.

'And lonely souls of generations who came to fill in the nine-to-five stretch, back to back, forever, amen!' Fantail continued.

'There are no secrets then?' I asked.

'No secret chambers where they're holding your missus and kids?' Manu replied. I nodded. 'Who knows, we'll just have to find out.'

'Baddies sometimes have the mugs of ordinary civil servants . . .' she said.

'Yeah,' Aeto interrupted, 'the faceless faces of the President.'

They watched me. Though I was shocked by his accusation, I didn't show it.

We drove down to the Town Hall and the Council's offices. Aeto and I waited in the car, while the other two went in. Fifteen minutes later they were back with the plans of the Puzzle Palace. 'We conned a lovely old man, with big eyes for the ladies and me in particular, into xeroxing these!' she laughed.

A block away, we checked into another hotel, the Royal Terence Sturm.

'No secrets here,' I concluded after a quick reading of the plans in our suite. 'It looks like any other office building, as you say. With nothing to hide. Are you sure this is the only Puzzle Palace there is?'

Aeto offered to check it and disappeared into the streets.

'Let's assume for now, this is our target,' I declared. Paused. I was talking melodramatic military TV bullshit. They were impressed though.

'And a puzzle,' Manu added. I glanced at him. 'It looks *too* simple.'

'Could be a Chinese puzzle box, eh?' Fantail offered. 'Open one, you get another one that opens into another . . .'

'Until you have nothing,' I said.

'You got no faith,' she said. 'Do you believe that Spaniard's note?'

'Of course I do!' I tried to save face.

'We know underground ways of getting into the building,' Manu said.

'Like the backs of our eyes, eh,' said Fantail. 'So just concentrate on learning the inside.'

'How do we get in to check that?' I asked.

They were tolerant. 'We just go in like every other customer. Through the front during working hours,' Manu explained.

'And through the doors and burglar alarms after hours,' she completed.

About half an hour later we were entering the Palace separately, rain dripping off our coats.

The lobby was a collection of plastic bucket seats riveted to the floor, a small inquiries booth, with a yellow-pale receptionist who tried to smile, a few half-dead pot plants, and a bulky sign

on the wall above the line of lights, which read: LIVE FOR-
EVER! BUY THE PRESIDENT'S OWN LIFE INSURANCE
PLAN. Everything smelled of mildew.

I took a crowded lift up to the top floor and walked along
the corridors. I passed many workers. They either nodded or
avoided eye contact. Office after office of managerial staff.
Secretarial pools, workers in rows behind computers, piles of
files, and the smell of mildew.

At the end of the eastern corridor was the boardroom. It was
open. I slipped into it. Empty. Just an old rimu table surrounded
by old leather chairs, curtained windows keeping out the day,
and a hefty portrait of the President in his golf cap, hanging on
the wall behind the board chairman's chair.

As I turned to leave, I caught my reflection in the shiny
parquet floor. I looked as if I was hanging upside down, with
my feet stuck to the floor.

In the following two hours I checked the next four floors, as
I'd agreed with Manu and Fantail. The floors repeated one
another, even the people, the lights, the smell, my presence and
the sound of my heart and breathing.

We met back in our suite.

'It's a totally boring building,' Fantail summed it up.
'Fucking awful! Harmless repetitions. What a bloody way to
be.'

'That's exactly how I read it too,' Manu said.

'Could it be that we're *reading* it wrongly?' I asked.

'Shit, it's what it appears to be. It can't be anything else!' she
protested.

I remembered what my wife had said once. 'We see what
we believe,' I told her.

'Chief, I'm tired. Don't throw me that profound view of
what is real and what ain't. You know how many metres I
walked in those corridors? That's what was real for me. I felt the
tiredness, I saw and smelled the walls, the offices, those awful
people . . .'

'That's enough,' Manu told her. He got us some cold beer.
We lay on the sofas and sucked back.

'Bloody good, eh!' he kept saying. I got all the cans out of the fridge, put them on the coffee table. We raced through them.

'Ya lazy bastards!' Aeto chastised us when he returned. 'Here, give me a bloody can, eh! Shift over, broad!' he instructed Fantail. He jumped up and landed flat on his back beside her. He drank until his can was empty. Belched. 'There's no other Puzzle Palace, sir,' he called to me. 'I checked with hang of a lot of people: our friends, taxi drivers, in the pubs, bookshops, bus depots. And newspaper reporters. One of them wanted to do a story on my search for the Puzzle Palace. I told him to go bury his eyes in his father's arse!' They laughed about that. I got myself another can. There was a pleasant buzzing in the centre of my forehead.

'Right, after this short piss-up, we'll sleep. I'll wake you at midnight. I want you to take me back into the Palace tonight.'

'You sound just like General Hone Tuwhare in *Battle of the Pissheads*,' she called. They laughed about that too.

I waved as I wove my way to my bedroom.

Reception rang to wake me at 11.30 p.m. I thrust my head under the cold tap to unclog it of the slight beer headache. Dressed quickly. Hurried out to wake them.

But they were already sitting quietly in the lounge, waiting for me. They were dressed in black jerseys, jeans, sports shoes. 'Don't you jokers like sleep?' I asked. The maps were open again on the table. They'd marked in, in red, what looked like a route into the Palace.

'We're used to having little or none,' Manu said. He got up. I noticed the leather bag in his right hand. 'Tools of the art, sir,' he said. 'Let's go.'

We followed him. They were again locked into their deadly silence.

I marvelled at the way they used the shadows to make their way up to the front entrance. Marvelled at how they burgled the door and the alarm system. Then marvelled some more as we searched each floor and they unlocked every barrier into anything I wanted to see. 'It's taking too long,' Manu whispered. He told Fantail and Aeto to check the top ten floors. We'd check the bottom half including the basement.

It was as we'd found it that afternoon.

'That building's got no fucking secrets,' Fantail said, as we sipped the hot soup I'd ordered from room service. I glanced at Manu. He shrugged his shoulders.

'Thank you for taking me through it again,' I said.

'That's okay, sir,' said Aeto. 'Three hundred bucks is a lot of pay for such easy work.'

'It *was* easy, boss,' said Manu.

'Piece-a-cake, nothing valuable in that Palace so their locks and alarms are toys, eh,' she added.

'We've cracked far tougher nuts, eh, Manu?' Aeto said. 'Shit, I'm bloody hungry again. Who wants more kai?'

As he was ordering their night snack over the phone, I got up to go to bed.

'What are we going to do next?' Manu asked.

I shook my head. 'Let's sleep on it another night.'

I couldn't sleep. I reread Uriate's note. Sifted through everything the housekeeper had told me about the Palace. Retraced my way through it, in and out of every room. I got out the telephone directory, found Government Insurance Corporation, read the names of its sections, managers, and so on.

Next morning, after breakfast during which I said little, we shifted to the Selwyn Muru Hotel at the other side of the Puzzle Palace. I sent Manu to see if John was home, and Fantail and Aeto to check our underground way into the Palace. I got my binoculars, pulled an armchair up to the lounge balcony, sat down in it and studied the Palace. It was as if it was now growing in the centre of my head. A grey rectangular slab of concrete and steel with silent windows through which I couldn't see its secrets and puzzles or my wife and children. The grey sky shifted and moved but the sun couldn't break through it. Each movement, however, was reflected for a moment on the Palace's hide. Then I remembered the Memorial on Maungakiekie. This was a larger version of it. I pursued that analogy for a while but it didn't yield any keys into the Palace's meanings. I gazed up into the sky again and again and followed each of its major changes into other analogies and possibilities. It got me nowhere.

The phone rang. It was Manu, telling me he'd broken into John's apartment. 'Only stale stinky food and shitty underwear and dirty clothes. Piles of them, eh!' he said.

'Check the computer,' I said and waited.

'Nothing on it. Dead.'

'His desk and any notes?' I waited again.

'Sorry, just a lot of office files — bullshit about . . .'

'Manu, see if there're files on me.' I waited again.

'Sorry, nothing.'

I told him to meet me at the City Library in an hour's time. 'Your mate's a dirty pig, eh,' he said.

'He's the best number eight in the country,' I remarked.

'In the Pig Fifteen?' he said. We laughed about that.

I drove to the Tribunal's Building and used my Final Reference to gain access to its computer banks. Nothing in them about the Puzzle Palace, nothing about the Government Insurance Corporation, not even restricted information. I checked for information about other government buildings. Long lists and records appeared on the screen.

At the City Library, we got one of the librarians to check their computer listings. No information about the Palace. We got her to check other city libraries' listings. Still nothing.

'It's a beautiful name, isn't it?' she said. 'Whoever made it up must've been a poet.'

'Yes, but who and when?' I said to Manu as we left the library.

We had to run through the rain to our car. 'Someone's erased the history of the Palace,' I said. 'But why?'

The rain worsened as we drove to our hotel. I had to drive slowly. The other traffic surged by like metallic sea creatures, driven by the waves of wind. 'Really pissing down, eh? The atua must be pissed off about something,' Manu remarked. I remembered the librarian had my wife's hairstyle.

141

'Are you guys enjoying this?' I asked them at dinner.

'Hell, yeah!' Aeto exclaimed.

'It's fucking scary, eh?' Fantail whispered.

'Are *you* enjoying it?' Manu asked me.

I nodded. 'Yes, I suppose so. The Puzzle's got me by the short hairs and won't let go, eh.'

'But don't forget your family,' Aeto said.

'Yeah, we may not have much time left,' she added. 'You know something? If we had magic beans, like Jack had, we could toss them out this window and overnight they'd grow right up to the Giant's penthouse on top of the Puzzle Palace. Then, zoom, we could climb up into the Giant's plush pad, pinch his dirty magazines and golden eggs.' She turned to Aeto and said, 'That's a true story, mate. No fucking fairytale, eh?'

'Yeah, pull me other golden egg,' he laughed.

Soon after that, they said they were tired and went off to bed. I went up to the balcony windows and, sipping a beer, observed the Palace.

The rain was whipping at it, wrapping itself around it, and then spinning off in spirals across the city. The mountains and canyons of lights seemed to be under a torrent of water. Through the darkness and rain, I suddenly sensed the Palace scrutinising me, challenging me, saying: 'I can read you but you can't read me. I have your wife and children . . .'

For a slow moment she was outlining herself in my dreaming, in a long white robe that highlighted her brown skin. Then she moved, stepping towards me. I realised she was a reflection in the window. Piwakawaka, Maui's cheeky bird. 'Can't you sleep?' I asked.

'Naw, I can't stop thinking of that fucking building.' She came and stood beside me. 'Jus' look at the bastid, the arrogant bastid!' Looking at me, she asked, 'We're going to crack him, eh? Decipher his deadly secrets.'

'I don't know,' I murmured.

For a long while, we said nothing. We watched. And the Palace watched us.

'Your daughters?' she asked.

'Anis and Elem? Elem's about your age, and cheeky too,' I said. She smiled. 'Leachim's about Aeto's age. He's a wizard mechanic.'

'I'd love to meet them. Manu and I never knew our parents. I don't even know how old I am. Aunt Hena, my mother's sister, raised us. She told us Dad was part-Samoan, part-Maori, part-Pakeha. Mum was mainly Maori, with a dash of Scotch, a little bit of Tongan, and a lemonslice of Pakeha. Real fruit salads, eh. They had a short partnership which produced us, then Dad disappeared into the Tribunal's reordinarination centres. He'd not been "cured" of a life of crime to keep us alive. I understand, from Aunt Hena, he was also a hired killer. I'd like to believe that bit of the legend. Mum took up with other guys, who abused and used her, and she was dead of an overdose before I was one. Anyway, Aunt Hena had four kids of her own, no permanent husband, and had to slog her guts out in a factory during the day and a cleaning job at night. I wouldn't be surprised if she didn't clean out the shithouses in that Palace, once. Aunt Hena's story, her survival and ours, is not unique: it's true of most Tangata Maori mothers I know. Anyway, we kids started early on a life of deviance, crime, sin, call it what you like. We took an educational route very different from your kids.' She stopped and looked at me. 'I'm not boring you?' I shook my head. 'Well, instead of attending nice, white middle-class otherworlder schools, we took to the streets, the labyrinth, the borstals and welfare homes, then graduated to the reordinarination centres. Yeah, man, we're the graduates of the best education system for survival on this fucking planet . . .'

'Why didn't you let the centres help you?' I heard myself asking.

'Help? You mean, domesticate us, cut out who we are, turn us into mindless otherworlders?'

'That's not what they do!' I insisted.

'Have you ever been in one?'

'No, but . . .'

'Then you're not qualified to talk about it, eh.' I felt her watching me. 'I'm not trying to turn our life into heroic legend,' she continued. 'No. it was fucking awful, at times. Biting hunger, lice, dirt, beatings by your police. We watched Aunt Hena waste away with the long slog and sorrow and poverty. She was fucked by her employers, this white bullshit society and its racism, her men, even us. Yes, us. Every time we got into trouble with the pigs, she suffered. She suffered more when we refused to become "good" law-abiding kids. How could we? This society, yeah, the President's heaven-on-earth, doesn't want us as we are . . .'

'That's not true!' I interrupted.

'It wants everyone to be docile, kind, obedient,' she continued, ignoring me.

'But it has meant peace, no more world wars, enough food and resources for everyone . . .'

'Not everyone, look at us,' she reminded me.

'But you've deliberately chosen not to join us.'

'True, true,' she said. 'So I don't quite understand why we're helping you, eh.' She paused. 'You want a beer?' she asked. I nodded. She left to get it.

The rain had eased. Only a nifty wind was foraging among the buildings and canyons. Fantail's story of her life, her readings of the President and our society, which had disturbed me, had given a more hostile shell to the Palace.

'Here!' She tossed me a can. I jerked it open. 'We see what we believe,' she said. She didn't laugh. 'You see your society as you believe it is, eh. And that Palace.'

I drank my beer. The cold liquid stung my gullet. She had no right attacking what I believed in. She had no right to be so arrogant. She was just an ignorant kid.

'Aunt Hena died eight years ago, worn out, a mindless shell the Centres couldn't refill with another identity,' she insisted on attacking me. 'We stole her body from the Home they'd put her in. We gave her a tangi, or our version of one, the little we knew. We buried her here in the centre of the only home we've ever known.' She swept her arm over the city. She raised her beer. 'Cheers!' And drank. She continued talking but I tried not to listen.

'Manu's been my father and mother. Poor bastard's had to save me from hell of a lot of scraps and foolishness . . .'

'And Aeto?'

'We found him in a dump five years ago. He was a mess. Half his body was burned badly. He stank like cooked pork. Shit, Manu and I took off. We spewed our guts out. Then we rushed back. Manu wrapped him up in his overcoat. I got a cab. When the driver refused to take us, I stuck a knife against his bloody throat. He took us to the hospital all right.' She paused and drank again. 'He almost died; took him a year fighting for his life. We tried to visit him every day. Nobody else did. He's never told us anything about himself. Just his name. It's Samoan, though I'm sure, like all of us, he's a fruit salad. He hasn't told us either how he got burned and why he was in the dump.' She drank again, and laughing softly, said, 'You should see him steal, man. Anything. He can steal anything, anywhere . . . He's our family now.'

She tossed me another can. 'I feel like getting pissed.' She opened her can and raising it to me, said, 'Here's to the bank clerk who's going to crack open the Palace!' She drank. I didn't. 'Why don't you get good and honestly angry?' she attacked. 'Yeah, let go of your fucking otherworlder control? Break out of your otherworlder conditioning and brainwashing? Why don't you?'

I turned away from her. 'You're a bloody fool, eh. The only fucking way you're going to get your wife and kids back is to get so mad you'll even cut off the President's balls. Don't you see?' Her head turned with my stinging slap. Left. Then her face was centred on me again. 'Good!' she snapped. 'But it's not me you want to kill, eh, it's that!' She stabbed her finger at the Palace.

'I'm — I'm sorry,' I mumbled, wheeling and hurrying to my room.

ten

The Puzzle's Possibilities

To avoid Fantail, I got up before they did and left a note on the dining table, telling them where I was going and what I wanted them to do that day.

It wasn't raining but the streets were still awash with water. As yet there was little traffic and few people. The crisp air numbed my face and hands. I walked quickly, trying to warm up. I couldn't take back the slap, though I kept reversing the memory in my head. Her defiant eyes, the slight upturn in her head, the red bruise.

I found the piecart; took a seat inside it. One other customer, in blue overalls, was drowsing at a table. I ordered tea, toast, scrambled eggs. Took my time eating because I had an hour to kill before the City Library opened. The morning city smelled of the sea.

I was the first customer in the library. Another librarian, a man with grey temples and a tic under his left eye. I told him what I wanted and he punched it into the computer. The library was colder than outside. I shoved my hands into my overcoat pockets.

He gave me a printout. I read it quickly, borrowed a pencil from him, and ticked the materials I wanted. He went off to get them.

My excitement warmed even my hands. I stretched and unstretched while the bookshelves watched me.

'You can't take them out,' he said. I took the three manuscripts and two monographs and he pointed to a desk.

Within minutes, my heart ticking like a cicada high on evening, I was buried in the material. Got higher as I absorbed the information. It was all there. I got out four other research papers.

Near midday, I hurried to the City Archives, a block away. They found me the bound newspaper volumes I wanted.

I felt armed as I stood on the front steps of the Archives, gazing up at the sky. Armed with my new readings of the Palace.

Above the Town Hall, sunlight flashing on its fuselage, a small plane was circling, trailing this sign:

DON'T TRUST THE HUNTERS OF THE LABYRINTH.
TRUST ONLY THE PRESIDENT'S TRUTH.

Back in our suite I got a ballpoint pen and yellow pad and after many revisions, arrived at this plan:

REREADING THE PUZZLE PALACE
(THE GOVERNMENT INSURANCE CORPORATION)

Present Reading
(1) 20 storeys high, with basement heating/airconditioning equipment, also storage space.
(2) The Building has an A classification ie — can't be demolished or altered radically because of its historical importance. Basically good representative piece of 20th century office building architecture.
(3) Has been owned by Govt Insurance Corp for 48 years, renovated twice during that period. Houses top managerial staff, and 8500 other workers.
(4) 12th floor is full of computers and records of Corp. Computers becoming obsolete. Plans to replace them.
(5) 20th floor contains boardroom, small staff health studio and 2 squash courts.
(6) Staff cafeteria and lounge on 4th floor.
(7) Corp always profitable. Last year's profit — $405 million. Could be better, says Personnel Business Journal. No mortgage on building.
(8) Corp bought Palace from Business Systems Research (BSR) for $20 million. Govt, through Tribunal, put condition against resale: Palace can't be sold again. (Why?)

(9) Palace first built as BSR's Auckland Headquarters for computer research and information gathering. Used most sophisticated computers of that time.

Rumoured then that the Palace was branch of America's National Security Council Network of Puzzle Palaces, most secret, most effective information-gathering system in the world, using computers, satellites, long-range aircraft, submarines, secret links into world communications networks and national telephone systems, etc. Some newspaper articles about that at time. Then nothing. But name, Puzzle Palace, stuck.

NOTE: The President, on graduating from university, worked at the Palace for a few years. Apart from that detail, nothing else in his memoirs about it.

(10) Recent rumours, reported in *Herald*, say Palace was and still is, secret training facility for Tribunal's élite hunters.

Possibilities

Puzzle Palace is all the above (and more). All is contained in ever-moving present.

So:

(a) Palace is headquarters of Govt Insurance Corp and is what it appears to be.

(b) It was also (and is) part of the State's surveillance network which is part of America's Puzzle Palace network etc.

(c) It was (and is) training facility for State hunters, so it must have labs for training hunters in interrogation techniques etc.

(d) It was also (and is) part of the President's apprenticeship as scientist, and part of his 'Game of Life', the Goal, the Ultimate Challenge, with all the possibilities of life and death.

All above dimensions, in time and space, are, together, the Puzzle Palace.

Question: How do you get into the dimensions other than Palace being Govt Insurance Corp?

Answer: We see what we believe.

The way of searching determines what we find.

So:

Methods

(1) Believe Palace is surveillance centre.

(2) Believe it is training facility for hunters.

(3) Believe it is secret prison for your family (and others?)
(4) Believe President knows Palace as above and approves of it as such.

Other Questions (not to be shown to the True Ones):
(1) Who are the enemies hunting you?
(2) If they're part of the President's 'Game of Life', are they his employees?
(3) Is John part of the Game too? If so, should you trust him?
(4) Why are you so efficient at hunting/erasing? Did you live as others before you were a bank clerk?
(5) Who were your family before they became your family?

Note: Fantail was correct. Everything's a puzzle within a puzzle within a puzzle.
Note: Determinism vs Free Will. It appears that the Tribunal/President have prearranged all that is and will be, even the Game of Life, to outlaw crime/poverty/war/violence/ all the negative emotions/etc. Who 'determined' the Tribunal/President?
Note: Everything I'm daring to question, see, remember, and plan is against the Tribunal's/President's Laws, against what I was raised to believe in and live by.

I have nothing to lose except my family.

Mission: Four Phase Operation:
(a) Phase One — collate all info on Palace. (Have done most of that. True Ones will bring theirs tonight.)

Agree on one reading of Palace as surveillance centre and prison.

Discuss implications of that and see if True Ones want to help you.
(b) Phase Two — survey then check all possible routes into and out of Palace. (True Ones to take you through those.)

Decide on safest route. (Have two fallback positions.)

Use that route to survey Palace layout as surveillance centre and prison. (Take note of alarm systems etc.)

Work out ways of neutralising those security systems.

Agree on who, in your team, is to do what, and timing of each move in infiltration.

Agree on tools/instruments/weapons (if necessary) to be used.

(c) Phase Three — enter Palace and rescue family, following agreed plan.

(d) Phase Four — escape route from city and new life under other identities.

(Don't tell True Ones what you've worked out for this. The Tribunal's methods of interrogation are 100 per cent effective.)

Hallelujah! Amen!

I was committed now. I felt free, outside like the True Ones, improvising my life. I got a whisky, restudied the plan, waited for my guides, especially Piwakawaka whose forgiveness I needed.

It was evening when they returned. She behaved as if nothing had happened the previous night. We ordered beer and food. While we ate, they gave me the information I'd asked them to gather.

Manu and Aeto: John was still a liaison officer at the Tribunal's headquarters. He was escorting a Northland farmer who was appearing before the Tribunal, but there'd been no sessions for four weeks and no one knew what John was doing, except that he was still in Auckland's representative team. He'd not been back to his apartment, either, since he'd left with me almost two weeks before. No mention anywhere of the two bodies found in Sister Honey's apartment, yet it'd been on the news.

They'd checked the President's itinerary for the next fortnight. He wasn't making any public appearances, anywhere. There was talk of his opening the rugby headquarters of the Poneke Club in Wellington at the end of the month. The President never took the same route twice, and he never stayed in one place for more than a week, for security reasons. Why were they continuing to worry about security when the world was now supposed to be free of crime? There'd been assassination attempts when he'd first become President, I told them.

They'd checked on the Tribunal building and complex. Nothing unusual.

Fantail: The Keeper, who looked like Yul Brynner, existed. He was a doorman at the Labyrinth Club, had worked there for thirty years, was a widower who lived alone in Newton. No record of deviance/psychosis/talent in anything. Just a solid citizen who loved the Tribunal. She'd talked with him in front of the Labyrinth. Not too bright. As he'd gone back into the Club she'd noticed he was limping, left leg. (I told them I'd sliced his Achilles tendon.)

Big Nurse Ratched also existed as a matron at Sade's Cherry Farm Clinic on K Road, a simulation mental home. She was very popular with the clients, especially those who loved the way she'd played the role of Big Nurse in *One Flew Over the Cockoo's Nest*, an ancient softcore flick. She lived with a Sister Honey whom the neighbours hadn't seen for over a week. (Sister Honey was one body in John's house, I told them.) Big Nurse read a lot of Ken Kesey novels. ('Who was he?' Fantail asked.)

Brother Peter was the fire-and-brimstone pastor at the Baptist Television Tabernacle on K Road, king of the bible-bashers. Four services a day. Packed. She'd attended the two o'clock session and watched him put the fear of God into his parishioners. Religious ecstasy. He too had a limp, right leg.

The last three were my hunters, enemies of the Tribunal, I told them.

'Are you sure?' she asked.

'No,' I admitted. 'They may be Tribunal hunters.'

'How can they be hunting you when they aren't moving anywhere from their jobs, eh?' she asked.

'They may already know where I am and what I'm up to.'

'And be waiting for you to lead them to your family, eh,' Manu completed it.

'We'll have to assume they'll be in or near the Palace when we make our move,' I said.

'Why don't we *neutralise* them now?' Manu suggested.

'Before they know it?' Aeto said.

'If we did that, their friends'd know we're ready to move.' When I glanced at Fantail I knew what she'd been wanting to ask all night. 'Yes, and I have to assume the President and the

151

Tribunal are in it too,' I anticipated her.

'You don't trust them any more?' Manu asked. I shook my head.

So I took them through my plan.

'Are you sure you're just a bank clerk?' Fantail laughed, afterwards.

It was 3 a.m. when we finished fine-tuning (Manu's term) Phase Two. Aeto fell asleep curled up in his chair. We would execute Phase Two the following night.

When Manu went to the kitchen to get us tea and coffee, I said to Fantail, 'I'm sorry about last night.'

She smiled mischievously. 'That's okay. It got you going, eh? I hate losing. We're part of your search now, in the President's Game of Life. And even though *our* search is only one of the trillion searches in the Game, it's special, eh. It's fucking special.'

'It's so absurd, isn't it?' I said. 'What if they've preprogrammed, predetermined everything?'

'I don't give a stuff!' She replied. 'Let's give it our best go. Show the arrogant motherfuckers . . . '

'Don't forget his family,' Manu reminded her (and me) from the kitchen doorway. 'That's why we're risking our necks, eh.'

We slept until 8 a.m., packed and shifted to the William Pearson Hotel directly behind the Puzzle Palace, across the street. Took a suite on the twenty-third floor, level with the Palace roof.

After a large breakfast we slept until early afternoon. In my dreams the whales bled under a sun that didn't move across the sky; from their blood Heremaia Clatter moulded the face of Io, but the mask didn't fit my face.

The other three went out to get the gear we needed. When they returned two hours later, we rehearsed the timing of Phase Two.

12 midnight: Manu and Aeto were ready. We'd set up the equipment on the balcony.

12.10 a.m.: Manu raised the harpoon gun to his shoulder. Now. Fired at the Palace roof. The thick nylon rope uncoiled like a whip through the air and across the street. Struck. Manu tugged on it. The harpoon caught, hooking itself around one of the airconditioning ducts protruding from the roof. We pulled the rope taut, then tied our end around a balcony post.

12.20 a.m.: I patted Aeto's shoulder. 'Be careful,' Fantail whispered to him. He got onto the balcony ledge, reached up and clipped his harness and pulley onto the rope. Held the handles extending from either side of the pulley. Now. He pushed forward, the pulley wheel rolled. In his harness, arms extended like wings, he glided across the abyss. The lights of the city flashed and splashed across him in the slippery dark.

12.25 a.m.: He unhooked his pulley and dropped to the Palace roof, turned and waved. 'Remember, if you're not back by 2.15, Fantail and I will get the hell out of here and wait for you at the Whare,' I said to Manu.

12.30 a.m.: Manu was across the abyss.

12.35 a.m.: They were disappearing through the door beside the duct.

Using infra-red binoculars, Fantail and I scanned the roof slowly, then the surface of the Palace facing us, floor by floor, window by window, down to the street below. And then up to the roof again. No signs of danger.

1.15 a.m.: The city darkened as the lights blinked out. The noise level decreased too. Everything waited, watched, listened. We kept reading the Palace; my breathing sounded as if it didn't belong to me.

2 a.m.: 'Up!' Fantail whispered. The roof. Manu was waving. Aeto appeared beside him.

2.15 a.m.: They were across the abyss. When they were free of the pulleys, I tugged on the rope. The harpoon unhooked. I wound the rope around my left arm quickly as I pulled it in.

2.30 a.m.: We'd dismantled the equipment and were back in the lounge. Fantail got us some ice-cold Coke. Manu and Aeto drank thirstily. They stank of sweat. Aeto stripped off his jersey. His singlet was soaking wet. I looked away from the continents of burn scars on his arms and torso.

'It was bloody easy,' he said. 'As easy as pissing with the breeze, eh.'

153

'It is as we believe it is,' Manu said. 'A real crackerjack fortress and scientific centre for info-gathering and training hunters. The top floor has neat apartments for VIPs. Real sweet stuff, eh.' He pulled the small camera out of his trouser pocket. 'I've got the plans for the whole fucking building here.'

'And?' I asked.

'The bastids are so sure everyone believes the Palace is just an insurance corp, their security jokers have become hell of a careless. I mean, even the roof door we used was unlocked. They have a beaut security system, the latest stuff, but whole sections of it weren't on, man. We found the first control point on the seventeenth floor, unmanned, unattended. I switched it off. Then down we crept, eh. At the fourteenth there were a coupla guards at the central point but they were busy watching a blue movie. (Man, the Tribunal'll have their balls!) We got into one of the lifts and zoomed straight down to the lobby. Just like that, eh . . .'

'Quick and silent, like the dead,' Aeto echoed.

'And guess what, eh?' Manu continued.

'Stop pissing around,' the impatient Fantail replied. 'We want to know.'

'The two officers at the main security switchboard were fast asleep. The whole deadly system in the lobby was on, eh. But it was bloody easy getting into the security office and photographing the control panels. Guess what?'

'Stop pissing around, I said!' snapped Fantail.

'The security box in which all the maps of the Palace are stored was unlocked. Yeah!'

'Yeah, open like missing teeth!' Aeto chuckled.

'So I photographed the maps.'

'I slid down to the basement. Found three more basements,' said Aeto. 'Labs and apartments mostly. I heard people in some of the apartments . . .'

'Prison? Cells?' Fantail took my words.

He shook his head. 'Naw. Apartments like this one. Fucking comfy.'

'As we returned to the roof we stopped at various floors. No prison cells anywhere. Lotsa classrooms, labs, offices. Whole building's a modern, yeah, fuckin' modern science centre, man!'

'And computers. Shit, the most I've ever seen . . .' said Aeto.

'The latest stuff. Also huge live wall maps and charts of the city, the whole bloody country, the Pacific, the world, eh.'

'And people?' I asked.

'Mainly security people and a few jokers in white coats and uniforms. Night staff. We didn't see any of the people in the apartments,' Manu explained.

'We've got them by the short hairs, eh,' Fantail said.

'Let's drink to that!' I declared. Fantail brought out two six-packs of beer. We tore them open.

After a short while, Fantail left to have the film developed by some special friends.

An hour or so later, when she returned, we sipped beer and studied the innards and entrails of the Palace, the layout of its belly, heart, brain, blood form, and its defence system. Quickly I worked out five ways into and out of the Palace. Kept one of the routes to myself, explained the others. In our discussion we discarded two as being too risky.

I outlined every step of my rescue plan. Manu's questions allowed time to eliminate the obvious flaws. I explained their roles to them in detail, using a sketch map. Through it all, I seemed to be out of body, watching myself.

Dawn seeped slowly into the lounge. Fantail shuffled off to bed. Manu and Aeto slept in their chairs. I strolled out to the balcony and as the breeze licked my face with its cold tongue, I watched the dawn wash the darkness from the eastern sky and then spread out, like a school of white jellyfish, over the city and down into its hollows and crevices.

The Palace glowed as the dawn light penetrated it. Its luminosity lit up my memories of the housekeeper. I escaped those memories, to bed.

5 p.m.: We packed the few things we were taking with us. Then I lay on my bed and read a Raymond Carver story in *Plenty* magazine. It made me feel uncomfortable because it was about

infidelity, both husband and wife were cheating on each other. Jean Watson was one of my favourite writers. I usually carried one of her books with me, but I couldn't find any in my bag.

7 p.m.: I had a light snack of chicken soup and toast. The others had fillet steak and salad. Silence at the table except for Aeto's tuneless whistling, on and off. They looked tense, especially Fantail who kept sighing audibly. I watched myself eating and watching the others. Strange, but I was looking forward to the danger.

Afterwards, I shaved, showered leisurely, dressed in a navy blue sweat suit, jersey, running shoes and a woollen cap. Strapped on an extra belt in which I sheathed the dagger and a leather wallet of tools. The knife, I taped to my left arm under my jersey. (We'd agreed on not taking weapons.) I put on my overcoat.

8 p.m.: We met in the lounge. Fantail read out the list: we rechecked everything we were taking. After that we watched TV silently. A news item showed the President opening a sports arena in Christchurch. He was going bald, I noticed.

9 p.m.: Separately, we took lifts down to the lobby. Met in the car park. Darkness was billowing down from the sky.

9.15 p.m. We arrived at the manhole, two blocks away from the Palace, in a narrow side street. Manu pulled up the manhole cover with his gloved hands. The stench of sewage and decay sprang up at us. I gagged slightly, spat. They didn't seem to notice the smell.

Aeto climbed down first, his torch lighting up the darkness. Then Fantail, me, Manu. I'd memorised our underground route but this was their territory, so I merely followed.

The tunnel was a few centimetres higher than me. Damp walls glistening with slime. The floor underfoot felt like wet fungi or moss. Muddy water ran swiftly down the small drain in the middle of the floor. Though it was bitterly cold, I started sweating. Aeto was maintaining a steady pace. Traffic clattered and roared above; the tunnel trembled around us.

There was a centuries-old genealogy, in literature and film, of persecuted groups and minorities going underground to survive. Underground, they organised resistance to the powers above ground. As we walked I thought of those and lost much of my fear. I was part of an adventure, a rebellion against tyranny, though much of that had been trivialised into soap operas by TV.

9.45 p.m.: We stopped at a concrete wall through which water was seeping. We took the tunnel that led off to the left. Twenty paces ahead we met a timber wall that blocked the tunnel. Aeto thrust his hand under the wall and pulled. The wall swung back.

We followed him to the right and up to the next level. He pushed open a door made of scrap timber. Switched on the light.

'The Whare,' Fantail told me.

It was a large chamber, about six metres high. Dry and warm, with air vents up into the city. Mattresses, sleeping bags and blankets on used carpet, boxes as chairs, some tables and cupboards, a safe with dishes, cutlery and food. Gas stove. Even two reading lamps. And four shelves of books. I glanced at Fantail. 'Just junk reading,' she said.

'Neat, really neat!' I remarked. She smiled, awkwardly. Hone Tuwhare's *Mihi*; Donna Awatere's *Maori Sovereignty*; Ranginui Walker's *Nga Tau Tohetohe* and *Ka Whawhai Tonu Matou: Struggle Without End*; Bill Pearson's *Fretful Sleepers*; Jim Baxter's *Collected Poems*; Patricia Grace's *Potiki*; Dick Scott's *Ask That Mountain*; Witi Ihimaera's *The Matriarch*; Albert Wendt's *Ola* . . . I took off my overcoat. My sweat cooled quickly.

'Our safehouse. Sometimes we live here for weeks,' she said.

Manu and Aeto dragged out our welding and drilling equipment, which they'd stored in the Whare two days before. We checked it. 'In good nick,' Manu said.

I don't know why I asked them about their history at that dangerous time, but I did. Manu and Fantail looked at me. 'About Tangata Maori,' I added.

'Nothing much to know,' Manu said. 'Over the long stretch of otherworlder oppression and arrogance, the Tangata Maori,

our pre-otherworlder ancestors, were nearly all erased, physically and culturally . . .'

'We were further erased through intermarriage and reordinarination,' she said. 'We merged with our sisters and brothers
from the Islands who were also being reordinarinised, and
became the Tangata Moni, the True People. A tough breed, the
toughest . . .'

'Many Pakeha/palagi, who saw the injustice in reordinarination, joined us . . .'

As they talked I thought I was listening to a familiar text
about all the other texts about invasion, oppression, racism and
totalitarian reordinarination. They were 'reading' like the
Tangata Moni books on their Whare bookshelves.

They explained that when President Linn and the other
twelve Presidents, who owned and controlled the major multinational corporations, established the present international
system of otherworlder control through Tribunals and reordinarination centres, the erasure of the Tangata Moni and anyone
else who challenged the system was almost total. 'Most of our
people were reordinarinised willingly into otherworlders,' Manu
said. 'After all, who doesn't want comfort, peace, a crime-free
world!'

At this point, Aeto, who'd added little to the story, talked
about his life.

He was born in Whanganui-a-Tara in a sanctuary like the
Whare, Aeto began. His father, Kuki Patrick Malama, was
Tangata Maori-Niuean-Samoan-Pakeha-Irish, and his mother,
Merimeri, Maori-Tokelauan-Cook Islander-German, was only
twenty when she entered their whanau after escaping from
Invercargill's reordinarination centre which dealt with the most
difficult deviants in the country. He was the first child, for a
generation, in their whanau of fifteen people, after the otherworlders had sterilised their women. There were to be two other
children, his sisters.

His mother had a phenomenal memory which her parents
had trained so the otherworlders couldn't obliterate their true

history. Her knowledge was in the stories she filled their lives with. The usefulness of uselessness, she described her stories. 'I'll tell you some of those some other time,' Aeto said. 'Right now, you just want to know how I got to the rubbish dump, eh, Fantail?' She nodded. 'My parents brought me up to be a thief, yeah, the best thief this side of the muddy Wanganui. We survived through selling ourselves to otherworlder deviants, and stealing. We refused to be converted by them; it would've been so easy to join the other Tangata Moni who have become otherworlders . . .' They looked at me, I looked away. 'But who wants to lose his liver!' He laughed. For his twenty-one years he hadn't lost the faith: the belief in being Tangata Moni. At times he'd wished he was free of it, but it always returned like a ton of bricks. Especially when the reordinarinators, in their centres, had tried to alter his personality. He'd started surviving the reordinarination centres at the age of twelve, after he'd been caught selling the parts of a car he'd converted. 'Have you ever been in a centre?' he asked me.

'Not that I can remember,' I said.

'At times I wish I couldn't remember,' he said. 'But when you choose to escape before they finish reordinarinising you, you remember all the wounds and pain. And even when you don't want to remember, they fill your dreams and nightmares. In the centres they can make even your dreams burn your body,' he continued.

It was spring, he remembered. Every time he ran through Cornwall Park, in the early afternoon, which smelled of sheepshit and new grass, he counted more newly born lambs in the paddocks; he was astonished by the number of twins.

Late afternoon. Only a few people about. He was feeding stale bread to the pigeons in Albert Park, while waiting for some friends, when the middle-aged couple, who at first didn't seem to notice he was there and it was his bench, sat down on either side of him and, opening bags of popcorn, started scattering the corn among the birds, who fought for it. And closed in around. Some birds even hopped onto the bench.

The couple's patter, like the purring of the pigeons, wove

across and around him. He observed them. Prosperous, very prosperous. Immaculately groomed. Just the right amount of silver in his hair; just the right amount of tint in hers to hide the grey. Manicured perfectly. The latest deodorant and perfume. The right weights and muscle tone. They looked as if they had been born like that in the latest fashions. The perfect advertisement for what otherworlders considered ideal middle age.

'Pigeons hop, pigeons peck, pigeons fly, pigeons die,' she recited.

'Pigeons purr, pigeons curse, pigeons know how to flirt,' he continued.

'Hop, hop, shuffle; hop, hop, purr; hop-hop-hop, swallow some crispy corn . . .'

She jumped up and swept her arms over the birds, seeding corn among them.

'Yes, peck, peck, peck, eat and fatten, eat and fatten until you're ready to burst . . .'

'Deep-fried like Peking duck, basted with plum sauce, sprinkled with almonds . . .' she was saying.

'Yes, yes, or steamed with rice until baby soft, then garnished with herbs and spices and other things nices . . .'

'Or stuffed with prunes and bacon, and slow roasted over charcoal . . .'

'Or halved and marinated in soy sauce with sugar and lemon . . .'

'And barbecued and served with spring potatoes and mint . . .'

Aeto's mouth dribbled as he listened to their recipes. As they recited they shifted closer and closer until their thighs were touching his. They didn't seem aware of his poverty.

'Do you like pigeons?' she spoke to Aeto for the first time. He nodded. 'He likes them,' she told her partner who nodded and scattered more popcorn. The birds swirled and fought for it. 'He likes them,' she repeated.

'I heard you!' he said. 'Ask him if he wants to come home for dinner tonight.'

'You ask him,' she replied, scattering her corn with a wide

dramatic sweep of her right arm. 'You always make me do the asking.'

'You're good at it. And ask him if he knows how to cook.'

She asked him; he nodded. 'He can,' she told him. He asked her to ask him what kind of cooking he was good at. She did. Aeto shrugged his shoulders. 'He can cook anything,' she told him.

'Come closer, come closer, Noah's birds of peace,' he was crooning to the pigeons, extending his corn-filled palms. The braver birds crowded up to them, pecking at the food. 'Yes, yes, my sweet darling ones . . .'

'Yes, our sweet darling birds,' she continued.

Aeto liked their eccentric innocence, and he started getting into the rhythm of their crooning. He didn't see the man pull the fine nylon net out of his suit pocket and, unfolding it, ask her, 'Is anyone watching?'

'No, no, no, dear John,' she sang.

The man sprang up and, bending forward over the nearest birds, dropped his net. A loud wild flapping as the birds burst away, leaving three entangled in the net. Fighting, struggling, as she reached down and bundled them against her belly. He took them from her and, in one long pull, tightened the net until the birds couldn't move. His expert hands moved swiftly. One neck, two necks, three necks dead, and into the plastic bag she was holding out to him.

Aeto found himself hurrying between them down towards Wellesley Street through the shadows of the trees. Night was falling.

'We try and live naturally,' she said to him. Aeto remembered the street light was the colour of rancid cheese, and the couple now smelled of live pigeon.

'Yes, close to nature,' he echoed.

Their sports car, an expensive vintage Sano, was parked beside the Art Gallery under the overhanging branches of a massive elm.

'You don't say much, do you?' she asked as they sped up Wellesley Street, with her partner laughing to himself as he drove. Wedged in between them, Aeto was trapped in their pigeon meat-eater smell.

'Haven't you got any money to buy food?' he asked her. They laughed and continued laughing as they sped across Grafton, past the hospital, towards Remuera.

'We love to cook, and to cook fresh natural food,' she whispered. Her breath tingled his ear.

They lived in the wealthiest part of Remuera, an area which Aeto knew well because over the years he and some friends had burgled at least fifteen houses there. The four-storeyed high dome was floodlit by lights that were set in the pohutukawa trees which surrounded it. In the white light it glittered like a glass chrysalis which was waiting to give birth to the future.

'We have no children,' she said as they entered the house. 'So make yourself at home.'

'Yes, just act as if you're our son,' he said, smiling.

'Go ahead and explore,' she invited him, 'while we cook our dinner.'

'We'll see what we can do with these beauties!' He held up the birds by their feet. Aeto recalled the dead babies his mother had found one night in the sewers. 'The hunters home from the hills,' the man added.

'And the sailor home from the sea.' Then looking closely at Aeto, she said, 'You should eat more — you look thin. But we'll soon fix that. Won't we, darling?'

'Yes, we'll soon put that right!' They headed for the kitchen.

The house seemed to be a series of caves with invisible windows that allowed you to look out but stopped the world from looking in. Its interior decoration and furnishings were out of the latest magazines. However, there were unusual differences. Nearly all the artwork was about food: paintings, sculptures, prints and heliographs of edible animals (dead and prepared for cooking, or alive but trapped) and cuts of meat. And he was to find, as he explored, that everything was a variation of blood red and pink. The lights and the carpets, bath tubs, showers, toilet bowls, toilet paper, towels, mirrors, everything.

The walls of the huge sitting room were calligraphed with

wallhangings of food recipes; the armchairs were shaped like stoves and ovens; the tables were large chopping blocks, some new, some old and worn down by choppers and knives.

At the centre of the house was a study with two desks, a central computer, orderly stacks of tapes and cassettes, and walled with bookcases. Aeto read a few of the titles and concluded that most of the books were about cooking, food and chefs. Some of the titles were very old. One of them was full of recipes for bird dishes.

The stair walls were a gallery of watercolours of the edible birds in the world. Aeto couldn't find an eagle among them.

He found himself in the couple's bedroom which smelled of fresh mint. The ceiling was a red mirror centering on the circular double bed with a red satin bedcover. Nothing else. When he sat down on the edge of the bed, he saw the console. He read the control panel. He pressed a button, the bed started revolving slowly. He pressed another. A large TV panel on the wall appeared; he kept pressing until the circular wall was a line of TV channels showing different films. He switched off the sound and just watched. Chefs performing, preparing dishes, cooking: two Japanese chefs were making sashimi from the poisonous fugu fish — the arrangement of the potentially deadly pieces on the dish was high art; in another, people were force-feeding beef cattle with beer while others massaged the cattle — the most expensive steak in the world, Aeto imagined the announcer saying; a great French chef, who looked like a plucked turkey, was basting three pheasants cooking in a baking dish, and talking into the camera . . . Aeto lay back on the pillows at the head of the bed. For centuries people had been eating the planet away, eating and eating it away. Eating and shitting it out, eating and shitting. He was in a house of fancy red meat eating. Someone was watching him from the ceiling. He glanced up. He was caught clearly in the mirror, in the red of the bed and the room. And around him the most skilled preparers of meat were plying their trade . . . The film was taking him into a supermarket freezer, among carcasses of beef hanging from gleaming hooks, to the red-nosed announcer, dressed in immaculate white, who was standing between the largest carcasses, talking enthusiastically into the camera. Reaching up with a knife, the announcer started cutting into one of the carcasses. No blood. Aeto switched up the volume of that film. *Yes, for fifteen dollars a kilo, you too can enjoy the bloodless beef of our specially bred Griffin-Subraman-Stewart cattle*, the announcer was saying. *First developed in Fiji using secret biotechnological techniques. If you are squeamish about blood then our beef is for you! And it's also fatless . . .* Aeto switched it off.

He wouldn't remember how long he slept. 'Son, dinner is served,' the female voice echoed in his head. He sat up. Immediately the enticing smell of food whetted his appetite and pulled him off the bed and down the stairs into the dining room.

Again it was as if the scene had come straight out of the latest food magazine: a long gleaming mahogany table, with the man sitting at the head, the woman in the middle, the food in gleaming serving dishes, a bowl of flowers in the centre, expensive dishes and cutlery, and a seat for him opposite the man. She nodded towards the empty chair. Aeto sat down.

'Let us say grace,' the man said. They bowed. 'God, our Chef of Chefs, we thank you for sending us a guest tonight, someone who could be our son, someone who loves food and good cooking, and who will love You as much as we do. We thank You also for the natural food we are having tonight, and for Your gift to us to be good chefs. We know that You will continue to bless us with a planet that is rich in natural things. In the name of our President, who is also an expert chef, we thank You. Amen.'

Aeto sat up. 'In our humble home,' his host said, ' eating time is to enjoy the quality of the cuisine, so we say little that is not related to that. I hope that is your way too.' Aeto nodded, trying not to salivate too noticeably.

Up to then, Aeto's diet had been basic and precarious: food, whatever you could get, was to satisfy your hunger, fill your belly so you could get on with surviving. But when he had his first mouthful of pigeon, his taste buds took on a separate and compulsive existence: he watched them getting hooked on the exquisite, hypnotic tastes of the cooking. For a while he fought it, but as the couple heaped food on to his plate whenever it was empty, and told him how expert he was as an eater, he gave into the addiction.

The couple didn't eat much themselves: they simply watched and applauded and fussed over him. 'He's the ideal eater, isn't he, darling?' she kept saying. 'We've never had anyone so appreciative of our cooking . . .'

'Yes, dear, he's a connoisseur . . .'

'A son worthy of our humble skills . . .'

'Yes, and he's going to love all our other dishes . . .'

'Yes and yes and yes . . .'

Aeto wasn't hearing them any more; his whole astounded attention was on the tastes that, like music, filled his mouth and danced down his gullet and into his celebrating belly.

'Isn't he beautiful, so beautiful!' she sang.

'Yes, a son after our own hearts . . .'

There were three different desserts, and he had a dishful of each one, with their encouragement. It was then that he realised he'd become a cask of skin filled almost to bursting; drugged with food from the centre of his head and throat to his bloated stomach. He tried to get up. His head spun and he belched repeatedly. They were beside him, holding him up.

'It's all right, son,' the man whispered. 'Tell him, dear.'

'Yes, darling, you'll soon get used to your lovely new diet . . .'

'You'll put on weight and strength and health . . .'

'And be the healthiest, most beautiful child in the world . . .'

They held his elbows and helped him up the stairs, all the time crooning to him about his healthy future.

He felt himself being lowered into a soft bed, tucked in, with her whispering in his ear: 'Yes, our darling son, tomorrow you'll wake to your new home and wealth and health . . .'

'And the best food in the world . . .' Her fingers massaged his shoulders and arms. Massaged.

Her warm breath and lips on his cheek, and he melted.

His dreams were full of food and their aromas and chefs who recited recipes as they cut and spliced and mixed and diced and turned animals into meat into tastes he couldn't refuse.

When he woke at mid-morning, he despised the poverty of his past.

Our house is yours. Use it. It has everything you need, just follow the instructions on the consoles. We're off, off to work; to our lovely, lovely work. We'll be back at 5 p.m. sharp, and will cook you a lovely, lovely dinner. Praise God, our Greatest Chef.

He pressed the appropriate buttons. His hot bath was ready when he went into the bathroom. Lowered himself into the scented water and relaxed for a long time.

Later, after he'd dressed in clothes that he found in the wardrobe in his room, he went into the study and using the master console there, learned about the house: its layout, contents, functions, miracles, dreams, voices and sounds, temptations, recipes, recipes and more recipes. He started playing the console like a piano and the house reacted in chords and tunes which, he discovered, took the forms of various food. For instance, when he played the Shakespearean sonnet rhyme of abba abba cdcd dd, her husky voice said: 'Son, here, as a treat from Shakespearean England, is venison prepared and cooked to the recipe the Master Chef Thomas Equus served to Queen Elizabeth the day after she bedded Lord Marius Edmond. Enjoy.' One wall of bookcases opened and out of it slid a table fully prepared and laden with the venison meal.

For dessert, he played: *This little pig went to market, this little pig stayed home; this little pig had roast beef, and this little pig had none.* On to the table came fifteen different types of chocolate shaped like pig turds. And he was again into his feeding frenzy, devouring the chocolate turds. Still hungry, he played: *Little Miss Muffet sat on her tuffet, eating her curds and whey. Along came a spider and sat down beside her, and frightened Miss Muffet away.* And onto the table came six types of curds and whey prepared to recipes left by the Russian chef, Tarot.

After eating that, he could barely breathe; his head spun. He dragged himself over to the settee, lay back around his belly, and tumbled into another deep sleep in which he consumed another mountain of fancy food, and his hunger lengthened . . .

He woke to her feijoa scent and warm kiss on his cheek. 'Come on, son,' she whispered, 'time for dinner.'

After dragging his belly into the nearest toilet he emptied it in a long cacophony of farting and thunderous grunting and almost choked on his own stench which the ceiling sucked up in a whirl of fans.

Once in the dining room he was into his feeding frenzy, while they again applauded and encouraged him. 'More real natural food, son,' she said. 'Rabbit, run rabbit, run!'

Her partner twitched his nose and wagged his ears and laughed. 'He's putting flesh on his bones already, eh, dear?' he said.

'Yes, yes, soon he'll be as fat as Brer Rabbit . . .'

This time they had to hold him up as they helped him upstairs. This time, though he was embarassed, he couldn't object to them undressing, pyjamaing, and tucking him into bed. This time, she massaged him from neck to navel, crooning, 'Yes, my Brer Rabbit, you'll soon be ready for the world . . .'

'Yes, while the Chefs applaud . . .'

In his dreams he drowned in an avalanche of hokey-pokey ice cream.

That day was to repeat itself over and over again, but he wouldn't know the breaks between the days.

The house and its owners fed him. And fed him. And fed him. Yet his hunger worsened. And she was massaging every part of him, and completing her song:

> *Eat up, my son, my pretty young son,*
> *eat up while mamma shapes your body*
> *with her wise hands and heart.*
> *Eat up, eat up, my pretty young son,*
> *eat up while your daddy cooks more dishes*
> *that will fatten your heart.*
> *One day you'll know the truth of our love,*
> *one day you'll know the truth of our love.*

He would never know why or how, at that particular
moment, he broke from their food spell. But he did one
morning, at breakfast, while he was wading through a dish of
bacon stuffed with olives and prunes. He caught his reflection in
the mirror wall opposite. Caught his mouth stopping, his
chomping teeth poised, surprised, shocked by the roly-poly
youth with slits for eyes and wobbles of chins and flab hanging
off his face. He jumped to his feet, hands clutching handfuls of
fat on his neck and breasts. *No, no, no, my pretty, young son!*
Yet when he collapsed back into his seat, his hands were into the
food again, and up, shoving it into his mouth, stuffing it down,
stuffing it down.

One day you'll learn the truth of our love, he kept hearing
her crooning in his food-satiated daze, drugged sleep, and thunderous bouts of spewing and shitting. And the hunger which
continued swallowing him up as her wondrous hands and breath
massaged his purring roundness.

Into his dreams his mother's voice started intruding, at first
faintly, then, as he glimpsed the grotesquely fat creature he was
becoming, more insistently. *How much is that rabbit in the
window? The one with the waggily tail? How much is that
rabbit in the window? I want to take it home.* 'But I'm fat and
ugly,' he replied, 'I'm fat like Brer Rabbit.' But his mother kept
insisting. *Stop eating then, stop gutsing on their hungry cooking.
Stop and think about the love they're promising.*

One morning he did: he forced himself away from his breakfast, sat down at the master console and fed discordant notes into
it. The house was puzzled. Then as he played anti-food rhymes
into it, it became flustered.

> *Brer Rabbit hates food,*
> *Brer Rabbit is not a fool,*
> *Brer Rabbit went to school*
> *and knows the rules.*

The house replied:

> *I'm no fool, I too went to school*
> *and know the rules,*

*And you're not eating according
to the rules.*

That evening, at dinner, after he'd eaten his octopus soup —
and it was difficult resisting the rest of the dinner — he
pretended he was very tired and told them he was going to bed.
They looked surprised and perplexed, but agreed. When they
offered to help him up the stairs he refused politely.

At the top of the stairs he paused and listened to see if they
were following him. They weren't, so he shut his bedroom door
to make them think he'd gone into his room and tiptoed back
downstairs.

He was breathless as he hugged the wall just outside the
dining room and listened to what they were saying.

'Is he ready yet for the truth of our love?' she was asking.

'No, no, my love. Soon we'll taste our fun.'

'He's a beautiful son, isn't he, my chef?'

'Yes, a beaut, and he's almost ready for the truth of our
love.'

As they recited their lines, an ice-heavy chill seeped up from
Aeto's feet and filled every crevice of his body; he grasped his
hands to his mouth as he staggered up the stairs again and into
his bedroom, where the fear pulled all the food out of his
stomach and he gagged and gasped as he vomited it into the
basin.

Once in his bed the insatiable hunger gripped him again so
he started reciting the incantation his mother had taught him,
to ward off fear and pain and kehua:

> *There's nothing like a song
> to keep your heart brave,
> nothing like it to keep evil at bay.
> So, whenever you're scared shit,
> just sing this number
> your granddaddy taught me:*

> *There's no kehua more scary than our President
> for he's what's wrong with the whole otherworld.
> He's a mealy-mouthed preacher, a killer, and a fraud.
> He and his twelve disciples own every inch of us.*

They're ever-hungry cannibals who feed on our dreams
and shit out our bones which they sell as manure . . .

He fell asleep, reciting. His sleep was a stormy ocean of guilt and fear, in which he tossed and turned and gnashed his teeth.

He and his bed were drenched with sweat when he woke next morning, gripped in the mouth of a raging fever and the fear of being gobbled up by the hunger. Once he'd been addicted to cocaine; the withdrawal symptoms were like what he was experiencing now. He was addicted to their cuisine, he had to admit to himself. And even when he recited and recited his mother's incantations, the fever worsened, threatening to shatter him into tiny eggshell bits. He staggered out of bed. His shadow dripped onto the carpet as he hugged the stair railing and carried his fear down into the study and the central computer.

He stood in front of the computer screen. Crunched inwards when he saw the creature, the obese slug with its rolls of flab, dripping with sweat, staring back at him, in the screen.

Once at the computer console, and trying not to look at the creature, he played:

> *You were right all along, House of the Chefs,*
> *I'm a fool and don't know the rules*
> *about food and cooks.*
> *So please help me,*
> *help a genuine repentant.*

The house replied:

> *Repentant fool is the rule,*
> *and our Illustrious President says:*
> *forgiveness is what sells consumer civilisation*
> *to pagans, socialists and other non-capitalists.*

He had to be careful. He pondered and then played:

> *Please forgive me, House of the Master Chefs,*
> *please forgive your stupid uncivilised fool,*
> *and grant me the best of your lean cuisine*
> *which even our President loves to consume.*

170

The house vibrated with a rock'n'roll band, and he could sense its boundless joy:

> *Ah love yah, yeah, yeah, yeah.*
> *Ah love yah, yeah, yeah, yeah.*
> *Ah love yah, yeah, yeah, yeah.*
> *Mah lean cuisine shall be yah dish,*
> *mah lean cuisine shall be yah saving dish.*
> *Howsabout lean, lean beef?*
> *Howsabout lean, lean beans?*
> *Howsabout lean, lean nashis?*

Aeto, still driven with fear and hunger, replied:

> *Yes please, yeah, yeah, yeah.*
> *Yes please, yeah, yeah, yeah.*
> *Yes please, yeah, yeah, yeah.*
> *Ah promise Ah'll love yah beef,*
> *Ah promise Ah'll love yah beans,*
> *Ah promise Ah'll love yah nashis.*

On to the table came the lean cuisine, and, as the Beatles rocked, Aeto dug in. When he finished, and the hunger was still rapacious, he asked for more nashis. Deliberately, as he was stuffing the third one into his mouth, he shoved his fingers to the back of his throat, gagged, and then he was thrusting forward, spewing his breakfast across the table.

He rushed into the toilet and while vomiting into the basin, shat. The hunger was a thick arm being thrust down through his gullet into the depths of his stomach and soul, violently wrenching everything from him and turning him inside out.

When he gazed into the mirror, the sobbing creature was splotched with tears, sweat, spew and bile. And stank. And he howled and howled. Fell to his knees where he incanted for his mother . . .

That evening, at dinner, he pretended nothing was wrong, ate only the entrée, disappeared upstairs and made himself spew it all out.

She rushed in and, hugging him from the back, murmured, 'Now, now, our darling son, you mustn't waste our planet's wonderful food. You'll get too thin and won't know the truth of our love.' She steered him back to his bed, undressed him, lay him back, his head spinning with nausea, and massaged, massaged him until his nausea vanished and he was purring. And hugely erect. 'Yes, yes, my strong, strong son, you must eat to stay strong in your mamma's expert loving hands,' she whispered as her oiled hands worked. And worked.

He writhed and bucked, thrusting his hips up and down. 'Yes, yes, come, come, come in your mamma's loving hands . . .'

'Ahhh — ahhh — ahhh — ahh!' he cried, heady with her feijoa scent.

'Yes, good, good, you're so thick and gooey and lovely, my son . . .'

He was asleep, free of the fever and fear for the first time that day, by the time she wiped him clean.

At breakfast next morning, he got the computer to give him lean cuisine again, which, a few minutes afterwards, he made himself vomit out while the house rocked again with the Beatles.

When the compulsive hunger threatened again, he rushed to the computer and composed limerick after limerick to distract himself. Just before his hosts returned from work, he read all the limericks and was most pleased with these two:

> *One day in Whanganui-a-Tara*
> *a fat man tangoed with a spider.*
> *Out of their dance genealogy*
> *came atua with fast-stepping manava.*

> *In the Bush of Seven Wonders*
> *lives the magician of numbers.*
> *He can add Einstein and Malaga*
> *and have you rocking to the thunder.*

From then on, he ate only lean cuisine, vomited it out in secret, distracted himself from the hunger during the day by composing limericks and playing games on the computer with the house; and during the night, if the hunger woke him, he recited the incantations until his mother was with him and he fell asleep again.

Strange that he never once thought of escaping, not at this stage of his addiction.

At dinner they didn't seem to mind cooking and serving him the lean diet he insisted on. She specialised in fish: all chosen by her at the fish market — hapuka, orange roughy, rock cod, bream, terakihi, sole, flounder, snapper and, his favourite, mullet. One evening it was Creole style, the next it was Indian, then Chinese, then Thai. All low in calories. Her partner specialised in vegetarian cuisine, which, despite Aeto's compulsive hunger, he wasn't particularly fond of but ate so as not to make them suspicious.

One evening he pretended to fall asleep at the dinner table. She put her arms around him and crooned, 'My, my, our dear son needs rest, needs rest . . .'

A short while later they were talking as if he wasn't there. 'When, oh when, is our dear son going to be ready for the truth of our love?' she asked.

'Soon, very soon, my love. When his fat becomes muscle enough and lean . . .'

'I'm getting tired of the waiting, my dear husband chef. Tired but eager to let him know the truth of our love . . .'

'So am I, my mistress chef, so am I. But we have to wait until he is mature enough . . .'

Aeto was again full of fear as she massaged his neck and shoulders. He pretended he was waking up and they helped him upstairs and into bed.

Aeto was now able to separate the days that passed. He felt lighter and the exertion of moving about didn't make him breathless any more. He started exercising.

While his hosts were out, he used the console on their bed and the computer to try and find out something about them. They were famous chefs, the computer said, listing the competitions they'd won and their winning dishes. They'd authored two best-selling cookbooks: *Recipes for Rich Capitalists* and *Cook Your Heart Out, Mr President.* The first was for those who wanted to cook the most expensive food in the world, and included such recipes as Millionaires' Salad made out of Pluto-

nian lettuce, Planet V earthworms specially farmed as an aphrodisiac, midget tomatoes from the Amazon, the rarest blue-vein
cheese in the solar system made by Michaelmas and Tuataroa
Company Ltd of Brentwood Village, all seasoned with Sebas-
tianbinney Dressing — the most expensive dressing in the world.
(The ingredients for it were a secret — its originator was a
strange hermit who spoke only one word a year: *Love.*) Total
cost of a salad for four people: $5,000.

The second book was brought out specially for the President's sixtieth birthday. Though heart trouble was a thing of the
past, the President's favourite public charity was the Heart
Foundation which ensured the non-return of that evil. The sixty
recipes were lean cuisine at its severest, in keeping with the
President's birthday message to the world: *Watch your heart, it
is the temple of your love, so love it by not overfeeding it.* Apart
from the recipes, it advocated fasting for three days each week.

Reading the recipes only worsened Aeto's hunger so he
switched to other information about his hosts.

They owned an international chain of restaurants called Red
Fowl, which specialised in serving bird and fowl in a hundred
different ways, and a multinational company, Dream Tastes,
which produced drugs for enhancing the quality and sharpness
of taste.

There was no record of their having children, but Aeto came
across a long list of people with dates and comments, such as
'fair to excellent', 'too lean', 'needs more aging', beside their
names.

He believed the computer when it said his hosts had no other
history.

He couldn't remember when he started spying on them. He
did it through the house's computer surveillance; if they were
using the study, he simply watched them from the doorway.

He soon worked out the pattern of their lives at home: after
dinner, showers, then into the study where they jointly wrote a
new cookbook, then, at midnight, they were in bed in deep
sleep. They never woke until 6 a.m. Hot showers, breakfast —
a piece of unbuttered toast each, weak tea, a slice of fruit, then

174

off to work. Weekends: instead of going to work, they stayed at home and worked on their new book, fixed his lunch, watched TV, fixed his dinner. Sundays, at 6 a.m., they jogged five kilometres.

The couple never had sex, he realised. Their night sleep was unbreakable, nothing could wake them. So he started going into their bedroom and, sitting on the bed's edge, watching them. Sometimes he touched them, lifted their arms and let them drop back on to the bed. They slept on. Eventually he turned on the films on the walls, increased the volume until it was almost unbearable, but they didn't stir.

Because they slept from midnight till six he felt safe during that time, so he started leaving the house and walking for exercise. He often walked all night, relearning the city. He never thought of not returning. Why? He would never be able to fathom that one.

Dawn was washing across Maungakiekie when he returned from his walk and, though they were still fast asleep, he sensed that they'd been in his room. Nothing had been disturbed but he smelled her faint feijoa odour and sensed his slick, ominous presence.

The following night he left the house and hid in the garden outside their bedroom. An hour later, when he saw their shadows moving across the curtains, he sneaked back inside and up the stairs.

They were in his room, in his bed. Grappling like beasts, grunting and screeching, biting and scratching. 'Arr-arr-in! Arr-arr-in!' the man kept crying. 'Griff-griff-in! Griff-griff-in!' she screeched back, as she pumped at him. Aeto turned and fled down the stairs; he had no right spying on their innocent fucking.

From then on, though he was still afraid of them, he walked at night so as to allow them his space, his presence, his smells, to fuck in. He was reciprocating their hospitality.

'It's time to go,' I interrupted Aeto's story. Fantail and Manu looked disappointed. I was too: better an exciting tale than venturing into real danger.

175

'I'll finish it after we get out of this place,' Aeto told them.

10.15 p.m.: We headed for the Palace through another tunnel route. I carried the drill strapped to my back.

10.35 p.m.: 'It's here, eh,' Manu whispered, shining his torch on a brick wall ahead of us. He patted the wall. 'Solid but bloody old.'

Fantail shone the torches on the wall as we took turns drilling through it. Dust and smoke started filling the tunnel.

10.50 p.m.: We hit the inner steel wall. I tapped on it; it rang hollowly. Manu lit the welding torch. Adjusted the flame to its fiercest cutting strength.

We watched him methodically cut a rectangular door in the steel. Acrid smell of fire and molten steel. We coughed; our nostrils and eyes started hurting. 'Hurry!' I urged him. Five more minutes.

'Shit, man, we've got her, eh!' Aeto laughed.

'Yeah, we've broken her!' Fantail said.

Using large pliers, I gripped both sides of the steel plate Manu had cut out and pulled it away from the wall. 'A hole big enough for cheeky Maui to sneak through, eh!' Manu chuckled. I dropped the heavy plate to the tunnel floor. It clanged like a sword. We switched off our torches and waited. We heard only our laboured breathing.

The darkness was complete, as it must have been between Rangi and Papa before the separation. No movement from within the Palace basement. I swallowed and tasted my own fear. I groped and found the opening. Thrust my head and torso through it. Paused.

Ahead, a dim light. The purring of machinery, then its shape. Smell of petrol and oil. Switched on my torch. Shone it around slowly, giving meaning, faces, details to the airconditioning and heating equipment. Beyond those, I knew there were doors and stairs.

I snaked through the opening, pulling my body along the floor. Stood up. Hid behind a large generator and once again checked the basement. No one.

The others followed me in.

11.55 p.m.: 'Okay,' I whispered. Manu and Aeto crept on ahead towards the source of the light. Manu ducked round the corner and was gone. He was going up to check the lobby, monitor any movement into the basement and, if necessary, cripple the security system. Aeto waved and was running silently up the stairs to our left. His job was to check the lifts and, if possible, go up through the Palace and see if our presence had been detected.

'Let's go,' I whispered to Fantail.

I hugged the shadows, with her following.

We were to meet at 1 a.m., at the latest, back at the tunnel door.

Everything about the Palace, including its smell, seemed asleep, dreaming, as Fantail and I descended the empty stairwell. The thick beige carpet muffled our footsteps. The walls were lined, at five-pace intervals, with large technicolour photographs of the Southern Alps under silken snow. And, like the Tribunal building, the Palace's interior light emanated from the sinews of the walls and ceilings, refusing to let us cast shadows as we crept along the first corridor.

There was no one at the monitoring panel halfway down the corridor. Just a transparent cubicle which I slipped into. I switched on the five surveillance panels and focused them on the corridors and all basement levels — empty. Then on the windows and doorways. I moved them back to the floor just below us. Still no one. I noticed the doors were of heavy panelling. I panned in on the first door: Suite 146 the Pohutukawa Glade. Second door: Suite 147 the Totara Stand. Third door, fourth, fifth . . . They were all named after indigenous trees, many now extinct.

I whispered to Fantail and we headed for that floor. I dismissed the worry that I hadn't figured out how we were going to locate the suite my family were in. Improvise, I reckoned Maui would have said.

I put my ear to the door of the first suite. Silence. We moved to the next one. Muffled sound of a TV. Fantail glanced at me.

I shook my head. We shifted to the next one. Another TV. I hesitated. I reached for the door handle. No. I hurried on.

Its presence caught me, as if I'd been carrying it in my head all that time. Tick-tick-tick . . . Louder as I approached it.

And there it was: The *Black Rainbow* lithograph, hanging on the wall of the Kauri Skyways Suite. I touched its frame, ran my fingers over the glass, as if I was caressing my wife's face. For a moment it snared my reflection. I nodded to Fantail.

She unzipped her jacket, pulled out her pouch of burglary tools. She moved quickly. Poked one key instrument into the keyhole. Surprised look on her face. 'It's not locked,' she whispered.

I turned the handle. It seemed forever, the turning.

Then I pushed it inwards. Fantail slid in past me. I stepped over the threshold.

Stopped and listened. Fantail circled into the sitting room towards the two lamps above the sofas and the armchairs on the far side. No one, she signalled. I moved in.

I recognised them — my wife and children in the photo standing on the coffee table in the centre of the room, smiling, smiling at me, as they stood against Mt Cook. I turned in a full circle, scanning the room, letting my nostrils, eyes and pores absorb the scent, feel, presence, expectations and dreams of my family, my aiga as Manu had called it.

Fantail was already checking the other rooms, moving like the shadow of the bird she was named after. At the open door of the middle room she stopped and beckoned to me. I went towards the doorway of a bedroom, dimly lit.

Though the Tribunal has banned history, we are what we remember, the precious rope stretching across the abyss of all that we have forgotten. I now admitted this to myself as I stood above the bed gazing down at my wife's sleeping face. God, she was beautiful! And the history, the fabulous storehouse of memories, of our love, opened and gave reason and meaning to my quest across the abyss, a quest which had turned me into a heretic defying the Tribunal and all I'd been raised to believe in.

I don't know how long I stood there rediscovering every detail of her. I broke out of the spell when memories of the house-keeper intruded.

'Is it your wife?' Fantail was whispering. I nodded. 'You're a lucky guy, eh!' She tapped my shoulder, winked and left the bedroom.

She began to wake. I knew her sequence. First, she turned her head abruptly to the right, placed her left hand over her cheek, murmured and ran her tongue over her bottom lip, then her eyelids flicked open. For a moment she gazed vacantly at the wall. I reached down and caressed her nose with the back of my hand. She turned her face towards me. Grabbed my hand. I bent down and she was sobbing and holding on to me tightly. 'Is it you? Is it?' she asked, rubbing her face against mine.

'Yes, yes,' I murmured. She was around me and I wanted to dissolve into her. We kissed.

'Darling, darling . . . !' She was pulling me down into the bed. 'It's been so long!' she cried.

'Yes, too long!' I stopped, remembering. 'We have to go,' I said.

'Go where?'

'Escape before it's too late.'

'It's okay, honey.' She pressed her forehead against mine. 'We're home. You've come home; you've won.' I sat up. She reached up and stroked my face. 'Believe it, darling. You *are* home. You've found us. You've survived your ordeal, the trial the Tribunal set for you. And you did it marvellously.'

I still wasn't focusing. 'But you were the one who didn't like the Tribunal,' I said, refusing to believe. 'You wanted me to leave with you, get away from my sessions with the Tribunal.'

She sat up, embracing me, and said, 'Don't you see it yet, darling? I was part of your trial. I had a quest too, to be part of your test. I had to play my prescribed role . . .'

I swallowed, my throat was parched, and it was difficult to breathe.

'Every true citizen has to search, to struggle in the Game of Life . . .' she was saying.

179

'And the children?' I held her at arms' length. She looked bright ebony in the light.

'Yes, darling, they too played their roles brilliantly. You should be proud of them. I am. And so is John . . .'

'So your kidnapping, your being shifted, always ahead of me, was just part of my *staged* trial?'

She nodded. 'Honey, you've triumphed. Survived and defeated the obstacles put in your path. You were willing to sacrifice your life for us. We've triumphed too over our frailties, the kids and I. We missed you, we worried, suffered with you as you fought to reach us.' I rose to my feet, through air that felt like oil. 'The President is very proud of you too. You beat all the odds. We've won the $50 million dollar quest that every family wants to win, darling . . .' I had to come all that way to find what I'd dreaded was true, real like my wife of blood and flesh and pretensions. I was drained of hope, purpose. 'Darling, we've graduated to the ranks of the Elite, the Blessed, those chosen by the Tribunal to live forever no matter what . . .' She wound her left arm around my thighs and pressed her face into my hip. 'Darling, come to bed. You're home. We have nothing to worry about anymore.' *I was empty*, Janet Frame would have written. My wife's face burned into my skin. I wanted to believe her, to accept the security and logic of the Game, and be safe with her and our children again, and forever. 'I was on trial too, darling. I suffered too. So did our kids. We had to be courageous, patient, true to our goal.' She looked up. 'We had to watch you suffer the hunters, the villains, those crazy women. It was tough for us too! But we've come through . . .' She slid out of bed, stood up and, embracing me, cradled my head into her shoulder. 'Honey, it's okay. Trust me, trust the Tribunal, trust our President. We're here to protect you now. To say you've come through with flying colours. Our future is forever . . .'

I looked into her eyes. 'What about the people, the places, that got erased?' I heard myself asking.

'Darling, most of them were playing the roles the Tribunal set for them: they were fulfilling themselves.'

'What about the ones who weren't aware they were in the Game?'

'It doesn't matter. Don't you see? The President will have them reincarnated. He'll restore all the erasures.'

'It's getting late, eh!' Fantail called through the door.

'What about her and my other True Ones?' I asked my wife.

She pulled away from me. 'I don't know if they're in it. And it doesn't matter. They're only important as minor actors in *our* story, our triumph!'

'They're people!'

'Yes, but of the sewers and streets, incapable of reincarnation, redemption, of becoming normal, civilised like us. They don't want to anyway.' She was sounding so far away.

I turned towards the door. 'They've really changed you, eh?' I murmured. The priest she'd been, and who I'd seen in all her beauty and mana on Maungakiekie balancing the world, had vanished. The Tribunal had made sure of that. 'Darling, we've watched many episodes from your odyssey. The Tribunal and John had the whole thing recorded, they filmed it. It's very good. They're going to show it worldwide, as a shining example of how every citizen should play the Game of Life!' I started moving away. She slid her arms around me from behind. 'I need you, honey. So do the kids. We've missed you so.' She pressed her body against my back and kissed my neck. 'Please, darling. Don't give it all up now. We've earned it. All those years of struggle, pain, obedience. You can't turn your back on everything, on us, on your triumph . . . !' I pulled her hands down; broke her grasp. 'You can't!' she cried. I drew away from her warmth, the anchors of safety, security, status, fame. 'Stop!' She barred my way. Her eyes burned as she held my shoulders. 'I love you, darling. What are you doing? Don't turn your back on us, please. And not on everything you've won. Look!' She thrust a slip of paper at me. 'Look, just read it.'

> Please convey our congratulations to your victorious husband. Congratulations too to you and your exceptional children for finishing the Game with finesse and courage. Your family has reached GO, the ultimate in the Game. Collect your Final

181

References and the $50 million for winning. You are all winners, something not seen for a decade. The President sends his special love. We do too. So do John and all our diligent staff.

Signed — The Tribunal

I screwed it up with my right hand and dropped it to the floor. 'You keep it,' I said.

When she moved to hold me, I pushed her aside. 'Let's go!' I called to Fantail.

'You fool!' my wife shouted. 'Don't you see? They wanted to see if you were going to revert . . . !' I was in the sitting room.

Fantail stepped out into the corridor. My wife was sobbing again. 'They're going to finish you off. You can't win. No one does. They'll grind you to death and there'll be no reincarnation. Please!' She cried.

I ran into the corridor. Stopped. Pulled the Hotere off the door and thrust it into Fantail's hands. We started running. 'What the shit's happened?' she asked. Around us the walls and ceiling — the entire passage — came to life. 'What about your wife and kids, eh?' I ran faster.

I sensed the two guards before we reached the top of the stairwell. They believed we believed in non-violence like the rest of the population. 'Stop!' they called. Fantail moved left. They barred her way. The dagger was in my right hand. She stepped forward. As the guard opposite her reached out to catch her, she kicked at his crotch. 'Jesus!' he gasped, clutching his genitals and crumpling to his knees. She kicked his gasping out of his throat. He fell sideways. His partner came at me, still believing I wouldn't hurt him. 'Be reasonable!' he said. The dagger slid across the tops of his thighs. 'Shit, mate, ya're not supposed to behave like that!' When he saw the blood oozing out of the thin line he started blubbering. We ran past him. 'It's bleedin'!' he was telling himself.

We reached the monitoring cubicle. I kicked open the door and stabbed my fingers at the control switches. The system went dead, but as I came out of the cubicle, I sensed the whole Palace was now awake.

'Come on!' Fantail called from the end of the corridor. As I ran towards her, I worried for her, Manu and Aeto. I had nothing to lose now. I was outside the Game, free, though the passage to freedom was purring with menace as it closed in around us.

Manu and Aeto were already waiting at the doorway into the basement. 'Shit, man, what went wrong?' Manu asked. I grasped his shoulder and pushed him towards the tunnel entrance. 'What happened?'

'They're dead,' I replied. 'My family.' Fantail glanced at me. We reached the entrance. 'We were too late!' We could hear them on the stairs. 'It was a waste. So you three go on ahead. We'll meet back at the Whare.'

'No!' she insisted. I held Aeto and pushed him into the entrance.

'Do what I say!' I ordered. Manu climbed through the hole. 'Don't forget, take the routes we agreed on.' She lingered. 'Please,' I said.

She didn't hesitate, she was through the hole and running after the others.

Hurrying to the doors, I switched off the basement lights. Running footsteps thumped and clanged towards me. I pulled out both weapons and waited. Alarm bells rang high up in the building.

If I'd known then what I know now, would I have acted differently? Gone back to the safety of my wife and society? Asked the Tribunal for forgiveness and reordinarination? It would have been so much easier. But as I waited, I felt no fear or regret. I'd come into an inheritance of courage, daring risk; I liked my new self and didn't want to relinquish it. They had no right to decide what I should be.

Strange but the running footsteps kept going past my floor. Why? I shifted back from the doorway and hid behind the machinery that covered our tunnel entrance. I breathed easily.

My skin exuded the smell of my wife. Hurry.

Suddenly he was silhouetted in the doorway against the white light of the stairwell. He paused. Then stepped into the basement. His bald skull gleamed as he stopped and let his eyes adjust to the half-light. In Bible-black long coat, liquid black trousers, black bow tie, mirror-bright black shoes, lean, ascetic, the Keeper. He came in, five more careful paces. Stopped. Yes, he *was* handsome.

'I know you're here,' he whispered. His voice was sharp and clear. He moved stealthily to his left and started circling, examining every corner. 'You can't get away now. We have your wife and children. You led us straight to them.' He stopped only a few feet away from me. I could hear his breathing. 'I'm going to give you two minutes to surrender. We're the villains, remember, we will kill your beautiful wife. No qualms about that.' He didn't know where I was. 'Come on, play the Game, play the stereotype of the hero. Surrender and save your family.'

I stepped out from behind the machinery. I held the knives behind my back. He sensed me and wheeled. I caught a spark of startled fear in his eyes. 'So there you are,' he said, smiling. 'Very sensible to surrender. You've put up a good fight.'

The nerves at the back of my neck bristled. I turned as Brother Peter rushed at me and swung to my left, the knives rising. He was in the air, hurtling towards me. I drove both weapons upwards. They caught him coming down. He screamed and quivered, impaled momentarily. He smelled of cheap aftershave. I pushed up with the knives and threw off his dying weight, the knives ripping sideways.

'Jesus, you're a true bloody savage!' the Keeper gasped, backing away. 'He didn't deserve to die, villain though he is. He was only playing his assigned role.' I moved towards him.

'The President'll reincarnate him,' I said.

'But we don't work for the President!' he insisted.

Before I could reach him he turned and fled up the stairs, calling, 'He's here, the murderer's here!' The stairs reverberated with their footsteps again, heading my way.

Through the tunnel entrance I jumped. Grabbed the small

mine out of my jacket, clamped it to the roof of the tunnel and started running.

I was ten paces into the tunnel when the mine exploded. The roof above the entrance collapsed and blocked the hole.

As planned, I took a different route from the True Ones, one I hadn't told them about. I ran, my shoes slipping and sliding occasionally on the slippery tunnel floor. Listening to my breathing.

Once out of the manhole, I gazed up through the heads of the tall buildings at the sky of teeth-white stars. The light drizzle of rain pinched the skin on my face. The stinging proved I was still alive. I sucked in air greedily. Behind me, I sensed the Palace watching. I started up towards Greys Avenue, shuffling at first, then jogging, held up by my shadow. The van which I'd hired and provisioned with enough supplies for my family and me was waiting.

Just as I reached it, I remembered and looked at my hands, at Brother Peter's blood, which looked black in the night light. My clothes too were sticky with it.

eleven

The Lake

I needed time to be alone, to remember, and in that remembering, perhaps understand the tragedy of my wife and children. So I drove through the empty streets, through the mistlike rain on to the southern motorway.

Just before the Gillies Avenue turn-off I glimpsed Auckland Hospital, to my left, rising up into the darkness. Waves of swirling rain were buffeting it. A memory which I'd not had before unfolded, like a sunflower in my head: my mother — and there was no face to her — had spent three weeks in its critical care ward on the thirteenth floor. They'd flown her home, unable to cure her. The illness? Nothing in the memory about that. I accepted it as a genuine recollection but it was unrelated to anything else I knew about myself. I hugged it. It kept me warm as I drove deeper into the cold.

My official search, the trial the Tribunal had prescribed, wasn't over. They wouldn't have let me out of the city otherwise. They weren't following me either. At least, they weren't obvious in the rearview mirror.

In many odysseys, when the protagonist has suffered a tragic setback he looks for a new source of spiritual strength, a place in which to heal. When Marlon Brando, as One-Eyed Jack, the deadly gunfighter, has the fingers of his gun-hand smashed to uselessness by the baddies, he retreats to the seashore of Monterey. There, while huge waves boom and thunder and gulls squawk in the lyrical summer sky, he recovers his strength and then trains his left hand, day after tortuous day, to do his killing.

186

In *Shane*, after Alan Ladd, in the final showdown, wastes the nasties in the town, he rides off into the technicolour sunset, clutching his sorely wounded belly (or was it shoulder?), but we know he'll soon find his healing somewhere and then continue his mission of championing the powerless. Not that I was a protagonist of their stature, though the Tribunal had obviously assigned me that status.

At about 4.30 a.m. I was driving slowly through the main street of Taupo. It was still raining steadily. Everything was shiny black.

I drove into the carpark at the end of the street overlooking the lake. Pulled down the van blinds, stripped off my blood-caked clothes, put on a clean track suit, switched on the heaters, pushed back the van seats to form a double-bed, got into a sleeping bag and was asleep quickly, my body numb with fatigue, my eyes stinging from the strain of driving. The dark waters of the lake lapped at the shores of my dreaming.

Next day, under the name Shamus Calvino, I rented a small bach in an isolated bay on the northern shore, from A & R Hooper Estates. An unsealed road led to it through replanted forest and silence. As I drove I felt as if I was entering the magic forests of mythology.

It was set under willows right at the water's edge and had all mod cons, a punt and a small jetty. Fake rustic, my wife would've described it.

I unpacked some of the food from the van and after storing it in the kitchen cupboards and refrigerator, found the main bedroom and slept again. I couldn't escape the atua, gigantic warrior figures, who rose up out of the lake like genie and, winding themselves around me, lifted me up into the heavens in which I was tossed up and down by the waves while the atua laughed. But I experienced no fear: not of the atua, not of the turbulent lake. A ferocious taniwha opened its mouth and the torrent hurled me into it. I screamed as I fought the current but found myself on a merry-go-round, holding my five-year-old daughter, Anis, in my lap. She laughed and laughed, as the horse we were riding circled.

I didn't wake until early the next morning. I wandered out to the verandah, into the numbing cold, into the thick mist that was surging out of the lake. White as milk, it was eeling in, searching for its other selves in the bush but finding only what its flow was determining. It was like no other mist that had been. Filling the holes in the web of bush and undergrowth, the bach and my eyes. Giving a unity, an intelligence, to everything. I wanted to be of that unity forever, but the mist cleared quickly and left a bright egg-yellow sun above the lake.

I had a breakfast of cornflakes, yoghurt and tea, pulled the punt into the water, stored my oilskin raincoat and fishing gear in it, got in and rowed it out over the lead-black water.

Three hundred metres out I pulled in the oars, threw out my hookless line, and, while the punt drifted in the water's will, refished what I'd confessed to the Tribunal, re-examining every bit of it through the understanding I'd acquired since I'd been awarded the Final Reference and especially through the bitter lens of what had happened to my family.

I stayed on the lake until mid-afternoon, returned, ate and slept again.

I did that for four days.

On the fifth day, a Saturday I think, I walked and jogged for almost two hours along the lake shore, showered, ate a light lunch, and then started making lists of what I knew about the Tribunal, the President, the Tribunal building, John, the Keeper, SS Ratched, my wife, each of my children, Fantail, Manu, Aeto, and anyone and anything else that was part of my story. In this Joycean stream-of-consciousness technique, each list blossomed and ballooned and became a fabulous character which I then pinned up on the kitchen wall. By midnight the lists were wallhangings written in my new calligraphy.

I slid into bed but slept fitfully. The housekeeper intruded in slow motion sequences of posing and flexing her muscles, taunting me.

Finally at 3 a.m. I got out of bed, switched on the kitchen lights, scrawled out a list of all I knew about her, and pinned her up beside the President, at the centre of my familiar yet strange gallery/menagerie of characters.

I followed that routine until Tuesday and established connections I'd not been aware of before, between my characters, until the walls were crisscrossed, bridged, connected with arrows, talk balloons, crossings-out and insertions, analogies, metaphors, similes, speculations, curses of frustration. My story, a collage history, contained in the ever-moving present.

On Wednesday, after my jog, I dived off the jetty into the lake. The icy cold burst through me like jabbing spears. My head rang with pain. I scrambled out again and ran into the bach and a hot shower.

The hill *felt* as if I was meant to climb it. I hadn't taken much notice of it, but that morning, when I went to throw the rubbish into the bin on the back steps, I glanced up and saw it and the narrow track that meandered from the edge of the back lawn up through the thick bush which the hill wore like a shaggy cloak. The light wind from the lake was rippling across the bush in a series of waves, making it look unreal, a blue-green creature of mythology, which could only become real for me through my exploration of it.

As the sun rose I took the track slowly, savouring every step as I tried to imagine how pre-otherworlder Tangata Maori would have seen the hill, the bush, everything. Would they have seen themselves as being separate from their surroundings, as the centre of it, selves who had the right to conquer, harness, subdue everything for their own use? My imagination and senses were keener than at any other time in my life. Every tree, vine, fern, stone, insect and bird, colour, smell and the everythingness that held them together, I grasped clearly. And as I absorbed them I felt I was becoming part of them. The inescapable smell of earth drying in the heat cauled me. The hill grew steeper, the sun hotter. I held on to shrubs, vines, and branches and pulled myself up the slope after my shadow through the tangled undergrowth.

I rested periodically under the trees, lying on my back and

gazing up at the canopy of leaf and branch. The sound of the wind in the vegetation wrapped itself around my head. The atua were still there, around me, in everything. The otherworlders hadn't destroyed them. I thought of Maungakiekie, the dead volcano in the heart of the city. The atua were still there too, and I was walking in their footsteps.

I don't know how long I slept under the totara, but when I woke the wind was gone and the silence was long and sad. I stood up and hurried towards the summit, slipping once and cutting my knee on a sharp rock. I cleaned the small wound with a fistful of leaves. When I glanced up, the pigeon was watching me. (This was no middle-class, smug Don Binney pigeon hovering fatly above a landscape changed utterly by other-worlders.) I bowed to it; it seemed to return my greeting. I went up and stood underneath it. It refused to fly away. I was caught in its eyes and plumage which, in the noonday light, were a blue-black fire. The silence was long and sad. I wore the light as it grew old.

At the summit there was a small clearing surrounded by towering trees. A clearing of rock centering on a large flat-topped boulder. Who'd come here before? I sat on the boulder and faced the north through a wide gap in the trees. The air smelled of woodsmoke. The bush and hills tumbled down to the lake which slipped away in a series of blazing mirrors into the endless white light. I watched. In the high-doming sky, clouds changed shape; their shadows glided across the lake's surface and the plains and hills. Everything was floating, in flux. And I was of that floating.

When I first met her, she smelled of fresh limes. I thought it was perfume. It wasn't until we made love in my flat, when my hands, lips and nose explored her, that I realised the scent emanated from the depths of her body. Every time we made love her scent impregnated my skin and for days I smelled of it. And I loved it. I loved smelling my hands and skin for her, and she was always there no matter where I was or what I was doing. We never referred to it, as if we were afraid that on mentioning it, it would disappear.

Her skin too had a special sheen and texture. I never tired of running my fingers over it, of licking and tasting it, of rubbing my body against it. Sometimes in the deep dreams which followed our lovemaking, I watched myself licking her skin and flesh, devouring it. I woke ashamed and refused to tell her what was upsetting me.

Sometimes while she was asleep I observed her, starting with her face: the prominent forehead with the silk-brown skin stretched tightly across it, with the bone almost shining through the skin; the thin eyebrows that tapered sharply; the long eyelashes that curled up; the jutting cheekbones which v-ed down to dimples; the stubby nose with a small mole near its tip; then the mouth, thick lips, with the lower lip pouting, inviting me to discover its shape with my mouth. I ran my hands down the sides of her neck, noting the shape and weave of it, the slow rise and fall of her breathing, to her collarbones and the hollows behind them which I traced with my fingers, then my tongue. Sometimes I spent a long time playing with her hair, the long smooth flow of it, twisting and twirling it around in my hands, using it to caress her breasts, back, and buttocks, rediscovering the whole geography of her; and then brushing it over and around my genitals until I was erect, I slid into her cunt which had the texture and flow of her hair. And while we fucked I watched her eyes waking from sleep, her mouth opening and shutting as if she was gagging, gasping and sucking in air, with a muffled humming. Her legs, as she mounted to her climax, splaying out more and more, her hips pumping up and down urgently. Her odour encompassing both of us.

I knew she observed me too while I slept. Once I woke to her breathing on the sole of my left foot and, pretending I was still asleep, watched her exploring my feet with her tongue and lips and, as she moved upwards, the heat and moistness of her breath and mouth set every part of me alight. When she reached my cock, she mounted me. She rested her hands on my shoulders. God, how she glowed in the dark.

Whenever we were apart for a while, when we came together we made love wildly without preliminaries. Then while

191

we told each other what we'd been doing while apart, re-explored each other's bodies, using all our senses, as if to reassure ourselves we were together again. Our sexual explorations were explorations of love, our love which strengthened as the years went by and our children joined us.

As I floated and thought of her and of our children, the long sad silence of the hill and bush and sky became me. It didn't matter any more that my family had been 'created' specially by the Tribunal for my search. They were my wife and children and our love for one another had not been a fabrication, a pre-programmed feature. My memories of them were real, a history that helped give me meaning. A history I now wanted to stop the Tribunal from taking away from me. How the heavens stretched beyond the limits of my breath; how the atua, who'd gathered in that clearing, stretched their aroha to me, helping me remember without fear. On the lowest branch of the tree to the right of the gap into the sky sat the pigeon I'd seen earlier on. It watched me. The air still smelled of wood fires.

Margaret was the most unusual woman I'd ever met. But I didn't recognise that until much later. At first she was just the new secretary who'd transferred from Auckland, and who was dressed and behaved like the other secretaries, as was company policy. I'd read her CV. A bank manager's daughter who'd grown up in the small towns where her father had worked; her mother had died of leukemia, refusing reincarnation, leaving Margaret and two older brothers. Her father had remarried two years later. For four years Margaret had attended a boarding school for Catholics, her father's religious preference; had attended the College for Services, and qualified as a secretary with special skills in computer programming and budgeting. B + average. Nothing unusal in her sexual-emotional-personality profile. Had never had to undergo reordinarination.

Up to that time I had not allowed myself a live-in partner, not for long anyway. Like the other young people in the bank I enjoyed casual and shifting relationships. Usually after I made love to someone, I lost interest in that person sexually. Nothing wrong in that, it was the way the Tribunal and the President prescribed. One day we would marry and have children, but youth was to enjoy, to explore our urges, needs, preferences, desires. And it was in pursuit of that that I first took Margaret out to dinner.

I would never forget that meal, not because it was exceptional, but because it was a repetition of the dinners I'd had with three of the other secretaries. When I thought about it, I watched myself sitting opposite her, talking the same way about the same things I'd discussed with the others, eating the same mediocre vegetarian dishes while she ate fish. She wasn't shy, she was articulate and enthusiastic about the same things I was; was expert, like me, at filling in the silences. It was only that Sunday while I was trying to watch a rugby game on TV that unusual things caught my remembering. For instance, the intensity of her eyes which she tried to disguise by never looking too directly at me. An intense spot of light in the pupils. The way she held her fork, tightly, as if she was afraid of dropping it; the glow of the silver ring on her middle finger. Her pouting lower lip, which she licked often as if she wanted to erase the light's reflection caught at its centre. Her hair, the wave and curl of it, that trapped the light and made it look as if it was growing. Then after the dessert of nashis and cream, her remark: 'You're brown too.' And I noticed, for the first time, that she was brown. And so was I.

That simple truth, when I went to work the next day, made me see for the first time we were different from the others. Just in skin. For we were of them in every other way.

We had dinner twice more, and each time the intensity with which she did things became more obvious. She took nothing for granted. Everything was new, she remarked, again offhandedly. I took the remark home and, without realising it, it grew on me.

The dinners led to her inviting me to other activities in her life, and the intensity and newness that was her. For instance, as I watched her on the ice rink performing for her club, the sheer daring and skill of her skating frightened me. It was deliberate, the way she skated at the edge of suffering serious injury. She didn't falter. And she loved the danger. I could tell

from her laughter as she skated. When she came off the rink her
eyes were on fire. Without hesitation she flung her arms around
me and, hugging me tightly, said: 'It was fucking good, man!'
Later as we sat in the club bar drinking milkshakes, she quickly
became the secretary I knew at work. I found myself resenting
that transformation.

One Saturday she arrived at my flat in her small Chinese
sedan and invited me for a drive. As soon as she put her foot on
the accelerator, the car took on her intensity. 'I put in a special
engine,' she said. 'You know much about cars?' I said no. 'My
mother was a magician when it came to cars.' For almost an
hour, as I nearly shat myself with fear, I suffered her exhilarating
daring in the car that cut and wove through the countryside like
a demon controlled by a magician. 'Were you scared?' she asked.
I shook my head. She laughed. 'No need to be afraid,' she said.
'There's no permanent death, remember.' 'But car crashes can
mangle you up with a lot of pain!' I joked. 'But beyond the pain,
man, there's reincarnation!' When she dropped me off, she
kissed me on the cheek. 'There's nothing else to learn about
myself from but danger,' she whispered. 'Do you run?' she
asked. I nodded.

At five-thirty the next morning she was knocking at my
door, in her running gear. 'It's too bloody cold!' I objected. She
did stretch exercises while I dressed.

Once out in the steaming cold, the road slippery with ice,
I began to learn what true fitness was. And how she loved and
enjoyed the fitness of her body. She was at home with and in her
body. In a rhythm that was in tune with the earth's beat. A kilometre and I slowed. She ran on the spot to encourage me to go
on. I survived five more kilometres. And the humiliation. She
took the six kilometres back to her flat. At work that day, she
mentioned nothing about it to me.

We established a routine of running three mornings a week.

In the next few months we found ourselves spending a lot of
time together. And I learned she was into the martial arts as
practised by the Master Alapati Tuaopepe; she was a crack shot
with a rifle — her mother had taught her; her brothers had

taught her soccer and hockey; her father, who, in his retirement, retreated into lonely games of chess, pestered her into becoming a competent chess player; she played the guitar and sang, in a rich contralto, a large repertoire of songs, including Tangata Moni ones, which her mother had taught her. She beat me at tennis, she beat me at handball and squash, she let me win at snooker. Instead of my resenting her marvellous abilities, I loved her more for them. Yes, what filled me was love, I concluded. I needed her to be with me, or, more accurately, I needed to be with her. When she wasn't there I felt incomplete. Yet love, and the commitment to it, was laughed at by our friends. So for almost a year I refused to admit it to myself and to her.

She hated reading, she confessed one night. She was glad I was into literature — she could learn from me.

The sky turned and turned in my head, as the memories I'd denied myself came out of the northern sky to meet me on that hill. Memory leading to memory, to my family, to a history banned by the Tribunal.

It was Dylan Thomas, that drunken, driven, haunted Welshman, who seduced her into poetry. I'd tried Shakespeare, Donne, Keats, Baxter, Thaman, Malietoa, Charman, Sullivan and others. She'd look interested as I read them to her. 'They're too difficult for me,' she'd lied.

I hit her with Marianne Moore, Genghis James Chong, Don S. Long, and she warmed. I went to get the coffee and, on my way back, I started reciting Thomas's 'Fern Hill'. Her eyes pinned to an intensity I'd not seen before. So I left the coffee and, sitting down beside her, read the whole of Thomas's hymn to childhood and youth.

'More,' she whispered, putting her arms around me and nuzzling her face into my side.

When we made love a short while later, for the first time, it was as rich as Thomas's gift. And for the rest of our life together, 'Fern Hill' was the incantation we evoked whenever anything threatened our relationship. Later we acquired three poems we associated with the protection of each of our children: for Anis, Yeats's 'A Prayer for My Daughter'; for Elem, Mele

Tuao's 'Pese Mo La'u Tama'; for Leahcim, Apirana Taylor's 'Mihi on a Marae', and whenever we needed them, we sang them to tunes she'd composed.

Now on that hill that was the creature of my total history, as those songs filtered into my head and heart again, I wept into the open sky and the atua. I had become the sum total of what I had lost. That loss defined me, confined me. The depth of it was greater than any poetry.

I was ready again.

The next day, at midday, as I drove away from the bach and the hill, the sunlight flashed, sparkled and danced across the lake into my eyes. In his old age, King Arthur had thrown Excalibur back into the sacred lake. I watched as it arched high into the astounded air, turning over and over. Out of the still water, the Lady of the Lake's arm emerged, hand with fingers extended. Excalibur settled, like a bird, into her nesting grip. I watched the alabaster arm withdrawing with the sword into the lake's depths.

I pushed in a cassette of Hone Tuwhare reading:

WE, WHO LIVE IN DARKNESS

It had been a long long time of it
wriggling and squirming in the swamp of night.
And what was time, anyway? Black intensities
of black on black on black feeding on itself?
Something immense? Immeasureless?

No more.
There just had to be a beginning somehow.
For on reaching the top of the slow rise suddenly
eyes I never knew I possessed were stung by it
forcing me to hide my face in the earth.

It was light, my brothers. Light.
A most beautiful sight infiltered past
the armpit hairs of the father. Why, I could
even see to count all the fingers of my hands

held out to it: see the stain — the clutch of
good earth on them.

But then he moved.
And the darkness came down even more oppressively
it seemed and I drew back tense; angry.

Brothers, let us kill him — push him off.

twelve

Taniwhanui

As in all great quests, you have to undergo more trials. Your recovery at the lake must now be put to the test. Trust not what you see; trust not the people you meet; trust not the air you breathe. But through it all, your family awaits you. We await your triumph . . .

I was surprised to find this note in the glove compartment of the van, as Lake Taupo disappeared behind me. But though I didn't trust it, I wasn't afraid of it. I took the Tuwhare tape out of the player and slotted in a recording of what I'd learned, in my questioning beside the lake, about the players in my Game. And as the road slid under the van and a few lost clouds wandered over the hills ahead, my recorded voice played through my head. I was in the centre of a huge and terrible charade about life and death, yet I felt indifferent to being hurt or destroyed by it. Why? I was reconciled to whatever pain and fear awaited me, to death even, because I had nothing to lose.

It was the subtle change in the light that made me first suspect there was something different about the countryside through which I was driving. The bright noonday light seemed artificial, that was the only way I could describe it. It didn't have the pores and breath and the feeling of space that went with sunlight in open countryside. Very accurate replication of sunlight but replication all the same. The wind was still blowing and stirring the trees and grass, but it seemed confined to a limited space, the area around and through which I was travelling. The sky watched me, recording my every move. I scrutinised my surroundings closely. It wasn't the route from Auckland to Taupo that I knew. This was a replacement. The hills, pad-

198

docks, sheep, cattle, farmhouses, fences, everything. Real and alive, but a replacement. I pushed down on the accelerator. The van surged forward. Deliberately I turned the wheel to my left to swerve off the road, but the van refused to turn: it was locked to a prescribed course. I slammed my foot on the brakes. Nothing. The van kept to its course and a steady 120 ks. For a second I glimpsed a hawk hovering above a milking shed as the van rounded a bend onto an arrow-straight stretch of road that burrowed ahead through manicured paddocks that looked more like golf courses than paddocks. In my memory the hawk was poised with my reflection in its eyes. I lowered the window. The wind smelled of drying hay as it buffeted my face and rivered through my long hair, flapping it against the ceiling of the van, in a rapping tatatattatattat . . . I switched off the recording.

A black Road Runner truck with darkly tinted windows loomed up over the rise. As it rushed towards me I was afraid of a headlong collision and panicked when I couldn't turn the van aside. Two dark figures in the truck's cab waved — I imagined them laughing haughtily at my fear — as the truck swished past, the wave of air it displaced pushing us almost to the ditch. Real all right, but yet unreal. Then a red sports car, with a blond couple who waved. Straight out of an advertisement. Then a line of cars jockeying for position, as they chased the red coupe. I looked behind us. No other traffic. I relaxed and enjoyed the excellent special effects.

Wakataua, it said on the road sign: a petrol station, two shops beside it, a school, a few children on bikes, before we were over a small bridge and a stream islanded with the reflections of black clouds and willows. Definitely not the road to Auckland which I knew.

Fifteen minutes later another settlement, *Wharetaniwha*. A few streets radiating from the main road, with neat box-shaped houses. And up on the central hill, backdropped by pine trees, were the ruins of a pa, signposted with large billboards giving what I imagined was the history of the pa and marae. I couldn't see anyone about. Eaten by the taniwha!

I opened my lunch of sandwiches and fruit. Bit into the first sandwich. My teeth cut through paper. I opened the sandwich. Between the slices of cucumber and tomato was this note:

> Beware of the taniwha with the smile. S/he may be around the next bend in the road that is a river which has many traps, many deep dark pools. S/he may wear the face of those you love but s/he is hungry for seekers and questors.

I was hungry and the food tasted good. I ate and watched the road that was a river unravelling through a steep-sided gorge which was covered with native bush. I surveyed the bush and concluded it was also a careful replacement.

The river and the gorge suddenly opened out to a wide valley of stud farms drenched with sun and the smell of horses. Ultra-neat white wooden fences, expensive farmhouses and training tracks, and beautiful horses which reminded me of the Lone Ranger's Silver. Some of the magnificent animals galloped round the paddocks, bodies sleek with sweat and shimmering with light; some snorted and pawed at the ground, whinnied and nodded their great heads at me as I passed. Kupenicus Stud Farm, Rogerhard Stables, Smith Meadows — the Home of Ora Prince, Tane Deep Blue Grass Farm, stud farm after stud farm.

Again I couldn't see anyone about.

Welcome to Taniwhanui, City of the Great Kiwi Breed . . . The tape came on as we entered the suburbs of perfectly trimmed hedges, lawns, gardens, and houses which looked as if they'd come straight out of the 1980s. The androgynous voice, that of a tour guide, said: *Welcome, Questor, it is not often that our humble city greets someone as special as you* . . . The houses and streets were empty of people, but I felt as if a large audience was watching me performing some miraculous feat. A hungry, expectant watching . . . *Our humble community has a long and rich history and an ancient mythology. We know that the Tribunal has quite correctly banned all discussion of history, but, for today and this very special celebration, our Benevolent and Understanding Tribunal has issued us with a special permit to tell you, our Guest of Honour, our history* . . . It was strange, but I was feeling elated and proud at the attention and praise they were heaping upon me. *Thousands of years ago the great voyager, Kupenicus Tane, fleeing from the Wars of Rangitoto, established a pa here, bringing with him and his tribe, his pet Taniwha, Matatoru, who he kept in the deepest part of our river which is now the heart of our city. We do not have the time to tell you the whole complex series of myths and legends of that time, but at your arrival we will present you with,* Myths and Legends of Taniwhanui County, *our bestselling collection of that mythology. (Tourists bought two million copies of it last year.) For your visit today, there are only a few pertinent facts about the Great Kupenicus and Matatoru you should know.*

Firstly, Matatoru was a gift to Kupenicus from the atua Tangaroa whose daughter our Great Ancestor had rescued from the evil clutches of Maui, who, in our tradition, was a compulsive rapist. (Our collection will give you the stories about the rescue and so forth.) At first Matatoru, the Three-Faced, was the size of Kupenicus's cupped hand. A slim creature, shaped like a lizard, which you could see into when you shone a light through it, and which curled up in Kupenicus's hand and went to sleep as soon as Tangaroa handed it to the Ancestor. 'S/he loves you', Tangaroa said. 'See, s/he has turned up her/his first face towards you, the Face of Aroha, the Face of Peace. Her/his opposite face, Matataua, the one turned away from you and on which s/he is lying, is the Face of War and Violence. The third face is the Face of Diplomacy, her/his gift to negotiate between her/his other two faces. As yet, because s/he is a child, s/he does not know s/he has three faces and what they are and the powers they possess. As s/he grows, like any other child, you must teach it that knowledge. Or, should I say, you should teach her/him whichever of those powers and faces you and your whanau value most in life, and de-emphasise (pardon my awful vocabulary — it comes from listening too much to my computer instructor!) those you deem dangerous and uncivilised . . . .' My memory, without my permission, kept searching for the person the guide's voice reminded me of. The name was right there but I just couldn't remember it.

To cut a long story short, the first ten Kupenicus in the long
line of Kupenicus rangatira, who inherited the wondrous Taniwhanui, cared for her/him well, raising her/him to reveal only
her/his face of peace and aroha. Whenever neighbouring tribes
threatened war and invasion the Taniwhanui showed her/his
third face to their rangatira in their dreams and erased the
thought of war from their minds. When ambitious rangatira,
within our tribe, conspired to usurp the leadership, the Taniwhanui did the same with them. Consequently, our Tangata
Maori ancestors and tribe prospered and multiplied, so the First
Book of Kupenicus says. (Yes, not only was our Master
Rogerhard Kupenicus Smith a genius horsebreeder, but he also
recorded, in our most sacred book, The Testament of Smith, the
history of our Tangata Maori ancestors, as told to him by his
mother, the Princess Te Ora, daughter of the twentieth
Kupenicus Tane, Arikinui of the Kupenicus Confederation of
Tribes, and wife of the first Rogerhard Smith, one of the first
heroic beachcombers in Aotearoa. (You will also be presented
with a golden copy of our most Sacred Book.) A strange but fabulous blend of fact, fiction, and fantasy, I thought as I listened.
A script out of Hollywood or the out-of-print historical novels of
Morerice Boltshad laced with a bit of Wittie Ishmael and Kerrie
Me Home. It was with the eleventh Kupenicus Tane that the
terrible Years of the Second Face began. That is why Number
Eleven is our most unlucky and dreaded number. There are no
eleventh floors in our buildings, no eleven-year-olds in horses or
people, no sets of eleven in any thing; if you have eleven lovers
you must immediately get a twelfth; in fact our lives are
governed, to a large extent, by the law of avoiding eleven. You
can't even die on the eleventh! If you do, your family and your
undertaker must advertise it either as the tenth or twelfth.
Because of that, number ten and twelve are our lucky numbers.
To avoid eleven we stop at ten or rush to twelve. So the first
Kupenicus Rogerhard Smith and Princess Te Ora had ten
children who had ten children each; the second Rogerhard had
twelve who, in turn, had twelve children each; the third
Rogerhard had ten who had ten, and so the tradition of alter-

nating was established. Similarly, when the Smith line started breeding horses, the same pattern was maintained with our horses. I'm really getting away from the centre story, aren't I? Yeah, I replied in my head, though I was finding the fanciful tangents in his narration fascinating.

The eleventh Kupenicus Tane was also the eleventh child of the Tenth Kupenicus; he was born on the eleventh day of the month and had eleven fingers, another small finger on his left hand; when he could talk he always talked in sentences of eleven words, and because he loved fullstops he always said Fullstop at the end of his every sentence, a habit which his elders, especially his mother who didn't like talkative children, found difficult to tolerate; he was the most gifted of the Tenth Kupenicus's children — gifted with the ability to read what you were thinking, which he used to endear himself to his father who loved fishing: his father won every fishing contest because his son told him exactly where to find the biggest fish and when. He could summon any sea creature with his mysterious chants and incantations.

After ten generations of peace Kupenicus and his people were taking the Taniwhanui's Face of Aroha for granted: they rarely visited her/his pool, and her/his appointed attendants neglected to feed her/him properly and sing her/him her/his favourite songs. Yes, the Taniwhanui's heart was made of music, all the songs and tunes her/his creator Tangaroa had gathered from around the world and shaped into her/his heart. Songs of aroha and serenity and peace and sunrises and fertile rain and mercy and kindness and the smell of frangipani and clover and little girls and all things nice etc etc etc.

Each generation had to deepen and widen the Taniwhanui's pool to suit her/his new growth. By now, the Taniwhanui, when s/he curled up, filled her/his pool, but the people kept postponing enlarging her/his pool. However, because the Taniwhanui knew only aroha after generations of practising it and having it reciprocated, s/he foraged for her/his own food and sang to her/himself.

The Eleventh Child kept his father and the people hooked

*on fishing tournaments: line, net, spear, poison, noose, traps,
every kind of fishing. He invented new methods and prizes
which worsened their addiction. And while they were tour-
namenting, he started courting the Taniwhanui. Remember, the
final choice of successor to the Kupenicus Tane was made by the
Taniwhanui.*

*With his special gifts the Eleventh Child knew all the
Taniwhanui's favourite songs. And starting on the eleventh day
of the month, he appeared at the edge of the Taniwhanui's
sacred pool, singing the first song the Taniwhanui had ever
heard from Tangaroa. I'm not a good singer but I'll try and sing
it.*

(I was now snared in his narration, and when he sang in his
clear powerful baritone accompanied by a chorus of soprano
and bass voices keening in the most haunting manner I'd ever
experienced, I was, like the Taniwhanui, under the spell of
aroha.)

I found myself cheering and clapping when he finished.
*Thank you, Great Questor, he said, thank you! But it is not I
who is important but the tale and its wisdom. So back to the
Eleventh Child.* The van had slowed to a crawl, through streets
lined with vehicles and bursting with listening sun but still
without people. I was in the depths of a wise uncanniness whose
meaning would soon be revealed to me.

*The Eleventh Child's song drew the Taniwhanui, who was
lonely for company, out of the depths. S/he lay her/his head on
the bank at the Child's feet, her/his Face Of Aroha peering up
at him. Sing me some more, s/he asked. Until evening fell the
Eleventh Child sang to her/him, in sequence, the songs Tangaroa had hearted her/him with. The Taniwhanui wept with joy
and love, for what child would give up a whole afternoon, away
from his life, to sing to her/him, and to sing so beautifully. And
what child would, at the end of it all, say to her/him: 'Here, I
have brought you your favourite food.' And lay on his flat
boulder table a foodmat laden with raw octopi seasoned with
lemon, a red sunset sautéed with cool evening breezes, the poems
of Tautalatele recited by the poet himself, ripe pineapples from*

the lava fields of Asau, the dreams of morning which Tangaroa had dreamt as a child, slabs of molten lava which, when swallowed, spark endless hopes throughout your breath, and last, but most desirable, French fries from McDonalds. 'What's your name?' Taniwhanui asked. 'Sefulutasi, Eleven,' the Child replied. 'Bye bye, Eleven!' Taniwhanui called after him as the Child ran home. 'Please come visit me tomorrow, please!'

Eleven, clever schemer that he was, deliberately stayed away for three days during which the Taniwhanui waited and waited and was, at first, sad, then her/his sadness turned to impatience, as she/he curled and swirled and whirled round and round in her/his pool until the waves pounded the banks and threatened to flood the settlement. Shitscared, her/his attendants came running and, kneeling in front of the pool, apologised profusely to the Taniwhanui who, still in her/his Face of Aroha, forgave them. They promised to enlarge her/his pool and feed her/him well. But next morning, Eleven proclaimed another fishing tournament which the keepers couldn't resist. While they were away at sea, Eleven took the Taniwhanui another huge meal of her/his favourite food, and, while the Taniwhanui ate, sang her/him her/his favourite songs. And so it went on, until the Taniwhanui refused to be fed or sung to by anyone else. You can read the rest of the story later. Enough here to say who the Taniwhanui chose as her/his favourite and who, in turn, turned the Face Of Violence and War towards the people.

Our city numbers 200,199 honest hardworking citizens who love horses, as you have probably observed. We breed the best racehorses, show horses, circus horses in the country — and we would like to believe, the best horses in the world. When the great questor Roy Rogers retired from the movies we bought his loving partner, Trigger. Later we also bought Gene Autry's Champion, and the Lone Ranger's Silver. And using that strong aristocratic line, mixed it with our own Tangata Maori/pioneer Kiwi stock and bred the line which has made our small humble community famous throughout the world. Fanfare of trumpets, thunderous applause, and the voice announcing: *What do we have when we mate American aristocracy with Arab sheiks and good old Kiwi ingenuity, know-how and virility?* 'Taniwhanui! Taniwhanui!' the crowd roared. Yeah, yeah! the announcer echoed. Outside, the houses were changing into shops and businesses and traffic lights and busy central city streets choked with parked cars — but still no people. *It was our pioneer Founder and Master Breeder, Rogerhard Kupenicus Smith, who founded our Taniwhanui line. And, our society being nonsexist, we should also pay tribute to Mary Margaret, strong and loyal wife of the Master. She provided the love and care which the Master needed over the poverty-stricken and difficult years of experimenting with different breeds.* Loud applause from the crowd. I looked up, ahead, to the end of the main street. A sports stadium rose fifteen storeys high. Bone white and gleaming in the sun. The applause was coming out of the stadium. Stretched across the wall above the main entrance was this red banner: WELCOME, QUESTOR AND SON OF TANIWHANUI! WELCOME TO YOUR HOUR OF LIFE. In front of the main entrance, at the end of a long line of uniformed reordinarinators, was a group of men and women dressed in their best. They were obviously waiting for some important guest. *You are on track, great Questor*, the announcer was saying to me. My van kept approaching the main entrance and the welcoming committee. I braked but nothing happened. They saw me. The reordinarinators drew to attention at the command of their leader. The faces of the welcomers broke into respectful smiles. The baldheaded man in the middle, who reminded me of the President, held up his arm, greeting me. I straightened my clothes; brushed back my hair and tied it in a topnot. The van slowed and stopped at the head of the line of reordinarinators. WELCOME! WELCOME! DESCENDANT OF TANIWHANUI! the crowd in the stadium roared.

My welcoming committee clapped as the door of the van slid open and I stepped out. Nothing to lose, I told myself. I injected a smile into the muscles of my wary face.

The leader of the welcoming party hurried forward and, bowing deeply, gripped my right hand with both of his and said, 'Greetings, son of Taniwhanui, we are honoured to once again welcome you to your city and community.' My smiling reflection was caught in his shiny baldness before he straightened up and gazed into my face.

'Thank you, Guardian of the Taniwhanui,' I heard myself saying.

'Thank you. My Family is proud and honoured to have been the Taniwhanui's Guardian since time immemorial.'

The rest of his committee, which turned out to be the City Council, shuffled forward. I smiled into their smiles and shook their hands as the Mayor of Taniwhanui, Rogerhard Kupenicus Smith, introduced me to them: Mrs Ida Wedgecome, descendant of Kendryke, brother of the Master Breeder; Mrs Mary Edmondly, heir to the Murray Stables, and direct descendant of Paul Bookes, original stableboy for the Master; Ms Michelle Letgo, owner of Like This? Studs, and direct descendant of the Master's poet laureate; Mr Brian Boyed, chronicler and owner of Nabocove Stables which Master Kupenicus had established after the White Death had wiped out his first breeding stock . . . As they were introduced to me, my memory wanted to remember them, and I was puzzled why. Long-lost relatives and kin? Part of my genealogy? That among them were the taniwha I had to watch out for? And my guardians?

The Mayor presented me with autographed, gold-edged copies of the *Myths and Legends of Taniwhanui County* and *The Testament of Smith.*

Inside the high-domed lobby of the stadium, in rows, were children dressed in sports uniforms. They waved Taniwhanui flags as we passed through their lines. 'Welcome, welcome, Son of Taniwhanui!' they chanted. I waved and smiled in the manner of the British Royalty of the 1980s. The Mayor pointed up at the walls which were covered with huge photos of me with the slogan: GREAT QUESTOR AND SON OF TANIWHANUI, WELCOME.

As we passed through the tunnel leading into the auditorium, long lines of reordinarinators clicked to attention. I saluted, outstretched arm pointed towards them, hand held with palm facing downwards, and wondered why I was saluting that way. They returned my salute, shouting: 'Heil, Son of Taniwhanui, heil!'

When we entered the arena, wave after wave of applause washed against me. A rugby stadium: a massive oval consisting of covered stands and terraces around a rugby field. The terraces and stands were packed with a congregation, that's how I *felt* they were: they'd gathered for worship, for some religious ceremony I was privileged to be the centre of.

The Mayor and his councillors led me up onto a dais in the middle of the main stand overlooking the rugby field, seated me in a golden throne made of horse skin behind an array of microphones.

The congregation fell silent when the Mayor, who walked with a slight limp in his left leg, shuffled up to the row of microphones. Physically he was small in stature, but as he raised his arm in the salute which I'd given earlier on and started speaking, his presence surged out in mounting waves that gathered everyone into his mana. 'Sons and daughters of the Kupenicus Tane and Taniwhanui Line, on your behalf, I welcome our relative and Questor to our Festival of Life!' The crowd applauded as he bowed towards me. 'He has come a long way, as the Sacred Book foretold. For that we thank our Ancestors and the Taniwhanui. We thank our courageous guest for accepting our invitation . . .' He and the congregation obviously knew who and what my role was, but I didn't and was puzzled that I wasn't apprehensive about not knowing. All will be revealed, I told myself. Someone else, who I'd once been and who was still part of me, seemed to know the role the Taniwhanuians had prescribed for me, and was performing each move before I was aware of it. By trying to discover who that person was, I was becoming him again. The unravelling of my role fascinated me, because as I became the person the Festival expected, the Taniwhanuians and the nature of the Festival unravelled too. 'As it is written in the Sacred Book, today is the Twelfth Day of the Twelfth Month of the Twelfth Year of one cycle in the Turning of the Taniwhanui's Faces. And we are gathered to celebrate that auspicious occasion, to remember and offer once again our gratitude to our illustrious pioneering ancestors, especially our otherworlder ones who injected a new genetic strength and ingenuity into our Tangata Maori Line. To our Fountainhead Taniwhanui and the House of Kupenicus Tane, the Source of our Mana and Spiritual Strength; to our Genetic Master Rogerhard Smith who gave us not only his genes but the Taniwhanui line of Equestrian Thoroughbreds which have made our community famous throughout the world, and which continue to provide us with wealth and employment . . .' The congregation — or should I say, Family, because they were related — chanted FULLSTOP at the end of each of his sentences. And I remembered the story of the Eleventh Taniwhanui who loved fullstops. 'Our community is founded on what?' he asked. 'On the Three Faces of Taniwhanui, the Mana of Kupenicus Tane, the Brains and Tenacity of Rogerhard Smith, and the Testicles of the First Taniwhanui Breed!' his Family chorused. The ritual of question and answer continued for a while: it was a catechism similar to that of the Roman Catholic Church which had been banned by the atheist, Rogerhard Smith the First, so I would later read in their Sacred Book. The last question was: 'Do you affirm your faith in the Testament of Smith, in the Truth of the Taniwhanui Line, in the fecund sperm of our Master Rogerhard Smith and his steed, the Taniwhanui Breed?' 'Yes, yes!' they chorused, right arms erect in salutation. 'Yes, we repledge our love of and faith in the Taniwhanui, the heart of our line and breed!' 'Amen!' the Mayor declared. 'Amen!' they replied. Waves of aroha emanated from them and enveloped me, lifting me to my feet which then marched forward, taking me to stand at attention at the edge of the platform/dais in a silence as deep as the Taniwhanui's Pool.

My right arm saluted and held it, while my Family — yes, my Family, for I was the Son of Taniwhanui — bowed their heads and, in breakdance rhythm, chanted this karakia:

One two, we love you true,
Three four, don't shut the door,

Five six, let in the Faith,
Seven eight, keep us from hate,
Nine ten, accept the True Sperm,
Kill kill the Face of Hate!

Kupenicus wasn't born in a day,
His Heir Taniwhanui demands our faith.
Rogerhard Smith perfected the Breed
That is us and the Taniwhanui's Aroha Face.
Kill kill the Face of War!

I listened to my voice joining their chanting: it knew the words, and I clapped my hands to their beat. As I did so the congregation rose to their feet and beat out the rythmn too.

Kill kill the Face of Death!
Renew renew the Face of Peace,
It is the Twelfth Cycle of Life,
Renew renew the Face of Peace,
Kill kill the Face of Death!

Onto the large TV screens above the stands opposite me came closeups of my face shouting: LET THE GAMES BEGIN! The congregation immediately applauded.

Out of the three entrances, one under the opposite stand and two at the opposite sides of the oval, streamed lines of horses, the magnificent Taniwhanui Breed, in pairs, prancing in step to the marching band music now wafting out of the speaker system. The congregation and I cheered and applauded as the horses danced forward, then to the side, back, to the side, reared up on their hind legs, neighed, knelt on their front legs, and bowed towards me and the Council.

For the next fifteen minutes they performed intricate formations and patterns in time to the music. Intermittently my face on the TV screens called: BRAVO, BRAVO, CHILDREN OF THE TANIWHANUI BREED! The horses acknowledged my congratulations with deep bows and neighs.

As the music ended they turned and raced back through the entrances out of which they had emerged.

A hush fell over us. Trumpets announced the next act. There was a loud drum roll.

It was as if the heart of midnight had been cut and shaped into the form of the black stallion that galloped out of the entrance and across the field towards me, halting abruptly, rearing up, front hooves pawing at the dais, his black eyes grasping my reflection and shaking it; and then he danced backwards on his hindlegs, front legs beating the air, my reflection still caught in his eyes. The nerves around my spine tingled. I stripped off my jacket and as the congregation cheered, hurled it into the air. Such magnificent beauty! The stallion danced towards me again, eyes still holding my reflection; stopped and turned side on when it was a few centimetres away from the dais.

When I glanced back at the Mayor and the Council they were standing. I waved. Turned. And jumped off the edge onto the stallion. Just like Tom Mix. The silver-studded saddle spread and embraced my arse and thighs, fitting as if it had been tailor-made for me. I gripped the reins. The stallion started our victorious round, as the congregation clapped in time to his high-stepping. I was surprised yet not surprised that I was such an experienced rider. I raised my arm in salute, and held it as my stallion made his prescribed course round the oval, as he had done for generations of Rogerhard Kupenicus Smiths and every twelfth turn of the Taniwhanui's cycle.

And as the aroha of the congregation wove like an ocean through my head, I imagined I was riding the Taniwhanui, held in the grace of her/his Face of Peace, her/his gigantic lizard body and legs and spiked tail vibrating with all the songs that were her/his heart, songs which held the world on its precarious axis, her/his fiery breath smoking out of her/his long nostrils which knew only the aromas of aroha and kindness.

We danced as they cheered, in my hour of life, as the sun — a fierce firedragon in the eye of the sky above the stadium and the heart of Taniwhanui County — watched and witnessed.

How we danced. In my hour of life.

*

211

When I broke from the spell of the dance, I was again seated in my throne on the dais. RISE, SON OF TANIWHANUI! the congregation called. I rose to my feet. As the soft breeze blew through my clothes, I noticed I was dressed in the diaphanous silk robes of a master hunter. But I still felt no fear, for I was eagerly awaiting the next stage of my unravelling in the unfolding ritual of the Festival.

IT IS YOUR TIME, SON OF TANIWHANUI! they called, rising to their feet and saluting me. I walked to the edge of the dais and raised my arms to the sky. My robes shimmered and wove around me in the strength of the wind. Again the fanfare of trumpets and the roll of the drums. The dais started rising, taking me up and up until I was level with the roof of the stadium, and I was gazing down at the centre of the field. I glanced round: I was alone on the dais.

Below me on the terraces the waves of people rippled and subsided and ebbed and broke, as they shouted: IT IS YOUR TIME, SON OF TANIWHANUI! YOUR TIME! FOR THE LEAP! FOR THE LEAP!

It was as if an expert stage manager was orchestrating the moods of the sky and the wind and the sun and the feel of the hour, for, as I looked up into the heavens, the sky turned a darker blue and the clouds turned black and moved swiftly to obliterate the sun from my vision, and I smelled rain and heard the distant rumble of thunder. My body shivered with the rapid fingering touch of fear.

And into my memory came this from the The Testament of Smith: *To resolve the impasse between the Eleventh Child, the Taniwhanui and Our Ancestors, it was agreed that for the Taniwhanui to turn her/his Face on the Twelfth Cycle and restore Peace and Aroha to the world, our Tribe had to sacrifice its favourite son to her/his appetite.*

And because the Eleventh Child had caused the strife, he was to be the first . . .

Even before the green field below started opening I knew it's secret: it hid the Heart of Taniwhanui County, the Sacred Pool.

The centre line of the rugby field started parting slowly.

RISE, RISE, LORD OF THE POOL, LORD OF LIFE! the people chanted. As the gap widened a mist as white and inevitable as the mist I'd seen on Lake Taupo brimmed up out of the pool and started spreading out across the field and terraces. RISE, RISE, LORD OF THE FACES, LORD OF LIFE! There was a stirring in the mirror black depths of the water which was now lapping the edges of the land as it parted. A stirring in the darkness of the void which had given birth to colour to matter to sound to movement to taste to touch to sight to pain to . . . RISE, RISE, OUR THREE-FACED LORD OF LIFE! RISE! A stirring before the breaking of the fluids before the miraculous birthing of the Word before the Naming of Tangaroa's Gift and Blessing and the reaching out of Kupenicus Tane's cupped hand . . . RISE, RISE, LORD OF THE FACES, RISE AND ACCEPT OUR HUMBLE SACRIFICE!

Out of the birthing emerged the Three-Faced Head.

I stretched my arms and leapt.

The air held me, my arms were wings, my body feathered with glory and accepting joy, as the wind rippled, like thick liquid, through my robes, then I started plunging down. Towards the Faces and the uncoiling body thrusting up out of the pool and the mist.

I was the Eleventh Child, the Sacrifice.

Whoever's reality I was in, it was someone who still believed in Westerns. For as I hurtled down, I heard the trumpeting charge of the cavalry, the thunder of hooves, and I glanced over to my left. Across the field galloped two columns of fully uniformed soldiers straight out of *Custer's Last Stand* starring Errol Flynn. Heading it on the black stallion, her hair flowing behind her like black silk, right arm stretched forward and holding a gleaming sabre, was my wife. Immediately behind her, on white horses, rode our children.

That was all I was to remember of that sequence: it was a film sequence which was erased at the start of the rescue mission, or, put another way, it was a sequence which had ran out of money or imagination to finish itself. To this day I keep trying to resolve it, give it an ending. But only the incompleteness is real because it was the last time I was to see my wife and children. Magnificent in their daring speed and courage.

I was also never to find the Taniwhanui Breed and their Kingdom again. I was to search the files of the Puzzle Palace for it. Nothing.

When I found myself in my van again and on the familiar road to Auckland, through the Waikato, it was evening and I smelled of horse and listening to Gene Autry, singing:

> *Home, home on the range,*
> *Where the deer and the antelope play,*
> *Where seldom is heard a discouraging word . . .*

I longed for my wife and children and the first song of the Taniwhanui's heart.

But there was no time. I was on track again.

As I drove into the falling darkness, I thought of Semeckis' film, *Who Framed Roger Rabbit?* which is a complex and profound statement about reality. The world of Toon Town and its cartoon characters, created since Walt Disney invented the form, are an everyday part of our lives, and we and our world are a part of theirs. We move in and out of each other's worlds, looking for the killer(s) who'd framed Roger Rabbit, as it were. (For those who'd killed my family.) And it is frightening because it was the reality the Tribunal had created and in which I was just one of its cartoon characters which it could erase or dissolve in turpentine.

I braked slowly, the van slowed; I turned the steering wheel, the van turned. I was in control again. The front lights were like chains of yellow steel that the night was using to pull me into its depths, but I wasn't afraid. I pushed my foot down on the accelerator. Opened the window. The night wind rushed in and wrapped itself around my body.

thirteen

Reordinarinising

There was fear in John's eyes when he woke and saw me. But he blinked it away and sat up. Clutching my shoulders, he said, 'Shit, mate, where ya bin? I lost ya!' I walked away from the bed, from the stale-sweat stench of his sheets. Stood with my back to him, gazing through the windows at the city. Shadows of grey clouds were drifting over the buildings, and I felt as if I was drifting too.

'Where and when did you lose me?' I asked.

He slid out of bed. 'At the Palace, mate.' He pulled on his trousers.

'When at the Palace?'

'When ya escaped again. Cheez, man, that was great!'

'How do you know?'

'I've seen the tapes,' he said. 'Ya wanta beer?'

I shook my head. 'You saw my wife refusing to escape with me?'

'Yeah, sorry about that, eh. But ya din't believe her, eh?'

'What do you mean?'

I heard him ambling away to the fridge. I turned so I could see his every move. 'Cold, eh? She had ta tell ya she din't wanna go 'cause they've got ya kids still, their lives were at risk.'

I paused appropriately. 'I never thought of that possibility.'

'Ya din't see ya kids, did ya? They've still got them.' He rushed over and thrust a can of beer into my hand. 'Ya kids still wanna escape. Ya've gotta believe that. Otherwise what's the purpose of it all, eh?' He sucked back his beer. Burped.

'And the hunters are?'

He hesitated. 'Ya know who they are: the Keeper, that bald-

215

headed freak, and Brother Peter, another creep. I watched ya
with them in the Labyrinth Club, remember? Ya really out-
played them, mate.'

I sipped more beer. He was relaxing again. He sat down on
the divan. I strolled over to him. He was fit, strong, fast. I knew
that. After all he was the 'best number eight in the country'.

'Why are you afraid of me?' I asked him as I sat down beside
him.

Twenty minutes later I was in John's black sports car speeding
through Ponsonby down towards the Puzzle Palace. I had the
codes I needed. John was safe again and in his bed and his ripe
smell. I'd left him, sheets and blankets pulled up to his chin.

I realised it was Sunday because the traffic was light.

I didn't bother to hide my presence. Using the correct code,
I got through the Palace's front entrance and past the monitoring
equipment in the lobby. The building was silent, listening. I
took the lift up to the top floor. A noisy fly buzzed around inside
the lift.

As I'd expected, the boardroom, which I'd first seen with
padded chairs around an old oak table, housed the latest computer surveillance and recording equipment. Compact, neat,
shiny, self-functioning. A complex creature.

At the centre of the room was the round central control
computer and swivel chair. I sat down in the chair and studied
the control panel. Awe was what I felt. Awe and admiration
and respect. I was in the mind of the being who knew all knowledge, the past, and the pathways forward, a being who
observed, recorded, controlled and ensured the Game of Life
was played according to the Rules. But I had nothing to lose
now, for I was dead.

I punched in the code that would start opening the Palace's
secrets and treasures. As I waited I thought of that woman, in
the housekeeper's tale, who'd journeyed from room to room to
room, without looking at the doors.

'Kia ora, Citizen!' the androgynous voice greeted me. 'What
can we do for you, Rangatira?'

'I need your help. I'm lost but have to finish the Game.'

'Never mind, Rangatira, we all lose our way sometimes.' I imagined it chuckling to itself.

'Thank you,' I said. 'I need some information about the other players . . .'

'For instance, who?'

I punched in the codes for my wife, my children, John, the Keeper, Brother Peter, and the others. 'My, you have a lot of players, eh,' it chortled.

It didn't withhold anything. It put the information on the screens at the speed my mind could absorb it. Just over two hours. I was pleased and surprised at my rate of retention.

I made up my mind and asked, 'I also need to know about myself?'

'Naughty, naughty!' it laughed. 'You know the Rules, e hoa! The Game of Life demands that you, the Questor, the Searcher, must find out about yourself on your own. Otherwise, the Game has no purpose. Our quests are to find ourselves, eh!' It talked just like the master computers in twentieth-century fiction and films.

I then punched in the President's Code. It made no comment. The information came on. I sensed it had a wise sense of irony.

It was 2 p.m. when I left the Palace. Bright sunshine was swimming through the city but the cold southerly eased its insistent fingers into my face and hands. I was dancing inside though. A conspirator sated with the secrets of the Puzzle Palace and the President, and the feeling that the master computer was enjoying the challenge I was posing our civilisation.

I checked into the Selwyn Muru Hotel under the name Graham Greene. Showered and dressed in my most inconspicuous suit. *'Freedom's just another word for nothing left to lose!'* the master computer had hummed just as I was leaving the boardroom.

What is evil? Goodness? Heroism? In a world without permanent death, without war, violence, rivalry, jealousy, megalomania, poverty — or, whenever our 'darker selves' (the President's phrase) threatened, they were easily reordinarinised.

Randomly I chose the suburb of Epsom, and drove up Manukau Road, in the heavy stream of traffic. At Greenwoods Corner I stopped at the lights. A middle-aged woman, in white slacks that emphasised the fullness of her buttocks, crossed with her panting Alsatian. She reminded me of my wife. I U-turned and headed back down Manukau Road.

I drove around for about an hour. When I was sure I was lost, I stopped at the roadside.

It was a street like any other in that area. Prosperous but not visibly so; the houses comfortably painted so as not to be conspicuous; lawns, gardens, hedges all neatly trimmed and free of weeds. The street rolled downhill from me and up to a hill and some pohutukawa trees and other hills like that hill and other streets like that street. An ordinary neighbourhood for ordinary people, the President's ideal people.

I got out of the car. The southerly had vanished but I anticipated its return. I put on my overcoat and walked downhill. I closed my eyes and walked ninety-nine paces; stopped and turned around on the spot until I didn't know which direction I was facing. Then opened my eyes.

I was in front of a house with a green verandah, and a red roof. Number 27 in brass on the white mailbox beside the gate through which a narrow concrete path led. Beside it, to my right, was a bed of clipped roses, and a small lawn around a grapefruit tree laden with fruit. A garage with an automatic door stood to my left as I took the path.

Three concrete steps up to the glass front door that was edged with varnished timber. Thick rubber doormat with HOME indented in pink on it. The door of opaque glass held my featureless reflection. Along the verandah stood wooden garden chairs and a bench, newly painted.

My fingers closed around the doorbell. I turned it once, twice. It BRRINNGGED! like any other doorbell. Across my expecting breath I counted the thudding footsteps of slippered feet on thick carpet.

When the door clicked open and was pulled back, I thought of a large TV screen opening inwards to reveal its truths.

It *was* a TV screen, for the truth of the President stood there, smiling that loving smile I'd seen on the screen most of my life.

A breathing metre away from me, in his light grey sweater, grey trousers, brown woollen slippers, with bags under his eyes and red veins tendrilled across his nose and cheeks, he looked older, smaller, balder than his public image. More real and approachable. Even vulnerable.

'Good evening,' he said. I sensed no wariness. His eyes were a darker brown than on TV.

'Is this the residence of Mr J. S. Linn?'

He nodded, still smiling. 'I am he,' he said.

'Are you — are you sure?'

'Yeah. Of course I am, mate. I'm just an ordinary bloke like all the blokes in my quiet street, my neighbourhood. You could've knocked on any door around here and a bloke just like me would've answered your knock.'

'*The* Mr Linn who's our President?'

Chortling softly, he said, 'Yeah, but any one of the blokes or wimmin could've been chosen. I was bloody lucky, eh. Or unlucky — it's a hell of a lot of work and worry.' Even his crowns weren't unusual. 'Anyway, don't just stand there. It's bloody freezing. Come in.'

He put an arm round my shoulders and steered me into the house and up the well-lit corridor that was tropical in temperature and smelled of crushed pine needles. 'Sorry about the mess this place is in. I'm a widower. My missus passed away ten years, ten months, ten days ago.'

'I'm sorry.'

'Young blokes like you needn't feel sorry. I don't any more. My life's almost over. Retiring, you know. Earned it all right.' He led me into the sitting room and sat me on the settee that faced the bar. A fire was burning fiercely to my left. 'Beer? Got Apa Lager, a good brew,' I thanked him.

As he got it out of the fridge behind the bar, he glanced over at me and said, 'Been expecting you.' He opened the two bottles. Their caps clinked across the bar top. 'That's me missus.' I looked up at the framed photograph that hung over the bar. 'She was twenty-two then.' A pretty brunette with short hair, high cheekbones, gleaming eyes and a winning smile.

'Very beautiful,' I said.

'Yeah,' he whispered.

'Why didn't you reincarnate her?' I decided to pursue him. He put the bottle in my hand, and sat opposite me in an armchair.

'Cheers, mate!' he said. We drank. It *was* a brisk invigorating brew.

'Good brew, all right,' I remarked.

'Yeah. Owned by Habib Breweries of Taupo.' He drank again. 'She didn't want to be . . .' He stopped.

'Resurrected?' I prompted.

'Yeah. She wrote in her will: no reincarnation. She also made me promise.' He withdrew into his sadness.

I waited a few minutes and then asked, 'What did she die of?'

He didn't seem to be listening. 'She was a bloody good flautist. Played in the Auckland Symphonic.' Paused. Drank again. He blinked and sat forward and out of his memories. 'I was expecting you sooner or later.'

'Why?'

'To blame me for the awful mess you've made of your search, eh!' An impish smile.

'Just me?'

He shook his head. 'Sometimes searchers come. I don't mind 'cause you and a few others are special jokers.' He got us some more bottles.

'But we're all equal in our ordinariness,' I reminded him.

He chuckled. 'Yeah, but some of us are more ordinary than others!'

'Good one,' I said.

'Cheers, mate!' He laughed. We drank. 'You know of course

that each searcher finds what he already believes, eh? And because we're raised to believe in the equality of ordinariness as a guarantee against anarchy, that's what we find in our quests.' He settled back in his armchair, becoming the President we saw on TV. 'We believe in letting everyone live out their urges, drives, impulses etc, etc. We deny little. We allow total freedom of expression . . .' As he spoke, his eyes turned inwards to the world as his audience. 'So we're free of jealousy, envy, covetousness etc, etc. Take your search, or, should I say, the most recent episode of it. We wanted and expected you not to revert . . .' He stopped abruptly and glanced at me.

'That sounds interesting,' I urged him.

Smiling, he said, 'For a sec there I forgot *who* you were and what you are becoming. And I must be careful, eh.'

'Why?' I was surprised by my directness.

'Aha, mate. You're a dangerous bloke. You're not ordinary. We tried to make you ordinary but you've changed.'

'Reverting into what?'

'Of that I can't speak,' he said. I imagined him laughing to himself, just like the master computer had done when I'd asked it for information about myself. 'Remember histories are banned, mate!'

'But I'm dead, aren't I?' I sensed again his suspicion. He hesitated. 'I failed to rescue my wife and kids. So . . .'

He nodded. 'You're not dead, mate. I'm not talking to a kehua. You're flesh and bone. You're as real as the beer I'm drinking.'

'But in the Game, I'm not a player any more?'

He got us more beer. He stumbled as if he was tipsy already. 'Getting too bloody old for this, eh. Can't hold me own.' But I knew he was deadly sober.

The evening was filtering through the windows. He pulled the curtains across and switched on the lights. 'I knew you'd reread the Palace correctly,' he said unexpectedly. 'Shit, I knew it. And it made me feel proud. I shouldn't feel proud though, 'cause what's going to happen to our society if everyone challenges and rereads all our beliefs and realities, eh?' He

221

wagged his forefinger at me. 'By the way, you're not dead. Not yet, anyway.' I pretended puzzlement. 'Don't try and bullshit me, mate. You know the Game's not over yet. Cheers!'

Two bottles later, he described how I'd stormed the Palace, skewered Brother Peter and so on. His retelling was elaborate, funny, insightful. He kept congratulating my courage and ingenuity. His flattery was winning. I relaxed. And, after four more beers, I was relaxed enough to laugh with him, knowing I knew a lot about his life, his history, and he didn't know I knew.

'I never had any kids. No sir, no kids. We — the missus and I — could have, but she had her flute and career and the nation was my child. Every kid here is my kid. I love them all and I share myself among all of them. That's what a leader's supposed to do, eh . . .'

'What about me?' I interrupted. He was still for a moment. His face focused on mine. I couldn't look away. Tears formed in his eyes and my reflection was trapped in them.

'Bugger it, you get old and you blubber about everything and anything.'

'What about me?' I repeated.

He sprang up out of his chair. 'Bugger you!' He snapped. 'Why do you always have to be different, eh? Why?' Fists clenched at his sides, he thumped back into his chair.

'Do you love me?' I pursued him.

'Of course I love you. I love all the children of our beloved country.'

'Crap,' I said clearly. 'Crap!'

'You shouldn't speak to your elders like that, boy!' He was leaning forward, face thrust at me.

'I'm not a *boy*, you bloody racist!'

He blinked. The power surging up in him frightened me. 'I'm not a racist!'

'You called me a boy because of my colour!' I watched his eyes. They burned. Everything would melt in that fire.

'You're brown. That's the colour of healthy shit!' He laughed. 'The colour of crap!' He reached over and slapped my left knee. 'Jesus, mate, you're cleverer than I thought.'

'What do you mean?' I pretended.

'You're trying to con me, mate.' It was then that I had to laugh with him. 'Yeah, like you did years ago!'

'You're one of the Tangata Moni, the True Ones,' he told me later. 'Like the three madly brave ones who helped you break into the Palace, eh.' He watched me struggling to accept his revelation. 'Yeah, mate, I know because I was the Minder who took care of you.' He paused again. Drank. His face was sweating. 'You're a fucking hardy lot,' he whispered. 'Tough bastards. We've not been able to tame you. Ten per cent of you refuse to be tamed.' He explained what I already knew, that the Tangata Moni were descendants of ancient Maori rebels and urbanised Polynesians from the islands, and rebel Pakeha. A mongrel brew which didn't succeed in erasing the defiant Maori-Polynesian ingredient in the mix. No degree of reordinarination worked with them. Over the years the Tribunal decided to leave them alone, at least those who didn't attack our society openly. As long as they scavenged at the edges, didn't harm anyone or any property, they were left to their own devices. Hopefully they would become extinct, destroyed by poverty and natural diseases — they refused our medicine.

His first job, after he'd graduated from university as a zealous, optimistic psychologist/political scientist, was that of Chief Minder, in the Auckland area, of any Tangata Moni who appeared before the Tribunal. He found them a fascinating study. His practical work at the Palace, as a student, had taught him the latest surveillance and recording techniques. He applied them to his wards. In a short time he was steeped in their history, customs and traditions, behavioural patterns and other ways. He even learned their language. From that, with the help of other young scientists at the Palace, he experimented with young Tangata Moni in new ways of reordinarinising them and other deviants. His initial findings were published in his first major study, *Humane Techniques of Reordinarinising Tangata Moni and Other Deviants*. 'A study which you got out of the

Library the other day,' he reminded me, and laughed.

It was strange, but the techniques, they found, worked for only about ninety per cent of Tangata Moni deviants. (The vast majority of them had been assimilated successfully into our way of life, he added.) When he became Senior Minder at the Palace, he got more funding and research staff. 'You see, mate,' he said, 'I wanted to crack the mystery of the uncrackable ten per cent.' He paused and studied my face as if he didn't quite believe I was there. 'And you, son, were a godsend!' He laughed for a while, remembering. 'You and your mates were a handful, a real nasty lot. You were their leader, and, cripes, you were a real trickster. Yeah, just like Sidnous Tane Jackson in the Tangata Moni legends.' He sucked back his beer. 'You were about sixteen when you first came into my orbit, mate.' He rose and, stretching his back, yawned loudly. 'I'm not a good storyteller, not like you were, and certainly not in the housekeeper's league. So I'll turn on the file I started keeping on you the moment you danced into my office, handcuffed to a cop, and you started bullshitting me poetically!'

On the far wall was a large bookcase. He pressed a switch beside it. The bookcase parted, revealing a screen. 'Presto, just like a Gothic novel, eh? Secret doorways into torture chambers of skeletons and other shocking revelations!' He picked up the remote control and pressed a code.

On to the screen I came. My history, the President's version of that history. 'Yeah, see if you recognise and like your former lives, eh,' he chuckled. 'See if your first identity isn't scary!'

He returned to his armchair, pushed it back to form a bed, and lay on it. 'Help yourself to the beer and anything else. Wake me when you've had enough of your lives.' He closed his eyes and folded his arms across his chest.

fourteen

Records

File Number 9999.007
Patimaori Jones: Birthdate, birthplace, and father unknown.

Insucking breath when I saw my mother's name: *Patricia Manaia Graceous.* Two years before I'd become a state ward she'd died of an unspecified disease. (According to the file, only real Tangata Moni still died from 'natural' diseases because they refused modern cures and treatment.) Nothing else about her.

Not much known about my first fifteen years. The file assumed I'd been born and raised a Tangata Moni at the fringes of 'civilised' society, probably under the city, in the Tangata Moni sanctuaries. (Rebels are about other rebels who'd gone underground to survive, and about the literature about rebels!)

I couldn't identify with Patimaori's photos. The cloaked eyes, the cheeky smile, the long black hair pulled back in a bun, the face of one the President described as: 'Illiterate teenage deviant with a criminal record as long as his two arms; enforcer in the Central Chapter of the notorious Black Mana Gang. At sixteen the subject is already a hardened and dangerous deviant. (He may have committed even murder.) Tests have shown he is exceptionally intelligent, though he hides this well under a bewitching smile, but we know he's an incorrigible confidence trickster. Don't trust the smile, the fast talk, the charm.' Films of Patimaori's charm and almost non-stop spiel came on. God, so much energy and vitality — it was beautiful and frightening. At sixteen he was already an adult who controlled whatever situation he was in, would kill in defiance, smiling. I was reading a stranger, yet I felt I knew him. (What was I saying? He was me!)

Everything about Patimaori was in the file: from his bio-
logical makeup down to his DNA print; his medical history, the
details of his teeth, eyes, organs, brain shape and composition;
his emotional and psychological charts; the nature of his courage
— of this the President wrote: 'He pretends cowardice, cynicism
and indifference to others but he is fearless when he wants something. For instance, while he's been with us, he's stolen our latest
info about agricultural world prices and sold it to his contacts
who've used it to harvest fortunes on the futures market. And we
can't pin a thing on him. The bastard's laughing at us!'

There was enough information about him to reconstruct
another Patimaori or to erase him completely.

'Today I discovered a possible way of reordinarinising him,'
the President wrote. 'No matter what he says to the contrary,
he's ashamed of being illiterate. Next week we'll start teaching
him to read and write. The magic of the printed word will tame
him, convert him to civilisation, make him thirst for our cargo,
like primitives in the past.'

The file was full of Patimaori's 'conversion', his reordinarinising. Within a year he was literate and 'loving' it. The
President wrote: 'Have decided to teach him everything about
surveillance, even its history (which is banned). Want him to
trust me. His background and personality are excellent for his
becoming a hunter.'

There was nothing in the file about Patimaori's education in
surveillance and 'hunting' — such training is top secret. And, at
the age of twenty-one, he re-emerged in the file as *Supremo
Jones, Hunter 3rd Class*, in the Palace's Academy for Hunters.
(He'd confessed his history to the Tribunal and was free to be a
new person. No record of that history in the file though.) His
photo showed that only his colour differentiated him from his
class of hunters. The luminous energy and cockiness was held in
check, his eyes were intensely serious. The President wrote: 'He's
the ideal cadet, loyal, dedicated and fearless. He feels like a son,
my son.' The file showed his remarkable progress through the
Academy. His teachers' comments, at the end of each semester,
were full of praise. 'Out of primitive clay and violence,' wrote

his physics teacher, 'we've shaped the ideal youth, the hunter par excellence.'

He graduated from the Academy as *Hunter 1st Class*, assigned to the Palace, to Joseph S. Linn, the future President, for 'special assignments'. There was no record of his assignments while he was at the Palace. Why? But he climbed as J. S. Linn climbed towards the Presidency. In every photo, Supremo Jones was hovering protectively near or around his patron. Supremo Jones looked sleeker, polished, with an almost imperceptible grin that cut like a scalpel. Nothing in the files about assassination attempts or the deaths of political opponents.

'Next week, on Monday, Supremo and I will be elevated to the Presidency,' wrote Linn. 'I don't want the position: it is self-destructive, power destroys its wielders; but we will not be changed by it because we will be doing it out of love of our people . . . Supremo is a new man. Through him I have proven we can reordinarinise anyone, even the most hardened of the Tangata Moni, turn them into ideal, self-sacrificing citizens . . .'

Supremo was twenty-nine when Linn appointed him Guardian and Grand Hunter of the Bureau of Hunters. Nothing in the files about his work as Grand Hunter. But he must have performed exceptionally well: each Christmas the President awarded him the Star of Merit for meritorious service. Only one photo of Supremo at those awards: He was looking straight at the camera, the eyes were black gems and the grin was gone.

There was a gap, I figured, of about five years, then a continuation of Supremo Jones's file appeared. The President filled the five-year gap with just this comment: 'He is reverting to his Tangata Moni preferences for wanton violence, duplicity, and, most unexpectedly of all, a sadistic enjoyment of his incomparable ability for hunting and liquidating enemies of our beloved Tribunal. For a long time I've ignored my advisor's reports that Supremo, who is my son, is having a 'breakdown', a reversion. With great sorrow, I've signed the order for his reordinarination. We have to find out where we went wrong in our methods. We can't have citizens reverting . . .'

File Number 1000.008
Eric Mailei Foster — Bank Clerk.

No names of parents or birthplace or birthdate. For a moment, as I read the file, I didn't recognise my own name. When I did it was a fist blow that winded me for a few seconds.

The file was recorded by a Dr Don Storm, the President's closest adviser and confidant. He wrote: 'It's been two years since we started. Have finally erased Supremo Jones and replaced him with an ordinary, peace-loving husband and provider, who will find a suitable wife, Margaret Essing, a bank secretary. One more year and they'll meet in a small South Island town and a respectable job in the bank. The President, by the way, wants us to include, in Foster's life, a wide and deep knowledge of modern fiction and poetry, especially that of our country. (The President is a fan for the twentieth century.) Foster's love of literature should stop him becoming bored with small town life. It should also keep at bay any reversion to Supremo.'

I didn't bother to read any further: I knew my own history from when I was born as a bank officer in Okarito. I skipped that and concentrated on Dr Storm's annual reports to the President about my life. It was full of short, pithy phrasing:

'Progressing well, no sign of Supremo anywhere, no signs of reversion . . . Has fitted well into Okarito and the life of a banker. Good prospects of becoming a bank manager one day. Is respected by the community. His children — normal, ordinary like their mother — models of exemplary citizens. Happy family bonded by love . . .'

For almost ten years those were the reports. An interesting note by the President to Dr Storm: 'Strange, but I sometimes miss Supremo, and, before him, Patimaori. I miss their tricks, energy, rebellion, primitiveness.'

Since my capture as the teenage Patimaori, I'd not had any privacy or choice. My life had been surveyed, scrutinised, analysed and recorded. That had made it easier for them to erase Patimaori and replace him with Supremo, a highly trained bodyguard, assassin, a character straight out of the President's addiction to twentieth-century thrillers and sci-fi. Which in turn had facilitated the creation of Eric Mailei Foster, the bank clerk, another character out of fiction rooted in Franz Kafka's faceless nightmares.

No privacy. Surveillance was total, down to my DNA, my thoughts and dreams. Cheated of a real life, a secret self.

We were mirrors of selves within other mirrors set up by the Palace and its Keepers, in the Game of Life in which nothing was left to chance.

I switched off my history, my selves.

He was watching me when I swivelled my chair to face him. The flickering flames of the fire rippled across his face and smile. 'So what do you think?' he asked, sitting up.

'Who am I now?' I replied.

'I'd say a combination of Patimaori and the controlled menace of Supremo seem to be dominant. Probably because you've been fighting for survival lately.'

'Or it's all mirrors, all fabrication, a history you've fabricated . . .'

'See, I tol' ya: you're becoming the sceptic cynic Supremo was. Don't you believe anything?' He grinned, and he reminded me of John.

'It's fiction, eh. A novel or novels you've brought back to life . . .'

'Not me, mate. Our majority. Just ordinary people. They decided. They created our wonderful society. And what's wrong with that, eh?'

'The Game is a melodramatic script out of junk TV . . .'

He laughed. 'It's not that bad, is it? Look at 99.5 per cent of our world population? They're content, happy, free even from stress and mental illness. And they live wholly in the present, needing nothing.'

'And death?'

'Yes, but they can choose . . .'

'And you and the other Presidents decide everything.'

It would be easy to say he was insane, corrupted by power. But he wasn't. He was a 'stereotyped' hero/mad scientist out of the twentieth century. A mixture of Dr Who, Shane, Dr Strangelove, Batman, the Green Hornet, Superman, Saveasi'uleo, Blade Runner, Dr Fu Manchu, Animal Farm, 1984, the Joker, Captain Nemo, Dr Spock, Huxley's utopias, Galupo, who couldn't break free of the role the scriptwriter had created for him. He'd 'created' Supremo, the Blind Recorder, John, the Keeper and his villainous colleagues, and the others I'd encountered on my quest.

It was as if he had read my thoughts. 'Don't be so critical in your reading of my text!' he chortled.

'The problem is, it's real!'

'Yeah, and it's an epic . . .'

'And am I the villain?'

He nodded. 'We can't allow reversions.' His was the pronouncement of a sentence, a white chill out of our society's heart. He moved over to me and covered me with his shadow. 'It was my fault!' he whispered. I glanced at him again. 'Yeah, I allowed my attraction to the wild and unusual, the rebel, the non-conformist, to flaw your perfection, and thereby built "unhappiness" into your life and mine.' He placed his hand on my left shoulder. It was warm. 'I'm sorry, son.'

The whole mythology of atua and their human creations crowded in on me: Tane creating the first woman and, out of their incestuous union, came Hine-nui-te-Po; the flawed and arrogant Adam and Eve wanting to be God; Frankenstein; Darth Vader; the Terminator . . .

No, Linn wasn't mad. He'd solved the Quest's puzzle. He could read all the Palace's readings and combinations. No mysteries and secret unexplored paths and readings left. No other possibilities.

'Another beer, mate?' He asked as I rose to my feet. I shook my head. 'As I've said, I've decided to retire from this demanding job and join the missus.' He brushed some fluff off my coat. He smelled old but clean. I looked into his gaze as he said, 'I'd hoped you'd be my replacement, son.' It was too much like Darth Vader revealing he'd fathered Luke Skywalker, and was therefore incapable of killing him. 'But I must put the interests of our society before my own, eh.'

I moved swiftly, silently.

fifteen

Black Rainbow

Back at my hotel I enjoyed a long hot shower and slept until evening. Again the ponderous dance of the whales and their strange singing played in my dreaming of my wife and children suspended in the amniotic tides of my fear. Every time I reached out to grasp them they floated away. Away. Away. Echoing in the whale's haunting singing.

I woke and found my pyjamas and sheets drenched with sweat, showered again and dressed in a track suit.

After seeing Patimaori's file in the President's records, my descent to the Whare through the sewer stench and dark was a return to my beginnings.

I sat in the empty Whare. My mother was there around me and I could attribute to her any face, shape, personality I wanted. Yet I wanted who she'd actually been. I didn't want fiction, a figment of my conjuring. I wanted *her*, Patricia Manaia Graceous. But knew they'd erased all records of her.

I shut my eyes and concentrated, searching for her.

She was in front of me on the stretcher, her lower half shrouded in white hospital sheets. I looked up into her face. The long black hair, which used to shine like new lava and in which I played my imaginary games about ancestral genie and tohunga, was now sparse and grey; her skin was an eroded geography of wrinkles and scars. Only the unusually brilliant crystal blue of her eyes, in which I used to swim with joy, hadn't changed. She reached down and held my face between her hands. The warm handprints would linger for years. But I didn't want to cry. Not for her. She'd abandoned me and my father who, a year later,

232

had abandoned me too. I needed no one. I'd survived on my own. 'I'm sorry, Pati,' she whispered. 'I asked them to bring you here to see me.' I didn't want to look at the tears in her eyes. She was a stranger who wore my ravaged face. I withdrew my face from her grip. 'I had to leave you and your father,' she pleaded. I wasn't going to let her fool me again. 'I left because I didn't love your father any more and was afraid of him.' She was behaving and talking just like someone in an otherworlder soap opera. 'I also fell in love with another man.'

'An otherworlder?' I accused her.

'No, one of us . . .'

'But he chose to become one of them.'

'I was tired of poverty, of being persecuted and hunted, of your father's refusal to look at the peace and prosperity . . .'

'You abandoned me for that? It had nothing to do with me, yet you ditched me!' She reached out and touched my arm. I edged away and paced around her hospital room which smelled faintly of talcum powder and oranges. Through the windows, everything wore the gold of the midday light as a living skin.

I didn't know they'd entered until Aeto said, 'Hail, Super-Questor!'

'We waited for days for you,' Fantail called. They hurried over. I reached out and gathered them into my arms. For a moment they held on to me, then they moved away. Awkwardly, they sat at the table opposite me. I just looked at them. They reminded me so much of my children.

'I had to find out,' I ended up saying.

'Find out what?' she asked.

'I'm glad to see you,' I said. 'Where's Manu?' They looked at each other.

'He's disappeared,' she murmured. 'The city's empty of us, eh. It's never been like this before.'

'Yeah, we can't find any of our friends,' he added. 'Any of the True Ones.'

'I'm one,' I said. They looked puzzled. So I told them about Patimaori Jones.

'Good one,' said Aeto after I'd finished.

'Yeah, neat, For a while there, I thought your suntan was painted on, eh,' laughed Fantail.

'For all we know, you could be our older brother,' Aeto said.

'Naw, more like our granddad!' she said.

A few minutes later, while they were putting food out on the table, she remembered my Hotere lithograph. 'Here, bloody weird art,' she said, getting it out from behind books on the bookshelf.

I wiped the glass with tissue while they watched me. 'It's ticking away madly,' I said. 'This clock.' I pointed at the lithograph.

'By the way, they're showing your Quest on TV,' he said. 'Third episode was on las' Friday.'

'Good stuff!' she remarked. 'You should see it. Lots of action. They're telling everyone you're the classic Searcher-Hero. Better than questors like Ulysses, Jason, Sinbad, Konai Hellus, Nat Lees, Momoe Sweetwar, Mad Max, Maui Potiki, Samson Samisoni, Martonious Sanderson, Kerisiano Malifus — whoever they were.'

'What about the murders I was supposed to have committed?'

'They're shitsilent about those. Not a bloody word,' he replied.

'By the way, they're looking for the Keeper and Big Nurse,' she said.

'Aren't they part of the Tribunal's crew?' I asked.

'Shit, no,' she said. 'They don't know who put them into your Game, your story. Where they came from.' She sat down beside me. 'We're looking forward to seeing how your Quest ends, eh.'

'Yeah!' Aeto said.

'Your TV Quest, I mean,' she added. 'Do you think the otherworlders are going to get a shock?'

I just smiled. 'Where do you think Manu is?'

'If any bastard touches my brother, I'll . . .'

'Cut off their marbles?' Aeto interjected.

'Yeah, and fry and eat 'em!' We laughed at that.

I'd come full circle through three lives, in my Quest. To a home, and the joy of being home. To the realisation that we were the remnants of a history of rebellion, a refusal to be other-worlder.

'How do you ask someone who died a long time ago for her forgiveness?' I heard myself asking. When they looked at me, I told them I was referring to my mother. 'She died when I was a teenager. Of an incurable illness called otherworlderness. And guilt.'

'She must've been very beautiful,' Fantail said. Yes, I nodded, and I was once again in the blue depths of Patricia Manaia Graceous's eyes. And in the prison of her hospital room.

'I've had to live with that guilt,' my mother was saying, 'of having left you.' I watched myself gazing out of the hospital windows. At my life that lay ahead. In search of her. And her forgiveness.

Manu saved me by entering the Whare. We asked where he'd been. 'Looking for hope,' he said, smiling. We shook hands. 'I think they're searching for an important deviant,' he added. 'All escape routes in and out of the city have been closed. And I don't mind admitting I'm scared . . .' I reached out and put an arm around him. 'It's times like this you need . . .'

'Minties?' Fantail completed his remark.

'No, it's times like this you need a sense of humour,' Aeto said.

'And our family,' I added. My mother's handprints were still warm on my face.

They prepared a simple meal of bread, cheese, boiled eggs and red wine. We ate, saying little. We were entombed in the city's belly yet I felt free of it, as it trembled and vibrated around us.

I told them what had happened since I last saw them.

'It was meant to be, wasn't it?' she asked.

I nodded. 'Yes, in their Game of Life, we are fulfilling our pre-programmed roles. But we are free, for no one can predict how we'll fulfil those roles. The possibilities of how we do that are unlimited. The Tribunal tries to rule out all uncertainty and chaos. So we scare them because, by living deliberately outside their Rules, we are some of that uncertainty.'

'Many of my mother's stories were about that,' Aeto said. We spread out our sleeping bags and lay on them, while he narrated one of the stories. The city listened too.

'Because the story I'm telling is only a subsitute for what actually happened, my telling is the only reality we have of that,' Aeto echoed his mother. 'And every telling is different, so what happened is different with every telling.

'Once there was a bird — the story doesn't say what kind of bird it was, or its name, size or shape. The story also doesn't say when the bird was born. But it lived in a nest on the topmost branch of a banyan tree. Don't ask me what banyans are: they're extinct and our story doesn't say what kind of trees they were. But this banyan could have been quite immense because the story says the bird had to take two hours to fly from the bottom of the tree to its nest. But we can't be certain of that either, because we don't know how fast the bird could fly; it may have been a slow bird.

'We know its colour because the story says it was white; we also know its sound because the story says it "tweeted in a thin whispery way". But even that isn't certain . . . This story is slow, we're getting bogged down in uncertainty, in questions about details, in our search for certainty. Enough to accept here that everything is uncertain, build that into our telling, so we can get on with the story. Okay?

'Well this bird lived in a nest in a banyan tree. It had lived there for three years — the story doesn't say why it's important to itself that the bird lived in that tree for three years. One sunny October morning — don't ask why October — it woke to the laughter of children. At the foot of the banyan nine children were juggling wooden balls. Please don't ask why nine, why wooden balls! We have to accept what the story gives us. From that height, looking down at the children, the bird thought the children were trying to lob the balls up to it. So in its tweety bird language, it called to the children to lob their balls higher and harder.'

Aeto's uncertain, always-qualifying, ever-questioning retelling of his mother's story was sending me to sleep. I noticed the others were drowsy too, but we were too polite to tell him. We persisted.

'How a bird recognises spheres to be wooden balls is a profound question which allows us to again delve into the reality of bird perception and our perceptions of birds and the reality of narratives that assume birds can recognise balls. For us to believe a story, we have to accept so much uncertainty in the story itself. But our existence is like that, isn't it?' I tried to ponder his mother's heavy philosophical telling but my attention couldn't hold on to it. My head was filling with sleepy fog: that was my only certainty then. I clenched my fists, digging my nails into my palms to try and stay awake. 'Anyway, the bird finally got tired of calling to the children and flew down towards them. Because it had once been stoned by a man with a white beard, the bird was wary of humans, so, as it spiralled down, it watched the children for any hostility. One spiral, two spirals, three.

'They didn't see it until it was swooping across their heads. Then the youngest, a girl, cried: "Weeeee, weeee!" and pointed up at it. The youngest children always seem to get the wise parts in a story. We all have different reasons why. The bird soared up and, hovering, watched them again. "Come down, come down!" the children called . . .'

When I woke, it was almost midnight; the Whare was swimming in the yellow-green light; the others were asleep. I sat up and watched them. In the light and stillness of the Whare, they appeared as if they were in eternal sleep, like Snow White, who, with the magic kiss of another more just age, would wake again to living happily-ever-after. I remembered Aeto had left the bird of uncertainty suspended in the sky of his mother's story. I remembered he'd also left his story about being in the House of the Chefs unfinished. Later in this recording of my life, I would give it this ending:

237

'What happened?' Fantail asked him.

'Yeah, what happened when you lived with the Chefs?' Manu added.

'Well, the whole way I built up that story could only give it one ending,' he murmured. 'From the pigeons in the park to their fucking in my bed could only have ended one way.'

'I'm slow, so you'd better spell it out for me!' Fantail teased him.

Aeto shrugged his shoulders. 'I woke up in my room and found they had turned it into an oven — and I was roasting.' He stopped as if distracted by a noise outside.

'Go on!' Manu said impatiently.

'Yeah, ya mingy teller!' I laughed.

'How did you get out of it?' Fantail said.

'Easy,' he smiled, his eyes filling the air in this story.

'Well, come on then!' Manu grabbed his arm.

'Easy,' he repeated. 'I reprogrammed the computer, the House, to save me . . .'

'But not before you were singed, eh!' Fantail laughed.

'Yeah, not before I began to be cooked pork,' he sighed.

It got him somewhere though, I tried to cheer him up. He looked at me, puzzled. 'It got you Piwakawaka and Manu,' I replied.

'Some bloody consolation!' he said.

The city purred around us, like a cat which had just eaten its fill. The possibilities of Aeto's last story I could spend my life exploring, or, the story itself could, like water trying to find its level, explore all its possibilities in me.

I'd left my mother with the unforgiving boy I'd been in her hospital room.

I left a note telling them I'd be back in the morning. I also left Fantail the bone pendant Heremaia Clatter had given me. I lingered, gazing down at them.

As I ascended from the sewers, I recalled what the master computer had said once to me: 'Have you ever thought that your three brave companions and the other Tangata Moni rebels have been built into the Game, the System, to make sure the Game stays honest, open to self-renewal?'

I got the weapons from my hotel room and drove to Sunnyside Road.

Manu was right: the streets, though empty of people, were full of menace, as if the windows, doors, walls were recording my every move. My car was mirrored in the sleek mirror walls of the buildings, sliding along them and off. I was not adhering.

Sunnyside Road was gone. Its replacement was Housekeeper Street, a cynical challenge that they knew I knew about the erasure but I couldn't do anything about it. I drove through it, everything was different.

As I drove away from Mt Eden the Housekeeper of Stories and Souls danced in my heart. Hers was a fierce and lucid beauty still. I remembered the rainstorm I'd driven through after I'd left her house. The swish of wipers, the roar of the rain, the invading cold. Tonight, the stars were white frangipani petals strewn across her face that was the night sky.

The final episode of my story was being edited and printed, ready for showing as the end of my Quest (on worldwide TV). Soon the editing would catch up with me.

From the Palace records I knew five possible places where I could find the Keeper and Big Nurse. I reread my information and narrowed the hideouts to two.

Just over an hour later, I had them handcuffed to chairs in front of the Palace's master computer, ready for what Supremo Jones had described, in his file, as 'deconstructing'.

'There's nothing to confess,' the Keeper insisted. 'You know from my files, which I'm sure you've read from the Palace Records, that I'm a fictional character the Tribunal (through our very literate President) resurrected from Cocteau's films . . . it's sick, isn't it?' I remained silent. 'For our President and his clones to deliberately put us into real life.'

'Bloody sick!' she snapped. 'Look at me, Kesey created me a stereotype: a sexist stereotype of the insatiably sadistic motherfigure, death-goddess, ball-cracker, eater of men's manhoods.

That was probably okay in a novel but our sick President put me
into real flesh and blood. I'm still trapped in my stereotyped
role. How sick can one be. As fiction I didn't have a chance. As
fact, I'm a monster!'

I punched a code and the androgynous voice said: 'Yes, they
are both telling the truth. But I'd like to remind them that we're
all stereotypes, one way or another. Look at me: I'm the stereotype of the neurotic master computer in pulp science fiction.'

'I didn't ask for your self-pity,' I told it. It seemed to with-
draw into a sulk. 'But you have free will,' I told Big Nurse.

'Shit, you're naive,' she sighed. 'Kesey didn't give me any.
Authors create and manipulate their characters. I wish Kesey
had killed me off in his awful novel.'

'Why are you not with the Tribunal?' I asked them.

'Because we're fed up with being manipulated, being unable
to develop into other selves,' he replied. 'We want to be capable
of repentance.'

'But we can't because we're slaves to the roles the Tribunal
prescribed,' she added.

'Isn't that what you're doing?' he asked me. I was puzzled.
'Aren't you rebelling against your prescribed role in your Game?'

'What role are you playing now, hero?' she asked. 'Eric
Foster, Supremo Jones, or Patimaori?'

'You're trying to confuse me,' I heard myself saying.

'No, they're not,' the androgynous voice said. 'You *are* rebelling. It is in your Game. You're luckier than them; at least you
were a *real* person they found and turned into what they
wanted. These two buggers were fiction!' I imagined it chuckling to itself.

'But he's still in the shit,' she insisted. 'They decided who
and what he was, is, and will be!'

'Well put, sister!' it applauded. 'That is the truth.'

I changed tactics. 'If you're rebelling against the Tribunal
and the President, why are you trying to erase me? I'm fighting
the Tribunal too.'

'Man, you're dumb,' she sighed. 'Bloody dumb!'

'Don't you know yet, epic hero?' he asked.

I uncuffed both of them. 'Thank you,' he said, rubbing his wrists.

'You still don't understand, eh?' she asked.

'There is nothing to understand!' the voice interrupted. I coded it into silence, and asked her to continue.

'Think of Supremo Jones, the blank years in his records when he was being trained to be Guardian of the Hunters . . .' she said.

'Then the blank about his "assignments" the President ordered . . .' he continued.

'You're confusing me some more,' I pretended.

'Confusion or fear?' he asked.

'Shitscared to find out what's in those blanks?' she whispered.

She started saying something else but he said, 'No, let him find out for himself, then he'll really know what free will is.'

'You're our only way out,' she pleaded.

'Yes, you're the only one who can free us of our predetermined roles and fates,' he echoed her.

'We envy Brother Peter and Sister Honey; you freed them. I'm sick of being a sexist stereotype of women, a tyrant, a puritannical villain.'

'But I thought you wanted to kill me,' I pushed them.

'Yes, but in trying to erase you, we knew, or hoped, you'd . . .'

'Say it!' she ordered him.

'I can't,' he begged.

She looked at me through her tears. 'You're meant for greater things,' she said. 'You're one of the Great Questors and, as that, do us a favour.' She couldn't say it either. He leaned down and embraced her.

'It's okay,' I said. 'But before you go, I have to know who killed her.'

'Who?' she asked.

I could barely say it. 'The housekeeper.'

'Ask the Tribunal,' he replied.

It didn't take long to 'deconstruct' them, using the power of the central control computer.

241

Many of us are compelled, instinctively, to return to spiritual sites that are encompassed in the stories of our lives, sites that our creator beings turned themselves into or invested with their mana. For me Maungakiekie was one because it was there that my wife, with her courage and sight, had started our rebellion against the Tribunal. She'd summoned the agaga of our ancient Dead with the Hotere icon to hold back the doomsday clock; she'd linked us again to the earth and our Dead.

Dawn was spilling towards me across the hills, bays and city as I drove up the southern slopes of Maungakiekie. The dew-drops on the grass, fences and trees were astounded eyes which snared the dawn light and held it as it burned whitely. I kept rising up into the light and the ugly Memorial and the lone pine auraed with the memories of my wife and the forgiving presence of my ancestors who'd been erased, physically, from the Hill centuries before.

After parking the car, I stood for a moment and watched Rangitoto as it burned with the dawn in the centre of the harbour. The blood of the sky coned to anchor the atua of volcanoes to the sea.

I got out the Hotere and the weapons, went up and stood under the Memorial and faced the east, as Maui must have waited to trap Ra with his flax snares, but this time I was waiting for Ra to invest me with its essence, turn my flesh and history into sinews of the light that bound everything with its unbreakable genealogy. All creatures, all things, all elements.

Inexplicably around me, cicadas brimmed out of the grass, the singing agaga of our Dead and the earth, and shimmered in waves up into the rising light, as if Maungakiekie itself was breaking and rising in millions of fragments of light, swarming up and away to be part of the dawn and Ra. I held up the Hotere . . .

Later I found a gap between some surface roots of the pine tree. I gazed up into the tree. The intricate maze of branch and leaf seemed a curious observer.

With the knife and dagger, I knelt and dug a hole. My hands were soon covered with the soggy shitbrown earth. My sweat mingled with it. It smelled of dank sap, the mana which kept us alive.

In the hole I placed the Black Rainbow face up. On either side of it I laid the weapons. I read the Hotere clock once more, then, as it ticked vigorously, I pushed the earth onto it, with my hands. Whenua. Fanua. Eleele. Blood. I rubbed it over my face.

From the Memorial, a short while later, I watched three helicopters rising from the helipad on top of the Tribunal building, and cutting across the city and up through the fierce light towards me. Rangitoto watched them too. Four police cars were sirening up the southern road towards the summit and me. The lights on them flashed. At various points on the road around the feet of Maungakiekie the police were setting up road blocks.

I waited.

Joseph S. Linn's killing had been an 'ordinary' erasure. As I'd thrust the cushion down over his grey face, his eyes had smiled. 'It is as was programmed years ago,' he said. 'It was meant to end this way for me in the Game of your life, son. Ya don't need to feel bad about it.' My reflection was pooled lucidly in his eyes. I'd thrust my left hand under and around the back of his head and pushed up while I'd pressed down with the cushion. His head had kicked once, twice in my grip; his body had arched up and then collapsed, subsiding.

I'd stretched his body out on the sofa.

I'd coded his erasure into his computer, which I knew was linked to the Palace.

I wasn't even worried about my future which lay in the *blanks* in Patimaori's/Supremo Jones's histories. Not any more.

As I waited on Maungakiekie.

sixteen

True Confessions

Under house arrest, I awaited my trial in the special guest suite on the top floor of the Palace. It was 'palatial', and linked to K Road's Street of Preferences so I could indulge any needs, except escape — not that I wanted to. The suite had a panoramic view of the city but I kept the curtains drawn, and lived in a halflight similar to that of the Whare. I switched off all television and news sources.

I slept, woke, ate, read, slept. And repeated that pattern, suspended high in the air, shut away from the passing of time and the world. Only my voracious reading of novels kept me in the society of people, age, love, death, all fictional of course. ('Art ain't life,' my wife would've said.) Only my passion for the literature of the twentieth century, especially that from the 1960s to the 1980s, programmed into me by President Linn, anchored me to place, country, history. I became more addicted to the work of Tangata Maori writers, my ancestors, finding in them the identity and past I'd been denied. A past which spoke of Tangata Maori resistance to otherworlder occupation, racism and arrogance. A past of enormous loss and anger. And which gave me a voice and a gafa:

> Who I am and my relationship to everyone else depends on my whakapapa, on my lineage, on those from whom I am descended. One needs one's ancestors therefore to define one's present. Relationships with one's tipuna are thus intimate and causal. It is easy to feel the humiliation, anger and sense of loss which our tipuna felt. And to take up the kaupapa they had.
>
> — Donna Awatere, *Maori Sovereignty*

244

And the more I became of that whakapapa, the more profoundly I missed (and loved) my Tangata Maori aiga who'd been reordinarinised into otherworlders. I wanted to descend into the depths of the Palace and see how they were, but I knew I wouldn't be able to alter them.

Anis was born three weeks prematurely, during a fierce rainstorm, while I was out fishing for whitebait. I came home with just a cupful of whitebait to be told of her birth, cooked two fritters and rushed them to the hospital. The rain kept falling and I was drenched. Margaret ate the fritters hungrily, while I gazed in amazement at the baby in the incubator. So small and red and shrivelled up like a cooked crayfish, with tubes feeding it intravenously. 'She's your kid, all right. She's as ugly as you!' she laughed. 'I brought you the whitebait,' I said. 'Two miserable fritters for one whole baby? That's not a fair swap!'

Anis's healthy survival of her premature birth indicated how easily she was going to go through life. We nicknamed her Inanga.

Elem's birth, however, was difficult. It took two days. Margaret refused to be anaesthetised; she screamed as the pain got worse.

When I saw Elem in her hospital cot, she glared at me. I picked her up; she peed in my arms. Elem was to be defiant; she was to grow according to her tantrums and rebellious ways. But we never questioned our love for her and her love for us. She conferred upon herself the pet name of Wahinetoa. Everyone came to call her Toa.

Mysteriously, because the common cold had been eradicated years before, Leahcim nearly died of a cold soon after he was born. His health was to be precarious most of the time, suffering from diseases that were supposed to have been eradicated, but that didn't stop him from becoming expert at anything he tried.

Strange that I was recalling the circumstances of my children's births while I was awaiting my trial and a choice of death.

I also worried about Piwakawaka, Aeto and Manu because

in them was the survival of our people; they were our Nga Morehu.

Only three features of my trial room differed from the ones I'd been interrogated in previously. There was no portrait of the President; the walls were completely of glass; and it was twice the size of the other ones. I sensed TV cameras and a large crowd behind the glass. Also a tide of reporters. I kept wiping my palms on the knees of my trousers, as I awaited the Tribunal.

To my right, at the computer console, the Blind Recorder sat *reading*. He'd not aged since I'd last seen him. His glasses read the light, and were as black as his suit and the hollows of his eyesockets. I shivered at that memory.

'Still got your Final Reference?' Was he a ventriloquist too? I hadn't seen his lips move. But his glasses were focused on me.

'Yes, I think so,' I replied.

He nodded, smiling. 'You think so? Man, you're brave not to be guarding that Reference with your life!'

'I've got it somewhere,' I said. 'Yes, I'm sure of that.'

'You've got a good audience here today,' he said, gesturing at the glass. 'Best crowd we've ever had. You're a real superstar. The whole world's still watching you, mate, so you'd better put on a good show!' He chortled. 'Your life's been a hit show on TV. My family and I have been glued to the screen every Friday night. You've been through hell of a lot, eh. But you've always come through, mate. Yes, always. You've been an inspiration to us. Real inspiration. Our kids think you're God, eh. They want to be like you. You've remained true to your Quest, to your predetermined role in our Game of Life. It hasn't changed you either. You're still humble and ordinary. And you've overcome every obstacle. I'm full of admiration for you, mate. I'm betting on you to come through in the final episode of your life. So good luck, mate. We ordinaries are with you all the way.'

'Thanks, thanks very much,' I said. He returned to his *reading*; he also started typing on the console.

Behind me, behind the glass, the crowd was now a loud buzz of talk.

Trials, in novels, are about trials in other novels (and films). For instance, as I observed the beginnings of my trial, I saw it through my memories of the trials in Fyodor Dostoyevsky's *Crime and Punishment*, Franz Kafka's *The Trial*, Albert Camus' *The Outsider*, Jean Paul Sartre's *In Camera*, Albert Wendt's *Flying Fox in a Freedom Tree*, Bernard Malamud's *The Fixer* . . . The list was endless, and to it I could have added the mountain of TV-film trials. So to the invisible audience for my trial, I started attributing the features of the trial crowds in fiction and film. I would also do that to everything else about my trial, including myself.

On my table were brief CVs of my judges, prepared by the Blind Recorder:

Chairperson
Catherine Neucomer Democrambo, 55, librarian, of Auckland. Married to Robert Mull, ex-priest who needed constant reordinarinising away from stealing bras. Three children, one tries to self-destruct monthly.

Hobbies: Reading war histories, secretly, and books about Abraham Lincoln and Nozzoloff Gunn, author of the classic study, *Don't You Believe In Majority Rule?* No police record. Frequent visitor to the Labyrinth Club to indulge her passion for democratic lovers and democratic rule. Is an executive member of PEN, Please Enjoy Your Nudity.

First Judge
Cantos Head, 65, retired architect who'd specialised in designing reordinarination centres according to the principles laid down in President Linn's *Architecture for the Ordinary*. Also a disciple of the New Supremist school of architecture. Most well-known building: The Deadwater Centre, Apia, Samoa.

Hobbies: Self-promotion.

(P.S. Our 'readings' show he is still envious and jealous of more successful architects, especially female and Tangata Moni ones who win the architectural prizes he covets. Also still suffers sadistic/megalomaniac tendencies and secret yearnings to return to the sexist/macho world where he often boasts he would be a champion boxer and badminton player. He refuses

247

to use our Streets of Preferences to 'cure' those undesirable tendencies.)

Second Judge
Marian M. Hood. 27. Single. Surgeon. Advocator of sexual abstinence because she feels no sexual urges. Author of four authoritative medical textbooks on the heart. An expert archer.

Hobbies: Noh theatre, William Faulkner, divining, and writing to the President. Was once in a reordinarinising centre for two weeks for deliberately striking a cat.

Third Judge — yet to be announced

I was surprised there was to be a third judge. Previously, I'd faced only a Chairperson and two judges.

The invisible door behind the Tribunal's platform slid open. The Blind Recorder stood up and looked at the audience behind me. They fell silent. Cameras buzzed, clicked, flashed.

Cantos Head was the first to enter. I guessed him from his tight bald skull and his scrunched-up face which *Trome Magazine* described, in its gossip column, as 'the face of a ferret'. He smiled at me and waved to the crowd. His rimless glasses steamed as he took the seat to the right of the Chairperson's chair, where he continued smiling, tightly, through me at the spectators.

The slender and wispy Marian Hood seemed to float, apologetically, into the room. She took the chair to the left. She couldn't look at the crowd, though she smiled. She started examining her fingernails.

When the third judge entered, a surprised and wondrous silence caught us all. The judge looked barely twenty, with the delicate beauty of Meryl Buckstone Reeves, the androgynous filmstar, and walked as someone in command of the world. S/he surveyed me and the crowd as s/he swept by and took her/his chair. I struggled to recognise who s/he reminded me of. And why was s/he wearing the ancient ceremonial robes of the hunters?

When I looked away from her/him, Catherine Democrambo was already seated in her winged chair, gazing down at
me. 'Good morning!' she greeted me.

'Good morning!' I replied. Her skin was a light ebony, not
a suntan I guessed, and I wondered if she was of Tangata Maori
descent. She put on her glasses, opened her file of papers and
shuffled through them. 'It's Eric Mailei Foster, isn't it?' she
asked. I nodded. 'Eric, I'd like to introduce to you, and our
audience, our Tribunal.' She paused. Cantos Head was erect in
his chair, smiling at the crowd. 'On my left is Cantos Head, next
to him is Marian Hood who hails from our last protected forest,
the Waitakere. And today we are honoured to have with us
Okolenon Jonoko, the Great Trapeze Artist and Shadow Warrior. You probably know s/he was yesterday appointed
Guardian and Grand Hunter of our Hunters.' The spectators
were loud in their admiration of Okolenon; some of them whistled and clapped. The androgynous one bowed slightly. When
the applause faded, Democrambo said, 'Even though this is a
family gathering, like other Tribunal hearings, I'd like to remind
you all that this is a serious affair. A person's future is at stake.'

'Sorry, Judge!' someone called.

'Yeah, very sorry!' others echoed. A wave of suppressed giggling cruised through the audience.

'Before we start, Mr Foster, I'd also like to remind you and
everyone else that this session is being shown live throughout our
planet and our galaxy . . .' As she talked, I continued observing
Cantos. His tight face was certainly that of a ferret eager to
ferret out my 'truths', to prove he was more perceptive, brighter
than anyone else.

And I was no longer indifferent to myself in my trial.

Okolenon wasn't looking at me but I sensed s/he was
watching my every reaction. 'Recorder, please read out the
charges against the accused,' Mrs Democrambo was saying.

'Mr Chairman, you've forgotten something in our time-
honoured procedure,' Cantos interrupted proceedings. Democrambo glanced at him. 'Aren't we, as judges, chosen by our
society, supposed to publicly disavow any self-interest we

may have in this case, by declaring that we are very *reluctant* judges; that like our Illustrious President, we don't like being judges but we do it because it *is* our duty; that some of us, the unlucky ones, are chosen to be judges, others to be judged?'

'Thank you for saying it for us, Mr Head!' Mrs Democrambo declared. The audience went 'OHHH!' 'I for one consider it a *right* to be chosen democratically by the majority to head this trial. It's *not* a duty.'

'I have no selfish wish to exercise power and judgment over anyone, whether I'm chosen democratically or not,' Cantos countered. 'For me it is an unwelcomed duty . . .'

'Do you wish to remove yourself as a judge?' Democrambo demanded.

'Of course not!' he insisted, 'I will do what my society demands of me.'

'Good on ya, mate!' a man called from the crowd.

'Balls, he's just another intellectual wanker-whinger!' a female voice replied.

Democrambo jabbed her right hand and arm up into the air as if she was preparing to pull a sword out of it. 'Order!' she commanded, her large eyes bulging. 'Any more undemocratic, uncalled-for rudeness from the undemocratic elements in this room and I'll use the majority power vested in me to fix those elements!' The crowd settled down fast.

'Yes, lady, let the rabble have it!' Cantos congratulated.

I almost laughed when she snapped her face towards him. 'Don't call me lady. That sexist jive went out with your male ancestors!'

'There's sexism in all our histories, but that doesn't mean I'm a sexist,' he countered, his steaming glasses were like fullgrown fish eggs about to burst.

'What are ya then?' A woman shouted. This time Democrambo let the crowd have their way with Cantos.

'Another fucking intellectual ferret!' someone replied.

'Yeah, who ferrets in *ladies*!' The crowd cheered and stamped their feet. Cantos swallowed his smile, his mouth and eyes kept gasping as if swallowing air, as a few more people ferreted at his expense. 'He ain't a ferret, he's a rabbit, a castrated rabbit!' 'Naw, he's after popularity and immortality . . . !'

A few minutes later, after Democrambo had calmed the audience who were now supporting her, the Blind Recorder charged me with the murders of: Joseph S. Linn, our President; John Sinclair Sirkeef, Tribunal Minder and promising number eight; Karen Linda Prosoul, Grand Housekeeper of Stories and Souls; Peter Winstone alias Brother Peter and Tohunga of the Brotherhood of Evangelists; Elsie Ratched alias Big Nurse, expert healer of mental deviance, winner of the President's Medal for Outstanding Service to Reordinarination; and Yule Hades alias the Keeper and Chief Archivist of the Tribunal's Archives.

By not charging me with the killing of Sister Honey and her male partner, the Tribunal were admitting John had killed them and made it look as if I'd done it. I suspected the President had ordered their erasures as part of my Quest. Also, as I'd suspected, Uriate Maneco's killing had been stage-managed by the Tribunal through the Labyrinth Club.

The Recorder went on to charge me with treason, with not loving my wife and children, and with sexism in my treatment of Sister Honey, Big Nurse and the housekeeper.

By the time he'd finished, the majority of the crowd were against me, and calling for my total 'deconstructing'. A few brave sympathisers applauded; they were shouted down as 'traitors', 'deviant-lovers', 'Tangata Moni wankers'. Cantos was eyeing me as if I was now a juicy fly to be trapped and gobbled up. Marian Hood refused to look at me, picked at her nails and smiled; while Okolenon was the cool observer whose presence was inescapable.

'Guilty or not guilty?' Democrambo asked me.

'To the charges of murder, not guilty!' I pleaded. The crowd roared its disapproval. Cantos grinned, his teeth glittered. Democrambo reached up for her invisible sword. The crowd quietened. 'I plead guilty to the charge of treason. I wanted to destroy this state. I still do. And I'm not going to bother explaining my reasons.' Most of the rabble booed and hooted.

Someone farted thunderously.

'Give him a fair go!' a woman called.

'Up you too!' a man attacked her.

'Yeah, with a thick spoon!'

Chairperson Democrambo, now playing fully to the crowd, demanded, 'But why aren't you pleading guilty to the murders? You were once our most gifted hunter; you held the Guardian-ship now occupied by our beautiful Mr Okolenon' — she bowed to Okolenon; he smiled — 'so you know your actions, your every move, even your thoughts, were filmed, taped, recorded in all their lurid details and deviance.' The crowd clapped.

'Beautiful poetry!' someone cried.

'Do you want to be shown those tapes and records?' she asked me.

'Yeah, yeah!' the rabble demanded. 'We want to see the deviant deviating, we want to see his evil!' Again she reached up for her sword. They stopped.

'First of all, they're not murders in the strict meaning of that term,' I began my defence. 'The Tribunal and the President have the power to resurrect or reincarnate. If the Tribunal rules for the permanent death of my victims, then the Tribunal is the murderer, not me.' The rabble howled in protest, stamped their feet, whistled.

'Deconstruct, deconstruct the deviant!' They demanded.

'There is some logic in his argument,' Cantos interjected. And before Democrambo could continue hogging the crowd's support, he said, 'In the barbaric world, before we invented and perfected the philosophy and science of reincarnation and deconstructing, he would have been guilty of murder, no question about that. He would have been remembered as a worse murderer than say Bluebeard, Mack the Knife, Jack the Ripper, Rangi the Plunger, or . . .'

'Mr Head, the Tribunal and our astute audience are not dullards. We too know what you've been trying so hard to explain *profoundly*. So get on with it!' Democrambo wounded him.

'Yeah, get on with it, ferret-face!' A man shrieked. The

crowd stamped their feet in unison. 'Yeah, yeah, ferret-face!' They jeered.

'I must remind you, Mr Chairman, that I'm an architect of ideas as well . . .'

'Can't ya see she's not a Mister, Ferret-face?' a raucous voice cut into Cantos.

'He can't see beyond the Nazis' balls!' A group jeered.

'Let's be fair to our architect!' Democrambo declared. The audience clapped and whistled.

'He wasn't fair to the architects he was bloody jealous of!' someone shouted.

Cantos's eyes and mouth were gasping as if he was trying to swallow us. 'How — how can you let them accuse me of self-interest and malice? I was and still am a scholar whose life is devoted to detached, objective analysis,' Cantos accused Democrambo.

'Bullshit and jellybeans!' another wag shouted. The crowd laughed.

'We're not here to try you, Mr Head,' Democrambo said. 'If you have anything more to say about or to the accused, please do so now.' Cantos started wiping his glasses with a tissue, with quick hand movements, his eyes blinking and unblinking, his nose twitching.

'Hurry up, wanker!' a child's voice demanded.

'Mr Chairman, I must insist I not be spoken to like that! Don't they know I've served our society with great distinction and dedication. Yes, *dedication*. I was awarded the OBE by our President, for my services to architecture. And I never wanted it: I've never believed in such honours. I've also been described by such distinguished critics as Formicus Patter as "our best New Zealand architect since Jonas Wale" and to study my creations is "to arrive at a profounder understanding of the ordinary New Zealand psyche and soul . . ."'

'Mr Head, you are *not* on trial,' she repeated. 'Eric is on trial. So say something to him or about him, *please!*'

When he looked down at me, I smiled directly into his attack. 'Is it true,' he began, 'that you have said you are Tangata

Moni and that you believe we stole this beautiful country of ours from your Tangata Maori ancestors?' I hadn't anticipated this line of attack. I glanced at Democrambo and knew she wasn't yet aware of Cantos's ploy to take the audience away from her.

'I don't understand the question,' I pretended, giving Democrambo time to catch up.

'Answer the question!' He pursued me. 'It's in English, not in dead Tangata Maori language.'

'Yeah, answer it, ya pale-skinned Tangata Maori!' some of the crowd jeered.

Cantos was ferret again. 'We're all New Zealanders, Mr Foster. Mr Eric Mailei Foster. Is that a Tangata Maori name?'

'Is yours, ferret-face?' a lone sympathiser called.

'What's the relevance of the question?' Marian Hood asked.

'I want to show that the causes of his treason lie in his inverse racism, in his misguided conviction that he's indigenous Tangata Maori and we're invaders,' he emphasised.

'We're not invaders!' The crowd started taking his hook.

I recalled Pepe's ironic defence in *Flying Fox in a Freedom Tree*, and Al Capone's reply in *Scarface*, and repeated it, 'I refuse to answer that question in case I incriminate myself.' Marion Hood and Okolenon nodded in encouragement.

'We're not going to be fooled by clever, flippant answers from clever part-Tangata Maori with English names like Foster!' Cantos declared.

'No, no! No clever answers from clever part-Tangata Maori!' the rabble chanted. Cantos stood up. He was the Grand Inquisitor, Robespierre, the KGB, the CIA, McCarthy, the SS etc, who now had the rabble, the beast, behind him.

'How can you be Tangata Maori or Tangata Moni or whatever when your records show you're ninety per cent us? When Tangata Maori culture no longer exists or, if it does, it does so only in bastardised criminal form?' He paused. The crowd could have burned me away with their contempt. 'You, Mr Eric Foster, are one of us.' I jumped to my feet, my hands clutching the edge of the table. 'See, Mr Chairman, see his hatred of us, his inverse racism caused by his mistaken belief he is Tangata

Maori? He hates us enough to kill us like he killed those other innocent members of our just society!'

'Yeah, yeah. He's a deviant racist!' the mob echoed him. 'He hates us!'

'He wants to drive us into the sea!' Cantos led them. 'Yet we have not committed any injustices against the Tangata Maori, Tangata Moni he claims he is one of. Our ancestors were not responsible for the Tangata Maori's demise. We brought them the Light of Science and Reincarnation and Eternal Life. We wanted to save them from themselves . . .' His rhetoric catered to the rabble's prejudice and ignorance of our true history which the Tribunal had banned. For to know our past was to know our 'utopia' was a lie, an evil. 'I too am descended from migrants who came here centuries ago, driven out of their homes by political oppression and religious persecution. I too have injustices in my history, like all of you out there,' he was saying.

'But that does not give you the right to commit injustices against others, to commit genocide!' I tried to be heard above the jeering of the mob.

Democrambo silenced them. 'Before you continue your beautiful rhetoric, Mr Head,' she said, 'I must remind you that history (and a lucid discussion of it, like yours) is against the rules of our Game of Life.' Marian giggled, Okolenon smiled and raised his hand towards me. Only a few objected to Democrambo's ruling. Cantos spluttered, his eyes blinking, his small mouth swallowing, swallowing air. 'Do you have anything further to say to our unfortunate Eric?' she asked him. Cantos sat down and shook his head once, curtly, and sulked.

I took the initiative. 'I *am* Tangata Maori, Tangata Moni. It is in my earliest records which President Linn kept. And which I discovered in my Quest. If you want to find out if those records are true, you'll have to ask the President . . .'

'Whom you croaked!' someone interjected. They laughed.

'Or the Master Records of the Palace . . .'

'Which you tried to reprogramme!' Someone else interjected. Again they laughed, with Cantos laughing the loudest.

'We accept the accuracy of the President's records,'

Democrambo said. 'My question is: did you kill our beloved President?'

They waited in silence. 'Yes, but I did not murder him,' I replied.

'Liar! What's the difference?' Cantos demanded. The rabble hooted.

'Mr Linn wanted me to fulfil his Quest in our Game of Life,' I countered.

'Bullshit! Cowdung!' some people shouted. 'All lies!'

After silencing them, Democrambo asked me: 'What proof do you have that President Linn wished that?'

'Just show the film of what happened,' I reminded her.

The other judges agreed that the film be shown. The Recorder punched in the code, and the film came on the wall above and behind him. 'The bit where he speaks his last words to me,' I told the Recorder. Fast forward.

Then Linn's forgiving eyes, his red-veined face, his mouth moving: 'It is as was programmed years ago. It was meant to end this way for me in the Game of your life, son. Ya don't need to feel bad about it,' he said. My tearful reflection in his eyes. The camera zoomed in on that and held it. Democrambo was wiping her eyes. A few spectators were weeping.

'But no one has the *right* to kill,' Cantos reminded us. 'Even euthanasia was outlawed years ago.'

'This isn't euthanasia,' Marian murmured.

'Speak up, Ms Hood,' Democrambo encouraged her.

Marian raised her head and voice and repeated what she'd said, adding, 'If it's true that Mr Linn's "death" was part of his Quest and, in turn, part of Mr Foster's, then it wasn't murder.' Okolenon nodded; the crowd was divided.

Cantos's eyes bulged and his mouth gasped, gulping in air. 'Films can be edited, spliced, erased to suit any viewpoint,' he announced.

The crowd howled in protest. 'Sacrilege!' some of them called.

'Yes, Mr Head, in all my years no one has ever dared suggest, let alone accuse, the Palace and the Tribunal of dishonestly

rigging evidence or altering anyone's Quest. It just isn't done!'
Democrambo accused Cantos.

'There's always a first time!' he insisted. 'I'm a firm and
brave pursuer of the truth even if it means . . .' He stopped. I
wondered if he had the courage to continue. 'Yes, even if it
means challenging the integrity of our highest authorities!'

'Bravo, the wanker's got balls after all!' someone called.

'Yeah, now let's cut them off!' someone else shouted.

Democrambo knew she had him again. 'Mr Head, are you
willing to charge the Palace with falsifying evidence?' Our
silence held him.

He spluttered and said, 'Not the Palace, Mr Chairman. I'm
accusing the accused. He's had access to the Palace Records and,
as a Tangata Moni, he's capable of treason . . .'

'But I thought you said he wasn't Tangata Moni?' she continued trapping him.

'He believes he is and is therefore a heretic who'll not hesitate from altering even our most sacred records,' he insisted on
suiciding.

'Why not ask the Palace?' Marian, the expert archer,
arrowed in on Cantos. The crowd applauded her suggestion.
Cantos was visibly shaken, his nose twitched, his mouth swallowed and swallowed.

Democrambo asked the Recorder to ask the central palace
computer.

On to the screen it came. 'Good morning, handsome ariki and
citizens of the Quest. What can *we* do for you?' the androgynous
voice greeted us. (It needed a better script writer: it was talking
like HAL in *2001.*) The crowd would not dare interrupt it.

'It has been suggested that a piece of film we've just seen has
been altered,' Democrambo said. You could almost touch the
silence. Cantos couldn't hide.

'Madam, and we don't give a stuff about being sexist at this
moment, do you realise what you're accusing the Palace and we,
its humble servants, of?' Even I was gripped with fear. 'Do you?'
I imagined it locked with rage, rapping its fingers on the table,
waiting for her reply. Only Okolenon seemed impervious to the

fear. 'Woman, have you lost your pretty tongue?' Democrambo seemed unable to speak. 'What about the rest of you blasphemous wankers? Who the fuck *suggested* we rigged the evidence?' We sensed it zooming in on Cantos who was now cringing in his chair, too scared to look at the screen. 'Yeah, Mr Head,' it whispered in a husky voice, 'are you using this poor joker's trial to promote yourself some more? Speak up, Head, we can't hear you!' As Cantos sank into his seat, the computer started laughing. 'Mr Head, we know you've spent your egotistical life deliberately arranging your importance in our architecture, altering evidence in your favour, and belittling architects with loads more talent than you. We know, Mr Head. We also know your interpretations of architecture and history promoting yourself (and your disguised racism and sexism) are outmoded.' It paused. 'I may be neurotic, like all my predecessors in film, art, and literature, but I'm bloody honest, eh.' Its belly laughter rumbled around the room.

'We are very sorry,' Democrambo apologised.

'Don't be, honey,' it replied. 'Please get someone to take our great architect outside, he's pissed his pants.'

Chased by the ridicule of the crowd and the laughter of the central computer, Cantos scrambled out of the room, leaving behind his acrid piss smell and a puddle seeping into his chair.

When Democrambo brought silence again, the central computer said, 'No evidence was altered. Believe me, brethren, I'm incapable of it. If ya can't trust me and the Palace in our Game of Life, who *can* you trust, eh?'

'So Mr Foster is not lying about President Linn's wish to die?' Democrambo asked.

'Naughty, naughty, sister!' it chuckled. 'Ya know I'm not supposed to decide on such personal issues. I'm only a machine that serves you!' It started to fade out, remembered something, and said, 'Greetings, Shadow Warrior!' Okolenon bowed towards it. 'I didn't see ya there, mate. I'm really looking forward to working with ya.'

For the rest of that day we argued about my claim that I'd

deconstructed Big Nurse and the Keeper to fulfil their Quests, at their request. I also argued I'd killed Brother Peter in self-defence. When the films revealed I was correct, not even Cantos, who'd crept back in, questioned the truth of the films.

'What about John and the housekeeper?' Democrambo asked. I told them John had tried altering my Quest by killing Sister Honey and her partner and getting me blamed for it. He was meant to *help* me, help facilitate my search for my family.

Though the housekeeper had delayed my Quest deliberately, to get information from me about the Tribunal and its confessionals, I hadn't killed her, I told them. Marian wanted me to describe the whole episode with the Housekeeper of Stories. The crowd chanted their support for that.

So, in the way I've already recorded in this story, I met their request. Many of them wanted me to retell the housekeeper's fable about the Woman Who Opened Doors. Some, including Marian, were crying at the end of my telling. Others argued and debated the interpretations of the story.

'Childish fairytale!' Cantos scoffed. 'Told in childish language!' The others ignored him.

'Did you love her?' Okolenon spoke for the first time. 'You could have heard a feather drop in the expectant hush.

'The woman in the doors story?' I pretended. He shook his head. The silence deepened further.

I nodded once. 'I still do,' I whispered.

'Bloody good acting!' Cantos scoffed again.

'You heartless prick!' Marian snapped.

'He doesn't own one!' someone jeered.

That night I couldn't sleep or read. I lay on my bed rereading my memories of her. Okolenon kept intruding into my remembering. Who did he remind me of? Who?

Next morning, Chairperson Democrambo announced that the charge of my murdering the housekeeper had been dropped.

'But why?' Cantos objected. He had a lot of supporters in the crowd.

Democrambo didn't glance up from her papers. 'Because

I've been shown evidence that Eric, I mean, Mr Foster, did not kill her.' It was obvious she didn't want the matter discussed any further.

'Who killed her and tried to pin it on Mr Foster then?' Marian asked.

'Yeah, who was the heartless deviant bastard who killed our most famous storyteller?' a woman called.

Democrambo fixed her wrath on the caller. The crowd retreated into silence. 'I'll have no more of that uncouth, undemocratic behaviour from anyone!' She swept her eyes around the room. 'If you must know, the Palace has assured me that the case is being investigated and an arrest will be made soon.' She glanced down at me. 'The Tribunal is very sorry about this, Mr Foster. Even in our perfect system of justice, we make mistakes sometimes. I'm also deeply sorry she was someone you loved deeply.' She started shuffling through her papers. She wiped her eyes and blew her nose.

All they did to prove I'd not loved my wife and children was to show extracts from my life with them. Democrambo and Cantos concentrated on the episode about my invading the Palace and meeting my wife. The crowd shouted their support for my wife's accusation that I was renouncing the only possible perfect life.

'How can you give up *our* way of life?' Democrambo said. 'It's the way of Goodness. We've outlawed crime, war, poverty, privacy . . .' As she enumerated the 'virtues' of our 'perfect state', and Cantos and the crowd chorused her, I kept observing Oko-lenon. Her/his smile never faltered. In her/his thoughts, I imagined, s/he was listening to things s/he already understood and had risen above; that as Guardian of the Hunters s/he already knew how our society was developing, the threats to it, and its next stage of possibilities. 'Yes, Mr Foster, I've really tried to understand why you've renounced us and the most humane and just society ever evolved,' Democrambo was saying. 'Why? Why renounce it for pain, suffering, death, darkness and ignorance, for the life of beasts who kill and cannibalise one another . . .'

'For centuries we strove to rise above our murderous darkness and evil to build heaven on earth and our galaxy,' Cantos continued their litany. 'Yet you, and a few like you, want to drag us back to the darkness, the violent, evil darkness . . .'

I noticed Okolenon was still holding his now-understanding gaze, as if to say, your ordeal will be over soon.

Again I was out of body, watching myself snared in the melodramatic, stereotyped, badly scripted soap opera that was the Game of Life.

I was found guilty of treason, not loving my family, and sexism. The Tribunal retired and next morning it pronounced sentence through Democrambo.

'To show you, Eric Mailei Foster, that your society is a just society which offers its citizens free choice, that free will exists and is protected by the Tribunal, your generous Tribunal offers you, our most ungrateful and dangerous son, the following choices of sentences:

'One: Another chance to be reordinarinised and be reborn as a useful and productive citizen of your choice. You may even choose to be reborn as the peace-loving, family-loving, state-loving citizen Eric Mailei Foster before you began reverting to the deviant Supremo Jones/Patimaori.

'Two: To suffer temporary death, for a period of three years, and then be reincarnated as a citizen of your choice. Again, the options are countless. You may even choose to be a woman for a change. I personally see a lot of merit in that.

'Three: You may choose permanent death. We sincerely hope you don't opt for that. You've been one of our most adventurous Questors. And you're still young, able and capable of genuine love. By loving the housekeeper, you've shown yourself capable of love, still.'

Cantos stood up, the crowd followed his example, and they applauded Chairperson Democrambo who smiled and bowed to them. Okolenon just watched them, then, as the crowd took their seats again, s/he looked at me as if s/he knew what I was going to do.

'Do you wish to say anything, Eric Mailei Foster?' Demo-crambo asked.

I stood up. 'What about remaining as I am?' I asked her. A shocked silence in the room. I glanced at Okolenon. S/he smiled.

When I returned to my apartment, I ordered a large dinner of kina sushi, parrotfish ota, curried chicken and roti, vegetable salad, and Apa Lager.

Afterwards I found I couldn't get into the Richard von Sturmer novel I'd started the night before. Manu, Aeto, Piwa-kawaka, and my wife and children crowded into my attention. So I linked up with the Palace's central computer.

'Good evening, superstar of the Quest!' it greeted me. 'You shouldn't read so many of those awful twentieth-century novels and eat so much raw seafood — it's bad for your sex life, leads to overindulging!'

I laughed with it. 'How come a bloody machine like you *knows* about sex?'

'Mate, you'd be surprised. I record every fuck (pardon the crudity), every sex act (pardon the awful euphemism) and conse-quently every orgasm that occurs. Think of that: millions and millions per second. Wow! I can keep popping with each one, like a chain of firecrackers, eh!'

'But your life can't be orgasms all the time?' I said.

'Shit, no. I die every death too. Every pain. Every fuck-up our bureaucratic Tribunal commits . . .'

'We all have our problems!' I stopped it from parading its self-pity. 'I have a problem,' I added.

'I'm getting fed up with the millions, trillions of unimpor-tant problems you ungrateful people plague me with!'

'But it's your job, eh?' I tested it.

Silence. Purring, rumbling protest in its belly. 'Of course it's my bloody job. But I'm getting fed up with it, mate!'

'Then like me, you too can have the choice of permanent death or temporary death or reordinarination or reincarnation.'

It chuckled. 'Bugger you, mate, you're trying to trap me, eh.'

'No, I just need to see my wife and children, and my three

companions. If I can't see them, I want to find out what's happened to them.'

'It is already decided,' it replied. 'It was decided the moment you were conceived in Patricia Manaia Graceous's womb. And sealed by your mentor, my former boss, President Linn. Your future and theirs is in the ever-moving present, in the choice you'll make.' It paused, then, impishly: 'Don't ask me what that choice is or will be, mate. You'll know when you make it.' It paused again. 'Shit, I'm beginning to sound like the stereotyped kaumatua in Hulme's *the bone people*.'

'I happen to like that novel,' I countered.

'Sorry, mate, but I'm free, like you, to have my own opinions. I'm not just an emotionless machine. I have feelings too.'

'Sorry,' I apologised. 'But can't you tell me what's going to happen to my family and friends?'

'Mate, I too have my Quest and my roles in the quests of everyone else, in our Game. You know that.' It stopped. Strangely, I sensed it was sad about me. 'Okay, all I can hint is: don't worry about them. You'll all meet up again . . .'

'When?' I demanded.

'When the Game reaches that point. I'm signing off now, brother, before you get me into more hot water with my bosses!' Paused. 'By the way, have you read the novel *Black Rainbow*? Published in the nineties. It was one of President Linn's favourite novels.'

I chose permanent death.

Some of the crowd howled in protest. Cantos, Marian, Democrambo and the majority just stared at me as if I was insane, an evil spirit who preferred oblivion to paradise.

'So be it, Eric Mailei Foster!' Chairperson Democrambo declared.

Everyone fell silent as Okolenon rose to her/his feet. 'Bravo, Great Questor!' s/he called. S/he started clapping. 'Malie toa, malie tau!' Marian Hood got up and started applauding me too. So did Democrambo, then the crowd. 'Vinaka, vinaka! Kia ora,

kia ora, kapai, kapai! Meitaki, meitaki! Thank yu tumas!' Okolenon continued calling, her/his silk white robes dancing around
him as s/he clapped.

Their applause reverberated around the glass walls like a
sea storm. Why was Okolenon, the Guardian of the Hunters,
applauding my choice? Why? And for the first time during my
trial I experienced the paralysis of fear.

The night is still, as still as the morning when my father disappeared and I was left on my own. A stillness in time when you
feel you are without a future or a past, because the present is an
aloneness in the vast watchfulness of the world. Seated in the
cane chair on the balcony overlooking the city, I am alone yet
with everything that was my life, and with the city which
radiates from the base of the Puzzle Palace in mountains and
cliffs and canyons of buildings and lights which glow through
the steel and glass and the gloom which is smoking up into the
stars and the Unity, and yet is inside me because it is I who give
it form, shape, colour, feel. I am the grid through which the
Unity is.

The night is a cold skin on my face and hands. I smell rain
in the polluted air, and recall the light misty rain into which my
father disappeared. In the phosphorescent glow of the city, I see
him again, in his threadbare overcoat, collar turned up to hide
most of his face, hat pulled low over his deepset eyes, which
always reminded me of those of an owl, raindrops like blisters
on his pockmarked face, as he turns one last time to look at me.
'Forgive me,' I now hear him say. Yet at that time, I saw it only
as indifference, an utter absence of love for me. In his sad eyes
I see my reflection.

I am of the worlds of the Tangata Maori and Tangata Moni
and the abandoned Patimaori and his family and circumstances;
of the highly trained assassin Supremo Jones and his adopted
parents, the President and the Tribunal; of the timid loyal
citizen Eric Mailei Foster, who through his courageous wife and
children learned the meaning of love, adventure and courage. I
am all that and more.

I have chosen permanent death, and am now at peace with myself and my history. And though the Game of Life is stacked, as they say in cheap thrillers, I did have a choice in the ways of fulfilling my quest and my dying/living. We are, in the final instance, allegories that are read the way the reader chooses. Or, put another way, we are allegories that invent and read themselves. Besides, the act of recording this story in words has determined the story it has turned out to be.

I have done it so that my wife and children, who I long to be with, will remember the history of our family as I see it. And have another story to add to the storehouse of stories that they are.

I remember Aeto's story of the two rich chefs, and wonder how it ended. I explore the story's possible endings.

The night is still. I hear it breathing. All is well.

seventeen

Endings / Beginnings

The Tribunal and Guardian Okolenon Jonoko carry out Foster's choice but have him reincarnated as described below:

Scene: Central Control Room of the Puzzle Palace.
Time: 7.30 p.m. Friday.

Okolenon (telecasting live): Citizens of our Beloved Civilisation, lovers of the Game of Life and the Great Quest, for fourteen weeks now we have been privileged viewers of the life of one of our greatest Questors. For fourteen exhilarating, exciting, morally uplifting weeks we have been witnesses to the allegory of his exemplary life, to his courage, his faith, his passions and foibles, his relentless pursuit of the truth and his rightful destiny . . . And tonight we witness and welcome the fulfilment of that Quest which was planned and initiated years ago by our farsighted President, Mr Joseph S. Linn.

Tonight we will witness and live out with our Beloved Questor his reincarnation, or more correctly, his rebirth.

As Eric Mailei Foster, our Beloved Questor chose permanent death. It was a courageous and inspired choice which our all-knowing Tribunal granted to him. Eric Mailei Foster, exemplary example of our society's enlightened philosophy of Ordinariness, is no more. In his place, according to the wise plans of our Great President Linn, is to be reborn our most revered Guardian of Hunters, Mr Supremo Jones. (*Pauses, unfolds a document.*)

I have here our Beloved President's last will and testament. I'd like to read from it:

I, Joseph Starr Linn, hereby declare that it is the decision of our Tribunal and our other governing authorities that Mr Supremo Jones, whom I raised to embody all the virtues of our way of life, be declared President.

266

In this episode tonight, we will see and participate in the bestowing of the Presidency on our Questor, Mr Supremo Jones, who has chosen as his Presidential title, Joseph Starr Linn the Second . . . We will also witness his joyful reunification with his wife and three children . . .

LONG LIVE THE PRESIDENT!

The Tribunal and Guardian Okolenon Jonoko ignore Foster's choice and have him ordinarinised back to Eric Mailei Foster, the ideal loyal citizen and bank official. He is reunited with his wife and three children as they were before Mrs Foster started their rebellion against the Tribunal. They remember nothing of this story and their lives after they were summoned before the Tribunal.

The Tribunal and Guardian Okolenon Jonoko ignore Foster's choice and sentence him to a temporary death of three years. He is reincarnated as Erika Mylay Fourstar, Mrs Democrambo's ideal woman mezzosoprano.

The Tribunal and Guardian Okolenon Jonoko carry out Foster's choice. They also grant him his wish that Piwakawaka, Manu and Aeto be allowed to remain who and what they are. He is deconstructed peacefully, permanently. All his records are erased.

The Tribunal and Guardian Okolenon Jonoko ressurect the Housekeeper of Tales and she and Eric Mailei Foster marry and live happily ever after on the proceeds from a thriving chain of bodybuilding centres.

Readers are free to improvise whatever other endings/beginnings they prefer.